KITCHEN
SINK

[signature]

KITCHEN SINK

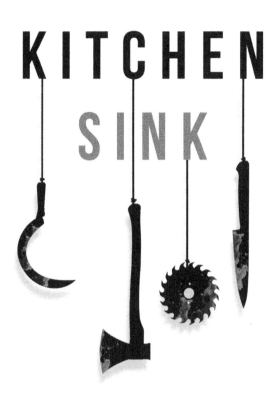

STORIES

SPENCER HAMILTON

NerdyWordsmith

Copyright © 2020 by Spencer Borup

These stories originally appeared in the following publications: "Promethium 147," www.lilymatilda.com (August 2018); *Café du Horror Book 1*, Kindle eBook from Nerdy Wordsmith (2018). "The Diary," *Shadowed Doorways: Fifth Annual NaNo Los Angeles Anthology*, ed. Elisabeth Ashlin (2018). "Shuffle," *It's About Time: 2nd Annual NaNo Los Angeles Short Story Anthology*, ed. Sara McBride (2015). "The Wormhole in Edwin's Cubicle," *Journeys to Uncharted Lands: Sixth Annual Los Angeles NaNo Anthology*, ed. Elisabeth Ashlin (2019). "Finite Forceman MDCLXVII," *Meet the Systems: Stories of Regimes, Formulas, and Schemes: 3rd Annual NaNo Los Angeles Anthology*, ed. Lisa Walsh (2016). "Truth Is a Dragon," *We've All Been There: 4th Annual NaNo Los Angeles Anthology*, ed. Elisabeth Ashlin (2017). "Maybe Tomorrow," originally published as "Tomorrow Never Came" in a chapbook for Folsom Lake College's Fiction Writing Workshop (2007). "Ten Thousand Steps," *7 Easy Steps for the Lonely Writer*, www.spencerhamiltonborup.blogspot.com (March 2016). All other stories are original to this collection.

Published by Nerdy Wordsmith
www.spencerhamiltonbooks.com
www.nerdywordsmith.com

Edited by Amy Teegan (www.amyteegan.com/editing)
Cover design by Kiss László (www.99designs.com/profiles/leslieworks)
Formatting by Sandeep Likhar (www.likharpublishing.com)

First Edition, January 2020

ISBN 978-1-952075-01-8 (paperback)
ISBN 978-1-952075-00-1 (ebook)

To my family
Mom, Dad, Landon, Alyssa, Lyrica, and BFJ
and Aunt Jerry

TABLE OF CONTENTS

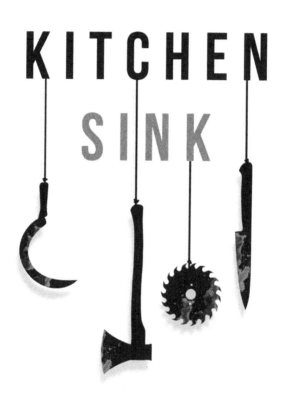

KITCHEN SINK

STORIES

INTRODUCTION

*T*HE MOST FRIGHTENING MONSTERS are the ones inside of us.

The most *compelling* monsters are the ones inside of us.

I've been on a quest to find and to tame my own monster over the course of the twelve years this book represents.

Quite the journey.

Humans are creatures united in their love of story. We make sense of the world and of ourselves through storytelling, whether through the stories we tell ourselves or the narratives we tell each other. History, novels, movies, stage plays, music, our own memories—these are all story.

My favorite form is the short story, because it is the hardest to crack, because it is the one most resistant to rules, because it is the most versatile and therefore the most adaptable.

Short stories haunt me. From a very early age, I was struck by the madman's descent in Edgar Allan Poe's "The Tell-Tale Heart" and the time-travel mishap in Ray Bradbury's "A Sound of Thunder," and they haven't let go of me since. The short works of H.P. Lovecraft have become a part of our cultural zeitgeist. Philip K. Dick's warnings of the future seem all too real—even as we *live* in that future. Short stories are powerful, my friend.

In this collection you and I will explore my own storytelling, from the beginning of my career to now. The earliest of these were written when I was only seventeen years old, the most recent as I approach my thirtieth birthday. All along the way I am grappling with the world around me and with the world inside of me.

Whether it be a more literal, Kafkaesque monster like in "Hive," or the monsters of denial like in "Promethium 147" and "The War on Christmas," or the million tiny monsters that compel us to do any number of atrocities to ourselves or to each other, the core of *Kitchen Sink* can be found in what I like to call the monster question:

Why do we do the things we do?

I believe this is a question Stephen King has been chasing and filmmakers like Vince Gilligan (*Breaking Bad*) have explored for decades. And the same is true for the book you are now reading.

The inception of *Kitchen Sink* began with a throwaway expression: "Everything but the kitchen sink." The idea was that I would gather everything I'd written and throw it out there and hey, maybe someone would like it. But this very quickly transformed—as all monsters do—into something else entirely. The title almost immediately changed from *Everything But the Kitchen Sink* . . . to what it is now.

Not all of the stories you are about to read are horror.

But all of them contain a monster.

Just like each of us.

Spencer Hamilton
January 2020

HIVE

QUENTIN KELLY'S MIND WAS EXPANDING. Not in a well-read sort of way. Not in a philosophical or psychedelic sort of way, though the latter got closer to the truth. Quentin Kelly's mind was expanding physically, as were his sight and hearing and smell and just about every other sense. Pushing themselves outside of his own body's limited perceptions to embody his entire bedroom, small though it was. Continued pushing out in a growing radius, with Quentin's body as its epicenter, out and out and out, consuming the walls and then the halls and then his mother's bedroom and the one and a half bathrooms and the kitchen. Consuming all that food in the pantry, then the fridge once its door could be pried open. Then the dog. What had the dog's name been? Quentin couldn't remember. It was silly tidbits of information like that which his mind had discarded first.

Quentin's mind halted its expansion in the confines of the house, but just barely. The walls pushed out like a distended abdomen, as if warped and swollen with water. The foundations, however, didn't stop his mind. They buckled under the weight of it, pressed themselves into the dirt, and Quentin's mind continued to quest and tendril down into the soil, down, down, down. Its richness and dark and damp excited him, so much that his body went through the hormonal changes of puberty in one sexual rush of boyhood. But this was also something his mind had thrown from its plane of observation. What was Quentin's body to it? Nothing but a closed circulatory system of blood and organs to support the hivemind.

Quentin didn't remember it now, but three days ago he saw his mother for the last time. She'd come inside his room, knocking three little raps—*knock-knock-knock*—before shouldering the door open and stepping through.

"Quenty, my dear," she cooed in her querulous voice, "I bring snacks!"

He hated the sight of her then, and the overwhelming rush of loathing was so foreign to him that it scared him. He *loved* his mother—he did! Promise! But for some reason, those limp locks of gray hair suddenly disgusted him. Those two simple glistening orbs she looked at him with, above that slight nose and quivering thin lips. The pale skin . . . it was vile!

She moved over to his bed bearing a plate of apple slices, and the way she stepped up and over the little mounds of musty laundry and other messes scattered across the carpet seemed blasphemous to him. A small part of his mind was aware that it wasn't usual, the amount of dirt he'd tracked into his bedroom lately, but he hated his mother for stepping over it all. As if she were too good for the dirt.

The apple slices were a welcome sight and smell, however, so he stifled his hatred long enough to snatch the plate from her and begin nibbling. Oh, that *juice*! How gloriously *moist*!

"Quentin . . ." his mother said, pausing as she looked down at him from beside his bed.

What was she waiting for? he thought. Leave!

"Quentin, darling," she said, "I know you've had a rough time this year. Those kids at your school . . . well, they're just *horrible*. Everyone deals with bullying, dear, but to have your entire class single you out like that . . . I've spoken to your principal. He says you need to come back to school. And I agree with him."

School? What was she talking about?

The forefront of Quentin's mind had attempted to discard this information, but there was still that small part in the back of his mind that held on. It was that same small part that knew Quentin was acting strangely as of late. That small part of his mind knew exactly what his mother was talking about, and shuddered at the memory.

This school year had started like any other, at least until lunch period on the second day. Quentin and his mother had moved here just a month before. He wasn't in a hurry to make any friends and was perfectly happy eating his lunch by himself. While he sat at an empty picnic table eating the peanut butter sandwich his mother had packed for him, he noticed a line of ants marching its way up the wood from the dirt below.

Quentin liked ants. He liked their teamwork. He'd told his father every year before Christmas that he wanted one of those ant farms, with the dirt in the frame and all the tunnels for the ants to crawl through as they worked. Every year he'd been disappointed, but this was his father after all. Quentin hadn't ever expected any presents. This year, however, he was holding out hope for that ant farm. It was just his mother and him now, and his mother actually loved him.

So when he saw the assembly line of ants creeping up the picnic bench, he pinched off a few crumbs from his sandwich and placed them on the tabletop. He watched the line progress up the table, and boy was he delighted to see how fast they found his little gift! He added more crumbs to the first, and soon he'd created a whole buffet line across the table, like Hansel and Gretel leading to the candy house.

He raised his sandwich in a toast. "Eat up, friends," he said softly, and resumed eating.

He'd almost finished when a shadow fell across the table. Quentin looked up. He hadn't been in this town long enough to know any of the kids, but the one standing in front of him was easy enough to remember. He didn't know the kid's name, but he'd heard some of the other students refer to him as "Dung." Quentin wasn't sure if this was because the kid smelled or if it was some reference to the amazing strength of a dung beetle. He'd read once that dung beetles could pull over a thousand times their body weight. This kid was huge for their age, big and beefy. And he smelled.

"Look what's happening over here," Dung said, sneering back at the group of smaller students which had followed in his wake. "Looks like the new kid finally made some friends. You sure you wanna give those bugs some of your sandwich, new kid? Looks like it's all you got."

Quentin didn't say anything.

"Maybe," Dung continued, "you're hoping they'll return the favor and bring you some of their crumbs tomorrow."

Some of the kids behind Dung sniggered.

"Not bugs," Quentin muttered into his sandwich.

Dung paused. "What did you just say, new kid? Speak up."

Well, Quentin had already said it. No turning back now.

"Ants aren't bugs," he said. "They're insects."

Dung gaped at him, then turned back to the growing crowd behind him, sneering. "Ya hear that? New kid here says ants aren't bugs. I didn't realize you were in love with bugs, new kid. Sorry—*insects*. You gonna marry 'em?"

Laughter.

"You gonna put some of that peanut butter on your wiener?" Dung asked. "Let your ants crawl all over it?"

More laughter.

Dung walked up to him. Quentin froze.

"I bet you wanna do that, don't you? Put the stuff on your wiener and let your friends eat it off."

Dung reached toward him, and Quentin shied away. Dung snatched the half-eaten sandwich from his hands. He threw it in the dirt.

"This is a school, new kid. Only sex offenders take their wieners out on playgrounds. Are you a sex offender?"

"No," Quentin said.

Dung acted like he didn't hear. He turned back to the other kids. By now, it looked to Quentin as if the entire class had gathered around the picnic table.

"I think the new kid here is a sex offender," Dung said. "That's probably why he moved here. The last school he was in ran him out of town and his parents had to move him here instead."

There was some laughter, but most of the class was silent, staring at Quentin. Quentin couldn't believe it. They weren't actually buying what Dung was saying, were they?

"Sex offenders aren't allowed within fifty feet of a playground," Dung announced to the entire class. "My dad told me, and he's a cop. That means the new kid here can't go near the playground."

Quentin looked up in time to see some of the other kids nodding. He heard a few whispers of *sex offender*. As if any of them knew what that meant.

"We don't want any sex offenders around us, do we?"

"No!" some kids shouted, with a few more mutters underneath the shouts. One kid, probably one of Dung's best buddies, screamed out a "HELL NO!"

And that was that. Quentin wasn't sure if any of the kids would have actually stopped him from going onto the playground—Dung would have, for sure, but the other kids? Maybe not. But Quentin didn't care to find out. He just wanted to make it through the day and to get home and to lock himself in his new bedroom (which was smaller than his *last* bedroom, though he'd never say that to his mom). Once he was there, he'd be safe. He could read. They were only two days into school, so they didn't have any homework, but yesterday Quentin had stopped by the school library and checked out a few cool encyclopedias all about insects and arachnids. He felt safer locked away, reading fascinating things like the difference between *Hymenoptera* and *Hemiptera*—a difference that Dung clearly wasn't aware of.

Quentin felt that if he could just have his ant farm, *then* he'd have friends. *Then* he wouldn't care if the entire *school* labeled him as a "sex offender." He'd stay home and drop out of school and learn things by himself, in his bedroom, with his best friends in the world. He'd watch them work in their farm and he'd talk to them and tell them his thoughts on the world. His friends would listen to every word he'd say.

Two weeks had passed since Quentin Kelly's classmates had labeled him as "sex offender" and made his name, his face, his very *presence* the ultimate taboo.

He hadn't gone back since.

It had been easy to pretend to be sick for the remainder of the first week. After the weekend, though, when Monday rolled around and he still refused to get out of bed, his mother had wised up to what he was doing. There had been fights, some of which had dredged up sore spots they'd been avoiding for months—about Quentin's father, and how his mother had been perfectly fine for years allowing her husband to beat her only child; how she would disappear for weeks at a time, letting Quentin suffer at the hands of his father while she was away. Quentin had told himself he'd forgiven her for all that the moment she made their move official and told him he'd never have to see his father again. But fights could get ugly fast when a child's safety hinged on their outcome, and Quentin no longer felt safe at his new school. Why couldn't his mother see that?

She'd caved eventually, and while he didn't get to be a fly on the wall during her many conversations with the school staff, Quentin was aware that she'd spent quite a few days talking to them about her child's absence and what could be done about it. While she was gone, Quentin would go exploring in the backyard. He'd spend all day grubbing through the dirt and mud looking for the insects he was reading about in his library books. At first he was disappointed that most of the specimens he found were beetles, but he learned quickly that this was to be expected. Beetle species, after all, accounted for forty percent of all insects—a staggering number, considering that scientists believed insects made up as much as ninety percent of the entire planet's living organisms.

When his mother stopped going to those meetings at the school, she had time between her working shifts at the hospital to notice the state of his bedroom.

"This *dirt*!" she'd shrieked. "What have you been *doing*, Quent?"

"I've been thinking of building my own ant farm, Mama," Quentin replied, sitting on his bedroom floor. "That way you don't have to buy me one this Christmas. What do you think?"

"A . . . an *ant farm*? What are you talking about? Are you trying to build it in the *carpet*?"

"Think about it, Mama!" Quentin said. He was very excited about his ideas, so much so that he didn't notice how upset she was at the mess. He wouldn't have known what she was talking about if she called it a "mess," anyhow. "In those little dinky ant farms you can get at the store, that entire colony of ants has only so little room to travel. There's tons of tunnels, sure, but eventually they'll run into a dead end every time. But in the *carpet* . . . the carpet fibers create natural tunnels for the ants, Mama. I'll put stops around the baseboards and by the door, of course, but they'll have this entire room! That's like a *hundred* ant farms in one!"

"Absolutely not, Quentin. I've surrendered on this whole school fiasco, but I refuse to let you turn this house into some kind of science experiment! For God's sake, Quenty, your mother is *renting* this house. Do you know how hard it was for me to get approved for this place so that I could take you away from your . . . your fa—"

But Quentin wasn't listening. He'd opened up one of his library books to read something to his mother. "Mama," he interrupted her, "do you know how many ants are on this planet? Enough so that . . . for every one person on this planet there are almost *two million ants.* Isn't that amazing? I could grow an ant farm of two million ants—probably the biggest ant farm ever! And there'd still be two million ants for everyone else. *You* could build your own ant farm in *your* bedroom, Mama!"

It was at that moment that his mother screamed. Quentin stopped dead and looked up from his book. It wasn't a scream of surprise or terror, he saw. It was a scream of frustration. Pent-up rage. From his mother? Quentin blinked in surprise, seeing her for the first time in weeks.

"We are not building any goddamn ant farms, Quentin Kelly! This house will not become some kind of bug infestation!"

Quentin jumped up, glowering at her.

"MY FRIENDS ARE NOT BUGS!"

And the door had slammed closed on his mother. Quentin jumped in surprise. It was as if a gust of wind had blown it closed. He looked at the window. It was open. He must have left it open sometime in the last few days. Sometimes, when he wanted to go looking for more insects but it was late, he climbed out the window so as not to wake his mother. Not sometimes, actually. That had become a nightly ritual by now. Quentin didn't actually remember the last time he'd slept.

But he didn't care. Now he kept his bedroom door closed and his window permanently open, and his mother didn't disturb him for days after that last fight. He'd built his ant farm, and the dirt accumulated at a rate that would have been alarming to anyone other than Quentin. His specimen collection became bigger and bigger, not just in overall size but in the size of the individual insects as well. Some of the library books had sections in which they described how to build an insect collection, and they made his stomach turn, so he quickly ripped those pages out and discarded them in the trashcan out his window and around the corner.

Kill the insects? Pin them up in shadow boxes? Embalm them in jars?

How could anyone do that to Quentin's only friends in the world?

Knock-knock-knock.

"Quenty, my dear, I bring snacks!"

Quentin looked up from where he lay in bed. It was his mother. She'd started coming into his bedroom a few days after their fight, ignoring the mess on the carpet in order to bring him snacks.

When she stood over him as he nibbled on the apple slices, savoring the juices, and she started talking about that *school* . . . that was when the voices began to prick at Quentin's mind. His mind, he'd found recently, was vast, and could support so much. To compensate, however, he'd begun propping up such a vast mind with different strings of consciousness, which he called his "voices."

She'll make you go back to school.

She'll make you abandon us!

Who will feed us? Who will protect us?

We need our friend! Quentin, aren't you our friend?

Aren't you?! Aren't you, Quentin?! Our friend?!

SMITH PUT THE CAR in park and killed the engine.

"Johnson, shut up," she said. "We're here."

The two got out of the sedan and Johnson looked at the house whose address he'd plugged into the GPS. "Jesus," he said. "I hope they're not renting."

The small house looked as if it were sweating. The boards of the walls bulged outward, and a thick black substance was oozing out of the cracks between them. It looked to Johnson as if the house could once have been painted a mellow yellow color, but now it was a graying, splintered mess. Shingles had popped off recently, and the place seemed to shimmer in Johnson's vision.

He rubbed his eyes, looked again. The house still swam in the air. "It's September, isn't it?"

Smith glanced at him. "Yes."

"So why is the air around that place dancing around like it's the hottest day of the year?"

"Good question," Smith said. "Let's go find out. Leave the file."

Johnson looked at her, then back down at the manila folder he clutched in one hand. "But . . . what if I need to reference something in the kid's file?"

"Maybe you should have memorized it beforehand,"

Smith said. "Or at least studied it on the drive over here, instead of jawing about dumping the kid in Antarctica."

"I'm just saying, it's *Antarctica*. Big block of ice, no bugs. He wouldn't have any power in Antarctica."

"*Belgica antarctica*."

"Gesundheit."

"Very funny, Johnson. No, *Belgica antarctica* are wingless midges. They live in Antarctica."

"Oh. Damn. So nowhere's safe, huh?"

"Just leave the file, Johnson."

Johnson sighed and stuffed the file through the cracked window, then adjusted his suit jacket. That shimmer in the air still unsettled him, so he took out his sunglasses and slipped them on.

Smith rolled her eyes. "You ready?"

Together, he and Smith entered the yard leading to the house's front door. The grass on either side of the cracked pavement was utterly lifeless. They hadn't been in a drought in years, but this grass was dried up and looked as though it'd been like this for centuries. The ground was just as dried and cracked as the little sidewalk. No weeds, Johnson noticed. Interesting.

They stepped up to the front door, and Johnson felt it the moment they stepped into that dubious shimmery air. Like oil on the skin. It also seemed to be a few shades darker in the awning than it had any right to be at three o'clock on a September afternoon. Johnson took his sunglasses off. Yup, it wasn't just him—the air was darker here. Heavier.

He was about to say as much to his partner, but before he could Smith reached out and rapped one fist against the wood.

Squelch.

Smith swore under her breath. Her knuckles had sunk into the wood as if she'd driven them into uncooked meat. She wiped the back of her hand against her slacks.

"Well, *that's* not up to code," Johnson joked.

Smith glared at him, searched around the doorframe, and pressed the doorbell.

The two stood there, shoulder to shoulder, waiting. They knew the doorbell worked, at least—the *ding-dong!* was perfectly audible from here, even if the house seemed to be underwater and the sun seemed to be a few more planets away than usual.

They waited.

Smith rang the bell again.

And a third time.

Almost immediately after the third *ding-dong!* the door opened. It didn't open quickly, nor did it make any kind of creaky-hinges sound a door should make. Instead, it fought with its frame before finally letting go of its moorings with a *SQUELCH!* much louder than the one Smith's fist had made.

Smith and Johnson stared into darkness. Johnson got the feeling he was staring into a black hole, and a shiver whispered up his spine like an insect.

"Hello?" Smith called out. Her voice was swallowed in the black hole.

"Who's there?" Johnson called out, louder.

Silence.

"We're here to speak to a Mrs. Kelly," Smith said, raising her voice. "It's about her son, ten-year-old Quentin Kelly."

A prolonged pause in which Johnson was expecting

another bout of silence, then: "Quenty?"

The sound made that insectile shiver run up Johnson's spine again. It was small and distant, much more distant than a house this size would allow. Like she was calling out from the bottom of a deep well.

"Mrs. Kelly?" Smith called back.

"You're here for . . . my Quenty?"

"Correct, Mrs. Kelly," Smith said. "Would you mind coming to the front door so we may have a word?"

After another prolonged pause, Smith inhaled to call out again. But she stopped when a noise reached them. A scuffling, like the murmur of a large crowd who'd grown restless. It scuffled and shuffled and all the while grew closer and louder, though still a long way off.

"This is creepy as f—"

Smith shushed Johnson, glaring at him.

A form appeared in the black hole before them, and to Johnson it looked human-shaped, at least vaguely so. A head, a torso, maybe wrapped in a bunch of quilts or something, but still an upright body. It looked to be maybe five or six feet away from the doorjamb, but it was still almost completely swallowed in the dark.

What was keeping the sun from spreading across the threshold? Maybe Johnson's mind was just playing tricks on him. It was his first mission. He was just nervous, that was all.

The form was saying something. Johnson caught the last two words: ". . . my . . . Quenty?"

"Yes, Mrs. Kelly," Smith said.

Johnson admired her for plowing through with the mission. She didn't seem to be letting all this creepy shit set her off. Johnson knew *he* sure as hell had. If she weren't with him, he'd probably turn heel and run and tell this crazy kid's mother to get fucked.

". . . my . . . Quenty . . . ?"

"Mrs. Kelly," Smith said, "we're here to see your boy. It's been brought to our attention that he may need our help."

". . . my . . . Quenty? Trouble?"

"No trouble—"

"Did . . . that *school* . . . was it the school . . . ?"

"No, Mrs. Kelly," Smith said. "The school isn't associated with this in the slightest. We deal with classification of supers. Your son has developed certain abilities that have blipped certain radars that you and Mr. Kelly wouldn't want—"

The form's voice rushed to the door from the bottom of whatever well it was in and slammed with full force, the sound bursting through the threshold as if some force field had been popped.

"MR. KELLY DOES NOT LIVE HERE!"

Johnson staggered back a few steps, but Smith didn't even flinch. Jesus, but his partner was tough. In the back of his mind, Johnson wondered what kind of shit she'd faced to make this just another day at the nine-to-five.

"Of course, Mrs. Kelly," Smith replied pleasantly. "I didn't mean to offend. I apologize. Our orders only concerned your son, Quentin, so we were not fully briefed on the home situation—"

"What . . . *home* . . . situation?" The voice was back to its weak, quivering dimness.

"I meant nothing by that, Mrs. Kelly," Smith replied. "Only that our business is with your son. We believe he may need our help."

"Quenty . . . he's a very special boy . . ."

"We agree, Mrs. Kelly. We only concern ourselves with those who are special."

"Yes . . . special . . . he has many, many friends, you know, my Quenty does . . ."

Johnson frowned. *That* was a strange thing to say. This woman was clearly touched in the head.

"That's *amazing!*" Smith filled her voice with honeyed enthusiasm, and it elicited a response from the form that sounded like a gurgly coo in the back of the throat. "We would love to ask Quentin about his many friends, Mrs. Kelly. Would you be so kind as to invite us in to see him?"

"No . . . you misunderstand," the form said. Johnson had to strain his ears to hear her words. "My Quenty . . . has many, many friends who keep him company all the day long. He's quite popular, you know . . . he isn't in need of any more visitors."

"You mean his friends are here with him?" Smith asked. "That's wonderful! We would love to meet your son's friends as well, Mrs. Kelly."

Like hell he would, thought Johnson. What the fuck was this fucking lady talking about? Her son was popular? Who the fuck cared?

"Yes," the form of Mrs. Kelly said. "Of course you would . . . come in, come in . . . I'll put out some . . . critters."

The form retreated back into the black hole and disappeared.

Johnson glanced at Smith. "You're not really thinking of following that thing inside, are you?"

"This is our job, Johnson. Grow the hell up and follow my lead."

Johnson blinked. "She just said she'd put out *critters.*

What the fuck does that even mean?"

Smith leveled a glare his way. "Watch your tone while we're inside the house, Johnson. I mean it. And if she offers you something, I don't care if it's an Antarctic midge, I want you to eat it and say 'Thank you, please can I have some more.' Got it?"

Johnson stared at Smith, his mouth agape. The thick air around them even *tasted* strange on his tongue. Like . . . *dirt*. He closed his mouth.

Smith stepped into the house, and Johnson followed.

It was dark, far darker than Johnson had anticipated, and the first thing that happened when they entered was that Johnson's leg bumped into a side table. There was no wooden knock, just a wet sound and a *thump* as the table toppled to the ground. Johnson bit his tongue hard to keep from swearing.

A few feet inside, he stopped. This was far enough, he reasoned. He looked around, but in the gloom he was better off using his other senses. The smell, the taste of the air . . . this was overwhelming. If Johnson managed not to be sick until they got outside, the first thing he was doing was rushing home to burn this suit and take a scorching hot shower. The second thing he was doing was demanding a raise.

He noticed a low mound in the darkness farther inside. Maybe an armchair? But it looked as if it were moving. Back and forth, back and forth . . . a rocking chair, Johnson realized. And someone was sitting in it.

Smith addressed the sitting form. "Mrs. Kelly, would you happen to have any candles on hand? We may need some light to find your boy's room."

"Quenty . . . likes . . . the dark," the form said, and

Johnson was very unhappy to hear that her voice was back to doing that bottom-of-the-well thing.

"Of course, Mrs. Kelly," Smith said.

"Fuck that," Johnson muttered, and before Smith could stop him he slipped out his cell phone and used the screen as a light.

"Johnson, wait—"

But Johnson didn't heed Smith's warning. He swung the beam of light up from his loafers in an arc toward Mrs. Kelly. "Time to shed some light on this bitch," he said under his breath. But then his breath hitched, and he formed a perfect oval with his mouth, but no scream came out.

Mrs. Kelly wasn't Mrs. Kelly. The skin of her face was pocked with decay, and as Johnson watched, maggots squirmed in and out of diseased holes covering her rotting flesh. Her skin crawled, actually *crawled*, and Johnson desperately wrenched his gaze down from her face, down her neckline, to . . . well, now . . . those weren't quilts like he'd first thought. Mrs. Kelly was wrapped in swaths of thick white gossamers, layers upon layers of the stuff— probably keeping her body together, Johnson realized.

Smith saw it too. "Arachnids," she said. She looked at Johnson. "This is worse than we thought."

Johnson didn't hear her. Insects, bugs, spiders . . . this house could be filled with crabs for all the difference it made to him. They were all small, creepy and crawly, and—something he didn't realize until now—held way more power over this planet than humans liked to admit. What, humans were the dominant species because we could send emails to each other? Because we could debate economics and philosophy and because we invented the cure for polio? We landed on the moon? Who the fuck cared? Johnson knew it was very likely that there was alien life somewhere out there in the universe, but you know what was even more likely?

That whatever aliens were out there . . . were fucking *bugs*.

"Johnson?"

He still didn't hear his partner. His mouth was stretched in that oval shape, soundless, and his eyes were growing larger and larger as he took the scene in. Quilts of spider webs, and sitting on her armchair . . . except *not* an armchair. What, an ant hill? Inside a *house*? Whatever it was, in Johnson's solitary beam of light from his phone, all he could see was that it was a writhing, shapeless mass that only roughly assembled itself into an armchair-like form for Mrs. Kelly to rest her feet. It was a giant globular mass of . . .

"Ants," he whispered.

There had to be millions of the things, all working to support Mrs. Kelly's squirming corpse.

"Johnson?"

He finally wrenched his eyes away and looked at Smith.

"Ants," he whispered again.

"Yes," Smith said. "Mrs. Kelly is gone, Johnson. She's been taken by Hive. We need to keep moving, but first you need to turn that light off."

"Turn . . . ?" Johnson couldn't even process such a command. "You're insane."

"Johnson, turn it off. Now."

"Fuck you."

"These things, Johnson? The things that have Mrs.

Kelly? They're working for Hive. They *are* Hive. And Mrs. Kelly's body just told us that Hive likes the dark. He's not going to let us take a single step deeper into this house—"

"Good," Johnson said, gulping. "Then let's get the hell out of here."

"Johnson, we have a *job*. Our mission is to evaluate the boy. Look around you. Look what he did to his mother. Wouldn't you say our evaluation just became a whole lot simpler?"

"You're right. Consider the little fuck assessed. He's a villain."

"So far, I agree with you. But we need to be sure."

"The fuck we do. I'm pretty goddamn sure the kid's a fucking monster."

"Johnson—"

"Shouldn't we at least call in some backup or something?"

"We need to get this taken care of immediately, Johnson. You see the spider webs. This is more serious than we'd thought, and I already thought it was pretty serious."

"All the more reason to call in backup."

"Johnson. Turn off the light. We're doing this."

"Smith," he said. He felt like they were at a turning point—and on his very first mission. But he liked his life. He liked Smith. Sure, she treated him like a stupid kid she was forced to babysit, but Johnson knew he was hard to take sometimes.

"Smith," he said again. Damn, his throat was so *dry*. It was that dirt taste in the air. It was cloying, overwhelming. He swallowed. "We should leave."

"We can't abandon the mission, Johnson."

"We're not, we're not. We assessed the kid. Look

around you. Look at his poor mother. She . . ." Johnson blinked back tears, swallowed again. "Look what he did to her, Smith. Let's get out of here, walk out that door, and call it in. 'Supervillainous.' We call it in, and we're done. Just like you said, we're done after that."

"I know you're scared, Johnson," Smith said, taking a step closer to him, moving slowly. "But we need to see this through. And I need my partner."

She pulled the phone from Johnson's slack grip, and he didn't protest when she turned off the light. He was just relieved not to have to look at that squirming mound of human organs and bugs for another second. That insectile scuttle up his spine came again, and this time he had to stop himself from reacting violently—how could he know this one wasn't an actual bug, climbing up his back? He couldn't know.

"Please," he whispered. He and Smith were inches apart now, but he couldn't see her at all in this overwhelming darkness. "We should leave . . ."

"Don't make me go in there by myself, Johnson," Smith whispered back. "I need my partner."

Johnson couldn't speak now. The lump in his throat was too thick. He nodded, but of course Smith couldn't see that. He made a soft choking sound and hoped that would be enough for her.

"Thank you," Smith said. He felt her fingers close over his hand and give a reassuring squeeze. Well, look at that—his partner cared about him after all.

That hand squeeze was just enough to get Johnson moving. He put one hand on Smith's shoulder and together they walked deeper into the black hole of the house. Johnson couldn't bring himself to reach out with his other hand to feel for their surroundings. But by the shifting of Smith's shoulder blade under his hand, he was pretty sure she was feeling ahead for the both of them.

It was then that Johnson became aware of a low buzzing sound. Had it been there this whole time? It was like becoming aware of the ocean's roar for the first time—not a roar, but a soothing static. But this wasn't soothing. It was a hacksaw buzz from miles away, and the sound was filling every crevice of this damn house—

BZZZZZZZZZZZZZZZZZZZZZ—

"Goddammit," Johnson muttered. "That noise."

Smith whispered back, "What noise?"

"That—"

BZZZZZZZZZZZZZZZZZZZZZ—

"—*noise*. You can't hear it?"

Smith didn't reply. Or maybe she did, but Johnson didn't hear her reply over that—

BZZZZZZZZZZZZZZZZZZZZZ—

—fucking *buzzing*. Was it getting louder?

Johnson did his best to ignore it and focus on their situation. He imagined that they had entered a small hallway. He remembered the house's layout: two bedrooms, a living space, a kitchen and bathroom, and . . . this hallway led to both bedrooms and the bathroom, right? They were close then.

SQUELCH.

Smith stopped in front of him.

"What was that?" Johnson breathed.

"My foot," Smith said. "The carpet's giving under our weight."

"Will we be able to make it?"

Johnson experienced another fleeting instinct: to yell

to his partner, *WE SHOULD LEAVE!*

"Yes, we'll make it," Smith said. "Just . . . just don't freak out if you get your shoes dirty."

"I'll be burning this whole outfit if we make it out of here. First thing."

"Focus, Johnson."

They continued down what Johnson hoped was the hallway, and after two steps—

SQUELCH.

Johnson's own shoe sunk into the floor a few inches. It felt wet. Like he was stomping through a marsh. *Bug paradise,* he thought, then shook his head—

BZZZZZZZZZZZZZZZZZZZZ—

None of that, Johnson, he told himself. He had to get it together. Smith was right.

They squelched their way step by step, and Johnson wasn't thrilled to learn that his shoes sunk deeper and deeper into the moldy floor the farther they went, to the point where it was becoming difficult to wrench his foot off the floor.

"I think it's here."

That was Smith. Johnson stopped, both relieved to not have to go farther and terrified to enter Hive's room. His *lair.*

Johnson breathed into Smith's ear in front of him: "What now?"

"Now we meet the subject and evaluate his psyche."

"Is 'totally fucked' a proper evaluation?"

Smith didn't reply. Instead, he felt her place his cell phone back into his hand, and he quickly grasped it with his fingers in fear of dropping it onto that squelchy carpet. No way in hell was he bending down to retrieve it, even if it was their only source of light.

"I'm going to open the door and call out to Hive," Smith whispered. "Don't use your phone's light except as a last resort."

"A . . . last resort? For *what?*"

"To get out of here."

Johnson didn't like how she'd left *us* out of that sentence.

There were some wet rummaging sounds directly in front of Johnson, and then Smith said, "Shit."

"What is it?"

"The door. It won't open. Something's . . . blocking it."

"Are you sure it's a push and not a pull?"

There was a pause in which Johnson could almost hear Smith's eyes roll, behind that constant—

BZZZZZZZZZZZZZZZZZZZZZ—

"Well," Johnson said, shaking the buzz from his head, "try pushing harder."

More wet sounds. Growing louder. A soft grunt from Smith. And then a *SQUELCH!* and sounds of breaking. Wood, Johnson guessed.

"Shit," Smith breathed. "The top half of the door broke off, fell into the room. The whole thing was rotten. We're going to have to step over the bottom half to get in."

"Wonderful," Johnson said.

"Just have that light ready." Smith aimed her voice into the room, away from Johnson, and called out, "Quentin?"

Silence. Except for the—

BZZZZZZZZZZZZZZZZZZZZZZ—

"Quentin," Smith called again. "We're worried about your mother. She doesn't seem well."

BZZZZZZZZZZZZZZZZZZZZZ—

Johnson pressed one finger in his left ear and tried to dig out that incessant buzzing. Was it growing louder? It was. Deafening, it felt like.

"Quentin," Smith said. "Aren't you worried for your mother? She's very ill—"

Without warning, that buzzing sound rose to a roar, and Johnson knew by Smith's crying out that she heard it too. Somewhere in that roaring sound, words formed, and Johnson knew it was Hive speaking.

—MOTHER DIDN'T LIKE MY FRIENDS—

"Quentin! We'd like to talk!"

—THERE'S NO NEED TO SHOUT—I CAN HEAR YOU PERFECTLY—I'VE HEARD EVERY WORD YOU'VE BREATHED SINCE YOU STEPPED INSIDE MY HOME—EVERY BREATH YOU'VE TAKEN—EVEN THE BLOOD MOVING SLUGGISHLY THROUGH YOUR VEINS—

Johnson shivered.

—AND I SEE YOU—I SEE EVERY INCH OF YOU—MY FRIENDS FEED MY MIND—I SEE EVERYTHING—I HEAR EVERYTHING—I KNOW EVERYTHING—

"QUENTIN!"

Despite Hive's admonishment that he could hear every whisper, Smith shouted louder than ever, and Johnson had to admit he admired her tactic.

"QUENTIN, WE'RE GOING TO COME INTO YOUR BEDROOM NOW! WE JUST WANT TO TALK TO YOU ABOUT YOUR MOTHER!"

Johnson gripped Smith's shoulder harder. Dammit, why didn't he know Morse code? He could squeeze out a message to her right now, tell her there was no way in hell they were going into Hive's lair. Well, he didn't know Morse code, sure. No fixing that now. But there was nothing stopping him from forcing Smith back from the door and manhandling her out of this house before she got them both killed.

—HAVE YOU NOT BEEN LISTENING—YOU DO NOT HAVE TO COME INSIDE TO TALK TO ME—I CAN UNDERSTAND YOU PERFECTLY—

"QUENTIN!" Smith called out against the roaring buzz. "WE HAVE TO SEE WHAT YOU'VE BE-COME! YOU KNOW THAT!"

—WHAT I'VE BECOME—WHAT I'VE BE-COME IS A MIRACLE—

"QUENTIN, YOU CALL WHAT YOU DID TO YOUR MOTHER A MIRACLE?!"

Smith, no, Johnson thought, preparing to pull her back. *Don't anger the little fucker . . .*

"YOU KILLED HER, QUENTY!" Smith yelled, and Johnson was horrified. She used his nickname, the nickname his mother used. The only way she could make things any worse was if she mentioned the kid's fa—

"MURDER, QUENTY! THAT MAKES YOU WORSE THAN YOUR FATHER!"

Oh God, no . . .

In an instant, the buzzing ceased, leaving Johnson's ears ringing. A *pop!* like an airplane climbing in elevation, and an empty *WHOOSH!* and Johnson felt Smith bodily yanked forward, out of his clutch. Like the side of that same airplane ripped away and her body was sucked out with all the pressurized air, one instant there and the next . . . gone. Swallowed by the black hole and left to die in the vacuum of space with those alien-insect fuckers. She didn't even have time to scream.

The light! Johnson's mind yelled at him over the—

BZZZZZZZZZZZZZZZZZZZZ—

He gripped the cell phone, almost dropped it with his sweaty fingers, but managed to catch it now that he had both hands available. No Smith to clutch on to now.

BZZZZZZZZZZZZZZZZZZZZ—

The phone's screen wouldn't do this time. Not enough light. He keyed through to the home menu and selected the flashlight app, and the second he'd clicked it on he raised it up, letting the blinding beam of bright white light stream from the phone. The light flooded Hive's room, and seeing what had become of his partner was nearly enough to rend Johnson's mind in two.

BZZZZZZZZZZZZZZZZZZZZ—

He staggered backward, his back crashing into the hallway's wall. The second he sank into the moldy wood, he felt the creepings and crawlings of little scuttling *things* advancing all around him. With a shout, he pushed off from the wall and went careening down the hallway.

Out. He needed to get out.

As he squelched through the hallway, he speed-dialed his office unit, desperate for anyone to pick up. Until they did, he would shout one word at the top of his lungs, in the hope that it would be heard over the buzzing.

Into the living room, now. His phone splashed light all around him, illuminating in seesawing snapshots pieces of the decaying and bloated house. Mounds of critters rose up in the light, and it was as if the house had come alive—it was groaning and breaking from its foundation, and a constant rush of insects poured from the walls and the ceiling and rose up from the floor and was that a fucking *dog*—

BZZZZZZZZZZZZZZZZZZZZ—

"SUPERVILLAINOUS!" he shouted at his phone.

—ZZZZZZZZZZZZZZZZZZZZ—

"SUPERVILLAINOUS! FUCKING SUPERVIL-LAINOUS!"

—ZZZZZZZZZZZZZZZZZZZZ—

QUENTIN KELLY'S TRANSFORMATION INTO Hive began three days before his final encounter with his mother, when he first heard the voices. His transformation was complete three days after his final encounter with his mother. For those final three days, he was less and less aware of what he'd done to her—which, for him at least, was merciful, for it threatened to consume him with grief at first. But by day three, the mental images of his ant farm—not so much a farm as an *army*, with two million soldiers—climbing up his mother's legs and dress and into her mouth and quickly swallowing her under a writhing mass, all those horrifying mental images no boy of ten should hold, were simply discarded along with all the other silly tidbits of information, like the name of his dog (and had he even had a dog?).

Once his mother was gone, and in her place his sentinel there to greet any unwelcome visitors, Hive expanded to the outer confines of the house and down through the foundations. Oh, but the soil was rich. So many ears and eyes to add to the hivemind!

It had only been a week or so since Hive had eaten his mother, but he'd long forgotten her existence. She certainly existed in the back of his mind somewhere, ready to be recalled if bidden, but he had other matters to spend his time contemplating.

His father, on the other hand . . .

Hive's father was the true villain here, Hive knew. Back when Hive went by Quentin Kelly, he was aware that he lived in a world of superheroes and supervillains. He'd known the government was responsible for intercepting any up-and-coming supervillains before they could rise up to full power. He remembered wishing with every fiber of his being that one day they would come to *his* house and declare his dad "supervillainous."

But they never came.

Nowadays, Hive sat in his lair and ruminated on his father. He thought he'd discarded trivial things such as his bullying at the hands of Dung, but really he'd just subscribed those actions to his father. It was all his father's fault. His father.

Besides thoughts of his father, Hive didn't think much of humans. He was content with his *real* friends. The voices even told him he was beginning to resemble them himself, which was just *so* pleasing! His human body was splitting itself into a thorax and abdomen, and the feelers on his head were growing every day. Yes, it was strange to feel the inside of his body breaking apart—but he knew from those library books he'd read what felt like years ago that this was just his blood rejecting the closed human circulatory system.

Bathe your organs in your lifeblood! his voices called to him. *This is the natural way!*

Hive's transformation was complete now. And all for the better. Humans were disgusting. But insects . . . insects were *beautiful*. Hive knew disgusting humans entered his yard at times—the mailman, mostly—but when the two humans in black suits came to his door, and when they *entered his house*, he became alarmed.

The idea that these two humans were actually coming inside his lair to declare him "supervillainous" never even crossed his mind.

But the voices told him not to worry. They would handle it.

Oh, what wonderful friends Hive had!

LOVE'S EMBRACE

SECONDS BEFORE SHE MET the love of her life, Crystal was just trying not to wee her wetsuit in front of her cute scuba instructor. But the streams of bubbles dancing around her like newly poured champagne conjured images of rushing water and made her bladder scream: *Is this some kind of cruel joke from the divorcée gods?!*

But then she plunged newer, darker depths, and she saw . . . *him.*

Love at first sight. It was real.

Maybe the divorcée gods would end her dry spell after all.

Her heart fluttered. Her bladder stilled. She watched his arms move sensually through the water like a hot knife through butter, like Cupid's arrow through her buoyancy compensator. He was gliding backward—it was adorable, the way he fumbled toward her without realizing—

And there he was. Her soul mate.

"You come here often?" she asked. But she was wearing a regulator so it came out—

"MMMMMMM!"

But they were meant for each other. They didn't need *words*.

And she was right. Of course she was right. Soulmates knew about these things, like mothers and horoscopes. He was gazing deep into her eyes. He was wrapping an arm around her waist. Another arm. Another. And five more beautiful arms, their suckers plop-plop-plopping onto her wetsuit until she thought she'd just die.

For their first dance, Crystal and her octopus spun round and down, round and down, in a shimmering tornado of warm champagne.

This was love.

PROMETHIUM 147

FRANK SIPPED HIS LATTE and thought: *These goddamned immoral monsters.*

It was inhumane! Was it so hard, Frank thought, to live one's life from creation to death without ripping another person apart? Look at what they'd become! No amount of cosmetics would get rid of *those* scars, Frank said to anyone who listened. He always added, just in case he hadn't fully made his point: Scars on the outside *and* the inside.

Frank couldn't believe how quickly this cannibalistic trend had progressed. This seemingly progressive Western civilization had gone from patting themselves on the back for finally achieving a "post-racism society" (whatever *that* meant) to ripping off the limbs of everyone now registered as "viable stock." And the transformation had been almost overnight.

Now Frank couldn't go anywhere without being reminded of what they'd become.

The library? No. The librarian was hopping around the stacks on one leg.

The grocery store? No. The cashier clerk bagged your items laboriously, one at a time with only the one arm.

He couldn't even enjoy watching his favorite TV shows. That was worst of all. The most beautiful people, supermodels and movie stars and actresses, now the most viable "stock" available. Every sitcom and drama and reality show was now full of gorgeous women with amputated limbs. Sure, the best cosmetic surgeons available had performed absolute magic, but it was still alarming to see. Noses carved from their faces; eye patches the new fashion trend; breasts lopped off as if there had been an outbreak of breast cancer. The most beautiful of them all were confined to wheelchairs, not an appendage left with which to express themselves. Within weeks of this overnight epidemic, every Hollywood set and every Hollywood lot had become handicap accessible.

But this was no epidemic, Frank knew. It was no disease in the true sense of the word. This was a disease of the brain—of the *male* brain. Every man in America woke up one day, saw a beautiful woman, and thought, *That's mine.* One could argue that this was no different than any other day, of course, but for one difference: in today's America, if a man liked a woman's tits or ass or legs, he didn't just catcall her or follow her around or rape her. No, he went to his toolshed, grabbed a hacksaw, and went and claimed what was his.

He took that nose, that eye, that breast, by any force necessary.

And since this was America, the world was pretty much okay with it.

It was like nothing had changed. Because, Frank conceded, nothing had. Men walked around today just like they did yesterday, swinging cocks between their knees as if they were their creator's gift to women everywhere, physically and mentally superior in every way. And if a woman had something a man wanted? Well, it wasn't really hers to keep then.

Even now, as Frank sat at his usual table outside his usual café, drinking his usual chai tea latte, he glanced around at the new normal in abject disgust. Women walked or limped or hobbled or wheeled themselves down the sidewalks as if nothing had changed, but if you looked close enough you couldn't miss it. They only traveled in large groups now, four or more, and Frank was willing to bet that those big purses each of them carried were filled with pepper spray and TASERs and little snub-noses, fully loaded and ready to go. He had heard that "girl nights" were now spent training each other on how to clean a gun or quick-draw. Nights at the bar were substituted for weekends at the shooting range.

Funny. Frank, a liberal through and through, used to protest gun rights in America every chance he got. As far as he was concerned, the NRA was the most evil group in the world. Now? Now he donated to them every month, little though he could afford. These women deserved to protect themselves, and no amount of gun laws were going to get in their way. It's their right to bear arms! It's right there in the Constitution!

"Anything else, sir?"

"Huh?" Frank looked up from his reverie.

The barista stood a safe distance away, hesitatingly making eye contact.

It broke his fucking heart. Here she was, just doing her job, and she couldn't even be sure she was safe in refilling his coffee at her own place of work.

God, he prayed, *please let her boss be a woman.*

"No," he told her, smiling his warmest, most sincere smile. He had practiced that exact smile; there was a balance between enthusiasm and showing too many teeth, lest you appear predatory. "Thank you. This was the most delicious chai I've ever had. You did a wonderful job."

She smiled back, but he noticed that the dirty cups she'd cleared from the table next to his were shaking in her hands. "You say that every day, sir. You're too kind."

"Well, I mean it every day. In fact . . . you know what? I just can't say no to you. Could I get another of these delicious creations of yours? And a nonfat vanilla latte to go with it?"

"Of course." She backed away several feet, not turning until she was well out of his reach, and headed back inside the café.

Frank sighed. The same barista served him every single day, and yet she still didn't trust him. At least not until Shelly turned up.

Shelly was Frank's wife. Unfortunately, he'd met her after this brutal new world, so she had her own scars already. But to him she was the most beautiful thing he'd ever known, and he made sure to treat her as such. They'd met at the hospital four years ago, mere weeks after women started showing up in the Emergency Room in droves missing body parts, desperately staunching the blood and just trying to survive. Frank had been in for his quarterly checkup. Shelly was there to treat the infection in her amputated wrist.

There hadn't been enough medical professionals to meet the sudden demand, so it was rather common for patients to bleed out in the waiting room, or for women to not bother coming in with infections and then dying at home from blood poisoning. In some hospitals, in fact, there were just as many security guards as there were doctors, because it wasn't unheard of for packs of men to rush a hospital lobby looking for easy pickings. The straggling lambs of the herd.

Frank, being the progressive feminist he was, nobly surrendered his slotted appointment to let Shelly see his doctor instead. Insisted on it, in fact. To thank him, she took him to this very café to buy him a coffee. "Chai tea latte," he'd ordered; "Nonfat vanilla latte," she'd ordered; he let her pay and just like that, their budding relationship began with what had now become a daily tradition.

And here she was, walking toward him now. It was only a couple blocks from their apartment building, but nonetheless she was speed-walking, furtively glancing around her as she went. Always the cautious one, Frank's Shelly.

The barista showed up with their drinks just as Shelly settled in her seat. Frank noted that the barista seemed noticeably more relaxed now that another woman was here. Silly, really. Frank met Shelly here every day. She really should know better. He clearly wasn't like any of these monsters. Couldn't this barista woman see that?

"Hey, sweetie," Frank said. He glanced at his watch. 1:47 p.m. A little later than their usual, but today was a big day for Shelly. "How was the showing?"

Shelly was a painter, a creator of art in her own right, and had spent the morning preparing a Halloween-themed art installation. Frank didn't quite get it, to be honest. Modern art was beyond his humble understanding, he would say to her when she asked for his opinion—while, inside, he'd stare at a canvas painted a solid shade of yellow and think, *Who would pay for this? It looks like a toddler pissed on it.*

"Oh . . . great," Shelly said, cupping her drink in her one hand and sighing out some pent-up tension she'd stored on the walk over.

"Yeah? Did you sell any?"

"Not exactly . . ."

"Not exactly? What does that mean?"

"It means I got an offer—"

"Great! So you *did* sell. Exactly."

"No . . ."

"No?"

She paused. "A private collector offered to buy the whole lot—"

"That's *great!*"

"—*if,*" she said, looking up from her drink, "I alter them."

Frank took a sip of chai. "Alter them how?"

"He . . ." She frowned. "You won't get it. It's stupid."

"Shelly," Frank said, fixing her with his reassuring smile. "Nothing you say is *stupid.* Come on. I'm listening, I promise."

"Well . . . this collector . . . he wants me to 'restore' them. Whatever *that* means."

"He didn't tell you what he meant by that?"

"He did, but . . . it's not restoring them, Frank, it's

fucking *ruining* them."

"How does he want you to alter them, exactly?"

"Well, my painting of the girl from *The Ring*, for example. You remember that one?"

Frank thought for a moment, recalling the installation in his mind. One of the larger pieces incorporated what Shelly called "three-dimensional mediums" and was actually made to look like an old TV set. On the television's screen was an image of a crumbling stone well on a dreary, desolate landscape. Made to look as if she'd just climbed from the well, this decomposing girl was frozen with one limb reaching from the screen. This was one Frank actually liked. Nothing "modern art" here. Shelly had very cleverly made the girl's arm poke through the TV's screen and actually reach out toward the viewer.

"Yes," Frank said. "I *loved* that one! Why would he want you to alter it?"

Anguish filled Shelly's face. "He wants me to give her a hand."

Frank understood now. The central theme in Shelly's installation was to show classic Hollywood horror films through the lens of today's social fetish of taking parts of the female anatomy for the male possession. Shelly had spent a large portion of her time on the art piece of the girl climbing through the TV because, Frank knew, she saw it as a reflection of herself. She had carefully created it, then just as carefully sawed the girl's hand off at the wrist—just like Shelly's own amputated hand—and made the arm to look as if it had been haphazardly sewn shut and turned green with infection.

"So," Frank said, "by 'restoring' them, this collector means he wants you to just make them look like the actual characters they're based off of, sans mutilation."

"Yes." Shelly sighed.

Frank considered this for a moment, sipping his chai. He looked out onto the street and saw one of the less fortunate women, one of those who had lost more than just her limbs. She was barely a torso with a head, and even that had been trimmed back piece by piece until she was truly terrifying to look at. One socket glared emptily, and the other still had its eye but no eyelid, so she was forced to constantly stare around at this new world with no depth perception. She was strapped to a wheelchair, and a man—her husband, her protector, Frank assumed—wheeled her down the sidewalk as he merrily chatted away to her.

Frank was too far away to hear what the man was saying, but nonetheless he thought: *Bless you, sir. You are one of the good ones. Here to support our women. Just like me.*

He turned back to his own woman and said, "I'm *so* sorry, Shelly. I know that part of the exhibit was very important to you."

"It was the *most* important part of the exhibit," she snapped back. "That was the whole goddamned *point*, Frank."

Frank held up his hands in defense. "Hey, hey . . . don't take this out on *me*. You know I'm one of the good guys."

Shelly almost dropped her cup. "One of the *good* guys?"

Frank blinked at her. This wasn't going as he'd hoped. "Yes. One of the good guys. I'm on your side here. You know I'm here to listen and to support you."

He shut his mouth, his teeth clicking together. He

hated these situations. They were becoming more and more frequent. How could he tell her he was here to listen and understand while still *listening* instead of talking? He wasn't about to mansplain to her. He *did* understand, at least as much as he could understand the female struggle, but telling her so would make this whole conversation about *him* and not her, wouldn't it?

How does one keep one's mouth shut without becoming complicit in one's silence?

Shelly still hadn't responded. She still hadn't picked her cup back up from where she'd placed it. And she still hadn't looked away from Frank's eyes. He was starting to feel very uncomfortable—but there was no way he would allow himself the comfort of looking away. He would bear this discomfort and keep firm eye contact with his wife to show that he was here for *her*, never himself.

"Frank . . ." Shelly began, then she too shut her mouth. She hadn't lost as many of her teeth as some of the other women, but it was enough for Frank not to hear the same click as his had made.

Frank didn't respond. *Let her speak,* he reminded himself. *This is her time to speak.*

"Frank," she said again. "Do you . . . you don't think you're completely separate from all of this, do you?"

He couldn't just ignore her question, rhetorical or no. "You know I'm not exactly going around cannibalizing anyone. I haven't taken a single piece of the female body from a single woman. I haven't even touched a hacksaw or a scalpel or anything. I'm not like those monsters."

Shelly squinted her eyes as if trying to look through Frank's.

Windows to the soul, he thought.

"And that's . . . what?" she said. "Noble of you?"

"No, of course not! It's not noble to do the *decent* thing, Shelly."

"The 'decent thing.' And what's that? *Not* ripping the female body to shreds?"

"That's certainly part of it."

Shelly leaned forward. She was shaking, he noticed.

"Frank, don't you dare tell yourself that you're not a part of this new American Dream."

"What . . . what are you talking about?"

"Goddammit, Frank." Tears welled up in her eyes, and one fell from her cheek directly into her forgotten latte. "You can't just call yourself a feminist because you don't fucking *eat women*."

"I . . . I *am*—"

"Oh, cut the bullshit, Frank."

Frank stared at her. She was absolutely quivering, and the tears kept coming one after the other. She used her wrist stump to wipe one side of her face, smearing her makeup.

"Where is this coming from?" he asked. "Is this because of your art installa—"

"It's not about the *goddamned art*, okay?" She was whispering now, and her hissed words whistled through a gap in her teeth. "Is the male ego so big, so fragile, that you are physically incapable of remembering your own mistakes?"

"Shelly, I've made mistakes. I'm not disputing that, but—"

"But they just aren't *that bad*, is that it?"

"Well . . . yes."

"Oh, fuck this." Shelly reached for her large purse

and spilled her latte with her stump in her haste. "I'm not going to spell it out for you, Frank. I'm going home."

"Shelly . . . *what* are you talking about?"

She stood up and looked down at Frank with . . . was that *pity* in her eyes? Or more anger?

"Maybe," she said, "if you're nice and condescending enough to our barista—her name is *Mary*, by the way—maybe she'll give you the key to the restroom so you can take a good, hard look at yourself in the mirror."

She turned and walked away, the same quick steps as the ones that had brought her here, only now she walked with hunched shoulders and a clenched fist and she didn't glance around for danger.

Maybe I should walk with her, Frank thought. *To protect her.*

"Anything else, sir?"

"Huh?" Frank looked up from his reverie.

The barista stood a safe distance away, hesitatingly making eye contact.

It broke his fucking heart.

"Um," he said, looking down at the table. "I'm sorry. It seems my wife has made a bit of a mess."

"Oh, no worries. Please, sir, it's not your problem. I'll clean up the spilled coffee as soon as you leave."

He smiled up at her, and then his smile faltered as he saw that she was shaking again. Just as if Shelly had never been here. Didn't she know she had nothing to fear with him? Hadn't he shown her that? Why was she treating him like this?

He remembered Shelly's parting words; his smile fell.

"Mary . . ." he said, again offering her his warmest, most sincere smile—though admittedly its warmth had waned. "It's Mary, isn't it?"

She nodded, her lips stretched into a semblance of a returning smile.

"Might I borrow the key to the restroom before I go?"

"Yes, of course!" she said, pulling a key attached to a plastic saucer from her apron and—well, not handing it to him as he'd expected when he held his hand out to hers. Instead, she placed it on his table within his reach and quickly stepped away.

Broke his fucking heart.

He smiled anyway, retrieved the key, stood up—slowly so as not to alarm her. Pulled out his wallet and placed a twenty-dollar bill on the table, careful to not place it directly in Shelly's spilled drink. "A little tip for you," he told the barista. "You deserve it."

He walked around her as she thanked him, careful to give her a wide berth—for her comfort, of course—and stepped inside the café and then into the small restroom in the corner. Closing the door behind him, he paused, facing the door. Was he really afraid to turn around and face the mirror over the sink? What did Shelly expect him to see exactly?

He turned around, but his eyes were fixed on the tiled floor.

He stepped to the sink. Placed the saucer-key on the porcelain beneath the soap dispenser. Grasped either side of the sink. Leaned into it. The mirror was now just inches from his face, but still . . . he couldn't bring himself to look up.

What did Shelly see in him?

Do it, he told himself. *Fucking do it.*

He brought his chin up . . . but his eyes were firmly shut.

Do it! Fucking do it!

Frank opened his eyes.

Look at what you've become!

"My God . . ." Frank whispered to his reflection. "Shelly was right."

He reached up with one hand and felt his face. There they were. The scars. He traced their zigzags across his face and down his neck and up into his scalp. The staples stood out from his skin and pricked his fingertips. His face was a collage of stolen flesh—pale white, tan, black, swarthy, green—like different countries on a map, the stitches as their borders.

How . . . how had he forgotten?

He looked just like all the other monsters. Just like all those goddamned immoral monsters he was so sick and tired of—the ones he condemned to everybody who would listen, telling them that no amount of cosmetics would fix *those* scars . . . not the ones on the outside and not the ones on the inside.

He hadn't lied to Shelly—he'd never lifted a hacksaw in his life, had never ripped a body part from a woman. But that hadn't stopped him from taking their bodies once they were torn to scraps, once another monster had destroyed them and he could simply seize opportunity. A piece here, a piece there . . .

A thought occurred to him, the implications of which filled him with horror.

Were any of them Shelly's?

Oh God . . .

Frank was a monster.

WHAT KEPT HIM UP AT NIGHT

MY MIND FEELS LIKE a physical extension of my body; it swings, above, unencumbered by the laws of gravity. I can taste it in my mouth: filling; expanding; whipping around me like a flag in gale-force winds, winds rushing from my head, straight up; violent, impossibly violent, as if mocking the ceiling fan sifting the darkness.

I have to open my eyes before I'm ripped from the bed by my mind, ground myself with my senses.

Sight: Shadows of shadows. The ghost of a computer screen glowing in my retinas' memories. Tenebrous tentacles of darkness spinning like a top: The ceiling fan. I'm staring into the ceiling fan. Focus on the ceiling fan.

Sound: the hum, the whirring of the ceiling fan, distant, beneath the constant ocean roar of a colony of tiny insects busy scuttling in my ear canal, the left ear.

Taste: the feel of my mind, still on my tongue; palpable. Chomp on it. It makes my mouth water.

Touch: pain, an assembly line of pain. The feathery chafe of the sheets against my fevered skin is lost in the pain . . . so much pain. My legs sit in a wood stove, feeding its metal maw, making its belly glow.

My mind is still there, extended above me, a dog straining on its leash.

Do I set it free? Where will it go?

I throw it a bone: imaginary conversations with the teenage kid from yesterday. Yell at him.

Explain to him how his insecurities are what make him. Explain to him that this can change. Explain to him that he is a disgusting, abominable fucking person who you should unleash your mind on. *Sic 'em!*

The kid said this, he actually said this to me, just yesterday, and it burst from him like a dam giving up the ghost, like he was reciting scripture: "I'm just saying, that I'm Mormon, and if a gay person tried to join our Scout troop we'd MURDER them!"

(He didn't shout the M word, but in my mind [*Sic 'em!*] the word is in all caps.)

Disgusting, abominable fucking person.

But you were a disgusting, abominable fucking person once, says the mind. *I know. I know this about you. I'm telling.*

I close my eyes. My mind is a physical extension of my body, struggling against its shackles; it swings, it flings; it expands. It whips violently. I chomp on it like a mother severing her baby's umbilical cord. It snaps, it's gone, it's passing through the ceiling fan, through the sky, the stratosphere, the who-knows.

Disgusting, abominable fucking person.

No, I've changed, come back.

My big toe itches. The kind of itch that you don't want to scratch; you want instead to take a bread knife and use the serrated edge to peel off your skin, or maybe just lop the whole thing off. But you can't. It still itches. You can feel it. I can feel it in my kneecaps, in my eyes, in my watering mouth.

No. I've changed. Come back.

I get up, waken those retinal memories of a computer screen, begin typing that my mind is like a physical extension of my body

(*it swings, above . . .*)

and hope that these words will soothe my mind back from Orion's Belt. Here's a treat. Sit. Good boy.

Play dead.

[*sic*] *'em!*

THE DIARY

HE BREAKS INTO JANE'S HOUSE to find the diary—
that's where his memory starts.

Feverish and furious, he slams his wool-wrapped
fist through the windowpane. Broken glass tinkles onto
the carpet inside with a sound like wind chimes. His boots
crunch the glass shards as he steps in through the window, and the chill night air follows him into the dark
house.

January 15

Dear Diary,

*I can't believe I just wrote "Dear Diary." I sound like such
a Judy Bloom cliché. I might as well have followed that up
with a story about having a "totally gigantic crush" on some
guy.*

This is what it's come to then—talking to a book. You're as close as I've got to a friend, so here goes.

I'm starting to feel like there's no hope for me, Diary.

ONCE HE'S IN, HE RANSACKS JANE'S BEDROOM. His only desire is to find her diary. The key to everything is within those pages—it has to be.

He tears the room to shreds in his search, tracking mud on the carpet then covering it with broken knick-knacks, shattered glass, ceramic figurines ground to a tchotchke powder. Dump her underwear drawer, check for false bottoms, ransack the messy closet. Nothing.

At some point he collapses on her mattress, feeling sore and sick. "Where the hell did you put it, Jane?"

The anger takes him again, and he springs up with renewed vigor, searching and breaking, breaking, *breaking.*

And in all that raging and yelling and breaking, he actually finds it. Typical Jane, hiding her secrets in plain sight—the diary was right on the bookcase next to her bed this whole time, disguised in the dust jacket of another book.

Fahrenheit 451. A book about burning books. He laughs so hard his chest aches, but then he's not sure why it struck him as funny.

His fever's definitely getting worse. No matter. He has found what he was searching for.

January 17

Dear Diary,

I know I need to get out and meet someone, but I barely

know where to start. I've never met anyone who understands the kind of life I've led. It seems like a relationship would be doomed from the start.

Still, I've been catching myself daydreaming about finding that one special guy. We'll run away together—me and the guy who loves my bad habits, who will sit and roll a guilty cigarette with me. A guy I can be myself with. A guy with sympathetic eyes.

JANE'S HUMOROUS DISGUISE—*Fahrenheit 451*, burning books, fire, ha-ha—gives him an idea that sets him laughing again, then coughing, then hacking. He's definitely coming down with something.

He stumbles to the fireplace, kicking angrily at that goddamn coffee table on the way. He dumps an armful of Jane's books on the hearth. Kicks them into the firebox. Searches his pockets. Though he quit smoking years ago, matchbooks have lined this coat for as long as he can remember . . . haven't they? God, why can't he remember? As hard as he concentrates, his memories keep returning to him breaking into—

Ah, there they are. Just like he thought.

Matchbook found, he sets about catching flames. He reads her diary by the glow of burning literature. Jane's cramped, careless handwriting hits him like a brick wall, and he remembers why he's here.

He spreads the diary open until the spine cracks and follows the lines of scribble with a trembling finger, reciting the words feverishly to himself. If Jane comes back and sees him with his scraggly beard and mismatched layers of clothing, reading aloud before a blazing fire of her favorite books . . .

He needs to hurry. Find his answers before she gets here.

January 27

Dear Diary,

Well, I did it. I forced myself to go out, in hopes of meeting someone.

I went to the best kind of bar: dark and smoky like an old noir film, complete with a bar-length mirror tilted behind the displayed spirits. I ordered an old-fashioned and sat in silence, soaking up the smoke and conversation and ambiance.

Before I could even finish my first round, I looked up at that tilted mirror and caught sight of a man, huddled over a pint of beer. He smiled at me and, even from that distance, it looked like he had . . . sympathetic eyes.

HE'S NOT FINDING WHAT he came here for. He rips the pages from the diary one at a time, as he finishes reading them, and feeds them to the flames.

Her first week of entries has no mention of him. Why can't he remember the exact date that they met? Every time he searches his memories, he just finds himself back at breaking into Jane's house.

What's wrong with him? Something's . . . getting in the way.

January 27 (cont'd)

I get so nervous around guys who act interested in me. They make me all tongue-tied and loopy. And then as soon as they're gone I think of a million "cool girl" things to say.

Tonight was no different.

As soon as Sympathetic Eyes smiled at me, I immediately turned into a mumbling idiot. I could barely answer the bartender when he asked if I wanted another drink. Before I knew it, I'd chickened out and left.

I know, I know. Pathetic.

I made a compromise with my dignity, though: Sure, I wouldn't go back into the bar, but I didn't have to go crawling back into my bed either. In the parking lot, I rescued my rolling paper and tobacco tin from the glove compartment, hitched down the tailgate, and sat on my truck, determined to enjoy the rest of my night.

I figured I'd celebrate my magnificent performance inside with a freshly rolled cigarette. I was just about feeling back to normal, enjoying the crisp night air, when I realized I didn't bring any matches.

"NO! NO, JANE, WHAT THE HELL? Where's the page?!"

It should be here, right here. January 27th—that was the day they met, he's sure of it now. She walked into the bar—what was its name?—and they made eye contact in the mirror.

. . . a man, Jane wrote, huddled over a pint of beer. He—

The page ended there, but when he turned to the next page . . .

Ripped out. The next one, too, along with the majority of the rest of the book. The jagged remnants on the inside crease of the spine taunt him.

His paranoia rears its head and he feels the beginnings of a migraine. Why would Jane tear out the pages? Does she still have them? What do they say?

He searches the book with renewed desperation, as if he's losing oxygen. But the only line he can find even remotely referring to him is written at the top of a partially ripped page. She wrote his name and then: *there's only a fine line between love and hate—* And then nothing.

Why does that sound so familiar?

January 27 (cont'd)

I was about to just call the night quits and head home when the door to the bar burst open, and out stepped Sympathetic Eyes.

He spotted me and headed right over to my truck, looking so calm and cool with his hands in the pockets of his wool coat. His hair was perfectly imperfect—something I've never mastered—with just the right amount of stubble on his chiseled jawline.

And those eyes!

He stopped a few feet in front of me. "Need a light?" His voice matched his appearance—rugged but charming.

And that, Diary, is how I finally met my Sympathetic Eyes.

HE'S READ EVERY PAGE of this damned diary. After that part about the "fine line between love and hate," there's nothing. No mention of him, of them, of what they had. They had something together, he's sure of it. Why can't he remember?

"What happened to us, Jane?"

February 13

Dear Diary,

I think I'm in love.

I can't believe I'm actually writing that, but I think, maybe, possibly, it's true. I'm in FREAKING LOVE! If you needed any more proof, you'd only have to see the goofy grin smacked across my face.

And I think you know who it is! Sympathetic Eyes. Except now I know his name is Ben. I even opened up to him about my mom and what she left me. Things I've only ever written in here. He understood me on a whole other level because— guess what? He's an orphan too. He wasn't left with a fortune like I was, but that's not the point. The point is, nobody's ever quite understood what it's like to feel this alone, but he does.

He did seem a little weirded out learning that I keep this diary. But I assured him it's only good stuff, of course!

So, yeah . . . we're kind of "together" now? Diary, you know better than anyone how I've been hurt before. I know you're worried. But it's okay. I'm keeping myself guarded. I just can't help feeling . . . safe with him. Still—I promise you I'll remain cautious. Cautiously optimistic.

Did I mention I'm in love?

HE KEEPS COMING BACK to that sentence: *there's only a fine line between love and hate.*

Why is it there, with his name? Why didn't Jane rip

that out too? She was pretty thorough with everything else.

Could she have left that one line on purpose?

"Are you trying to tell me something, Jane? Are you trying to say that you hate me . . . or love me?"

A car's engine startles him, and he drops the diary. He runs to the front windows, squinting against the headlights streaming in. A truck pulls into Jane's driveway, killing its engine and its headlights in one fell swoop that chills his spine.

Jane is home.

Christ. She's home.

August 23

It all started with resentment—my money, my house, my truck, my clothes, my healthcare. I guess even orphans can't understand each other. We're all just hopeless.

I've got to write the whole thing down before I end up losing my mind. Maybe if I get it all down on paper I can get it out of my head.

I came home to find him on the couch again, beer in hand, watching one of his heavy-metal DVDs. His boots were flaking dried mud onto the coffee table.

"Hey, Janey-baby."

"What the hell? How'd you get in here?"

He turned back to the TV, took a swig from his Stella. "You should just give me a copy of the key, babe. Much easier that way."

I threw my purse down and stared at him in disbelief. "Easier? What, so you don't have to break in?"

He gave me a wink, but his charm didn't work on me like it did the first time I caught him breaking in. Or the second.

"You can't do this!" I said, trying to force the quiver out of my voice and show I'm not a doormat. "You can't just come in uninvited, break in and help yourself to my beer, track mud on my carpet—"

"Babe." He sat up and faced me. "You know me. You know my story. I wasn't left with some trust fund—"

"It's not a trust fund!"

"Whatever. Sorry I can't afford my own suburban two-story home with a white picket fence. If I could, I'd be over there, drinking my own beer, watching my own television. If that was my life, you'd be allowed over whenever you wanted. But I'm the penniless orphan in this relationship, remember?"

"You can't use the 'orphan' card on me—we're in our thirties! Grow up."

He slammed his beer down on the coffee table—inches from the coaster, just to push my buttons—and stood up from the couch, ignoring the blaring TV.

"What did you say to me?"

"I . . . look, I'm not letting you use me. You need to show me some respect. We've only been dating for, what, six months? You need to act like I'm more than just a credit card and a place to crash."

"Jane," he said, taking a few steps toward me. We were within arm's reach of each other now. "Jane, you know I love you. You love me too, don't you, babe?"

That's when the tears came. Love? I hadn't gotten the courage to say the words to him yet. My mind reeled. He'd broken into my house. What else had he broken into? Had he been reading my diary?

Is he reading you now, Diary?

I sniffed, holding the tears back. "Maybe this is going too fast."

I tried to turn away, but he reached out and stopped me, holding my arm. I could smell the beer on his breath.

It scared me.

"What are you saying?" he whispered, fixing me with those eyes. Steel gray. No sympathy anymore.

"Let go of me, please," I whispered back.

JANE'S HERE. Christ, she's back.

He runs back to the fireplace, and *God* he feels so sick, burning up but it's so *cold*, and he's dizzy and stumbling and he's got to get to the fireplace, because he left her diary there on the hearth, in the ashes, and he needs to search it again, before she sees what he's done, he's got to—

He trips on the upturned coffee table and falls the last few feet to the fireplace, slams his head on the brick, and sudden blackness—

August 23 (cont'd)

The screaming started when he wouldn't let go.

I yelled at him, and he shouted and shook me and called me a spoiled bitch. I pushed him and called him some ugly name, I don't remember what. When I'm angry I get flustered and my words don't make much sense.

We fought for what felt like hours. You'd think a six-month-long relationship wouldn't have much baggage to unpack, but it was as if everything we learned about each other's past was a land mine, and we'd managed to step on every single one. Through it all we kept coming back to it—back to whether or not we loved each other.

He was pacing back and forth between the coffee table and the television. "So what is it, Jane? Love? Hate? Do you love me? 'Cause right now it feels like you hate me, just like everyone else in my life."

"Stop throwing this pathetic pity party already. Nobody hates you."

"Don't they? Can you honestly say that if I wanted to stay here, in this house—us, together—that you'd love me? 'Cause I will! I'm desperate, Jane. I'll crawl if that's what it takes. Would you like that? Is that what you want?"

I couldn't see through the tears. I couldn't breathe. "No!" I gasped.

He stopped, gestured wildly toward me. "See? See?! You wouldn't! You don't love me, Jane, so just admit that you hate me just like everyone else in my life from the moment I was born, and I'll leave!"

I couldn't answer. I was sobbing so hard my chest was seizing up. In retrospect his words seem laughable—can a person really feel so sorry for themselves, Diary? But in the moment it all felt so real. Now the memory's a ghost of what it was.

He rushed to me, arms still out, and got in my face. "Admit it! You hate me! You don't love me, you never loved me, you just love your house, your truck, your stuff, but you can't love me—"

"SHUT—UP!" I screamed. I slammed both hands against his chest.

He stumbled backward, the force of my shove enough to send his body right over the coffee table. He crashed to the ground in front of the fireplace.

"It's not one or the other, Ben. It's not love or hate—that's not how it works! The world isn't out to get you just because you never had a mom to tell you she loved you. You think, Ben, there's only a fine line between love and hate, but maybe there's a middle ground. Maybe I just need a little more time to let you in!"

Ben didn't respond. He didn't move from where he'd fallen.

"Ben?"

Silence. Cold dread filled my chest. I waded past the couch like I was in a dream. Past the television, the coffee table . . .

"Ben . . . ?"

That's when I noticed the blood.

His head had smashed into the hearth, and dark blood was pooling in the cracks between the rustic red bricks.

"Oh my God . . ."

I can't write about it anymore, Diary. I just can't. The pain is too much.

The evening ended with a 911 call, an ambulance, and a body bag.

—BRIGHTNESS, SUDDENLY.

He wakes up where he fell just moments before, barely registering the deep red stain on the carpet beneath his head. Rolls over, grabs the diary. She hasn't come in yet. There's still time.

He starts at the beginning, again, just the same as before. *I can't believe I just wrote "Dear Diary." I sound like such a—*

Wait a minute. He already read this. He already . . . didn't he? He already ripped through these pages, already watched them curl themselves to ash in the fire. How could he . . . how could he have ripped out the same pages from the same diary and set them each ablaze—and yet they're still here?

This doesn't make any sense.

What's happening?

"Think, asshole, *think*, dammit."

How did he get here?

His memories begin the same way each time.

His memories begin each time with him breaking into Jane's house.

There is nothing before that. There is only this house. This moment.

Behind him, he hears a small sound. *Click.* A tumbler turns. A door creaks.

He looks up.

His memory ends with Jane whispering:

"Ben?"

October 10

Dear Diary,

It happened again. I must be going crazy.

I came home, relieved to escape the cold, and when I opened the door . . .

When I opened the door, I saw Ben.

He was kneeling at the hearth, just like last time and the time before that, reading this very diary. He looked up, saw me, but didn't say anything.

And, just like last time, I whispered his name.

My hands are shaking so much I can barely write this.

I whispered his name, and he disappeared.

My diary keeps showing up by the fireplace. Either I'm sleepwalking or what I'm seeing is really . . .

Ben, if you're reading this, or if your spirit is . . . I'm so sorry. I know it was an accident, but that whole evening keeps going through my head in an endless loop. If only I hadn't pushed you. If only I'd answered truthfully when you asked if I loved you. I wish you could have at least had that.

If you're reading this, Ben, then this is how I'll end it. I'll leave the diary by the fireplace, and I'll write your answer right here, and maybe you'll find what you're looking for. Maybe you can find some peace and some rest.

Ben . . . I love you.

Love,
Jane

HE BREAKS INTO JANE'S HOUSE to find the diary—that's where his memory starts.

SHUFFLE

Timejump #1

HE WAS A FRIGHTENING MAN. His wild eyes shone beneath a thunderous brow and his hair swept from his scalp as if struck by lightning. He busily paced his dim quarters, killing the fire beside the hearth, gathering papers scattered about a table into his satchel, shrugging on a greatcoat over his stiff collar and velvet cravat. All the while he whispered feverishly, as if memorizing some paramount speech.

His name was John C. Calhoun, and he was woefully ignorant that a team of specialists from the future was watching him from the comfort of their time machine. The team stared in wonder at the giant portal before them, showing this impossible scene from the past.

"It is up to you, Dodge," said Dr. Veltman.

Dodge lifted his round form from his armchair, quivering with anticipation, chalk dust settling about his shoulders. "At the risk of repeating myself, Dr. Winnow, all I must do is distract Calhoun from relieving himself until he has no choice but to ride to the bank with a full bladder?"

"Yes," she replied.

"And Peppercorn, my good chap," Dodge said, "in order to do that, I must first step through this screen?"

"Er, portal!" squeaked the mechanical engineer from the back.

"Yes, this portal, quite. Mr. Foible, would you be so kind as to hold my tea? Thank you, young sir. Well, as they say, I will be seeing you on the other—"

And then John C. Calhoun and the year 1812 vanished and everything went wrong.

Before the jump; 6:58 a.m.

TIME STRETCHED LIKE TAFFY for Mora Winnow as she approached the door. It was an intimidating door, industrial steel and looking like the top-secret entrance to Area 51 itself. But this wasn't Area 51. She could almost feel the weight of the 450 metric tons of concrete above her head, sealing her in this bunker deep underground. Where in the world *was* NOMALA? She had no idea. The American government sure didn't want her to know. She only knew why she was here.

NOMALA had built a time machine.

And she was here to show them where to take it.

Her footsteps echoed down the long, stark corridor, the clipped hammer strike of heels on stippled steel. Her eyes never left the looming door, as if she were challenging it to a staring contest. *Just try to keep me out, door. I dare you.*

Her manicured nails clicked the laminate of the glossy ID in her grip: DR. MORA WINNOW, STATISTICIAN, N.O.M.A.L.A. SECTOR 7.

Sure, it wasn't Area 51, but then, everyone and their grandmother had heard about Area 51; nobody outside of this bunker even knew NOMALA existed.

She held her ID before the red LED eye above the door's handle. The red blinked green in recognition; the echo of her footsteps died in the roar of a circuit breaker. She opened the heavy door, victorious.

Mora didn't know what she expected to find here: a room full of cackling mad scientists? The TARDIS? A DeLorean? Certainly something equally dramatic to suit the situation outside in the real world, where impending doom literally flew above their heads in every direction.

What she found on the other side of the door was her team, deep in a political debate, shouting over one another, surrounded by towers of mysterious machinery. An undercurrent of electrical power hinted at hidden hardware; its sonorous hum vibrated through the floor and walls—she didn't so much hear it as she felt it deep in her bones.

"Russian involvement is minimal, bloody nonexistent if you ask me."

"I can assure you, Ringbauer, that is a myth, no doubt encouraged by your Australian Navy's blockade south of—"

"A blockade that wouldn't have been necessary, Veltman, if those sackless Americans hadn't pulled their forces from Japan back in 2029!"

"I say, please do calm yourselves, gentlemen! History has shown us our future: not some Third World War, as the media delights in calling it, but an event more like the Seven Years' War of the eighteenth century, or perhaps another Thirty or even Fifty Years' War!"

"Er, please, sir, not on her machinery, eh? If you must sit—"

"If you truly believe in the fake news that the Russians are minimally involved—"

"I would hardly call smuggling nuclear war heads into China *minimal*."

"Precisely, Dodge, thank you. If this is what you truly believe, Ringbauer, then I do not doubt you also believe Korea to be neutral?"

"Actually, Veltman, my good sir, Korea has yet to sign the Eurasian Treaty—"

"Bloody 'ell, Dodge, you'd believe an African swallow if it told you it was from Alaska!"

"Ahem."

Mora had finally interrupted and the argument halted in its tracks, the quartet of men turning to stare at her like deer in headlights. She lifted her chin and acknowledged each of them in turn.

"Good morning, gentlemen," she said. "I am Dr. Mora Winnow. Your statistician. We are not here to point fingers or postulate theories. We are here to do our job, and I suggest we begin immediately."

After a beat of silence in which the men's shock was deafening, one of them stepped forward. He was a short middle-aged man in a tweed jacket, belying his plump features with a quick step that sent a haze of chalk dust into the air. Coughing to clear his throat, he bent in the lowest bow his round belly would permit.

"Ah, Dr. Winnow, allow me to introduce myself. An historian, academic, professor, and research fellow of Cambridge, Oxford . . ." As he straightened, he caught Mora's eyes reading the nametag clipped to his breast pocket. "Yes, my official title is rather long—" He chuckled, his proper English accent eliciting Mora's instant adoration. "Clayton Roundhill Dodge, Conspicuous Gallantry Cross, Member of Parliament, PhD, MA, BA, Cambridge Philosophical Society, Royal Historical Society—but where are my manners? Would you care for some tea, Dr. Winnow? I've just sent Veltman's intern, Foible, to fetch some. He should be—"

"Dodge!" snapped a much older man in a white lab coat, bringing his full height up beside the historian. "Did you not hear the woman? Presently we must attend to our mission, as we do not yet have the luxury of time!"

Dodge chuckled, looking embarrassed. "Ah, a *time* joke—"

"Dodge!" the man repeated. There was a fire in his eyes, which sunk deep within his skull-like bald head. He resembled a skeleton shrink-wrapped in wrinkled skin, and his German accent clipped his words with a stern authority that made Mora think he could have been a schoolmaster in a previous life. Or a Nazi general.

"Please, gentlemen," Mora interjected. "Dr. Veltman, I presume," she said to the man beside Dodge. He nodded. The man standing before her was indeed Dr. Herbert Veltman, the famous physicist who, along with his colleague Dr. Jorge Gaspar, invented time travel. *This man is one of the Fathers of Time!* And yet, Mora had to admit to herself that his taciturn manner did not impress her as much as his innovations in science.

She turned to the remaining two gentlemen on her team who had the good sense not to waste time with niceties. One wore green fatigues; a thick hat squatted over his heavy brow and stern features. Judging by his attire and the accent she heard earlier, Mora placed him as Major General Garth Ringbauer of the Australian Army. His file listed him as the team's Special Operations Commander, but Mora knew he was just here to assuage the doubts of a few politicians. A pawn. *A pawn with a gun,* she amended.

The other man, wearing a lab coat similar to Veltman's, hovered protectively about the black towers staggered throughout the room like giant sentinels; blips and decimals blinked in rapid patterns of red and green along each ten-foot-tall tower's surface, which his bottle-thick glasses reflected in his comically magnified eyes. Wispy white hair exploded from his tiny head. He whispered to himself, completely unaware of the rest of the team. *Albert Leonard Peppercorn.* Mora tried not to smile; she had heard of his eccentricities. But a person can afford all the eccentricities they desire if they also possess in their mind the blueprint of a time machine.

"Take your seats," she said, gesturing farther in the room to what resembled a private home theater. Two rows of leather armchairs faced a floor-to-ceiling screen on the far wall. To Mora it looked as if they were ready to show a marathon viewing of the *Terminator* films . . . if it were not for the ominous computer towers surrounding the theater area like a strange, space-tech forest, and the ever-present *hummmmm* emanating from the entire room.

Mora's teeth were beginning to ache.

Mora waited until the men had taken their seats—minus Peppercorn, who refused to leave his computer towers—then marched in front of the giant screen, faced her team, and said, "I am sure you have all been informed of the situation, but there have been new, dire developments. The world above us will, any moment now, become an apocalyptic wasteland if we do not succeed. Let us begin our mission at once."

Timejump #2

MAJOR GENERAL GARTH RINGBAUER'S instincts kicked in the moment he saw, through the portal, an armada of Viking longships advancing full speed ahead over a stormy sea and straight for the time machine. He dropped to one knee, effortlessly drawing his pistol and leveling it at the enemy, before he even registered who the enemy was.

"Are those bloody Vikings?"

Nobody answered him. They were busy shouting and shrieking in alarm at—he was right—bloody Vikings.

Ringbauer had trained for this—well, minus the time travel and the swords and horned helmets and ram-headed ships. As SOC of this mission, he had to keep his wits about him to protect his team.

He glanced at his team and groaned. They were like pubescent teens screaming at a horror film. One of them—the young intern, Foible—had even escaped from his armchair's harness and was climbing over it as if to escape.

"What in the blue blazes just happened?" Ringbauer

roared at them.

The fat historian, Dodge, was the only one to respond. He stared dumbly back at Ringbauer and said, "Vikings didn't wear horned helmets. That's a myth!"

The raiding party of Vikings loomed ever closer to the portal, disproving Dodge's myth with bestial battlecries.

Ringbauer steadied his firearm in futility and prayed the time machine would make another leap. The army never trained him for anything like this.

Timejump #3

SOMETHING HAD GONE WRONG. Terribly, horribly wrong.

"Mr. Peppercorn?"

The engineer popped up behind Mora, startling her. "Yes, Dr. Winnow?"

"Do you know what's happening? Why did we leave 1812?"

The tiny man flitted around a computer tower behind her, pressing his bug eyes to the blipping machine's readouts of data. "Haven't the foggiest, Doctor. She's only supposed to travel to a single time, specified by coordinates I designed myself. Quite the mystery, eh?"

Mora turned back to the portal, numb. She stared with the others—the engineer, the historian, the physicist, the soldier, and the intern—at the full moon illuminating the macabre scene before them. Two men had stood over a freshly dug grave before one hit the other's head with a shovel. His body crumpled into the grave, and the murderer used his murder weapon to begin shoveling dirt back into the ground.

To Mora, the whole thing tasted of metaphorical irony.

Before the jump; 7:08 a.m.

"THE QUESTION LIES with the inciting event," Mora said, facing her team as they buckled themselves into their armchairs. "Or, rather, what and when the inciting event *is*."

Ringbauer interrupted immediately. "Why the fu— Why's that our only solution? Just take the Chinamen's nukes away *now*!"

"The correct term is *Chinese*, you bigot, and they are not some child with a toy, Ringbauer," Veltman said.

"Gentlemen," Mora broke in. She felt as though she herself were the one dealing with children, which she had found was typical whenever she was the only woman on a team. In the academic world, her gender and her black skin often presented themselves as obstacles over which Mora's tenacity and brilliant mind delighted in bounding. "To answer your question, Major General Ringbauer, no, we can't, because the Chinese no longer have nukes for us to take away. As of 6:30 this morning, they have launched enough nukes to send the world as we know it back to the Dark Ages."

Silence. Humming electricity from the walls.

"This team, gentlemen, is quite simply humankind's last hope."

More charged silence. Dodge barked a startled cough.

Mora continued, "It was my job to create the computer that would tell us which event in our past will right this wrong. There were many factors to compute:

causation, data analysis, years of probability and statistics . . . I digress. All you must know is this: the single historical event predicted to successfully derail this nuclear extinction—because yes, gentlemen, it will be an extinction, it will be the apocalypse—is the War of 1812."

"You are saying," Veltman said, "that we must stop a war from over two hundred years ago in order to prevent this current war from occurring?"

"Precisely."

This was greeted by quiet contemplation, followed by Veltman shouting to the back room, "Foible! The A/C! It's hot as hell in here, I am sweating bullets!"

"Stopping the War of 1812," Mora continued, "would greatly remedy America's problem with debt, which will in turn . . . but I'm wasting time. The *how* is immaterial at this stage. Suffice it to say that stopping the War of 1812 will lead us down a path without a nuclear Holocaust."

Dodge gave a polite cough. "How do you suggest we stop an entire war? A war, I might add, that has been written in our history for over two centuries!"

Mora smiled. "Quite simple, really. Thanks to cause and effect—or, for fans of Ray Bradbury, the butterfly effect—all we must do is stop a man named John C. Calhoun, on the morning of January first, 1812, from going to the bathroom."

Ringbauer burst out in laughter, making Peppercorn jump in fright from behind a nearby computer tower. "What the hell would that do, sheila?"

"Please, call me Dr. Winnow," Mora said, "and to answer your question, you would first need to understand the equations and scatter plots and computer systems I have spent the last six years of my life developing. Do you?"

Ringbauer grumbled at the floor in embarrassment.

"Just trust me when I say," Mora resumed, "that keeping this John C. Calhoun's bladder full when he rides to a certain meeting at the bank on a certain restless horse will sufficiently throw a wrench in his chain of events, and will set in motion—or rather, *un*-set in motion—the dominoes that lead to China nuking the planet."

Timejump #9

DR. HERBERT VELTMAN looked at the new scene framed in the portal and felt a sense of familiarity, followed by guilt, then obstinate justification, and then guilt again.

It was a laboratory, lined with walls of cages filled with rhesus monkeys, some sleeping, some screeching. In the corner of the lab were two scientists, each wearing white lab coats and holding clipboards. One said to the other, "This is a lemur. Patient 50K is a lemur. Who put a lemur in here?"

"*Mein Gott,*" Veltman breathed.

He could not bear to watch, nor could he tear his gaze away. He was trapped, like the monkeys (and the lemur), but his was a cage of his own making. His mind was his own time machine, transporting him to a time in his past that mirrored the time in the portal. He had been there, once, with the monkeys, experimenting on them. Those poor creatures, with no control over their fate.

Like us. We cannot control our fate. We are monkeys in a cage.

He finally broke his trance, wrenching his eyes from the portal.

"These monkeys," he whispered to no one. "These monkeys make me feel guilty."

When he managed to look up again, the scene had already changed.

Timejump #14

A MAN IN FILTHY RAGS and with a beaten demeanor hunched over an oak desk with a feathery quill quivering unsteadily in his hand, while a second, better-dressed man leered over him, roughly guiding his hand.

For Dr. Clayton Roundhill Dodge, after the initial shock of learning Vikings did indeed wear horned helmets, the timejumps had turned into a kind of game of *I Spy*. He eagerly scanned the scene through the portal for some clue to their new destination. The drawn curtains, the coatrack, the mouse nest in the corner . . .

There! A nameplate before the two men at the desk, like a placard describing an exhibit at a museum. Dodge recognized the name instantly, smiling in childlike wonder. *Can it be . . . ?*

Beside him, Dr. Veltman sighed heavily. "Where are we now?"

Dodge leapt at the opportunity. "The man sitting is the blind poet John Milton, I believe. The other is the publisher Samuel Simmons. This must be the day Milton sold his magnum opus, *Paradise Lost.*"

Exquisite! The detail! Better than any textbook, treatise, or documentary Dodge had ever seen! If he could just procure a little privacy with this magical machinery.

Another sigh. "What year?" Veltman asked.

"The date is the twenty-seventh of April," Dodge said, dizzy with glee, "in the year 1667."

The room was silent in what Dodge imagined was reverent awe.

"Milton," he continued, "claimed his purpose in writing *Paradise Lost* was to 'justify the ways of God to men.' "

Veltman replied, after a pause, "Perhaps this is God's way of saying one should not tamper with the past."

Timejump #23

THE GIANT SQUID FLOATED through the abyss in perfect peace, where time meant nothing, until her territory was invaded by a colossal behemoth, which appeared out of nowhere. She spun her arms through the water to swivel her left eye—her good eye—to face the behemoth. It was gigantic, towering over everything in the depths, like a living volcano.

Attack!

The squid propelled herself at the leviathan, wrapping her arms about her enemy to feel the satisfying *schlikk* of her suckers sinking their razor-sharp teeth into its impossibly hard exoskeleton. She struggled to gain purchase against its unyielding armor. Her beak smashed into the behemoth, whose skin gave off a static charge not unlike the electric eel that had blinded her right eye. Wary but determined to reign supreme over her territory, the giant squid prepared for the inevitable counterattack.

And waited.

* * *

Timejump #24

ALBERT LEONARD PEPPERCORN'S world exploded with sea monsters and fireworks.

"NO!" he screamed. "That cannot be possible!"

Dr. Veltman found the courage to jump from his armchair and turn his back on the horrifying image through the portal to face the engineer.

"Peppercorn! What is this?"

"It . . . it's a giant squid!" he squeaked.

"Goddamn monster's what it is!" Ringbauer yelled, still on one knee, aiming his useless pistol at the time machine's new stowaway.

Everyone stared in abject terror at the portal—all except Foible, who was crying quietly behind his armchair. They could make out nothing through the screen, to which now clung a throbbing mass of flesh writhing with rows of suckers. Water dripped from its pink skin in rivulets, sizzling down the portal's screen. Worst of all was the thick beak, gnawing at the time machine and screeching like some Lovecraftian beast from another dimension.

"Peppercorn!" Veltman repeated, raising his voice over the squid.

"The squid must have attached itself to her, Doctor—er, to the portal, that is," Peppercorn shouted back. "Somehow, it has followed us through time!"

A blood-red light suddenly washed over the faces of the team, completing the horrific image. A *BOOM!* accompanied the explosion of fireworks from behind the squid. Sounds of celebration and music swelled in discordant counterpoint to its shrieks.

Dodge pointed at the portal. "I say, a dragon!"

Peppercorn squeaked indignantly, "It's a *squid*! A giant squid!"

"No," Dodge insisted, "a dragon, in the background. You can just see it between the squid's seventh and eighth tentacle. See the way it flows and billows? This is Chinese New Year! We're in China!"

Ringbauer laughed madly, still not lowering his weapon. "That's a step in the wrong direction, eh, mate?"

But Peppercorn had become deaf to the banter of his teammates. He staggered to the front of his time machine, using the computer towers and armchairs to pull himself forward and keep from dropping to the floor. His head reared back to take in the entirety of the squid. Another *BOOM!* and more fireworks reflected in his large glasses.

"Something's . . . happening," he breathed.

Cold sweat plucked gooseflesh down his skin. The squid . . . it was changing. It didn't seem to be attacking his time machine anymore; it was squirming and turning and . . .

"The squid isn't afraid of you anymore, my girl," he whispered to his time machine. "It's afraid of the fireworks. It's—"

With an escalating scream, the squid unleashed its last defense mechanism.

It squirted ink.

Timejump #25

MORA WINNOW WAS LOST. She had entered this machine as a confident, intelligent authority, determined to be the woman who saved the world. But no matter what she did, she was helpless to the whims of the time machine. She didn't control her fate anymore; the black shroud was descending.

Not a shroud—ink.

A splat of Rorschach inkblots erupted from the massive squid just as the Chinese New Year celebrations disappeared. Now, the ink bled black down the portal's screen, obscuring the new scene behind the tentacles: an impossible image of flying cars and a sparkling metropolis . . .

. . . from the future?

Mora stood up, determined to do something. She placed her hands gently on the shoulders of the engineer, who had fallen to his knees before the portal and was weeping into his hands, his glasses forgotten on the floor.

"Mr. Peppercorn, it'll be all right. Please, just . . ."

He allowed her to escort his frail figure to an empty armchair, where he gathered his lab coat around him like a quilt and curled into the fetal position. She scooped his glasses from the floor and handed them to him, to which he whimpered with gratitude.

Mora stood and faced her team, still numb with shock. The sounds behind her changed in regular intervals, but the portal was now almost completely covered by the squid and its ink. They were on a dark carnival ride with no end.

"Gentlemen," she said, "we need to talk this through. What went wrong? Why did we leave 1812? Why do we continue to leap through time? What patterns can we discern?"

Veltman gathered his wits faster than the others. "There is no pattern, Dr. Winnow," he said. "The times, the places . . . they seem to be without reason. Random."

Mora nodded. "I've been counting our trips. The last one, after the squid inked, was our twenty-fifth, and I glimpsed what appeared to be a city from the distant future. So we can agree that we're not just jumping through the past, but the future as well. This may even confirm that time is not set in stone."

Ringbauer snorted. "Or it means the jet set used their hoarded riches to survive the end of the world and build themselves a utopia."

"Maybe," Dodge spoke up, "if our esteemed Dr. Veltman cared to explain how time travel works—"

"This is not a damn Michael Crichton novel!" Veltman yelled, his accent thickening with stress. "I will not waste my time explaining the complexities of time travel!"

"Doctor," Mora said, raising her hands, "let's stay civil."

Veltman breathed out his tension and regained his composure. His exhaustion, coupled with the dim light, made him even more skeleton-like. "The problem, Dr. Winnow, obviously lies with the *mechanics*."

They all turned to the engineer still sobbing in his chair.

"Mr. Peppercorn?" Mora tried to sound gentle.

Peppercorn peeked through his hands and considered her for a moment. Then, replacing his glasses onto his tear-stained face, he shook his head, defiant.

"I made no mistakes," he said, his voice raising an octave. "She . . . my machine made no mistakes. There's nothing wrong with her! I couldn't begin to speculate—"

"You lyin' bastard!" Ringbauer bellowed.

Peppercorn curled back into a ball and resumed crying.

"Please—stop! Gentlemen, listen!" Mora waited until

she had everyone's attention. "There must be a solution. Stop blaming one another, and instead recall every step you took, every surface you touched, and every word you spoke since entering this machine."

After a pregnant pause, a small voice Mora had almost forgotten piped up from an armchair to the side. The intern. Foible.

"Oh God," he said. "I think I know."

Before the jump; 7:07 a.m.

EUGENE FOIBLE BURST into the time machine, almost spilling the mugs in his hands. Trying not to trip on his own feet, he bumbled to the team already sitting in their armchairs.

"Columbian roast for you, Dr. Veltman," he said, handing one mug to the bald physicist. He turned to the seated historian. "And your tea, Dr. Dodge—"

He almost dropped the mug for a second time as he saw the woman standing before the giant screen. Dodge rescued the cup from Eugene's hand and smiled. "Ah, yes, thank you, Eugene. May I introduce you to Dr. Mora Winnow? Eugene Foible, Peppercorn's intern, I believe."

The most gorgeous woman Eugene had ever seen. Without question. His complexion burned the same color as his messy hair—*Why didn't I comb it this morning?*—as she smiled, holding out her hand.

He stood frozen until a harsh word burst from behind: "Foible!" *Veltman.* "Please make yourself useful and find the A/C. Peppercorn treats his machine like an incubator. No, Peppercorn, let him go on his own. We need you for Dr. Winnow's briefing. Proceed, Doctor."

The woman gave Eugene one last smile and turned her attention back to the team. The intern hastened to the small side-room on the opposite side of the giant portal, looking into the time machine through bullet-proof glass, his thoughts muddled with smiling lips, delicate brown fingers, and a sensible pantsuit. He tripped over a thicket of cables humming with electricity, spotted the A/C box, and reached over a console to check the thermometer, his eyes never leaving the woman speaking across the room. Her melodious voice washed over Eugene. He leaned one hand on the console, mesmerized.

"As of 6:30 this morning," she was saying, "they have launched enough nukes to send the world as we know it back to the Dark Ages."

What?!

Eugene, balking at the enormity of her words, slipped, accidentally flipping a switch on the console with a soft *click*.

"This team, gentlemen, is quite simply humankind's last hope."

He read the strange symbol under the switch. What did it mean? He fumbled frantically with the switch, flipping it back and forth, unsure if he had flicked it back to its correct position. Sweat dripped into his eyes. First China nukes the planet, and now this.

On or Off? On or Off? Oh, why me?

Eventually, he returned his gaze to Dr. Winnow, still briefing her team.

"Some say time should remain unsullied," she was saying. "That we should face the consequences we have built for ourselves. But mistakes have been made, time is irrelevant, and we will be the heroes of yesterday, today, and tomorrow."

Eugene Foible was in love. He put the switch from his mind and turned on the A/C.

Timejump #29

MORA, AND EVERYONE ELSE in the time machine, stared in the dim silence at Eugene Foible.

"You think you know?" she prompted.

Foible's red hair had wilted, plastered to his pasty face with sweat—they'd left the A/C behind in the present. He pushed his glasses up the bridge of his nose and they immediately slid back down.

"Y-y-yes," he stammered.

"Would you care to elucidate your thoughts for us, Foible?" Dr. Veltman's words dripped with acid.

Foible's eyes never left his loafers. "It was when you sent me outside to turn on the A/C, Doctor." His voice wobbled like Jell-O. "I accidentally flipped a switch on the back console, and . . ." His Adam's apple bobbed with a gulp. "I got distracted, a-a-and . . ."

"Foible," Veltman said, his voice deceptively calm. "To which switch are you referring?"

His lower lip began to tremble as he mumbled, "I'm—I'm not sure exactly. Its label had two arrows crossing each other, like train tracks."

Veltman held his chin in one hand, pulling his face into a frown. "Two arrows crossing each other? Well, Peppercorn?"

The tiny engineer squeaked a single word from his armchair: "Shuffle."

"Shuffle?" Ringbauer asked. "Like a bloody iPod?"

"Peppercorn," Mora said, turning to the engineer, "can you turn the shuffle feature off?"

Peppercorn stared at her dumbly for a few moments before shaking his head. "No," he squeaked, pointing to the back of time machine. "The console is in the back room, at NOMALA headquarters. I can't open that door, because . . . well, we don't physically exist in 2034 right now—"

"That is a serious design flaw!" Ringbauer laughed. "You drongo—"

In the gloom, everyone jumped at the sudden roar of white noise outside the portal. They must have shuffled near a waterfall.

"So," Dodge said, after some time. "We're stuck here then?"

"No," Peppercorn said. "We shuffle to a new place in time every few minutes. We're not stuck anywhere, technically speaking."

"Is that supposed to be a fuckin' joke?" Ringbauer shouted.

"Why would a time machine need a *shuffle* switch?" Eugene Foible asked, but nobody heard him.

Mora raised her voice over the static roar of the waterfall. "What about John C. Calhoun? China's nukes? Did we change *anything*?"

Veltman uttered a soft, humorless chuckle, a sick staccato that echoed percussively with the water. "Einstein's theory of relativity," he said soberly, "suggests that time is a river. I would like to amend that: time is a torrential waterfall."

"And we," Mora whispered, "are a pebble in that waterfall."

The time machine shuffled through time once more, the sounds of the water fell away, and all was silent.

1 January 1812; South Carolina

ON HIS WAY TO HIS meeting at the bank, an image of a torrential waterfall, apropos of nothing, burst the floodgates of John C. Calhoun's mind. His bladder began to protest, louder and more urgent with every thump in his horse's saddle.

"Damn," Calhoun swore under his breath. He really couldn't be bothered with such agitations on a day like this. He couldn't be late, not today.

But no, his bladder would not be denied. He pulled his horse off to the side of the road, dismounted, led him by the reins to a shrubbery away from prying eyes, and set about relieving himself.

As he was urinating into the bush, he wondered why the image of a waterfall had come to him, until a whinny broke his contemplations. The damn horse was running off!

There was no helping the matter now: he would just have to be late to the meeting. He hoped his business associates wouldn't hold it against him; he was a Congressman, for God's sake! It didn't mean war!

"War?" he muttered, buttoning up his trousers. "What a ridiculous thought. And what of that waterfall? My, Calhoun, what's gotten into you this morning?"

GRAVITAS MORTEM

*T*HE WEIGHT WAS CRUSHING HIM.

Beck could feel it in his chest like acid reflux, feel it on his eyelids like a migraine, feel it pressing down on him like gravity. But it was none of these things. It was a beast, a monster. An utter nightmare. And like nightmares always go, no matter how hard he pushed himself he couldn't escape. Running wasn't running so much as it was running in place.

Beck was in his house. Just moments ago, being safe and secluded in his own home had been just what he needed. Moments after that, just what he needed was a quick drive—a change of scenery, an escape. Maybe to the grocery store? Energy drink, ice cream sandwich, book for him or magazine for his wife—these things would help, surely. Then, moments after *that*, he found he couldn't grab his keys from the vanity by the front door or slip on his sandals in the mudroom. He couldn't grab his phone and play a podcast as he drove, couldn't say goodbye to his two cats.

He couldn't even move.

That was when the weight began to crush him.

When it first pushed down, Beck didn't know what it was. His thoughts were sluggish, and he couldn't process . . . what . . . what *is* this? The air around him and moving in and through and out of his lungs and clouding his vision, its viscosity or density or *something* has clouded and thickened and it's filling him and *he's going to drown . . .*

Beck manages to roll himself from the bed. He knows his feet are pressing on the hardwood floor, but the pressure beneath his toes registers as happening to someone else, not to him. He vaguely wonders if this is what being poisoned feels like.

Did my wife poison me? he thinks, adding, so she knows he's joking, Ha-ha. The laughter is disjointed. When he laughs Beck has always imagined it as a bubbly, continuous stream—Hahahahaha!—but this vague, staccato laughter arrives with a definite hyphen.

Ha-ha.

It must be the poison.

He realizes—also vaguely—that he has switched to present tense. When did that happen? He decides he doesn't like it, decides to switch back to past tense, where Beck felt more at home at the moment.

He walked from the bed, out into the hall, still with this *presence* pushing down, down, down on him. He looked around but saw nothing coming down on him, no visible weight on his shoulders. Yet it followed him through every room as he meandered around the house.

Where was his phone? He needed his phone.

There, in his pocket. Beck pulled it out, letting it scan his thumbprint to confirm his identity. For a moment he grew violently afraid that his phone would tell him that he *wasn't* Beck. Then who was he?

But it opened for him.

Paranoia, Beck thought. Ha-ha.

That disjointed hyphen worried him, but he tried to ignore it.

He didn't know what else to do except to text his wife. He typed nonsensical words that, thankfully, auto-correct correctly translated for him. When he pressed the *send* arrow, he reviewed what he'd written:

I'm in pain. Every inch of me. I feel like I'm being crushed.

He read the words again. Was that right? Pain?

He decided that it was.

When people are in pain, Beck thought, they take something for it.

Take something? What did he mean by that?

It was getting harder and harder to think.

But it wasn't just that it was getting *harder* to think. It was that he didn't want to think at all.

No. Even that wasn't right. He didn't want to think or not want to think, he . . .

That vague, viscous, disjointed ha-ha. Thinking hadn't become a more difficult task, and thinking hadn't become something he'd decided he didn't want to do. Hell, deciding anything at all would require some of that *thinking* muscle. No, it was that he didn't give a fuck one way or another. He couldn't think to decide whether or not he gave a fuck, and so by default he gave no fucks.

Something about this felt dangerous to Beck, but he

didn't know what, and he wasn't sure if he cared anyway. Here he was, standing in the middle of the living room, surrounded by thick, darkening air, feeling something akin to gravity pressing down on every sense of who he was.

What was wrong with that? He didn't know.

His phone went *ping!*

His wife, texting him back: *I'm sorry, Beck. What kind of pain? Physical?*

It sure as hell *felt* physical, but he responded to her with a metaphor, typing: *I'm falling into a dark hole and some-one's filling it back up with me at the bottom.*

Jesus, that was melodramatic—but it felt right. His vision was even filling up with little black specks, as if kernels of dirt were beginning to block the light with every shovelful of the stuff whoever it was above him flung down. But no, that was impossible. Beck was an atheist—no way in hell would he buy the idea that some-one, omniscient or not, was hovering unseen above him and plucking his strings like a vindictive puppet master. Even if his brain told him that was exactly what he saw *with his own two eyes* . . . the brain was a powerful sack of cats; it couldn't be trusted, especially if it was missing something.

Missing something? But what . . . ?

Ping!

Reply from his wife: *That sounds awful. So your depression?*

He stared down at the phone. He was depressed?

No. This felt way heavier than anything sparked neurologically.

Another reply from his wife: *Your pills are in the medi-cine cabinet. In the kitchen. Take one if you haven't yet, okay?*

Pills?

Take something . . . missing something . . .

Shit. Maybe this *was* depression.

Knock-knock.

Beck jumped at the sound. Someone was at his door, and by that hyphenated knock they sounded unfriendly. Maybe it was the mailman? He didn't trust mailmen, so it wasn't a stretch to imagine them as unfriendly.

Knock-knock!

"Coming!" Beck said.

He walked the short distance in as large steps as possible, to help evenly distribute the weight pressing down on him, and opened the door.

Two large men in black suits, black sunglasses, and crew cuts stared back at him from his front step.

"Can I . . . can I help you?" Beck asked.

"Sir," the taller one said, "have you been in contact with your wife today?"

Beck just barely managed to stop himself from reaching for his phone, which he'd put back in his pocket. He prayed to the maybe-nonexistent puppet master above that it wouldn't *ping!* again and give itself away.

"My . . . wife?" he asked. "I'm sorry, but who are you?"

He instantly regretted apologizing for no reason at all. This was *his* house, dammit, and she was *his* wife.

The taller man ignored his question, brushed past him and into the house.

"Hey!" Beck said, chasing after the man. "You can't just walk in here. Don't you need a warrant or something?"

"Your wife," the man said, not bothering to turn around but plunging deeper into the house, "has been colluding with the Russians for months."

"The—" Beck paused, staring at the tall man inside his house and then the less-tall man still standing on his stoop. "What are you talking about?"

"I'm sorry to have to inform you like this, sir," the man said, eyeing the large white cat staring up at him from the ottoman. "But I need you to understand that your wife has been taken into custody, and—"

"That's ridiculous!"

The man paused, staring at him as if seeing him for the first time. "What is ridiculous about betraying the United States of America, sir?"

The waterlogged cogs of Beck's brain ground into motion. There was something off here. What was it?

His brain went *ping!*

"If my wife has been taken by the FBI or CIA or something, then why haven't you said her name or my name once?"

The man stared, not saying anything.

"This doesn't make any sense," Beck continued. "If any of this were true, this is not at all how it would happen."

"And how would it happen, sir?" the second, less-tall man asked, who was suddenly standing next to his partner by the ottoman. The cat leapt off the furniture and ran out the open front door, hissing.

"I have no idea how it would happen!" Beck said, surprising himself by not being worried about the cat running off. Under the weight still crushing him, he somehow managed to raise one arm and angle an accusatory finger up at the ceiling. "But I also know that *he* has no idea how it would happen either!"

The two men just stared, blinking at him, and Beck

noticed with a vague curiosity that their sunglasses were now missing. "He?" one asked. Neither looked up at where he was pointing, almost as if they refused to do so.

"Or *she*," Beck said, "though I suspect it's a *he* since I'm also a *he*, and you're a *he* and you're a *he*, and the only *she* present in this story is a name on my phone. Hell, even the cat you just scared off is a *he*!"

The two men looked at each other. Moving as if by silent agreement, they simultaneously reached into their coats and withdrew handguns.

Aimed.

And shot.

Beck didn't know if the slow motion from the movies was a thing in short stories as well, but he wasn't willing to wait and see. He focused all his vague, sluggish, disjointed ha-ha unthinking thoughts on that same hand that was still pointing at the ceiling and willed it into motion. It swung through the thick air, and he formed his hand into a shape he'd known since grade school, one he learned along with the game Rock, Paper, Scissors. And he cut.

The bullets fell from the air, as if they'd hit a brick wall and bounced right off. The two agents lowered their guns, staring down in disbelief.

One asked in a whisper, "How the fuck did you do that?"

"That's what I've been trying to tell you," Beck said. "You don't know my name, you have no real purpose here, and your descriptions keep changing. You don't exist. It's not depression. I'm not depressed. I'm just stuck in a bad story."

"Bad . . . ?"

"Well, a bad storyteller, anyway. Or maybe a depressed storyteller, puppet master, who the fuck knows. So I cut the strings to those bullets, and they fell. Here, I'll do the same to you."

Beck swung his hand up again, in the Scissor position, and pressed his index and middle fingers together in the universal motion for *cut*.

The two men's bodies vanished before they even hit the ground.

And everything was silent. Even Beck's front door was closed again. It was as if nothing had happened.

He paused. "As if nothing happened . . ."

Take something . . . missing something . . .

Was his wife right? Was this depression? He knew such complex chemical reactions could manifest themselves in strange ways. Perhaps . . . maybe it wasn't that the two agent men were the product of some omniscient asshole. Maybe it was all a product of a brain that needed medication.

All the emotions rushed into him in a single moment—fear, desperation, anger at himself and at his wife and at his brain—and he flung himself toward the kitchen. He landed on the hardwood and crawled sluggishly forward. He was vaguely aware of moans coming from his own throat. He pulled and pulled and flung himself and tried so hard, but still the weight crushed him.

Beck knew the weight now. The weight was depression. And if anyone told him right now that this wasn't a physical weight or a physical pain, he'd gladly retrieve one of those bullets from the floor and force it down their throat.

He made it past the refrigerator, past the cabinets and

the sink, and pulled himself up using the counter. Now he was leaning his elbows on the counter, staring at the cabinet that held the medication. He rested his head against the wood of the cabinet door.

Oh, the weight . . . it was unbearable.

That was the moment when Beck began to entertain the idea of killing himself.

It would be easier. Easier than continuing. Easier than reaching the medication. The knives were in a drawer beneath the cabinet, and therefore easier to reach. Where could he stick the blade? He read once there was a carotid artery in your thigh that could bleed you out in minutes. But what part of the thigh?

His phone chose that exact moment to *ping!* and he knew he couldn't kill himself. He couldn't answer the phone, either, but that was okay. Baby steps.

He lifted his forehead from the cabinet door, raised one arm, and flung the cabinet open. His movements were more frenetic now, swinging arcs of desperation, like someone who knows he's drunk but is trying with all his will to clean his house before his mother-in-law arrives for dinner.

The bottle is large in his fumbling hands. Damn child lock. He twists and twists and twists and twists and twists and twists and twists and twists and—

Click.

The lid spins through the air and lands in the sink, and he's distantly aware that he's switched back into present tense. He doesn't care now because he has the pills right here and he's even okay with entering a stream-of-consciousness voice just as long as that means he can get his medication—

Dammit. He needs water.

Beck drops the bottle to the floor. Dozens of pills scatter. No matter. He has two clutched in his hand. He places one foot in front of the other and somehow manages to get to the fridge without falling. Even as he pours water into a cup, he's aware of the humor in this situation—even when he feels as if he's on the brink of dying (and vaguely relieved by that fact), he can't bring himself to drink tap water; he needs the filtered, cold water in the fridge. Ha-ha.

Beck has the cup of cool water in one hand, the two pills in the other. He tosses the pills back. They taste a bit like . . . *dirt* . . . and when he lifts the cup to drink, he sees that the water isn't that cool, filtered water anymore. It's . . . *mud*.

What the hell? Is this another hallucination? Should he drink anyway?

Doesn't matter, someone called from above.

"What the fuck?" I asked.

Great. Now it was back to past tense *and* first-person narrative.

The cup fell from my hand and shattered on the floor, spraying the floor with rich brown mud. And spraying. And spraying. The mud was now far more than could have ever been in my small cup. I was knee-deep in the stuff.

Now waist-deep.

"Oh hell," I said.

The mud was rising and rising, and when it reached my hands I wasn't surprised to find it room temperature and not all that much different from the foggy, viscous air I'd been wading through for the past however-long.

And now the mud was up to my neck, and its weight was crushing me.

What was going on?

It's depression, Beck, I heard that all-powerful voice say. **I'm sorry.**

"Puppet master?" I asked, though now my throat was filling with the mud, so it came out as though I were gargling.

I craned my head back to escape the final climb of the mud, and I found that the ceiling and roof of my house had disappeared, or perhaps been stripped away by the puppet master. I was staring up into the blue, cloudless sky—

—and into the blue, cloudless eyes of my puppet master.

He was a giant and he was shoveling dirt onto me, and it was cascading down in showers of speckled brown. The light was slowly blotting out. The last thought I had before everything turned black, and the weight crushed me, was:

It's like looking in a mirror.

THE WORMHOLE IN EDWIN'S CUBICLE

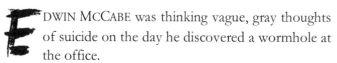

EDWIN MCCABE was thinking vague, gray thoughts of suicide on the day he discovered a wormhole at the office.

The elevator ride up to the eleventh floor hadn't been enough to derail his thoughts (which in that moment had revolved around deep, dangerous elevator shafts), and neither had the long walk across the entrance's black marble floor before that, nor his passage through the revolving doors at the front of the building before *that*. He'd kept contemplating how he'd do it—kill himself, that is—throughout the long subway ride, with its collage of thundering tracks and flashing light, then dark, then light again, and crowding strangers who scared Edwin to no end. He'd kept his eyes fixed on his black loafers and refused to look up even when one of the strangers boxing him into his tiny corner of the subway jostled him. He'd tightened his hold on the railing above his head and tried not to jostle them back. He'd read once that diseases were transmitted via these subway railings. Maybe he'd contract hepatitis and die that way. He'd be okay with that. Before that, when he'd stood waiting for his train to arrive, his eyes had been glued to the tracks leading into that dark tunnel. All it would've taken was one step and he'd have fallen onto the tracks. Whether he met his end at the spark of that infamous third rail or at the wheels of the train itself, it would've made no difference to him. Before that, his walk from his apartment building to the subway entrance hadn't interrupted his suicidal thoughts—in fact, the gray, overcast sky and rainy drizzle may have even turned up the volume, like a moody score in an indie film. The thoughts hadn't started as he'd left his building, or before that as he'd got ready for the day with his single cup of black coffee, or before that as he'd dressed in his gray suit, or as he'd brushed his teeth, or even as he'd woken up inside his tiny, badly decorated studio apartment.

Now that he thought back, Edwin couldn't remember the genesis of these thoughts. They'd slipped seamlessly from his dreams to his waking, and who knew how far back they went before that? But today, those thoughts came to an abrupt stop, as if he'd pushed them in front of an oncoming train, the moment he entered his firm's floor and rounded the corner to his cubicle.

He stopped in his tracks, still five cubicles away from his own.

Edwin didn't enjoy his coworkers and went out of his way to avoid social interactions with them—including arriving at work at least thirty minutes before they did. So no one else had arrived yet to see the blue glow surrounding his cubicle, stark in the dim lighting. No one else had yet seen the dancing blue glow or Edwin frozen in place, staring at it.

The sphere of blue light almost perfectly encapsulated his gray cubicle. But "blue" couldn't possibly describe the hue, he decided. Cerulean? Azure? It was a shade of blue that reminded him of . . .

Childhood.

Not only the shade, but the vibrancy of it. It appeared to be alive, and the glowing sphere of blue danced and *thizzed* in the air as if it were conducting an electrical current.

Whatever the case, Edwin decided he'd stood there for too long already. What if his coworkers started showing up? He'd have to interact with them.

He approached his cubicle one step at a time, his eyes glued to his black loafers. They reflected that strange azure hue more and more with each step. He ticked off each cubicle in his mind as he passed them. He didn't know the names of most of his coworkers, but the final cubicle before his belonged to a very loud man named Stan. Stan acted as if he and Edwin were best friends and, no matter how much Edwin ignored him, he refused to stay at his own desk. He'd peek his head over the cubicle walls and tell Edwin about his weekend's romantic "conquests"; sometimes he'd even come into Edwin's cubicle to "pick his brain" about some work-related problem or other. Edwin had considered requesting a new cubicle almost every day since meeting Stan—but that would require going and talking to his boss. That was just too much.

Edwin closed his eyes for the final three steps past

Stan's cubicle. He stopped, eyes still closed, and pivoted ninety degrees so that he faced the inside of his cubicle. He could feel the light in front of him dance against his closed eyelids. That dancing scared him. He didn't trust things that couldn't hold still.

At first, he thought maybe he wouldn't open his eyes. Maybe he'd just retrace his steps, go home, and spend the day in bed. That sounded nice.

But no. Just minutes ago, he'd been entertaining thoughts of suicide. If he couldn't simply open his eyes right now, how would he ever build up the nerve to kill himself?

He opened his eyes.

Before this moment, Edwin would have thought he was different from most people. He would say that most people would exclaim their awe, that most people would find beauty in such a thing as this, but that he was different. He didn't see beauty in the world—only pain and drudgery. But perhaps Edwin had been living in the darkness and the rain and the cold for so long that something like what was in front of him, inside *his* cubicle, was just too much for him to ignore.

The entire back wall of his cubicle had vanished. No calendar, no kitty-cat-dangling-from-a-tree HANG IN THERE! poster (a present from Stan), and none of the other useless things Edwin's cubicle had accumulated over the years. In its place was a circular, swirling mass of blue light that bathed his workspace in an electric azure wash of color. The light felt warm on his skin, like UV rays. Edwin once read that ultraviolet sunlight was good for a person's endorphins, and therefore a natural antidepressant; but he'd also read that ultraviolet radiation caused skin cancer. Perhaps *that* was how he'd kill himself.

He stepped to the edge of his cubicle entrance. His new, blue, dancing companion didn't reach his desk. Tentatively, he stepped inside, sat, and swiveled his office chair to face the source of the blue light.

What was it?

He hadn't the slightest idea.

The elevator *ding!*ed and the susurration of his coworkers' conversation broke the silence like a wave.

He sighed and muttered, "Better get to work."

EDWIN HAD BEEN IGNORING the blue thing in his cubicle for over an hour by the time Stan showed up. He seemed to get away with showing up late to work every day. This always perplexed Edwin, because Stan was startlingly loud when he entered the office—drawing attention to his tardiness and disrupting the other workers. Wasn't that enough for the boss to step in? Apparently not.

"Ay-yo!" came Stan's daily arrival call. Edwin dreaded hearing that non-word shouted across the office each day. It was like a countdown to their inevitable interaction.

Edwin sat rigidly at his desk, his back to Stan. He'd been able to ignore the massive glowing blue wall just two feet away, after all. Maybe today was the day he ignored his aggravating coworker. Maybe Stan would finally get the message.

"Eds, my boy!"

Edwin shut his eyes and braced himself. He hated that nickname. Nobody called him *Eds* before Stan was hired, and certainly nobody had called him a boy. Not since . . . he couldn't remember when.

"Eds, there's someone here I want you to meet."

Edwin opened his eyes. This was new. Meet some-one? Maybe it was a replacement. Yes, Edwin was being fired and he could go home and never look at the glowing thing in his cubicle again.

Despite his earlier convictions, he turned toward his cubicle's entrance. There was Stan, tall and smiley and gelled and stuffed into a starched button-up shirt a size too small. Next to him was a man Edwin had never seen before: fancy three-piece suit, Rolex watch, tanned skin . . . definitely not a cubicle worker.

"Eds, this is Roland. Roland, Eds."

Edwin was immediately uncomfortable. Should he stand? Shake the man's hand? He gulped and stayed seated, managing a small nod up at the man in the expen-sive suit.

"Roland is the new district manager," Stan was say-ing. "He's just informed me things are gonna start changing around here, for the better. Lots of shake-ups, and an overhead you can be proud of."

"That's right," Roland said. Just like his clothes, his voice sounded rich, coming from a mouth of perfect white teeth.

Edwin sat awkwardly staring up at them. Something seemed off. What was it?

Edwin blinked. Of course. Neither of the men stand-ing at his cubicle entrance seemed to have noticed the glowing blue wall next to Edwin. But how could they not? It was bathing them both in light so bright he was sur-prised they weren't squinting.

Stan was talking. "I was telling ol' Roland here, 'You know who you need to meet? You need to meet my cell mate, Eds.' " Stan laughed at this, and Roland joined him, but Edwin only managed a weak smile. "And so here we are, making the rounds. Why don't you fill Eds here in on what you were telling me, Roland?"

"I'd love to," Roland said. "But first . . . cat got your tongue, Eds? Or do you not like being called Eds?"

Edwin immediately liked this man far more than he liked Stan, which was none at all. It had taken Roland all of two seconds to figure out that a grown man probably didn't appreciate being called *Eds*.

"Ed . . ." He cleared his throat. "Edwin."

"Edwin," Roland repeated, nodding. "Fine name. And I'm glad to hear you can speak. Got anything else to say?"

And then Edwin surprised himself by actually having something else to say.

"Yes," he said. "I'd love to talk more, but . . ." He gestured at his computer. "I've got work to do, you see."

Roland laughed, taking Edwin aback. "Stan said you were a hard worker. Said he barely got five words out of you a day, you were that focused on work."

Stan laughed with him. "Hang in there, Eds, my boy!"

I'm not a boy, Edwin wanted to say. But instead he just nodded and turned back to his computer.

And, amazingly, they left.

Edwin smiled at his reflection on the computer screen, which, thanks to the new glowing wall next to him, was tinted blue.

EDWIN DECIDED IT MUST be a wormhole.

He wasn't familiar with what wormholes were,

exactly, but it sounded right. In Edwin's mind, wormholes were like doorways, or tunnels, leading to only God knew where.

Actually, he thought a *slide* was a better simile.

He thought back on the days of his childhood spent on playgrounds—by himself, of course. He remembered how he would sit atop the slide, the breeze playing with his hair as he looked over the vast expanse of the playground and the park surrounding. It was breathtaking, how the world would steal the words from his mouth every time with its unspeakable beauty. Then, anticipating the butterflies which he knew would flutter in his tummy, he would push off the top of the slide and *swwooooop!* down he would go. The breeze in his hair would strengthen and sting his eyes, and the ground would rise up to meet his feet, and suddenly he'd be in a new world: the park ground. Gravity would take hold once more.

That sounded nice. Perhaps that was what this wormhole was like.

Deciding it was impossible to work with a literal wormhole beside him, he opened an internet browser and began searching for answers. Most of the articles about wormholes went over his head, but he was electrified to learn that they could be visualized as tunnels.

Or slides, he thought.

Even better, wormholes were said to connect two points of the *spacetime continuum*. Edwin didn't have the slightest idea what this term meant, but he loved when they mentioned it in the old sci-fi television shows he liked to watch. *Space* and *time* together in one word? Edwin wasn't sure why, but it seemed almost romantic to him. *Spacetime.*

Apparently nobody knew whether or not wormholes actually existed, but he was pretty sure that if they just paid his cubicle a visit, they'd change their minds. The possibilities thrilled him—the idea of visiting different universes, or different points in time.

Despite his growing excitement, or maybe because of it, his thoughts returned to that dark elevator shaft . . . that noisy subway tunnel with the high-voltage third rail . . . those disease-infested subway trains stuffed full of frightening strangers . . .

And then all of those images vanished, replaced by the memory of that playground slide and the breeze and the view of the park and the blissful feeling of being the only person in the whole wide world.

Edwin closed the internet browser and pushed away from his desk, swiveling his chair as it rolled back so that it came to a stop with him facing his spacetime continuum slide. Its vibrant swirl reminded him of when he'd visited the carnival as a child. His father had lifted him up so that he could see how the confectioner made the cotton candy. It had swirled just like the wormhole before him did now—soothing, almost hypnotizing.

"You going to lunch, Eds?"

Edwin ripped his gaze away from the blue swirl. There was Stan, peeking over the wall that joined their cubicles. Edwin returned his gaze to the wormhole. *His* wormhole.

"No," he said. "I'll stay inside."

"Predictable Eds," Stan said, laughing. When Edwin didn't laugh with him, Stan said, "You gotta get a sense of humor, Eds, my boy."

But Edwin wasn't listening to Stan anymore. His

mind had drifted into that cotton candy swirl just inches in front of him.

Unprompted, he thought again of throwing himself into that dark elevator shaft. *Why* did he want to kill himself? He wasn't sure. Was he really so unhappy that he wanted to just give up? He wasn't sure of that either. Where had the boy on the slide gone? The last handful of years had been gray and lifeless. Gray sleep, gray suits, gray cubicle.

But here, today, in his cubicle with his wormhole . . . he saw *color*.

Would he die if he stepped into that color? Scientists weren't even sure if wormholes existed, so they were probably clueless about what would happen if somebody tried to enter one. Maybe he would simply bounce off the shimmering ball. That would sure be a letdown. Maybe he would fall down the slide forever, and would then have to wait until he starved to death, and even then his dead body would just fall and fall and fall and— That actually sounded a lot like his life here, inside his cubicle. Maybe the wormhole would take him to another dimension, or an alien planet, or back in time, or some combination of all three.

But what sounded most likely to Edwin was that his body would be torn to bits the moment he stepped into the sphere. He'd read once that black holes were so incredibly dense that a human simply could not exist inside one. Maybe that was how this wormhole functioned. He'd step inside and just stop being Edwin. His last conscious moment would be filled with this beautiful, childlike swirl of azure blue.

That sounded wonderful.

He paused. Edwin might be the only person able to see this wormhole, but maybe everyone would *feel* it if he touched it. Maybe attempting to enter it would cause it to explode or implode and kill everyone in his office. Though Edwin didn't know any of his coworkers except for Stan, and he didn't *want* to know his coworkers (especially Stan), he didn't want them all to die because of him either. The possibilities of the wormhole crumbled at this thought.

But wait . . . why was it so quiet?

He stood up and lifted onto his tippy-toes (one hand on his desk for balance, lest he trip and fall into his wormhole) and scanned the office floor. From what he could tell, he was the only one here. It seemed everyone else had gone off to lunch.

He sat down heavily, his head once more dizzy with possibility.

On the day he found a wormhole in his cubicle, he also happened to be the only person inside during lunch. That couldn't be a coincidence . . . could it?

He decided it couldn't.

In a burst of action, he stood back up, his office chair spinning out from beneath him and coming to a crashing stop at the cubicle across the way. He stepped back so that there was a little breathing room between him and his wormhole. His *slide*.

For a moment he was back at the top of that childhood slide with the entire park spread out before him. He could almost feel the breeze in his hair, and the butterflies filled his stomach just like they did as a kid. The breeze at the subway tracks had reeked of garbage, but this breeze was fresh, new, invigorating. And there'd been butterflies in his stomach as he'd contemplated that dark elevator shaft, but those had been more like moths, not exciting at all and filled with an empty dread. These butterflies seemed to lift him up, making him weightless. Fluffy, like cotton candy.

"Come on, Eds, my boy," he said. "Just push off."

Though he'd always hated it when Stan called him that, somehow it felt right in this moment. It was, after all, a childlike name. Fitting for a boy about to launch himself down a slide on a bright and sunny day. Fitting for a boy about to taste a thick swirl of blue cotton candy.

Edwin stepped forward. His right loafer touched the wormhole's blue boundaries and then slipped in without resistance. He stepped through the portal as easily as gravity had pulled him down the slide.

EDWIN MCCABE didn't get torn to bits that day or any other. He also was never seen again at the office. And by the time his coworkers returned from their lunch, the swirling blue mass in Edwin's cubicle had vanished. Not that anyone else would have noticed.

Over the following months, as Edwin's coworkers accepted the theory that he'd finally had enough and abandoned his life at the office (and they weren't wrong), Stan would often peek over the cubicle wall at his boy Eds's old desk. He would often wonder where Eds had gone off to, and why Eds never said goodbye. But Stan liked to imagine that his good ol' pal Eds had gone off to find a little adventure in his life.

Stan wasn't wrong.

HAPPY HOUR

M IKE DAVENPORT NEEDED TO GET LAID, and he knew the perfect spot to score some pussy:

Suck It.

For one, the name of this particular bar made him laugh—"I'm going to Suck It," he imagined telling his buddies, laughing and adding "no homo" so they knew he was no homo—but also, he'd heard his buddy Dean say he'd seen some of the hottest chicks dead or alive entering Suck It just the other night.

"I'm telling you, man," Dean had said, punching the nearest arm in his circle of friends. "Chicks with fuckin' alabaster skin. Pouty, blood-red blowjob lips . . . Angelina Jolie types. *Eyes Wide Shut* sex and shit, I bet you. Place is guaranteed to be a nest of vagina vipers."

" 'Alabaster'? Fuck you mean, using gay-ass words like 'alabaster'?" one of the guys said, punching Dean's arm back.

Dean gave him a wounded look, as if he'd insulted his mother. "I'm talking about hot chicks here and you call me gay, bro?" When the other guy just scoffed, Dean added, "Swear to God, bro. Suck It's the new spot."

That settled it for Mike—he was going to Suck It. He didn't say this out loud to the other guys. Truth be told, the others just weren't the type he'd want to be seen with around babes like the ones Dean described. Too many dick jokes. Mike was the smart one of the group, knew fancy words like "figuratively" and "irregardless," regularly used phrases like "as it were" and "if you will." On a deeper level, though, he knew that if he were seen with this crowd out in the wild, away from work, all those vagina vipers would see him as one of a group of idiots. But he knew he was different. He was better than that.

So his buddies could suck it—no pun intended and definitely no homo.

He would be going to Suck It alone. More vipers for him. A small, niggling voice in his head asked what he would do if he struck out. What if all those chicks looked at him and still only saw a desk-job dude-bro without a fancy college degree? Didn't matter. He'd get trashed on their cheapest beer and try again. When there was no last call, three strikes never meant you were out.

But what truly decided him was the sign he saw when he drove past Suck It the next day on his way to work. He'd spent the previous night holed up in his shitty studio apartment keeping warm with cheap potato vodka and cheaper ramen, trying to watch cable on his ancient tube TV but invariably drifting his gaze to the loose moulding. The chipped paint. The growing waterstain on the ceiling.

The stinking fireplace that seemed to do nothing but let in cold drafts. He didn't invite people over—not even his buddies from work, whose pads were just as putrid. It was one aspect of his life he could only drink away. There's no facing a broke-ass living situation head-on if your bank account has more overdraft fees than deposits.

But when he drove past and saw that sign, a rare frisson of hope surged with the blood in his veins. Here was a sign, a literal sign, of better things to come. All at once Mike saw flashes of boundless opportunity in his future—a new girl, who would give him the confidence to score a better job, which would lift him out of Chicago's poverty trap and into the echelons of high society. And all it would take was a confident strut through those doors, a nod toward the bartender, and a sexy blonde would catch his eye. The rest, as it were, would be history.

That sign hovered in his mind's eye the rest of the day in his musty cubicle:

HAPPY HOUR
FROM DUSK TILL DAWN!

HAPPY SAINT PATRICK'S DAY,
LOVIES!

SUCK IT

——————BAR & LOUNGE——————

That word, HAPPY, repeated twice because it sounded so nice, burned into his brain like a brand marking cattle for the slaughter. He wanted that word to describe him,

Mike Davenport.

HAPPY . . . HAPPY . . . HAPPY . . .

Admittedly, Mike couldn't remember the last time he was happy. Maybe the last time he'd been laid? If so, it'd been far too long.

When he entered the place, he knew immediately that Dean hadn't been lying. Sure, Suck It was nearly empty right now, but a swanky place like this just *had* to attract some choice chicks as the night wore on. All crushed velvet and lacquered cherrywood gleaming under a wash of bloody mood lighting; no pool table, but one of those large, fancy billiards tables; leather wingbacks and chaise longue by the largest fireplace he'd ever seen—no way *that* thing would let in a single wisp of Chicago pollutant.

Yes, this place was literally *dripping* with HAPPY.

Mike walked through the empty lounge area and sat at the bar on a cushy stool. Truth be told, he was glad to have the place to himself in the beginning. This way he could strategically choose the perfect spot, cradle his drink in a cool, relaxed, approachable manner . . . and wait.

The bartender had his back to him but turned around at his approach.

"What are we having tonight, sir?"

Mike paused, taking the man in. He was a Dracula-looking motherfucker, with precise, oiled-back black hair coming to a widow's peak and a pale face with sharply angled cheekbones. His three-piece suit made Mike feel extremely underdressed. He took an immediate dislike to the man.

"Here for the Happy Hour," he said, jerking his thumb over his shoulder toward the entrance as if the bartender could see the sign from in here. "I'll take the cheapest beer you got on tap, and I'll keep taking it till Happy Hour's over." And then, to make sure this bartender—and any ladies lurking in the shadows—knew Mike could be just as fancy as anything else in this place, he added: "If you will."

The bartender stood perfectly still, staring at Mike as if appraising what he'd just said, biting the words to test for fool's gold, and upon finding them twenty-four karat, turned away, returning shortly with his drink. Mike sipped the beverage from a fancy stein, one of those thick glass mugs with the big-ass handle. The bartender had frosted it, turning the edges of the glass opaque and chilling the liquid at its lip. A little gay, as it were, but Mike wouldn't begrudge the man his preferences. Besides, maybe the chicks would dig it. He sipped, sipped some more, all the while that one word pulsing in his throat.

HAPPY . . . HAPPY . . . HAPPY . . .

He was the only patron in the bar for the first three drinks, just him and Mr. Dracula. The fire raged—there'd been a recent cold front that blasted its way through Chicago—and he was starting to feel itchy in his big woolen coat. But the coat was the nicest thing he was wearing. He'd need to keep it on to show he had some "class" or whatever. As it were.

After his third drink, a woman entered the bar. She paused just inside the door to slide gracefully out of her pea coat and deposit it on an ornate coatrack as if performing a ballet. She was gorgeous. Breathtaking. Boner-inspiring—literally. Her beauty was almost too blinding to look at, but Mike told himself you couldn't *be* a pussy and *get* pussy, and so he kept his eyes on her. Just as Dean had promised, to the word: full red lips and alabaster skin. Her heels on the parquet floor clicked hypnotically with the crackle of the fire.

Please come here, he thought, still watching her from the corner of his eye as the bartender plunked a fourth drink in front of him.

And she did. What's more, she'd sidled up to the stool just two places to his right.

HAPPY . . . HAPPY . . . HAPPY . . .

Time to make his move. He placed his fourth, untouched drink on a coaster and slid it halfway between them, smiling at her.

"Interest you in what I'm having?" he said, secretly thrilled at how fucking suave as fuck he sounded right now. Like James motherfucking Bond, if you will.

She gave him a scrutinous look, then arched her eyebrows and looked down at the hefty stein between them. She pursed those red lips. Paused. Then she turned to the bartender.

"Cranberry juice, please, Harold. On the rocks. Thank you, lovey."

Cranberry juice? Fucking cranberry juice?!

Mike couldn't believe this bitch. She'd ignored him, as though she were better than him, then proceeded to order a fucking cranberry juice? What was she, on her period?

And she'd called Mr. Dracula "Harold," as if she knew the guy. Maybe they were fucking. But who came to a bar so much that they were on a first-name basis with the bartender and then didn't even *drink*?

Mike left the drink between him and the bitch and said, "Pour me another once you're done with that cranberry juice, *Harold.*"

The man did so without comment, and Mike proceeded to down a fifth, sixth, seventh, eighth, and ninth glass of beer until he'd effectively wiped that stupid idea of HAPPY from his brain. As if anyone like him could be happy. It was people like this bitch, like fucking *Harold*, who kept people like Mike in their place. This bitch would never let him be HAPPY.

He finally circled back to that fourth beer languishing away on the countertop and sweating condensation all over the coaster. Studiously ignoring the bitch, ignoring Harold, ignoring everybody as patrons began appearing at an increasingly steady trickle, Mike downed the beer. He was gonna have some strong words with Dean come Monday. Dean hadn't mentioned the chicks who came to Suck It were stuck-up celibates.

When Harold appeared before him, he thought the bastard was going to cut him off. All nine empty steins cluttered around Mike, and he had the sudden urge to go all DiCaprio in *The Departed* and smash one of those steins over Harold's oily head. He glared up at the man, waiting to be cut off, waiting to demand another drink. Instead, what the bartender said surprised him:

"Sir, our Happy Hour is nearing a close. As a thank-you for your patronage, from Suck It to yourself"—in his drunken stupor, Mike barely registered the man's twitch of distaste as he said the name of his own bar—"we would like to offer you a new specialty drink. On the house."

Nothing about this sounded strange to Mike. In fact, drunkenly, he felt he *deserved* a special drink on the house. He'd *earned* it.

"Good man," he slurred, leaning heavily on his

elbows. "Lay it on me, if you will."

Harold indeed would. The drink was in a large shot glass, a cherry bobbing just beneath the surface. The cherry was a sickly red, and sent a bloody tint through the liquid. Mike almost downed the whole thing in one go, but he paused with his hand on the glass.

"What's it?" he asked Harold.

"Our specialty drink, sir, as I said. A new one, which we hope to make a Suck It staple."

"Whass *in* it?"

"The finest brandy, sir, with a dash of red flavoring. The cherry is meant as a chaser."

Mike hiccupped with derisive laughter—he didn't need no fucking chaser. He plucked the cherry from the glass and tossed it over his shoulder, then downed the shot.

The last thing he heard was a second order of "Cranberry juice, Harold, my lovey."

And then, black, with that glowing word pulsing in the night:

HAPPY . . . HAPPY . . . HAP—

"FUCK AM I?"

Bright lights, stabbing into his head like shards of crystal into exposed nerve endings. Cold steel and ugly cement, all hard edges and merciless. Mike blinked, willing his surroundings to still, to stop swimming as if in a strobe light. Underwater and bone-dry at the same time.

He was *parched*.

"Water . . ."

None was offered.

He blinked more rapidly and the bright lights became less sharp. He was sitting upright yet slightly reclined, as though waiting for a haircut. The pleather upholstery was faded and cracked, the chair grimy on his skin—his woolen coat was gone. What the hell? That was an expensive coat; he better get it back.

Then he realized he was strapped to the chair. Immobile. And—*fuck*, he was thirsty.

"I need water," he called out, his voice louder now.

His words echoed, alone, just like him, in what looked like a meat-packing factory or something. Gone were the parquet floor and mood lighting and posh high-society patrons of Suck It. All he saw now was a dingy backroom, maybe a warehouse. Cracked cement floors with intermittent oily patches of something viscous enough to reflect the overhead sodium lights. Rows of meat hooks swung lazily from a rig snaking across the ceiling; some of those hooks held unrecognizable lifeless torsos of meat—carcasses bled dry and stripped beyond recognition. Were they cows? Pigs? Mike couldn't guess.

"Help—"

"Shit!"

Mike jumped in his restraints, swearing, surprised to hear another voice so close. He wasn't alone after all. His head was also strapped to the back of the chair, a leather thong cinched across his forehead, but he had just enough freedom of movement to see that his was just one of a row of chairs. And in most of them—four? five? he couldn't be sure with just his peripheral vision—sat men like him, strapped down and either vaguely stirring from unconsciousness or out cold.

Or dead.

"You know where we are, dude?"

But the man who had called out for help didn't answer. Seemed Mike was the first of the group to fully gain consciousness. Probably meant he was the smartest. Probably he'd be the one who had to figure a way out of this mess. As it were.

Becoming aware of the chairs lined up beside his own had also brought something else to his attention: a skinny rod of aluminum, standing upright immediately to his left. There were similar contraptions beside each of the chairs.

IV stands.

A cold dread came with this realization, ice spreading through his veins. A clear tube of plastic ran from a bag, which in turn was attached to a pump; the tubing snaked down from the apparatus and into his arm.

"The *fuck*?"

Mike started thrashing, straining against his restraints, but there was little give. All this did was make his head pound even harder and remind him how motherfucking *thirsty* he was.

"Hello?"

Nothing.

"Hello?"

Still not a stir. He gave up, stopped struggling, and just lay there, his heart racing, his head throbbing, his eyes still squinting against the light, his throat like sandpaper.

What was going on here?

What *the fuck* was going on here?

Where was he? Who were the others? Who had put them all here? Why the fuck was he tied up?

What was in the IV drip? Definitely not saline solution—he was pretty sure there were only a few liquids that would be as horrifyingly red as what coursed through the tubing. Was it a blood transfusion? Was that red stuff going *into* him . . . or coming *out* of him?

A wave of dizziness washed over him. Spots danced in his vision.

He felt weak. And more thirsty than he'd ever been.

All signs pointed to that red stuff being his blood, being steadily hoovered from his veins.

They were taking his blood. All of their blood.

We're all being harvested.

But who was doing the harvesting?

Then, this thought, hot on the heels of that realization: *Fucking Dean!*

He would literally give that guy a piece of his mind when he saw him on Monday.

If he'd see the guys on Monday. For all Mike knew, he'd been in this chair for days, weeks, *years*, his captors keeping his body alive so that it continued to produce more blood for—

For what?

Mike didn't want to think about that.

He steadied himself, waited to calm down. The spots in his vision danced and fizzled out, but his heart still raced—no slowing it down, either, not with this much adrenaline spiking in such a weakened body.

He took a deep breath.

"HELLO?!"

In the afterlife of his voice's echo, there was only silence. Then:

"Uhnn . . ."

Well, he hadn't managed to get anyone's attention outside this large room, but he seemed to have woken up his fellow captives.

"Water . . . please—"

"Fuck . . . fuck, fuck, fuckfuck*fuck*—"

"My *head* . . ."

"Hell am I?"

"Ugh, that *smell*—"

"Water, I need—"

"—*fuck*, get me the *fuck out*! FUUU—"

Muted sounds of struggling against leather straps, metal buckles, rusty chair stands scraping on the cement floor. One of the guys a few chairs down, the one who'd taken to yelling the F word incessantly, somehow managed to jostle his chair enough to tip it over. There was a deafening crash, followed by a smaller metallic skitter as the IV stand was pulled down as well, that elicited pained moans from the rest of them and more cursing from the fallen guy—

"—*FUCK*, MY FUCKING *ARM*!"

Seemed he'd snapped his arm in the fall. And Mike could just make out the beginnings of a puddle of his blood. Poor guy.

"Dude," Mike said over the others' groans. "Chill."

" 'Chill'? *Chill*? I'll fucking chill with my dick up your ass!"

A bit aggressive, Mike thought, but he understood the sentiment. "Fuck off with the gay shit, man. We're all stuck here just like you."

Spitting, gasping noises, like a fish out of water. "None of the rest of you are being pressed into the cement in a pool of your own blood!"

Mike realized the guy must have his face pressed into that puddle. Damn. But that only reminded him how thirsty he was. Mike snorted, which didn't help his headache. "Yeah, well, none of the rest of us were stupid enough to *put* ourselves there, now, were we?"

"Oh, *fuck off*—"

"*Both* of you fuck off," a new voice said. Mike thought maybe it was the guy who'd first asked for help, but he couldn't be sure. "We're all in the same situation, okay? Shut up and let's see if we can change it."

Mike and the guy on the floor kept silent.

"Okay," the new voice continued. "Let's sound off."

"What is this," the guy on the floor scoffed, "the fucking Boy Scouts?"

"Just do it, asshole. We're on the same side here."

Mike broke in: "Name's Mike Davenport. From what I can see, I'm the furthest person on the left." Or was it "most far"? It was difficult to sound smart when his head was throbbing like a cock with blue balls. "Who's next?"

A pause, then a voice immediately to Mike's right, barely more than a whimper: "Chad."

"Mike, Chad, next is me—Brock Richards."

This was the voice that had reprimanded them and called for a sound-off. Brock had ostensibly assumed leadership of their little group, and that was okay with Mike. At this point, he didn't care about getting laid, didn't even care about looking smart. Not anymore. He just wanted to get back to his shitty apartment so he could drink all the water he wanted, jerk off, drink more water, and jerk off again.

Brock's assumed leadership wasn't, apparently, okay with the dude on the floor. He was next, saying in his most bitingly sarcastic voice, "*Such* a pleasure to meet you, *Brock*. I'm Wyatt, the asshole drowning in his own blood."

There was a lengthy pause.

"Okay," Brock said, "looks like it's just the four of us. Mike, Chad, Brock, and Wyatt."

"Sorry to interrupt, Brock," Wyatt said, still acerbic as hell, "but your count's off. There's one more dude next to me, a little farther than the rest of you."

Silence. The fifth guy wasn't speaking.

Wyatt added, his attitude gone, "I think he's dead."

That last word injected a dose of reality that weighed heavily on the group for a moment, before Brock forged forward.

"Still just four of us then. For now."

Mike didn't like those words—*for now*. Was he implying more of them would die? Or a new captive would be brought in to replace the dead one?

"Mike," Brock said, breaking into his thoughts. "Start us out. What's your last memory, before waking up here?"

That was easy enough. "Suck It."

He'd expected laughter from this, or at least a scolding from Brock that he needed to keep the jokes to a minimum, but none came.

Chad, still soft and whimpering: "Me too."

"Yeah, I think it's safe to say we all got fucked in the same place," Wyatt said.

"So we all came from the same bar?" Brock asked. "The one on Martin Luther King Jr. Avenue?"

"Pretty sure that's the only Suck It," Wyatt said through gritted teeth. Mike couldn't imagine how uncomfortable and painful it must be, down there with a broken arm, an open vein, and possibly congealing blood pressing into his face.

"So then the question is," Brock said, "where are we now?"

Mike's eyes returned to the hanging blocks of meat and bone. "Butcher shop."

"No." This was Chad, his voice growing a bit stronger.

"Why do you say no?" Brock asked.

"Those . . . those aren't animals."

"What do you mean, 'those aren't animals'?" Wyatt still spoke through gritted teeth. "How the fuck would *you* know?"

"Grew up helping my dad in the shop," Chad said. "Those aren't animals. I'm sure."

"Then what the fuck *are* they?"

"They're . . ." Chad paused, as if hoping it was obvious and thus unnecessary to say out loud. "They're human."

Mike didn't want to think about the implications of Chad's words. "Doesn't matter if they're fucking *aliens*. Irregardless, we're in a butcher shop. Those meat hooks could carry cows and pigs just as easily as"—he choked on the word—"humans."

Chad didn't argue with Mike's point.

Brock put them back on track: "Okay, so we all have the same last memory of being in the same bar, and now we're in some kind of butcher shop somewhere. Tied to chairs and being drained of our blood. How long do you think we've been here?"

It was then that Mike realized all the windows had been boarded up, conveniently blocking out any clues as to the time of day.

"I'm definitely still hung over," Mike said. "Can't've been more than a few hours."

"Few hours from *when*?" Wyatt asked.

Mike's mind sang: HAPPY . . . HAPPY . . . HAPPY . . .

He shook the words away. "Happy Hour."

Wyatt laughed.

Brock asked, "Had anyone been to Suck It before—"

"Before Saint Patrick's Day?" Mike finished.

A pause, after which each of them confirmed that this had been their first Suck It experience.

Other things they learned: they'd all gone to Suck It alone, hoping to score with the amazingly gorgeous women rumored to be seen entering and exiting the new bar; they'd all gone during Happy Hour and struck out with, seemingly, the same blood-lipped bitch; and—most telling of all—they all shared the final hazy memory of being offered the "Suck It specialty" by the bartender, Harold, all told that the drink was "on the house."

Chad remained his soft-spoken self throughout the discussion, and Brock's leadership skills remained intact, but Wyatt seemed to slowly drain of his facetious attitude—perhaps at the same speed his open vein drained of his lifeblood. Or maybe the gravity of their situation had finally crushed his bravado.

One thing Mike was too embarrassed to share was his stupid decision not to tell anyone he knew where he was going that night. Nobody, not Dean, not his landlord, not his mother, knew that Mike spent St. Patty's in a new bar downtown. So no one would know even remotely where to start looking for him if he didn't show up after a few days. It hadn't felt like a stupid decision at the time—he wasn't that dude from *127 Hours* who'd supposably gone hiking and had to saw off his own arm—but in hindsight it was an incredibly unfortunate decision.

The weight of mortality settled over him. He felt a

sudden itch to thrash around again, desperately wanted to hulk out and burst from these restraints; but Wyatt, still on the floor, was a constant reminder to keep his cool.

Another constant reminder: the unrecognizable hunks of meat hanging from hooks not a dozen feet away. Mike felt as though he were staring into his future: there hung the former Wyatt, Brock, and Chad, sucked dry to the bone and salted for tomorrow's meat buffet.

And Mike was next.

WHILE THEY WERE DECIDING what to do next ("deciding" was a laughable choice of word; their options were rather limited while securely strapped down and immobile), a door opened.

None of them could see the door—not even Wyatt with his adjusted floor-level perspective—as it was somewhere behind their line of chairs. But the sounds were unmistakably those of someone entering the room through a door.

The turning of a bolt.

The almost imperceptible sigh of well-oiled hinges.

Purposeful steps over a threshold.

The firm shutting of the door, then more purposeful steps, tracing an arc around the group, away from Mike and toward their fifth, recently deceased cell mate.

A pause, some muffled maneuvering and grunts, then the head-pounding *SCHKKKKKK* of metal over concrete.

The man entered Mike's peripheral vision, dragging the dead body in its chair behind him.

It was Harold.

Did that mean they were still at Suck It? Or had

Harold found someone to cover his shift while he played his sick games?

SCHKKKKKKK—pause—*SCHKKKKKKKKK*—

"Give it a rest, man," Wyatt said. But his voice was weaker than before, had lost its sarcastic cut. Or maybe his heart was running out of blood to pump.

Harold stopped, as though he were just now seeing the others in the room. He steadied the chair he'd been dragging and left it, walking slowly toward Wyatt.

"Hey, man, I'm just saying," Wyatt said, his voice getting nervous as the man got closer and closer. "That can't be good on your hearing either."

Harold didn't reply. He stopped when he got to Wyatt, staring down at him, his patent leather shoes just a hair's breadth from the outer circle of Wyatt's pooling blood.

Wyatt tried again, his voice still weak: "Mind helping me up?"

Still no reply. Harold just stared down, his face void of expression. One oiled lock of hair had come free of the rest, curving down past his widow's peak and resting over eyes cold as steel.

That one lock of hair scared Mike more than anything thus far. Any form of imperfection, any sign of control lost, subtle though it was, spoke of the possibility of an unwinding of character. Harold—boring and polite Mr. Dracula the bartender—could be one breath away from snapping, or he could simply smooth his hair back and it would be business as usual.

The not knowing was what unsettled Mike the most.

As Harold stared, pinning Wyatt's mouth shut with his gaze, he rolled up his sleeves. Purposeful, firm gestures: first the unbuttoning and removal of cufflinks, which he stored safely in one pants pocket, followed by the methodical rolling of the right sleeve and then the left, both stopping in a perfect crease at his elbows and apparently needing no more incentive to stay folded than their master's insistence that they do so.

He stayed there for a long moment, a statue. The air was thick with his intent. The rest of them remained still, staring at him, wondering what he would say, if he would say anything. Mike felt short of breath.

The man's eyes flicked to the puddle of blood lazily reflecting the lights above. He lowered himself in one fluid movement, resting on his haunches, his now-bare forearms casually balanced on his wrinkle-free slacks.

After a moment in which a decision was made—Mike could feel the change in the air—Harold rose from his haunches and circled around Wyatt, back toward the out-of-sight door. He rummaged around what Mike thought must be a table full of tools—and his imagination brought the tools to sharp, gleaming points, and colored their serrated edges with rust and old blood.

"Listen, sir . . ." Even the feigned leadership had drained from Brock's voice. "We've spoken, and you have our promise that we won't say anything, not to friends or family or police or any authorities in any official capacity. No one. That's my promise. That's all our promise. Just let us go, let us go home, and we'll forget this ever happened."

Harold remained silent, now circling his way back to Wyatt.

"We'll—" Brock's voice broke. "Please, sir . . . you can even keep the blood, if that's what you want. Just . . ."

But Brock never finished that sentence.

Just what? Mike wondered dully. *Just nothing.*

Harold returned to his crouching position over Wyatt, this time with something in his hand. Mike couldn't see what it was, but with his limited vision he had the impression of a black cord snaking from the object to the wall behind them . . . and of the object's vaguely gunlike shape.

"What are you—"

But Wyatt never got to finish the question. Harold brought the object forward, to Wyatt's head, maybe, and pulled a trigger. What followed wasn't a gunshot, nor was it a gunshot muffled by a silencer, but the *pffft* sound it emitted spoke of point-blank death nonetheless.

It happened quickly: Wyatt's "What are you—," Harold's *pffft*, and then Chad's screaming.

Harold stood and walked a few feet to stand in front of the other captives—now the only remaining three. He let the object fall to the ground, and Mike now saw it for what it was: not a gun, but a firing mechanism of sorts, like the ones used to "humanely" slaughter livestock; the steel bolt had already recoiled back inside its muzzle, the whole thing gummed up with thick strands of blood and gray brain matter.

Chad stopped screaming long enough to catch his breath, then he yelled:

"What the fuck, man?!"

Harold turned his stare on Chad. Blood from Wyatt's execution stood out in brilliant scarlet specks on those perfectly rolled sleeves, starched white speckled with glistening red. Once Chad stopped yelling, Harold turned his gaze to the group as a whole and said:

"You are the libations this evening, gentlemen. I wish to thank you for properly tainting your blood with my establishment's cheap beer. It is a spice most desirable."

"Look, man," Mike said, finally speaking up for the others. "What the fuck are you talking about?"

Harold frowned at him. "I do apologize for the inconvenience, but you will have no need of further information. Thank you for your patronage at Vino Veritas—"

"Fuck did you say?" Mike interrupted. "Vino *Veritas*? I thought this was Suck It."

It was absurd, Mike knew it was absurd, getting hung up on this one detail instead of the fact that this man had roofied them, kidnapped them, harvested their blood, and just executed one of them. But that one detail, that one simple, obvious error, was something he could focus his anger on and further ignore the impossible things happening to him right now.

Harold scowled for half a second before returning his expression to one of austere hospitality. "*Suck It* is hopelessly vulgar, don't you think?" He paused, then answered his own question. "No, you wouldn't think that, which is precisely why we've written such a childish entendre in large letters across the façade of this building. To attract a particular breed of patron. Yourselves, if you will."

Mike perked up at that.

"Vino Veritas," Harold continued, "is a name with such grace, such subtle wit, as would invite a respectable class, one whose subsequent disappearance would bring law enforcement upon us like sharks to blood." He grinned grimly, eyeing the pouches of blood. "So *Suck It* we shall be. But that is enough palaver. Thank you, again, for imbibing at our establishment. Do not feel the need to tip your bartender."

Without even a hint of a smile at this perceived joke, Harold turned back to the fifth chair he'd interrupted moving in order to attend to Wyatt, and resumed its *SCHKKKKKK*ing movement to a separate section of the room, in the far corner, cordoned off by a hanging wall of rubber sheets.

As he returned from behind the curtain and began attending to Wyatt's body, the rest of them just sat there, too stunned to say anything more. Or perhaps they were afraid of drawing Harold's attention and consequently joining Wyatt and the other guy behind that rubber curtain. Mike's lips and mind were empty as Harold righted Wyatt's chair and dragged him behind the curtain. Mike remained silent as Harold fetched a mop, and as he filled a wheeled bucket with soapy water, and as he rolled it over and began to clean, pushing Wyatt's blood toward a drainage grate in the floor.

Once this incongruously pedestrian chore was completed and the mop and bucket returned to their cleaning station in the corner, Harold turned his attention to his next chore.

Retrieving their blood.

He went to each of their IV stands, Mike's first, not meeting their eyes or answering their questions. Like they weren't even there, weren't even human. Once he had five full pouches of blood (he'd retrieved a bag from both Wyatt's fallen stand and the dead guy's), he proceeded to patiently feed first Mike then Chad then Wyatt each a full juice box of electrolytes. Mike hated drinking anything offered by this monster, seeing as the last drink Harold gave him landed him in this chair, but dammit if he wasn't too thirsty to resist.

This final, sickening chore done, the three remaining victims sated and hooked up to a fresh blood bag, Harold left them alone once more.

The second the door closed behind him, Mike's eyes swiveled in their sockets, drawn like magnets to the new IV bag, already spotting red as it sucked him dry. It was all he could do—watch his body's contents be displaced one clear pouch of plastic at a time. The drip of his blood hitting the inside of the bag was like Chinese water torture, was like the stuttering fade of that word—

HAPPY . . . HAPPY . . . HAPPY . . .

Drip . . . drip . . . drip . . .

As his blood reached the pouch's 150 mL mark, his mind making the pitiful *Is it half full or half empty?* joke, there came a loud *BZZZZ* that made Mike jump in his chair, jolting him out of his stupefied daze. It was like the sound of an electric circuit being broken. Inside that jarring buzz, Mike felt a release and realized—

"Oh thank God!" Chad exclaimed.

The restraints at their arms had come free of their buckles, released by some mechanism likely facilitated by Harold on the other side of the door.

They were being freed.

But why?

"Come on, guys, let's move," Brock said, trying to sound hopeful.

Together they found the buckles for the straps at their heads, then, when they were free to bend down, the straps at each of their ankles. And then—

Thank Jesus fucking Christ.

Mike was free.

He looked over. Chad and Brock stood apart from their chairs too. Seeing them separate from those chairs, from the maw of what Mike had been sure would be their final resting place, was like meeting them again for the first time: Brock, with his flaming red hair and short-man syndrome; Chad, a pudgy, gentle giant.

Chad had a goofy grin pasted on his still-pale face. "Where to now?"

Brock's warning made that grin falter. "Don't think we're out of the woods just yet. Come on, need help?"

Brock had pulled the needle from the crook of his arm, letting the rubber tube dangle from the IV stand and drip his blood all over the just-cleaned cement. Now he was at the table behind them where Harold had chosen his tool. He'd found a roll of duct tape, bit a length off, and slapped it crudely over the wound to keep it from leaking blood.

Chad nodded and Brock tossed him the roll of tape. Once Chad had followed in Brock's steps, he turned and threw the tape to Mike, who did the same.

"Good ol' duck tape, right?" Mike said, grinning.

Fuck, it felt good to be free of that tubing. Dopamine flooded Mike's system. He spun around, reveling in his ability to take in the entire three hundred and sixty degrees of his surroundings.

Brock was already rushing along the perimeter of the large room, searching for any doors or windows that could be exploited for weaknesses. He turned to the others.

"Nothing."

Chad pointed at the section hiding Wyatt's body. "What about . . . ?"

"Nothing." Brock shook his head emphatically, his eyes pained. "Don't go in there. Seriously."

Neither Mike nor Chad asked him what he meant. They wouldn't go back there.

Mike stood in the center of the room, a bit too close for comfort to the grate where Wyatt's blood had been drained. He looked at the others, spread out across the warehouse.

"What now, then?"

Neither one responded, but Brock turned his gaze pointedly to the one door in the room—the door Harold had disappeared through.

Mike almost laughed at the idea—the dopamine coursing through his system had turned everything around him into a carnival of dancing clowns, and somehow Brock's suggestion was an uproarious joke.

"You can't be serious, dude."

Brock shrugged. "What other options do we have?"

Mike looked at Chad for an answer, but he just shrugged his hulking shoulders.

"But . . ." This time Mike *did* laugh. "You don't really think the bartender just left the door unlocked, do you?"

"My guess is that he's the one who released those arm bonds," Brock said. "And if that's the only door in or out, it follows that he released us so we could go through it."

They stood there, trying to absorb this absurd possibility. But Brock was right—what else could they do?

They were gathered at the door, about to leave this nightmarish room behind and step into a new, unknown one, when Mike held up a hand to stop Brock. There was something he had to do.

"Wait."

Brock looked him askance, his hand paused on the door's handle.

Without explaining himself, Mike turned and crossed the room in just a few strides. Once back at his chair—not *his* chair; he hated that he'd come to think of it as *his*—he worked quickly, disconnecting the blood pouch from its stand and pump and then taking it to the grate in the floor. He yanked the tubing from the bag, slicking his hands with his own blood, then dumped its contents down the drain. The bag was only half full, or half empty, or whatever, but it felt right.

No way in hell was Harold taking another drop of his blood.

Chad and Brock appeared at his side, dumping their own bags' contents. He looked up and was relieved to see it in their eyes: he didn't need to explain himself; in fact, they were grateful to him for making sure they did this somewhat ceremonial final act before they faced whatever was waiting for them outside this room.

Together they stood, the bags discarded like used condoms on the cold cement. There was a shared look in their expressions, one that labeled them as brothers now. Wyatt had been a brother, too, as had the fifth guy whose name they'd never learned.

And brothers had each other's backs. Womb to tomb.

THE DOOR WAS INDEED UNLOCKED. It felt sacrilegious for some reason. That the final checkpoint to escaping their prison could be so accessible felt . . . wrong. Like they hadn't *earned* their escape, and thus it wasn't actually an escape.

It felt like a trap.

Which is exactly what it was.

Mike knew it was a trap the moment they reached the end of the long, dark corridor running parallel to their prison/warehouse. He felt it in the pit of his stomach, yet he couldn't bring himself to stop Brock as he reached for the second door—another door which he and all of them knew would obviously be unlocked.

The door felt *hungry*. Eager for their admittance.

Brock's hand rested on the brass knob. Mike let it happen despite his unease; after being unable to move a single inch of his body for so long, a part of him *needed* to push through any and every barrier keeping him from the outside world—damn the consequences, damn whatever waited past the door.

From the look in Chad's shining eyes, he must have shared Mike's dread of walking into a trap, but the most he did to stop Brock was little more than a squeak. Brock looked back at the two of them, and in his own wide eyes their sense of impending doom reflected back at Mike.

But then something else passed between the three brothers. An acknowledgment of the inevitable trap they were undoubtedly strolling into, yes, but another, more affirming acknowledgment, shared between them in the form of a firm nod of the head. A promise.

We go down together, that promise said. *Womb to tomb.*

The moment passed.

Brock faced forward and pushed open the door at the end of the dark corridor.

He, Chad, and Mike strode single-file into the unknown.

* * *

BUT NO. NOT ENTIRELY UNKNOWN. Familiar, yet different.

They were in a large room, shadows pooling in the corners like thick spiderwebs. Huge swaths of plastic sheeting stretched over every surface, again covering any windows that would show the time of day, though Mike thought that if it were daylight the sun would glow through the sheets anyway; it must still be night. Mike recognized the fireplace along the far wall, its fire now a pile of glowing embers. He thought he recognized the table covered in plastic sheets—hadn't that, once upon a time, been a fancy billiards table?

To their left was confirmation: the bar, the one uncovered surface of the room, an even richer mahogany now when surrounded by milky white plastic, its stools removed yet dirty glasses still littered across its length . . . and its tender, Harold, standing perennially behind it, his austere smile of hospitality gleaming back at them.

They were still inside Harold's Vino Veritas.

"Gentlemen," Harold said, his voice barely above a whisper yet easily carrying across the large room. "The final course."

Figures melted out of the shadows. Tall, thin specters that coalesced into a swanky nightclub crowd as they stepped fluidly farther into the room. Seven or eight of them, converging on Mike, Brock, and Chad with gleaming, wicked grins.

And suddenly Mike understood.

"They're fucking vampires," he muttered.

Chad glanced over at him. He tried to laugh, but it came out as a cough.

Brock said, "What?"

"Suck It is a vampire bar," Mike said, awe in his voice.

As the vampires stepped closer, Mike knew he was right. There, peeking out of each of their perfect mouths, were incisors well over an inch longer than a human's. Even in the gloom their pale skin was arresting. Some of them had chosen to remain in their evening attire, silky three-piece suits and velvet form-fitting dresses; some had stripped naked, no doubt hoping to save their wardrobe from an awkward trip to the drycleaner.

Mike couldn't help but stare at the nude bodies, even now, just moments before a no-doubt violent death. There was the first bitch who'd refused his offered drink and ignored him, her lithe body far better than he could have imagined. He remembered now how he had daydreamed earlier, while sitting next to her—dreamed of making her laugh, of charming her, of taking her back to his shitty apartment that in his daydream somehow wasn't shitty at all, of peeling her crushed-velvet dress from her body and finally seeing every supple inch of her, of taking her into his mouth . . . and now his daydream had come true. Not word for word, if you will, and it might be she who would be taking him into *her* mouth, but still. His eyes hungrily took in every inch of her exposed skin, and he felt himself getting an erection. Absurdly, he hoped Chad and Brock wouldn't notice.

But the she-vampire sure did. She winked at him lasciviously.

"Happy Saint Patrick's Day, lovies," she said.

As she stepped closer, one hand snaked down her body to touch herself, and she moaned. The moan morphed into a full-throat laugh, her fangs tilted back and gleaming in the gloom.

Brock turned his head, his eyes still on the vampire,

and whispered to the other guys, "Am I the only one kinda turned on right now?"

Mike didn't answer.

Chad only whimpered.

As the she-vampire stepped forward from the mass of naked bodies, her hourglass figure transitioned so smoothly from a feline predator's statue-still prowl to that of a ribbon dancing in the breeze as to be imperceptible to Mike were it not for some distant clanging alarm in the very back of his lizard-brain. Before any part of him could react to that klaxon of survival screaming *RUN! LOOK AWAY! SHE IS DEATH! YOU MORON, YOU—*, he and Brock and Chad were all struck dumb, hypnotized, swaying where they stood, jaws slightly ajar and drooling, like three zombified sunflowers dying in the dark.

"So nice of you to stop by and help a lady with her complexion, boys." The words dripped from her mouth (which Mike no longer thought of as having "blowjob lips") like honey. Like milk. And these boys were lapping it up.

The other vampires converged, fanned out and just behind the she-vampire who had stolen the humans' attention. To Mike they were specters in the twilight of the dying fire, pale ghosts melting from the shadows. His final thought before he was caught in those dizzying eyes—

(*Dracula is real ... Dracula is real, Dracula-is-real draculaisreal*)

—spun through his mind like a drunken carousel, its engine sparking in overdrive. The mantra swatted away all other thoughts like flies, especially the one that went *HAPPY ... HAPPY ... HAPPY ...* , and a small part of him, perhaps that lizard-brain part with its klaxon call, knew he should run, knew he should defend himself, knew he should do *something*.

But his body wouldn't respond. Couldn't.

The she-vampire lifted one slender arm toward him. A pinky nail, painted blood-red, whispered across his skin and tickled the patch of duct tape covering his tender puncture wound. That single touch projected a memory in Mike's inner eye: Wyatt's execution, like that of an animal, and that hydraulic-gunshot sound—

(*pffft*)

The memory of that death-knell sound sparked movement in Mike. It sent a signal from his lizard-brain down to his limbs and out. He took one unsteady step to the side, away from the source of the memory, away from that delicately reaching vampiric hand. His foot caught itself in the feet beside him, and together, like the Three Stooges in a bowling alley, Mike and Brock and Chad tumbled over in a mass of entangled limbs.

Their hypnosis broke the same moment their bodies thudded onto the hard, plastic-covered floor. Mike coughed then screamed, so loud it burned his throat:

"*RUN!*"

The next thirty seconds stretched ahead of Mike like a running track, and he scrambled to be the first to cross the finish line. Limbs entered and left his field of vision faster than he could track, an absurdist's puppet show, but he slapped them away and barreled through, yelling wordlessly and thrusting his elbows at anything still in his way. He was unaware of who was vampire and who was not, but in this moment all were obstacles just the same. He'd done his part, he'd broken the spell and told them to run, and if Brock and Chad didn't take the chance to bolt to freedom then that was their own goddamn problem—

The door handle appeared in his sweaty grip as if from nowhere, and for a moment Mike stood with a stupid grin of utter bewilderment mixed with assumed entitlement: of *course* he'd managed to fight his way through an army of blood-thirsty vampires and back to the outside world, he was Mike Davenport, he was no pussy, he—

"Fuck," he said.

The door was locked.

He turned to the bar, screamed "Fuck you, Harold!" and slammed a shoulder into the locked door. It barely shook in its frame. He reeled back and slammed into it again. There was a distinct, heavy *thunk* and he realized the motherfucker hadn't just locked the motherfucking door, he'd *chained* and *reinforced* the motherfucker. Mike could see just barely through the drawn curtains the back of that motherfucking sign whose promise of HAPPY he'd bought hook, line, and sinker, and what was he going to do now—

Screams.

He froze.

More screams.

The screams went on endlessly.

The most tortured and utterly hopeless sound he'd heard in his life.

He spun around, his back to the useless door.

One of the others, Brock or Chad he did not know, was drowning beneath a pile of writhing naked bodies. His screams built in intensity while at the same time becoming muffled and farther away beneath the orgy of pale body parts.

Goddammit, how was Mike still so *aroused* by these monsters?

A different scream split the air, like a mythological siren calling to her sisters from the sea. "You *monster*!"

"Mike! Dude! Help!"

Hearing his name pulled his attention from the orgy of bodies to another drama being played out near the fireplace. There was Brock, his red hair striking in the gloom (a small part of his brain told him the person being devoured in the vampire orgy was Chad, poor, lucky Chad), and if what he was seeing was correct—but how could it be?—Brock had somehow succeeded in bashing a vampire's head in against the fireplace's brick mantle and was standing over the unmoving body.

"How *dare* you! *Monster*!"

The original she-vampire bitch who'd snubbed Mike's advances was approaching Brock and her fallen comrade, hissing and screaming her siren scream.

"I'll *kill* you, you warm-blooded *whelp*!"

"Mike!" Brock yelled again, staring at him wildly. "Dude, help me!"

But Mike didn't hear him. He was focused on the she-vampire, her bare back to him and perfect apple-ass beaming up at him out of the dim. He experienced, in that moment, a surge of anger like none he'd ever felt. This vampire, this bitch, had turned down his advances, had turned down his beer, and was now trying to *kill* him . . . and she had the nerve to call *Brock* the monster? Mike and Brock and Chad and Wyatt and whoever that fifth dude had been were just trying to survive. They had just come to Suck It for some drinks and picking up chicks, but this fucking bitch with her fucking *cranberry juice*—

Before he knew what he was doing, Mike lunged at the bar and grabbed an abandoned glass, cranberry-tinted water sloshing out. Before he could try for a better weapon, he'd leapt across the room, actually *leapt* over a few limbs on the outside of Chad's dying orgy, and, instead of cupping that perfect ass with one hand like he'd daydreamed, Mike brought the glass tumbler crashing into the back of the she-vampire's head. The fragrance of her conditioner and the ghost-scent of cranberry juice and the sex-and-death smell of Chad's orgy hit Mike's nose like a dream. He probably would have been hypnotized again just then, so close to this naked beauty, but the jagged edge of the broken glass stabbed into his palm and woke him up.

The she-vampire fell to the ground, her ass now vaguely tilted up in the air, as if inviting Mike to bend down . . .

"Nice shot!" Brock said, bringing him back to reality again. "I came over here thinking I'd use the fire iron or something, but there ain't shit." He gestured around the bare fireplace cloaked in sheets of plastic. "Should've thought of the bar first." He grinned down at the fallen naked woman between them, waggling his eyebrows suggestively at Mike. "She's pretty hot though, right?"

She was more than pretty hot, Mike thought, but she was also stirring, still awake.

"Come on!" He threw the broken glass down onto the vampire, but in the face of that perfect ass the throw was only half-hearted. "Another door behind the bar."

He turned and Brock followed him back to the bar, and the two of them vaulted over its surface like James motherfucking Bond—or at least Brock did. Mike's was more of a slither than a vault, and it ended with him flipping over and falling sprawled out on the sticky concrete on the other side. He sprang back up.

"Harold!"

It was the she-vampire, fully upright and cradling her wounded head as she followed them. Brock and Mike exchanged a glance, surveyed the bar top, and selected their weapons. Brock had chosen a stainless-steel cocktail shaker; Mike went with one of his trusty beer steins, the handle firm in his grip. They turned to the door and found the person she was calling for.

Harold.

"Vino Veritas is a douchebag name, bro!" Brock yelled, charging him.

The man didn't flinch. He took Brock's shaker blow and shouldered him into the lip of the bar. Brock fell to the bartender's still-immaculate patent leather shoes, groaning. Harold turned his attention to Mike.

"I'm afraid last call has passed us, gentlemen."

Sure, the man had just shrugged off Brock like an NFL fullback, but Mike stepped toward him, unafraid. Where was his execution gun now? His sleeves weren't even rolled up anymore. The dude was a pansy, was nothing more to these vampires than a servant.

Mike hefted the beer stein in his right hand and swung at Harold's head.

If he were being honest, he probably would have missed, or Harold would have easily blocked the attack, if Brock hadn't chosen that exact moment to punch straight up from where he lay on his back—straight up into Harold's crotch. Turns out the one place this bartender couldn't plant like a statue was his balls. He couldn't protect both ends. At the exact moment Mike swung the stein, Brock's fist made testicular contact and Harold's eyes bulged out of his head, arresting his ability to block the stein's thick base with anything but his face.

THUD.

Mike had often heard that your life is supposed to flash before your eyes when you die. In that moment he learned that the same is true when you cause someone else to die. As he fell upon Harold's crumpled body, bashing him over and over in the head, Brock pinned to the floor beneath them and shouting his encouragement like they were at a baseball game, Mike saw Harold place that first frosted stein on the bar top. *THUD.* He saw Harold grimace as he said the name of the bar, the name he looked down his nose at just like he looked down his nose at people like Mike and Brock and Chad. *THUD.* And Wyatt, the sound the end of his life had made, that *pfft* and then nothing. *THUD.* Collecting Mike's blood as if he were livestock. *THUD.* Holding a juice box straw up to his lips as if he were two years old. *THUD.* Dragging that unnamed body across the floor with a *SCHKKKKKK.*

THUD. THUD. THUD.

"Dude." Brock's voice was soft. "He's dead."

Mike paused in midswing. His vision had misted over in his rage, but now the stein fell to the floor with another *THUD* as he took in the pulped mess that used to be Harold's face. The crisp, freshly-fallen-snow white of his skull poking out of the muck shocked Mike into the reality of what he'd just done and he fell back.

"Oh my God . . ." he breathed, horrified.

Brock shoved Harold's corpse away and scrambled

onto his knees, leaning his nose as far away from the soupy mess of Harold's face as he could. "Don't sweat it, bro. The dude was a sick fuck. Any one of us would've done the same if we could."

Mike met Brock's eyes and nodded, grateful for his brother. "For Wyatt."

Brock nodded back. "For Wyatt. And Chad."

The fifth, unnamed brother was an unspoken glimmer in their eyes, and they nodded for him too. Then the sounds of the carnage that had claimed Chad returned them to their situation. Brock's eyes shifted to something past Mike and he swore.

Mike didn't need to turn around. He knew who he'd find.

The she-vampire.

"You'll pay for that, lovies."

Without turning, Mike said, "You gotta catch us first."

And he ran, grabbing Brock and dragging him the remaining few feet to the door. A new door—not the one intentionally left unlocked like a rat's maze, not the entrance Harold had barricaded shut. This one was unlocked, but it wasn't a trap. It was freedom.

He hoped.

Unlike every other door in this place, this one squealed on its hinges, and in response every vampire in Vino Veritas hissed and screamed and took chase. Also unlike every other door in this place, this one let on to a flight of stairs. Not expecting this, Mike and Brock stepped into empty air and tumbled down a steep, narrow staircase.

At the bottom, too flooded with adrenaline to feel

any pain, they were back up on their feet and running. But running where? They didn't know. Everything was black except for the small rectangle of weak light hovering at the top of the rickety stairs. Mike was running blind. His feet squelched in damp, maybe mud or mold. He held his hands out in front of him, groping the dark.

"There's gotta be another way outta here," Brock said behind him. Brock said something else, but Mike couldn't grasp his words amid the shrieks and howls descending from the bar above.

Mike didn't bother to reply or ask for him to repeat himself. He just ran, praying he wouldn't trip and fall prey to the pursuing vampires. He ran into a wall, a slimy barrier against his fingertips, bounced off and around it and down a corridor, careening off the walls like a pinball. Moldy boxes collapsed under his feet, empty bottles clinked together or shattered, and still he stumbled on.

"Mike! Mike, dude, wait up! Dude, where are we going?"

Brock's voice was falling behind, but Mike didn't wait for him to catch up, nor did he bother answering. He didn't know; he didn't *need* to know. All he knew was the sound of vampires catcalling after him and the weight of his trusty stein missing from his grip.

Why had he left his only weapon behind?

An object flew out of the dark and whacked his head, and now he was ducking as he ran, avoiding the maze of pipes pressing down from the ever-lower ceiling. Brock was still calling for him, sounding farther and farther away, almost drowned out by the *drip-drip-drip* of the walls and the ringing in his head, that dripping reminding him of the *drip-drip-drip* of the IV bag with his blood and of the *HAPPY-HAPPY-HAPPY* of that sign, and still he ran, he ran desperately toward some semblance of that happiness, and now there was another sound, what was this new sound?

It was his own, screaming voice.

After some time—a few seconds? hours?—the low ceiling opened up and Mike got the distinct impression that he'd entered some vast, cavernous space. It was a quality in the air, in the ambient noises around him opening up and thickening. He slowed to a shamble and stopped when he felt as though he were in the center of this new chamber. Was he still under Suck It? While running, he'd felt an almost imperceptible sloping decline, and now every bone in his body sang to him:

This is something else. This is the deep. This is a secret.
This is wrong.

The silence echoed around him. Water dripped down the walls. There were furtive movements somewhere nearby, or maybe all around him . . . scuffling, snuffling, shuffling. He wanted to ask who was there, but his voice was strangled in his throat. He couldn't speak. He couldn't even scream.

That's when he realized he couldn't hear Brock anymore.

Did that mean they'd caught up to him? Of the five, was Mike the only one left?

And then: *Are those eyes?*

Staring at him out of the darkness, from this chamber's entrance or elsewhere within he did not know. Glowing, malevolent eyes.

And then another pair of eyes.

And another.

Two more.

They popped out of the dark faster than the gooseflesh could prickle his arms. He was surrounded by a swarm of eyes, tiny luminescent eyes like the yellow of radioactive waste. After so much darkness, they hurt Mike's vision.

A stream of larger glowing eyes poured into the chamber from a tributary tunnel, and Mike instinctively knew this was the group that had chased him down from the bar. This was the group that had undoubtedly just devoured Brock.

"You look lost, lovey."

It was the she-vampire, calling out to him from this new group of glowing eyes.

Mike finally found his voice. "What'd you do with Brock?"

Her laughter bubbled across the cavern. "You know."

Mike swallowed. "So you'll kill *me* now?"

She suddenly sounded bored. Or maybe that was petulance. "On a normal evening, yes. But you've complicated things."

Her voice was coming closer. A pair of eyes near the front of the new group peeled itself from its fellows and came hovering closer and closer to Mike, but he stood his ground. Not like he had anywhere to go. As it were.

"I would love if we could just do our usual," she went on. "Drain you, strip you, fuck you, hang you to dry."

Mike tried to swallow again, but he couldn't. Was she saying what he thought she was saying? If things had gone according to the menu, he, Mike Davenport, would have actually gotten lucky with Blowjob Lips? Her naked body rushed to his mind. To be able to touch that alabaster skin . . . cup one ass cheek . . . feel her writhing on top of him . . .

He finally managed to swallow. "I've still got enough blood in me if you . . . if you wanted—"

But he couldn't say it, couldn't make his move, even when faced with death, even in complete darkness. He was a coward, and she was laughing because she knew it too.

"That ship has sailed, I'm afraid. But, believe me"—one glowing eye winked at him—"you would have loved it."

"So you'll let me go?" he asked, hating the quiver in his voice. "You had your fill with the others?"

Laughter floated to him from the vampires at the room's entrance. The she-vampire's glowing eyes came so close he could smell her warm, fruity breath.

"No, my lovey," she said, not unkindly. "But we do face a dilemma. My brothers and sisters wish to feed you to the children, but I've reminded them that you've left us without a herald."

Children . . . ?

At her mention of that word, titters and chirps and mewling swept through the ring of small glowing eyes like a wave. Mike stared around him at the dark, his mind reeling.

Children . . . ?

At some unseen command, the circle of glowing eyes constricted, rushing toward him, and Mike saw by the light of their eyes a mass of tiny bodies climbing over one another. Pale, bone-thin bodies, mouths of needle-like teeth hissing beneath their animal eyes.

Mike couldn't scream. He couldn't breathe. He saw this nest of—not vampires, not sophisticated and human-esque like the she-vampire and the others he'd encountered upstairs in Suck It—this nest of vampire creatures, *children*, she'd called them her *children*—he saw a squirming wall of them at his back and at all sides and all he could do was jump forward—

The she-vampire caught him in her arms and held him against her, her grip like iron. Her skin was cold to the touch, but not unbearable. Not unbearable like what was coming at him from all around—

"Shh," she whispered, her breath feathering his ear. "You're safe with me. The kiddies won't touch you while you're in my arms."

Mike rested his head in the crook of her neck, his body relaxing in her grip. Her touch was like chamomile, dulling that klaxon blaring through his skull to that of a sea shell's ocean call.

"What will we do?" Mike managed to mutter, unconscious to the fact that he had said *we* instead of *you*.

"My Harold is gone," she said, only a hint of sadness in her singsong voice. "You took my Harold from me." She pulled her head back and locked his eyes in her gaze.

"I'm sorry," he breathed. And he truly was.

He was also HAPPY.

"I'm sorry," he said again, his voice thick with tears.

She smiled with understanding, hovered ever closer, and kissed him.

It was the most glorious moment of Mike Davenport's life. Bright, neon tubes pulsed in his mind, singing HAPPY . . . HAPPY . . . HAPPY . . . as his lips pressed and enfolded themselves with her own. He felt her naked body against him, and his erection throbbed achingly along her bare thigh. He had just enough freedom in his arms to reach and, *Yes!*, cup his fingers along the smooth slope of her bottom.

She pulled a hair's breadth back, licking his bottom lip, and there were tears in her eyes.

HAPPY . . . HAPPY . . . HAPPY . . .

"You will be our herald now," she said, and kissed him again.

MIKE DAVENPORT WAS ABSENT from work the next Monday.

"Bros, I'm telling you, he's ditched us for greener pastures," Dean told his buddies around the water cooler. One of them, Steve, punched him in the arm. He took out his phone to show them proof. "Seriously, check it out. He texted me saying he scored a new gig as a bartender. Remember that joint I told you about, with all the chicks? Dude, that's where it is! Says we should drop by and check out all the fuckable chicks."

But they all scoffed, walked away, disbelieving. No way did *Mike* of all people get lucky like that.

Dean didn't much mind. He didn't want any of them to come anyway.

Dean Milhouse needed to get laid.

And he knew the perfect spot.

THE SEUSS

THE DOCTOR HAD NEVER HEARD OF SUCH A THING.
Absurd, really. Patients driven to speak only in
rhymes? She had studied medicine for over twenty
years, thank you very much, and she had come across
nothing even remotely reminiscent of diseased syntax.

And for the patient to suggest that
    his symptoms could be *contagious*?
        Why, it was outrageous!
The moment *this* doctor was forced to rhyme
    would be the moment she'd quit on a dime.
Look at the PhDs on her wall!
    Why, she'd studied it all!
A person would have to be obtuse
    suggesting she could *catch* "The Seuss"!

JOE BUILDS A SUNSET

OLD JOE WAS DYING, and he knew it. But he couldn't leave before telling his best friend that he'd figured out the answer to life's ultimate question.

The meaning of life. Life after death, and how to get there.

"It's not what you think," he told his basset hound one afternoon.

He was sitting on his porch, in his favorite spot, exactly so that when the sun set it looked to him as if it was split in half by the oak beam supporting the roof. His chair rocked and his hound nodded sagely back at him. Basset knew this was all in the strictest confidence, of course. Joe didn't need to tell him twice to keep this to himself. What is said on the porch stays said on the porch—that's the rule.

"It's not what you think," Joe said again. "I mean it,

Bass. Heaven . . . hell . . . whatever. It's not up or down or in another realm of reality or dimension or whatever they preach in those churches or mosques or anything. It's— Bassie, you listenin'?"

Oh, Basset was listening. His droopy eyes stayed on his master, and Joe could have sworn that his dog raised one eyebrow in response. As if to say, *I'm always listenin', Joe. Tell the damn story.*

"All right, all right," Joe said, resuming rocking in his chair and letting the split sunset warm his old bones. He needed the warmth. The sun was something like four billion years old and some change. That ain't nothing to shake a stick at, Joe knew; but he also knew that ninety-six years weren't nothing to shake a stick at, neither, and that was how long Joe'd been on this damned planet. So he figured he'd earned this warmth. The sun and Joe? They were like old friends now, and he knew the sun didn't mind sharing its rays.

"I'll tell ya, Basset, I'll tell ya," Joe said.

Basset waited.

"It's not a heaven or a hell or up or down or nothin' like that. It's all . . . *in the brain.*"

Joe pressed a crooked finger to his temple to illustrate to Basset where the brain was—right through the skull.

"Ya get me?" he said. "It's all up here. In the brain. We got a . . . well, I don't know if *you* got it, Bassie, but I sure hope you do. But we humans? Our brains have the answer, sitting right there the whole time. It's actually . . . it's actually kinda fuh-fun—"

Joe cackled, bending over in his chair, taken by a sudden bout of hysteria. But damn it all if it weren't so *funny*! He just couldn't stop laughing at it.

"Think . . . think about it, Bassie," Joe said between laughter and hitching breaths. "Our whole lives—our *entire existence*—we damn humans been looking everywhere to find the answer, and the funny thing is . . . it's been sitting right there in our noggins the whole time!"

Joe cackled again, and Basset humored him with a low howl.

"That's right, Bassie! Ain't that funny?" Joe took another deep breath, calming down. That was good. He needed to tell Basset the answer. He was ninety-six, dammit. The sun would be setting for good soon.

"It's all in our dusty attics," Joe said, resuming his rocking. "Ya see, Basset, the brain's got these chemicals, firing around like . . . aw, I ain't no scientist, Bassie, you know that. But it's in there, I tell ya, in the brain."

Basset nodded, then placed his snout back on his paws to rest. He wasn't young neither, no he wasn't, old Bassie.

"Survival mechanisms," Joe said. "The brain sees it— a bullet to the head, a car crash, a heart attack, or maybe just old age after a good long life."

A moment of companionable silence passed.

"Whatever the cause. That point of death. The singular instant where your body switches from living to dead." Joe snapped his fingers, *crack*. "It sees that moment, and it panics. The brain has these reflexes, and it just floods the system. Hits that red *DO NOT PUSH* button. Serotonin, dopamine, endorphins, whatever the hell they're called. It starts that final LSD party. And it's all right there, in that moment. That's the answer, Bass. Let's say you got this image in your head, an image of some dog heaven. You get to run through a field and sniff other dogs' asses all day. That's your vision of life after death. Ya with me?"

Basset was with him, all right. That sounded wonderful.

"Now, yer not young, Bassie. You and I both know that someday soon, you'll die. Sixteen years ain't nothing to shake a stick at. So let's say you're about to die. You hit that instant between life and death and your brain panics and opens the floodgates, and . . . *boom!* Your version of heaven is projected in your mind in this vortex of dopamine, and your brain tricks you into eternity. One single moment that, for all you know, stretches out forever. And your brain has successfully scammed you into thinking you're in doggy heaven, sniffing butts for all time."

Basset snorted.

"I know, I know, you don't believe me," Joe said. "But I'm tellin' ya, boy, that's what happens. Say those nice young men come by here again, the two on the bicycles and the Mormon Bibles. Say I took my shotgun down from the mantel and filled them with buckshot for trespassing on my property."

Basset raised his head from his paws and his ears flopped up.

"Nooo," Joe said. "I wouldn't actually *do* that. Come on, Bass, you know me better than that."

Basset settled his head down again, pacified.

"Say," Joe continued, rocking his chair, "that I shot those kids. They die, but their brains trick them into thinking they're going to Mormon heaven. I dunno what's that, maybe some cloudy, golden-gated community? Whatever it is, they get it."

Joe chuckled. "Those radical suicide zealots, them crazies what blow themselves up? They do it for some virgins in the sky or something, I don't know. But I can guarantee that when they do it, if they truly believe that's what they get . . . *their brain delivers*."

The sun had almost finished setting. A gold band hung above the railing of the porch, golden in Joe's eyes and fiery on Joe's wrinkled skin. The warmth was nice. He'd miss that.

"So whaddaya say, Bass? How do we want to live when we die?"

Basset didn't respond except to look at his master, patiently and faithfully waiting for him to go on.

"It almost makes me feel sad for them Catholics. Believing all that fire-and-brimstone bull must really put a damper on that brain's final acid trip. Or—"

Joe sat up in his chair, energy renewed at a sudden thought.

"Or those damn *atheists*. Oh, that's terrifying, Bass, you better believe it. What do their brains give *them* as a finale? The brain shoots out those chemicals and delivers . . . nothing? Nietzsche's black abyss, staring back at them?"

Basset snorted. Like Joe knew Nietzsche.

"Oh, those poor, poor bastards. Ignorance is bliss, Bassie. That's why I'm glad I ain't no scientist."

Basset nodded. He was glad he wasn't a scientist either.

"I wanna die just like this," Joe finally said after a long pause. "I wanna live on this porch, with that sun setting."

Basset grunted his agreement.

"No," Joe said. "I wanna . . . I wanna visit the sun!"

Basset grunted again, but not in agreement this time.

"No, listen to me, Bass! Think about it! That sun . . . it's millions of miles away, so huge ya can't even fathom the thing. Hell, it's so far away that it takes a full eight minutes for the damn light to hit your skin. I think I read that somewhere. Eight minutes. Imagine that, Bass. The sun will always be eight minutes ahead of you, no matter how quick ya are."

Joe paused. The sun was almost gone.

"That's how I wanna go. I wanna go be with the sun. I like it. But I think I like it best when it's setting. Tell me, Bass, if a sun is always setting but never set, is it actually setting?"

Basset didn't tell him. That's all for naught, figured Joe. He didn't quite understand the question himself. But it sounded pretty.

"I wanna go with the sun," Joe continued, "and I want my best friend with me. That's you, Basset, and you better sure as hell know it."

Joe bent down to his best friend and said, "But that's where it gets even more cuckoo, Bass. If I want you there with me in the afterlife, then my brain will deliver. You'll be there with me. But *you* won't actually be with me. Maybe your brain's afterlife is far away from the sun and nowhere near me because you've been secretly hating me all these years. So there we'd be, me hanging with my best friend Basset, and you finally free of your begrudging roommate Joe."

Joe chuckled. Stretched down to touch Bass's head. Basset craned his neck so that it was in reach. Joe was old, the old dog knew, and he didn't want his master hurting himself. Ninety-six ain't nothing to play fetch with.

Joe paused from his chuckling, his gnarled fingers resting in the velvety folds of skin atop his best friend's head, his eyes reflecting the last dying light of the sun. His skin was losing the sun's warmth. The sun had stopped shining for him and the basset hound eight minutes ago, in fact, but his skin didn't know it, so he let it enjoy the last rays. But he was growing cold.

"I think I might go find my own answer tonight, Bassie," Joe said. "Right here, in my favorite chair, next to you. I'm sorry, boy. Not sure if I'm gonna be getting you your milk tonight. Not sure if I'll be getting up from this chair, actually.

"Let's answer our question together, Bassie. We ain't entering death so much as we're building our own after-life. Like I built that beam right there when I built this porch. You weren't around yet, but I built that beam from oak and was mighty proud of it. I like to sit here and let it split my view of the sun as it sets, and ya know why? Because that sun there is the same on either side of the post. And life is good. So why shouldn't death be the same?"

With his hand still on his best friend's head, and with Basset still reaching his head up for his best friend's hand, they met that single instant, let their brains fire away, and together they set with the sun.

FINITE FORCEMAN MDCLXVII

"**W**HERE DID THIS—"

"Don't ask me, please don't ask me where this came from, okay? I don't have the energy."

"Just trying to do my job, sir."

"And nowhere in your job description does it require you to bother your superior with questions about the meaning of life, the Universe, and everything. You're just a grunt, kid. Doing grunt work. It's your job, right now, as a grunt, to take this file I'm handing you, grunt a 'Yes, sir, right away, sir,' and get the Hell out of my office."

"Yes, sir. Right away, sir."

"Apology accepted. Look, kid—sit back down. Now, in case there was even the slightest whiff of facetiousness in what you just said, even just a dab of sarcastic insubordination, with the 'Yes, sir,' and the 'Right away, sir,' I'll do you a favor and elaborate: You don't need to know where this file came from. All you need to know is it's here now, and I'm pressing it into your hands to take to the Executor's office. Don't bother with the *where*s, the *why*s, the *what*s. That big stamp across the front, still glistening with the Boss's signature chartreuse ink, can you read to me what it says?"

"FATE, sir."

"And fate it is. We don't question fate, kid, and we certainly don't question Fate."

"Y . . . yes, sir."

"You're questioning, aren't you?"

"No, sir. Wouldn't dream of it, sir."

"*Hah.* Grunts don't dream, kid. That wouldn't be another whiff of your sarcastic wit I detect, would it?"

"No, sir. Never, sir."

"Kid, I can see it on your face."

"See what, sir?"

"The question."

"The question, sir?"

"It's as clear as that FATE stamp, kid. The where-did-this-come-from question."

"Yes, well . . ."

"Yes, well? Yes, well, *what*?"

"Well, it's just that . . . you asked me not to ask you that question, sir."

"You're a smartass, you know that, kid?"

"Apologies, sir. My assigned father-figure always told me it was better to be a smartass than a dumbass."

"HA! Hahaha, humph. 'Yes, well,' indeed! I changed my mind, kid. I like you."

"I like you, too, sir."

"Don't brown-nose. What's your name?"

"MDCLXVII, sir."

"Come again?"

"I'm a grunt, sir, as you know. A team member of Fate's Finite Force. We are assigned call numbers as names. Mine is MDCLXVII."

"That's a nightmare! Mind if I just keep calling you 'kid'?"

"Not at all, sir."

"Well, kid, it's like I said: I changed my mind. I'm still not going to answer that stupid question. It's stupid. But I may have found just enough energy at the bottom of this Bottomless™ coffee mug to explain a few things about what we do here. I will admit that we tend to overlook you grunts over at Finite. I mean . . . *finite*, for Fate's sake! You follow me?"

"Can't say I do, sir."

"And I can't say I'm surprised, if you'll forgive the insult. I say again—finite. The point is, you've got questions. You've got a Helluva lot more questions than just *Where did this come from?*, and we've never been good at addressing them. Sure, I'll shoulder some of that blame. But maybe if I feed you some premium knowledge about why you're here, who knows? Maybe you'll soak it in and spread said knowledge to all your little grunt buddies. And maybe said knowledge will give you Finites a better sense of direction, and therefore your performance will improve. And maybe, just maybe, then the Boss'll give me a raise!"

"Maybe, sir."

"That last part was a joke. About the raise."

"Very good, sir."

"So these questions of yours. Any of 'em so pressing that you just have to have it answered first?"

"Hmm."

"Hmm?"

"Well, sir, there is one question that I always ponder on my monthly coffee break. A question that just may hold an answer satisfactory enough for all my other smaller questions."

"Efficiency. Love it. Ask away, kid!"

"Why is it that every file we're handed is just a copy of another file that another Finite Forceman filed with an Executor before, which was a copy of another file of another file of another, and so on?"

"That— Jeez, kid, that question's more of a nightmare than your name!"

"I understand, sir."

"No, no, I didn't mean I won't answer it for you. Please. Sit back down. What I meant was, is there a better, simpler way of phrasing it?"

"Oh, I see. Well . . . hmm. How about: Why must history repeat itself?"

"Why must history repeat itself?"

"Yes, sir."

"How about: That's the way it's always been done? Would that pacify you? Would that quench yours and your grunt buddies' insatiable thirst for knowledge?"

"That's the way it's always been done, sir?"

"Ah, your hearing's fine then."

"Yes, sir. It's just that . . . wouldn't you agree that that answer is a little—"

"Kid, let's not parse words."

"No, sir, no parsing. Can I speak plainly?"

"I've invited this discussion, haven't I, and it's come this far, hasn't it? Please don't feel you must edit your words on my account. We Ultimates deal with *the* Complexity—that's *our* job description—so you can bet your sweet grunting ass I'm made of thicker stuff than whatever abstract thought you grunt my way. I'm a big boy, kid. Speak plainly. Knock yourself out."

"Very well, sir. Wouldn't you agree that that answer—that's the way it's always been done—is a little . . . willfully ignorant? Cognitively dissonant? Juvenile? Puerile? Naïve?"

"*Puerile?* All right, who gave you grunts a thesaurus? Was it Larry from Accounting?"

"What I'm trying to say, sir . . . I don't think empty-headed tradition, the belief that that's the way it has always been and so that is how it shall always be, is an acceptable answer."

"Empty-headed?"

"I believe, sir, that you said you could handle whatever I *grunt* your way. That you're a, what did you say? Big boy."

"Ohhh, you little—"

"But if my words did indeed find their way through that *thicker stuff* of yours, I'm more than happy to allow you another chance at a more suitable answer. Sir."

"I think maybe I don't like you anymore, kid."

"I'm very sorry to hear that, sir. May I remind you, sir, that you gave me permission to speak plainly."

"All right—how 'bout you try this one on for size: It's in the system."

"Sir?"

"And the *system* can't just change on account of a few

stir-crazy grunts thirsty for some adventure, to live vicariously through a file that offers something fresh."

"You think I ask why history must repeat itself because I am bored?"

"That's exactly what I think, kid. You familiar with war?"

"War, sir?"

"War. It's this sick game humans play, down on Earth. Civil wars, religious wars, revolutions—nothing the Boss would condone *here*, but down there it's all the rage. Those humans, they can't get enough of it. *World* wars, even. They have places like Hollywood that go so far as make *movies* of war—movies, uhhh . . . pictures that move—and humans go *watch* wars. *For fun!* Sadistic bastards, every last one of 'em.

"These wars, kid, they tick like clockwork. Humans build up their lives, entire civilizations rise up, and then it's time for the cleaning lady, Miss World War, to come sweep 'em all away like so much dust. And just in time for the next minimum-wage nine-to-five, so that the humans can begin building their civilizations again, straight up out of the rubble. And they do this over and over again. Lather, rinse, repeat."

"And none of them question this?"

"Question *what*, kid? Come on, specificity."

"The necessity of war, sir."

"Oh, sure they do! There's humans of all sorts, kid. That's an inevitability. But so is war."

"And what do they tell these humans that question war, sir? 'That's the way it's always been done'?"

"Not in so many words, but yes. Most of the time those sorry saps are wasting their breath. The humans that run Earth—or *think* they run Earth—they don't even dignify it with a response. You see how lucky you grunts have it, with Ultimates like me taking pity on you? But humans, they just keep building and then destroying, keep building, keep warring . . . and you know what? It *works*. If it's not broke, as they say, don't challenge a human's base need for senseless murder. And if that doesn't penetrate your grunt intellect, then you just don't get it."

"Get what, sir?"

"The *system*."

"Ah, the system again. 'It's in the system.' "

"You're damn right, it's in the system!"

"And what system is this, exactly?"

"What system? *What system?* Where do you think you work, kid?"

"I work for—"

"No, no, not the company, the *where!*"

"I . . . I don't know, sir."

"Holy grunting Destiny, kid, where's your high horse now? You can't expect to understand an answer to your question if you don't even know where you work. It's, well, it's everything! Stand up."

"Sir?"

"Stand up! Walk around my desk and open the blinds."

"The blinds?"

"The blinds, kid. Open the blinds!"

"Yes, sir. Right away, sir. Where do I . . . ah, here, just a mo— *AH!*"

"Ooh, that had to hurt. Aw, crap. I forgot. You've never seen outside, have you, kid?"

"I'm blind!"

"You'll live, no need for the dramatics. Aw, look, kid, I'm sorry. Completely forgot. Call it even—you call me empty-headed, I blind you with the Sun. But you gotta believe me when I say I forgot. I'm so used to the view in my office, I didn't think about how you grunts never . . .

"Here, here, put these on. Special sunglasses, Solar-Flares I think they're called. I've never needed 'em, what with my enhanced vision and all, but we've got a whole drawer-full just in case. I guess you're the just-in-case. Hey—maybe I'll start calling you Justin Case! *Hah!* Get it?"

"Ah. Hah. Clever, sir."

"Ah, you'll be all right. Just keep blinking. Keeeeep a-blinking. That's it. Thaaaaat's it. When your vision's clear again, describe to me what you see out there. Take your time."

"I— I . . . a ball of fire? It's a sun? And planets. I see planets, going clockwise in orbit. It . . . it's beautiful!"

"Yes, yes, all that crap is there. Real knock-out. True. But what do you *see*? What's the big picture?"

"I see a solar system, sir."

"Yes, a solar system. A system so large, you cannot begin to fathom it, even when it's staring you in the face."

"Yes . . . sir."

"And yet it's all pretty delicate. One wrench in the works—a big wrench, granted—and it all implodes. All those planets, each with their own moons and atmospheres and problems, orbiting around that big, fiery star. What enables this system, this miracle, to work? Do you know?"

"Gravity, sir?"

"Sure, gravity, I'll take that as an answer. So this

gravity you speak of. Let's say Fate has a *severe* lapse of judgment, gives over gravity to you grunts at Finite. Grunts everywhere are clamoring for something new, maybe you just can't get your jollies off with the same ol' gravity anymore. You're screaming, *We've seen this gravity a thousand times! It's always the same! We want new gravity!* And so you write up a hot new file with an original, fresh take on gravity. This file then gets a chartreuse FATE stamp, it's delivered to an Executor by Grunt MDVX—"

"Finite Forceman MDCLXVII, sir."

"Whateverthefate. You take it to an Executor. This exciting new gravity is sent out into the Universe, and what happens? *BOOM!* Because a few grunts craved a little excitement in their lives, the rules of gravity have been broken. What goes up must not necessarily come down. Newton just rolled over in his—"

"Newton, sir?"

"What? Never mind who he is. As I was saying: gravity. All of a sudden! Planets spin around, smash into each other like the break shot of the Boss's billiards. That solar system outside this window, so vast you cannot begin to fathom it—it's *destroyed.* And now I've got the distinct pleasure of firing half my workforce. All because you wanted originality."

"I see, sir."

"Do you? Or am I still speaking in terms too *puerile* for your taste?"

"Well, sir, if we're still speaking plainly . . . do we have to be so dramatic? I wasn't questioning the laws of physics."

"Oh? My mistake. What were you questioning then?"

"The laws of *meta*physics."

"What do you think we do here, kid? Sit around and

philosophize? Wax poetic on the topics of war and peace while reciting passages from *War and Peace*? No. What we do here is scientific. Hell, it's a science all on its own. An *exact* science."

"I don't quite follow, sir."

"Then quit talking and listen. That's what grunts like you do, kid. *Listen.* I'm assuming, since you're observant enough to notice that, as you put it, history repeats itself, that you've opened up those files on more than one occasion. Maybe only what you're able to glean on the short walk from the Ultimates to the Executors? Well, I'll save you the trouble of having to read FATE reports and walk at the same time—go ahead, open the file.

"Seriously, kid. Open it. Go ahead. You won't get in trouble, at least any more than you're already in, seeing as you've already admitted you've read FATE reports before. So go on. Open it. I'll wait, give you some time to read it.

"So. You see now. This file isn't like most others. Sure, it will follow the same laws of physics, or metaphysics, or what have you. But this is the final stamp of Fate— literally—on an Eleventh Hour emergency. My boys downstairs have been working on this one for months. You see what we're calling it? Right there, at the top of the stack."

"Shuffle?"

"That's the one. The Shuffle file. Maybe you've heard of it. Anyway, it's all right there in paper and ink, you'll see. Basically, some humans down on Earth too smart for their own good built this thing called a time machine, something that had only been in stories until now. Stories? You know, kid—falsehoods, fictions. Consult your thesaurus.

"So these smart humans, they jump in their time machine and attempt to undo one of Fate's most lucrative orders just to stop their World War Three. But what they don't realize is, by changing the rules—by creating something *original*, you could say—they're breaking the system. Insert planets-smash-like-billiards metaphor."

"So you're saying that history repeats itself because . . . history is a law of nature?"

"Not history, no. *Fate* is a law of nature. And stop saying history repeats itself, kid. It's called historic recurrence."

"And that's why the humans with the time machine have to be stopped? Because another world war has to take place?"

"Sure, three world wars—those humans love their trilogies. As I said, kid: lather, rinse, repeat. You gotta give 'em simple instructions, or nothing will ever get done. Much like you grunts."

"You really don't have a high opinion of humans, do you, sir?"

"Oh, listen, let me stop you right there. This is a job, kid. But that's why you can't wrap your head around what we do here and why we do it. You're too invested."

"You're saying I shouldn't care about my job?"

"Of course that's not what I'm saying. But it doesn't matter what I'm saying. You know why?"

"I don't, sir."

"Exactly! You don't know. You're a grunt. So why am I even wasting my time trying to explain anything to you? You, frankly, can't handle the kind of scientific technobabble needed to fully explain this stuff. To be fair, I probably couldn't handle *saying* the technobabble, but that's not my job. And that's okay. It's not your job either. It's my job to compile a report, get the Boss to stamp Her chartreuse FATE of approval, and deliver it to an Executor via a Finite Forceman—which I have done, and then some. It's your job to take this file out of my sight. I currently can still see it sitting on my desk. In fact, I see it open and spread out. So collect it, close it, pick it up, wipe the look of confusion off your face, and—"

RING!

"Oh for Fate's sake! Look, kid, I gotta take this phone call. Go do your job. You can keep the sunglasses.

"Hello, office of an Ultimate, how can I direct your complexities? What? Yes, I've got the file. I've actually got a grunt here to collect it as we speak, he's still standing here like an idiot, doesn't know the meaning of— His name? Yeah, it's . . . hold on.

"What's that ridiculous name of yours again, kid?"

"Finite Forceman MD—"

"Okay, it's MD—"

"—CL—"

"—CL—"

"—XV—"

"—XV—"

"—II."

"—II. Yeah, that's him. Why do you ask? *What—?* Hold on, just *hold on one hot second.* What do you mean, he's taking it back to Fate? The *Shuffle* file? But—he can't do that! Do you know how long I've— That's just not how things are done around here. No, I don't care if— Wait. No, before you hang up, answer me one goddamn question. Where did this come from? From *Her*? She . . . okay, okay. I'll calm down. Yes . . . yes, yes. Yes. Bye."

Click.

"What the Hell are you playing at, kid?"

"I'm afraid I don't know what you mean, sir."

"Oh, don't start. You're not taking this FATE report to an Executor!"

"No, sir."

"You're taking it upstairs."

"Yes, sir."

"To Fate Herself. You're taking it to Her so She can . . . can . . . *rewrite it!*"

"That about sums it up, yes, sir."

"You know, I'm starting to think all those 'sirs' are sarcastic."

"I wouldn't know, sir. I'm a grunt."

"Why, you little—"

"I wish I could stay and chat, sir, but I really should be getting this upstairs."

"You think taking this upstairs is gonna change anything, kid? You think—"

"Did you even *read* the Shuffle file, sir?"

"*Read* it? I *wrote* the damn thing. And stop calling me *sir*!"

"Then you must have seen the lengths these humans, the ones you say are too smart for their own good, are willing to travel just to save their own kind. They're stuck in a time machine skipping through history, and you're ready to condemn them and the billions of lives they are trying to save based on your own inability to let go of antiquated ideas like historic recurrence? You may be on the wrong side of history, but we at Fate's Finite Force— grunts, kids, whatever you want to call us—are ready for a revolution. And Fate is listening."

"You asked me where this came from. You waltzed into my office to ask *Where did this come from?* and you knew damn well the entire time what was in that file and where it came from."

"I also know where it's going. Upstairs. Those humans are going to live."

"I want those SolarFlares back. That's Ultimate property."

"I'm sorry, but you already gave them to me. And Fate is waiting. Sir."

"Get the Hell out of my office."

"Yes, sir. Right away, sir."

TRUTH IS A DRAGON

*T*IME, ONCE MINED AND SMELTED, is liquid metal, and you are the blacksmith.

The anvil is time's clock face, and your hammer is the clock's minute hand.

Just as you cannot hold molten steel, cannot cup mercurial iron in your callused hands, lest you lose your mind, neither can you grasp pure time. Unwrought time kills; it is unrefined truth, which poisons the mind. You must shape it. Mold it, to fit. Therefore, memories are a kind of metallurgy. You, the blacksmith, must transform the truth into memory. With no memory, the truth is forever lost to all but the dragons, those perennial truthsayers.

You stare around the dimly lit smithy at the many memories you have shaped and hung on your walls, then focus your attention on the memory at hand. You strike. Flattening and folding the molten steel of time, shaping your memory. Memories are the alloy of the rememberer: the blacksmith. You yield the hammer, you shape the sword, you hold your own key to time. It is backbreaking work—*heartbreaking* work, if you are being honest with yourself—but it must be done. Remember: one cannot carry distilled veracity.

Do you see it, in the rivers of silvery truth? Do not look away—especially as you strike it, change it, throw sparks from it with your hammer. You must see what that truth becomes, when folded upon itself and hammered in place, then turned, then folded, then struck, over and over.

Do not look away.

Strike it.

Strike it now.

Are you watching?

STRIKE.

It's 1990, '91. Your first memories, now rusted with disuse. Of running, of wind, of sand, of seagulls, of living on the beach. But no, you've seen pictures of yourself: a baby with a sand-crusted face, wispy hair, a pacifier. Are these truly your memories, or have the photographs planted these images in your head? The mind is a trickster.

Are you watching? Are you looking for the source of your truth?

STRIKE.

Somewhere in the mid-nineties, hovering in the thick dragonsmoke pouring from your furnace, is a memory, a story of your childhood recounted for the first time to a friend on a tarry rooftop in the new millennium. But is it truth, or simple certitude? What are memories but our versions of the truth? History is written by the conquerors, and we are all conquerors of our own thoughts. You were still a child on that rooftop, and children tell each other tales whether they are true or not and then come to believe those tales themselves. Children are tricksters. But this story of a younger you in the backseat of your mother's van, playing a game your older brother told you was called "Vampire," where you had to suck the blood from each other's— . . . Was it real?

Were you watching the truth and intentionally altering it? Turning fact to fiction so you could feel safer, like a child tucked in with a fairytale?

STRIKE.

True love, the first. Not the love you whispered to a girl in her driveway when you were ten, but true love, circa 2005. The year you lay on the couch beneath a girl, in the dark, beside a heap of laundry, with her breath cascading down and mixing with your own heated breath; the year you learned what a woman's body feels like. Later, on another couch, you replay these memories of skin and warmth and first love, while you are stuck at home reading scriptures with parents. Your own personal VHS tape. Press Play, Rewind, repeat. Play, *Mormon 8:24*, rewind, *yea, even the fiery furnace*—repeat—*could not harm them.* Rewind to your favorite part. *Neither wild beasts nor*— rewind again—*because of the power of his word.* Again. Overused memories wash out, edges fray, holes appear, but you can fill in those holes. You are the conqueror.

You are still watching. But is it a fantasy? A rerun? Or is it truth?

STRIKE.

People are weapons in your arsenal. They leave your life, they are finished, cooled, hung up in neat lines along your wall. How do you remember this friend? Hilarious. This one? Narcissistic. This girl? Cold. But then you take the sword down from its mount on the wall and examine it: a love you'd thought of as the last, the love to end all loves, back in 2009. Reexamine. No, she was not *cold* . . . one word cannot capture the sword's beauty, her intricacy. What have you done to it? What has it done to you?

Are you watching truth become a word? A weapon?

Stop watching. You can't.

YOU PAUSE, MINUTE HAND HELD ALOFT, the hammer slick in your grip. You paw the sweat from your brow and look back at the clock face, the anvil. The warm glow has cooled, the dazzling white—was it ever that hot?—to a dull red. Something has changed. What are you missing?

The memory you strike. Is it yours? Is it true? The memory you strike is of your younger self, when you first entered adulthood, found your independence, when you walked down the wrong path. Did you choose this? Were you coerced? And then, after righting the wrongs, you again chose self-destruction. Now, in your suffocating smithy, you stare at this memory. You see yourself speeding off the cliff, careening into that telephone pole. Dream of arsenic, of coolant in liquid spirits. Of death.

Of murder.

Was that you?

"Yes," you whisper to the furnace. "But I've changed."

Have you? Or have you concealed the truth? Struck the memory with your hammer and reshaped it?

You heft the hammer. Furrow your brow. Grip the memory. Prepare to strike.

"Time," you say, "is a liquid. Shape it. *Shape it.* Or it is lost."

And you strike.

STRIKE. TIME IS BROKEN. *STRIKE.* "I must fix it," you say. *Strike.* But you can't. *Strike.* "I must try," you say. *Strike.* You are the rememberer, the blacksmith, the conqueror. *Strike.* You are immortal. *Strike.* Lift your hammer. *Strike* the clock face. *Strike* the memory. Mold your immortality.

Strike. While it's hot.

"I CAN'T."

The hammer falls from leaden fingers, thuds against the packed dirt at your feet. You look up, unable to watch your work another second. The barn door is slightly ajar, its lock neglected in your haste earlier this morning; the rays of the dying sun bleed between its planks. The daylight is a relief after such a long vigil staring at the malleable metal with its covering of black fire scale.

You let the sculpted metal drop. It sizzles as it rests against the hammer.

"I cannot do this," you say. To nobody. To yourself.

You have no striker, a blacksmith's apprentice, to wield the sledgehammer for you; your own minute hand has always sufficed. You have always preferred shaping your truths away from prying eyes.

Away from judgment, maybe?

"I cannot *do* this," you say again, to nobody, to yourself, perhaps to the dragon. "I cannot forsake the truth for my own bastardized version." You stare at the walls showcasing your years of work. "Cannot perfect the art of *lies*. These are lies I have made and hung in clear view. Lies!"

You burst into a flurry of motion, ignoring the creaks in your knees as you move them for the first time in . . . hours? Years? Straight to the furnace, to the door atop it, to feed the beast below—

But no, not the furnace dragon yet. You're rushing things, frantic—manic!

"The memories first," you say. Then, louder: "All of them!"

The beast far beneath the smithy floor coos hungrily in response.

You shuffle about, kicking up dust in a fevered dance; it clings as grit to your sweat. You're scouring the walls, knocking your created memories from their hooks: axe heads, anchor chains, shipwright tools, swords . . . so many swords. You fling them all—all of them!—in the direction of the furnace as you go. Run, almost *leap* to the furnace now. Yank open its door on hinges that shriek, making the dragon whine. Throw the weapons in, one, two at a time. And holler your litany to the empty air as you do:

"I want to remember the *truth*!"

The beast roars back as if to take up the challenge. The floor vibrates with its hunger. You collect the weapons faster.

"I want to hold the truth in my hands. What am I hiding from? Why is the truth so dangerous to me? I can change. I *want* to change."

You pause to stare at a sword in your hand: it is her, the cold girl, from 2009.

"Or . . . I can change the *truth* instead."

Fling it into the open maw of the furnace. Keep tossing the heavy, sharp memories into the heart of the furnace until there is no more room and they spill out of its top like spikes, or perhaps a crown. In your haste, a sword glances off the nearby forge and sends a flurry of embers across the smithy like neon snow. One lands on your forearm; the cherry glow sizzles your arm hair, but that's fine. Just another truth you can reshape.

The beast can sense you above it. You give it what it wants, throwing a few final bits of reshaped memory into the furnace. The truthsayer is fed, and it knows what the master wants. It knows you want it to spew its fiery breath up into the furnace above. It knows you want liquid truth.

You leave the beast to its work and turn away from the blasting heat, feeling it on your exposed neck as you step back to the clock face. Kneel down. Pick up the dropped minute hand; pick up the half-formed sword that fell beside it—now the only memory outside of the furnace, the memory of telephone poles and coolant and murder. Stand up. Examine this new, incomplete lump of a memory in the crosshatching of dying sunlight and living dragonlight. Farther down the blade is an unformed lump you have yet to shape, and in that dull gray you realize that the memory extends beyond what you'd previously seen.

There is more, and it is worse.

You are watching.

YOU ARE DRIVING.

You are driving, and she is laughing in the passenger's seat, trying not to spill her drink as you speed through the back country roads. She pauses to take a sip. Can she taste the coolant you've spiked it with? She makes no indication that she does.

This is not the cold girl from 2009, of course, though she still held her own sort of court in your heart. You swore off marriage because of Cold Girl, didn't you? But you eventually changed your mind and proposed to this laughing girl beside you, and now here you are. Here you are, slipping her poison, staring at each thick telephone pole as it zooms by on the roadside. Willing yourself to have the courage—or is it cowardice?—to jerk the wheel, to careen the passenger's side into an oncoming pole.

Your last thought flickers like a dying bulb between images of freedom, prison, funerals, wedding vows—

Strike!

YOU STOP WATCHING.

The walls stare blankly down at you, as if in accusation. In the belly of your smithy, the truthsayer has grown quiet, pleased with its work. The memories are melted, now mixing with one another in the furnace to make a silvery amalgam of your life.

The foundry whispers to you: *Finish what you've started.*
The hammer in your hand says: *Heft me and strike.*

Together, with the forge, they chorus: *Weld new memories, new truths.*

You lift the hammer, the minute hand of your life, above the anvil, the clock face of your life, where you hold this final memory. You prepare to strike it . . . and you pause.

"I cannot," you say, surprised by your own words.

You must! The truth will kill!

"So be it," you say, and, pivoting in the dirt, you toss your hammer into the air. It arcs as if in slow motion, like a VHS tape rewound and replayed too much. With a splash of roiling metals, it disappears into the still-open furnace.

"The truth," you proclaim to nobody but yourself, "only kills because it is ugly, like the beast beneath. But even beauty is a matter of perception."

You step closer to the furnace; it hisses at you.

"I must be at peace with my own reflection," you tell it.

You pivot again, this time throwing the unfinished sword in your hand. It turns in the air, end over end, that horrifying memory of that countryside drive, and comes to a stop quivering in the barn wall—its sharp tip, after all, was the first part you shaped.

Your boots scuff the earth as you approach your rack of tools. You may not have need for a striker—may have been too ashamed of your own truths to employ an apprentice—but you still have a sledgehammer. You reach for it now.

Behind the furnace you walk. You raise the

sledgehammer firmly in both hands and roar, *"I WILL SEE MYSELF TRUE!"*

The dragon roars back.

You bash the sledgehammer into the furnace. Again. And again. Your head is ringing from the sound of the metal and from the cries of the truthsayer. You can feel the vibrations of your strikes climbing up your arms, jarring your bones.

Strike.

Again.

And again.

Until the truth can flow freely.

The sledgehammer falls to the dirt. You step over it with one boot, then place the other boot upon the furnace's backside . . . and you push. The metal contraption rips from its moorings with a shriek of metal on metal and cascades heavily down. Liquid truth flows from its gaping maw; the silvery stuff pools and spreads and reaches for the corners of the smithy floor.

Quickly now, you step onto the overturned furnace and leap from its hot hide to your clock face. Standing on the anvil, one boot on its heel and one on its horn, you gaze about. The silvery river has run quickly, has covered the floor in its entirety. Only a matter of time, mere minutes, before it cools and hardens.

What will you see? Will you be able to face it?

——*STRIKE.*

Your boot strikes the floor as you step down from the clock face. It is no longer dirt, but a thin layer of hardened metallic reflection. You step across it in awe, afraid to look down but unable to resist. You see . . .

A beast.

"No," you say to your reflection. "The truth does not have to be ugly."

Is it your imagination, or does your reflection nod in agreement?

Now you see not a beast, but a man of middling to late twenties with blue eyes—not icy gunslinger's eyes like you'd imagined, but gentle, rather small eyes—hiding behind slightly askew glasses. Your beard has come in scraggily and red, and your blond hair is retreating at the temples.

You see an honest man.

Don't you?

You expect the truth to kill, but it does not. You expect the truth to drive you mad, but you remain sane, at least as far as you can tell. That will have to suffice.

As you walk, you keep your gaze on the man reflecting up at you. You are not surprised when you find yourself approaching one of the blank walls. When you look up, you discover the only remaining weapon in your arsenal, still impaling its tip in a wooden plank—the memory of you, driving, and the girl, laughing, drinking, swerving, dying. You pluck it from the wood, which splinters upon the sword's release.

The walls are empty once more.

You examine the unfinished blade. You can still see in the unmolded metal something of the truth. Not a man on the cusp of marriage, not a woman on the brink of death . . . but a man who has yet to take responsibility for his own life and a woman who will not give up on him. Perhaps never will. Why did you give up on yourself?

You stare at that cold lump of metal, and you say: "This is the truth."

You have found a way to hold liquid truth. Not in your hands, but in the furnace of your heart. The proof of this is shimmering at your feet.

The dragon is quiet now. Sleeping, perhaps, its job now done.

You hang the sword on the wall.

"Truth cannot be tamed . . . but it can be faced."

THE MOVIE MASSACRE

"COME OUT, COME OUT, *wherever you are . . .*"

These words echoed across the dark gymnasium. In spite of the singsong lilt, they were not kind words, not one bit friendly. They dripped with menace.

Cassandra knelt behind a rack of basketballs at the far end of the gym, hiding in fear from the man taunting her. Rivulets of sweat dripped into her eyes, stinging, yet keeping her alert. These last few hours had been harsh and unrelenting. She forced herself to focus, to control her heart rate; she had to think of a way out of here. She knew the danger she faced, knew that if she could not escape . . .

No! There was no worrying about that now; it was either act or be acted upon.

Wiping the sweat out of her eyes, she squinted in the gloom. Her eyes had not adjusted to the darkness like she had hoped. She strained to hear, hoping the slightest of sounds might give away her pursuer's position. Nothing. The silent blackness closed around her, choking her, giving her the panicky feeling of being underwater. But she was not underwater; she was hidden behind this sports rack, the rubber grips of the basketballs it held becoming slippery under her clammy hands. The wooden gymnasium floor was harsh and bruising against her bare knees.

Tap. Tap. Tap.

What was that? Cassandra remained completely still, an animal alert for its predator. All she could hear was the hammering of her heart, *thump-thump*ing against her ribcage. No *tap-tap* sounds, although she was positive she had heard *something*.

She had heard footsteps.

She had to move. She would not just sit there, waiting for this man to find and kill her. Slowly, she lowered herself to her hands and knees, praying that the newly waxed gymnasium floor would not make any squeaking noises. She forced herself to painstakingly place one hand and knee in front of the other, moving inch by inch, her sweaty palms threatening to slip on the floorboards.

Once she cleared the basketball rack, something jumped into her vision, the brightness momentarily blinding in the dark world around her. She almost gasped, but caught herself when she recognized what she was seeing.

In the distance, hovering in the darkness, was a neon sign.

A sign that read EXIT.

Thank you God, thank you God, thank you thank you thank you.

These words echoed in Cassandra's head as she

changed her course and began her strenuous crawl to the EXIT sign—her lifeline, her gift from God. Cassandra had never been very religious; she had never believed in divine intervention. But that EXIT sign changed everything.

After what seemed like hours of crawling, of carefully lifting one bruised knee up and setting it in front of the other, she found herself just three yards away from the EXIT sign. From its blood-red glow she could just barely make out the outline of a door. She could imagine a metal bar on the door's surface, could hardly wait to push it and break over the threshold out of this hell. But she would need every second available before the killer would follow, and so she continued to inch her way to freedom.

"Fishy out of water."

The words were so close to her, she could feel the tepid breath on the back of her neck. Cassandra jumped in surprise, her heart skipping a beat. She desperately lunged to her feet, making for the door with the EXIT sign, now only steps away. A heavy weight fell onto her from above, driving her into the unyielding floor. Large, rough hands yanked her hair. Cassandra cried out in agony, arching her neck. She felt the hands, clutching her hair, ram her head into the floor. Forehead and hardwood made contact with a resounding *CRACK!*

"Uhnnn . . ." she moaned.

Pain shot through her head in blinding torrents of light, the blood pounding in her eardrums. Warm liquid seeped out of her head wound, gushing into her eyes. She struggled frantically against the large man attacking her. She blindly swung her arms and kicked her legs out, making little contact. She screamed and screamed, until a fist pounded into her jaw, momentarily stunning her.

When she came back to her senses, Cassandra realized she was free. Her head throbbed with excruciating pain. She could feel the cold floor beneath her; she was still in the gymnasium. It was difficult to open her eyes; there was something in them. She reached up with aching fingers and found her eyelids stuck shut with dried blood. She rubbed the flaking crusts out of her eyes, hesitatingly raised her head, and looked around her. It was still extremely dark, all except for the bright EXIT sign above her. Perhaps she had only been unconscious for a few minutes.

What she saw made her gasp.

The silhouette of the murderer stood upright, looming above her. His feet were mere inches from her head, and he stared down at her in the gloom. Something in his hand reflected the red light from the EXIT sign.

A knife.

Too weak to scramble away, Cassandra watched as he knelt down and brought the knife toward her throat.

It's over, I'm done for, it's over, she thought. *So much for divine intervention.*

The edge of the knife's blade tickled her bare neck, hovering before her eyes.

She heard the words "Tag, you're it," and then the knife slid forward.

"AAAND *CUT!*" SHOUTED THE DIRECTOR.

The lights in the movie studio pounced to life in big *SWOOP*s that lit the backlot piece by piece. The film crew—just a gaggle of film students, barely entered adulthood—scurried around the set, gathering up equipment.

The director stood beside the monitor, staring at the set: a gymnasium in a high school, with a polished hardwood floor. He waited as the prop crew rolled the rack full of basketballs off the set, and then raised a microphone to his mouth.

"That's a wrap, ladies and gentlemen. Good work!" This was greeted with excited cheering from the crew. "We'll shoot the next scene in Studio B next week. Until then, get tons of sleep and stay away from dark gyms!" Chuckles at this remark. "See ya later, and keep up the good work!"

The air buzzed with chatter as all the students walked out of the studio. The director placed the microphone back in its box, then strolled over to the one person who was not exiting the building: a tall, dark man with blood spilled on his shirt.

"Hey there, Charles. Another great take. You're the perfect killer for this movie," the director said, the hint of a smile in his eyes. "Where's Cassandra?"

Charles smiled, a leering, predatory smile. He nodded at the EXIT sign. "She went out back. For a breather."

The director nodded. "Good work. The both of you."

The two men began their walk to the studio's exit. By now, they were completely alone.

"So," said Charles, "who do I get next week?"

"Next week . . . I believe next week is Sabrina."

Charles smiled his unpleasant smile.

"Excellent."

SABRINA GAZED DOWN at the stack of crisp, white sheets

of paper sitting in her lap, newly opened, the ink fresh from the printer.

What sinister secrets does Kale have in store for us today? she wondered.

Kale. She'd already had plenty of laughs at that one. An up-and-coming big shot in Hollywood named after the new superfood in a city full of body-conscious health nuts? No *way* was that his real name.

Just last week, on her first day of shooting, she'd read the title on the top page of the sides and laughed.

SCENE SIX
"The Theater Thrashing"

These cheesy B-horror horror titles were hilarious, if not cringey. "The Theater Thrashing"? Wasn't the last scene called "The Gymnasium Guillotine" or something? What would Scene Seven be? "The Hospital Homicide"?

"Horror as a genre is always just one flop away from the grave," Kale had told her when he'd called her personally to offer her the role. "These days, sadly, you need a gimmick. The *Blair Witch Project*s and *Final Destination*s of the cinema zeitgeist understood this, and we do too."

"We do?" Sabrina had tried to keep the hesitation out of her voice, but . . . gimmicks? Really? Was this where she wanted to take her career?

"Absolutely," he'd replied, his voice almost abrasive in its conviction. "A gimmick so gimmicky it'll start a whole subgenre, like *Saw* did for torture porn."

Sabrina winced. Gross. "And our gimmick is . . . ?"

"Method."

"Method?"

"Our movie is going to be so method people will think it's a snuff film. I'm talking full embrace of reality, Sabrina. Loose scripts, with plenty of room for the actors to improvise—"

That got her attention. She'd taken an improv class just last fall.

"—all of whom, by the way, may be nobodies now, but just you wait . . . soon *everyone* will know their names. This movie will have Johnny *Depp* knocking on our door. Every scene will start with a closed set, and I mean *shut tight*, just the actors. No crew, no director, no cameras—"

"No cameras?" Sabrina laughed nervously.

"No, no, that's the beauty of it, don't you see? Of *course* there will be cameras, but at first they'll all be hidden, out of sight. The actors will be essentially on their own, so they can fully immerse themselves in their characters' lives . . . and deaths. We'll do pickups to fill in close-up shots, and without a boom mic following you around we'll definitely do ADR, of course, but for the rest of production we'll be creating some of the most visceral, seat-of-your-pants performances ever caught on film. And, Sabrina, I need you to be part of it."

Sabrina was no dummy—she knew part of his reason for calling no-names like her was the movie's shoestring budget. That was also why there was no CGI—just practical effects and a lot of fake blood. But apparently it was working. Rumor on set was that a film student best boy had lost his lunch while watching the dailies early in production.

In the end, it was the pure excitement in Kale's voice that convinced Sabrina. Besides, she was growing tired of the long drive from her parents' to Hollywood for commercial auditions, where she'd sit in a hallway full of identical yet *prettier* versions of herself, that always led nowhere. He'd gone on to say she was the perfect pick for this particular role, with her theater background, but at that point in the conversation she'd already decided to accept.

And so Sabrina felt electric with nerves as she skimmed through the ending of Scene Six. It had been her name on the call sheet for over a week now, and a part of her would miss it. She'd spent the last week running around like a chicken with its head cut off.

Her character's was a typical story that lacked all originality: girl stars in her high school play, girl's entire drama class goes to the local Denny's after their final performance, girl gets a text from cute boy inviting her to the empty theater, girl is stupid enough to go there, by herself, *at midnight* . . . finds pretty boy's dead body in the prop room and is subsequently chased all around the theater and high school campus by crazy serial killer. And today her character would finally fall prey to the killer's blade.

She was determined to give the performance of her life. To go full method, as Kale had said. She would embrace this improvisational, method form of filmmaking; she'd go on that stage and fully envelop her role and feel *real* fear and *nail* it. This was going to be her shot if it killed her.

Anyway, it would be a relief to wrap her scenes; she was beginning to get a bit homesick. She missed her mom. And her dog.

Having completed her read-through of Scene Six, she felt confident about her character's role in this scene. She slid the pages of script back into the manila folder on the coffee table and stood. Stepping down the three stairs to the exit, she opened the door. Sunlight poured into her trailer, raising her spirits. Sabrina loved the sun; she always believed that a bright, sunny day was a good omen before a performance.

Crossing the threshold and stepping down from the VFX trailer (where a makeup artist even younger than herself buried her with enough pancake to cut through the darkness of the set and fit a squib of fake blood behind a prosthetic, just above the gentle pulse at the hollow of her neck), she looked around her. She was at the back of a large, concrete building, next to a door with the words STUDIO B printed on it. She made her way to the door, a smile on her lips and confidence in her stride.

The Theater Thrashing? she thought. *How about Macbeth, Mac-death?*

"AAAND *ACTION*!" SHOUTED THE DIRECTOR.

Sabrina stood shivering at the front of the stage. The sweat had dried on her skin, and her breathing had finally quietened in her pounding eardrums after what felt like hours of running. Running away. Being chased. Chased here. It was dark, and cold, and the air was suffocating. She felt enclosed, trapped, alone. But she knew she was not alone.

He was here. Somewhere.

She stood there like a statue, not daring to move a single inch. *Maybe he won't know I'm here,* she thought.

As if the murderer had heard her thoughts, there was a *BANG!* and she was suddenly surrounded by a glaring light. Sabrina let out a high-pitched squeak of surprise.

Squinting, she raised an arm to shield her eyes. Specks of dust swam lazily in the golden shaft of brilliance, a myriad of patterns, sparkling to the low hum of the machine that created it. She saw that she was now in a circular beam of light, coming from the back of the audience.

The spotlight, she realized. The last time she'd been in its glare, bowing to the audience's standing ovation, already felt lightyears away.

"I spy with my little eye . . . a girl about to die."

The words came to her across the vast expanse of the theater, probably from the same place as the spotlight. The man's voice was rough, *mocking.* It seized her heart.

Sabrina remained frozen, her legs locked into place with fear acting as her anchor. Although the intensely concentrated beam of light was making her perspire again, she continued to shiver uncontrollably. A lump rose in her throat, but she attempted to swallow it back down.

She lowered her arm and defiantly stared into the glow of the spotlight.

"What do you want from me? I didn't do anything wrong! And neither did B-Buh-Brandon . . ." Her voice broke into dry sobs.

In answer, the man shouted, "Ready or not, here I come!"

The spotlight powered off with a low droning of power, killing the theater's only light. Sabrina stood there, unable to gather up the courage to move, to *do* something. But as she stood there—center stage, as if she were about to begin her solo performance—the many shadows surrounding her like gargoyles started to establish themselves as more prominent shapes. She could now see the couch on stage right, with the coffee table just down-stage of it. Now the wooden coatrack next to the doorframe on stage left. Behind it all rose a ghostly scrim, like a death shroud waiting to envelop her.

Her ears picked up something in the silence surrounding her. Heavy breathing. Her time was growing shorter; the man was climbing the stairs onto the stage. But no matter what she told herself, she couldn't move; fear had temporarily paralyzed her. And there he was, advancing past the couch and coffee table, coming closer and closer.

Almost . . . he was almost upon her . . .

As he came to her, she regained movement, retreating, the man still trudging toward her. She backed away from him, moving stage left, until her back hit the door in its frame. She had found what was perhaps the only dead end.

Brilliant, Sabrina, she thought.

The man was only feet away. As he drew nearer, he reached for something at his belt—*A knife,* she realized—and sneered horribly. He pulled the weapon out, its blade long and threatening.

"Is this a dagger which I see before me?"

"Macbeth," she blurted, thinking: *Mac-death.* Then the drama-kid side of her whispered, "Isn't it bad luck to say the *Mmmbeth* word onstage?"

With a laugh, the killer brought his knife up to her throat with the precision of a surgeon and went in for the kill.

Sabrina was not an actress who breaks character in the middle of a scene—especially when she was expected to embody this role to its core. And although she knew that this was supposed to happen, that everything was going according to the script, something did not seem right to her. Perhaps it was how real the situation seemed to her—far more real than "method." The knife looked a little too sharp; the killer's eyes looked a little too evil; the blade's edge looked a little too close to her neck.

She expected the director to yell "Cut!" any moment, but it never came.

All of these things were highly unsettling. Enough so that her survival instincts took over for a split second, and she did something that she knew was not part of the script.

She dodged the blade.

She swerved her body toward the coatrack so that the knife missed, just barely. She knew that the man was not going to actually *stab* her; this was a movie, not reality. But, then, why didn't he stop the movement of the blade? Why did the knife's edge nick her bare neck and draw real, definitely-not-corn-syrup *blood*?

This is real, her brain told her. *Get out of there!*

She shoved the arm holding the knife out of her face. "What are you trying to do, *kill* me?"

The man smirked at her. "You catch on quick," he replied.

"Kale? Can we cut?" she called out.

But the only response was the killer's mocking laughter.

Sabrina's eyes went wide with shock. *Oh my gosh, oh my gosh, is he serious?* Her head spun with the implications of his words. *You catch on quick.* Was that just him improvising? Or was it—

No, her instincts told her. *That's your blood, no special effect. It's real. Fuck "method," this is real.*

It was a set-up. From the very beginning. Kale wasn't going for the "snuff film" effect; he was *making* a snuff film.

What now? she wondered.

And then it dawned on her.

The coatrack!

With a burst of pure adrenaline, Sabrina bulldozed into the man, sending him staggering back a few feet. She grabbed the coatrack and swung it in front of her in a wide arc, hitting the man squarely in the side of the head. He dropped to the floor with a *thud* and lay motionless.

Sabrina stood there, overwhelmed, for a second. But only a second. Then she leaped over the fallen killer—*the actual killer,* she thought—and crossed to the stairs leading down into the orchestra section of the house. She judged where to place her steps by the pieces of glowing tape secured to each step's edge.

Once down the stairs, she ran up the aisle between the rows of seats. She ran to the very back of the theater, where she saw a door with a neon red EXIT sign above it. She broke through the door, into a room she guessed connected Studio A and Studio B.

She entered a small, sound-proof room with white-washed walls. Once she was inside the room, she quickly turned and made sure the door closed securely behind her. Was there a lock? She couldn't see—

What's that smell? she asked herself.

It was too powerful to ignore. Her whole body wanted to reject it. What could be so . . . revolting? She slowly turned back around to face the room she had just entered, unsure of what to expect. What she saw was—

Oh my God!

Sabrina reeled back around to face the door to Studio B. Her stomach turned and flip-flopped. Bile came to her mouth.

Before she could even consider what she had just seen, the door reopened.

She took a tentative step back, waiting for the inevitable.

"Sabrina?"

It was Kale, her director. She looked up as he closed the door behind him.

"Kale, what the hell is going on? Charles tried to *stab* me! It's all supposed to be a goddamn movie—*pretend*. Call the police!"

"Sabrina," Kale repeated, "calm down. What Charles has done is unfortunate, I know, but we have detained him. I promise you I had no idea—"

Sabrina was beside herself. "*Unfortunate?* He's a murderer, Kale! He tried to *kill* me!"

Kale placed his hands on her shoulders reassuringly. "Sabrina, please. You're safe now."

Safe. That word was a key and opened an emotional box inside of Sabrina. Tears welled up in the corners of her eyes, streaming down her cheeks in fat drops.

"Safe. Kale, *I'm* safe, but . . . but what about the others?"

She couldn't bring herself to motion behind her, where three bodies sat piled together in one massive heap of blood and death, each one in a different stage of decay, like layers of sediment. Dozens of flies had been attracted to the smell, and were busy buzzing excitedly about the pile of dead actresses.

"Don't look," Kale whispered. "It'll be okay." His eyes were soft and sympathetic. "Everything'll get better soon, I promise."

He brought her into a warm hug. Sabrina lost herself in his arms, sobbing into his chest, sobbing out of fear and anger and sorrow.

"I promise," he repeated.

Sabrina stood in her director's protective arms, shedding tears and pain, wanting more than anything to return home to her mother. And her dog.

As she continued to cry, pain broke into her senses, flooding them full of a screaming white flame, blossoming out from her back and consuming her mind and its train of sensible thought. A stabbing pain between her shoulder blades—the agony was unbearable.

She looked up into the face of her kindly director. It had changed from a face of compassion to one of evil, a face that smiled at her affliction.

She staggered out from his grasp, staring until she could not see anymore, until she crumpled to the floor, until she knew no more.

THE DIRECTOR STOOD FOR A MOMENT, staring down at the body of Sabrina—face down, with the long knife jutting from her back. Then he pulled a cell phone out of his coat pocket and hit the speed dial.

"Yes, Kale?" answered the man on the other end.

"We had to let Sabrina go. Creative differences."

"How unfortunate. I was enjoying her improvisation skills."

"That might just be your concussion talking, Charles."

A staticky chuckle. "Shall I send the crew home?"

"Yeah." Kale looked at the blood on his hand. "I've got my hands tied up over here for the moment."

"Understood. And the girl's family?"

"I'll take care of that. Hollywood's a dangerous town,

and I will of course play the concerned director whose leading lady failed to show up on set."

He paused, the room's fermented stench tickling his nose. He'd need to have words with Charles for leaving a mess for this long. He couldn't have another member of this film stumble upon all these disposable actors. But they could wait for now. They weren't going anywhere. Their acting days were over.

"Good work today, Charles. Get yourself to the doctor for that blow to the head. Can't have my star losing his edge."

He killed the call and dialed a second number, casually standing over Sabrina's body. He kept his back firmly to the rotting corpses behind him.

"Yes, Kale?"

"Erin," he said into the phone, switching his voice to haughty anger. "What the hell is this?"

"I-I'm sorry?"

"Sabrina. The new girl."

"Did something happen to her?"

"*You* tell *me*, Erin. The bitch didn't even bother showing up to film her scenes. Thousands of dollars of our budget, wasted."

"Oh! I'm so sorry, I don't . . . she seemed excited—"

"Yes, well, clearly you were wrong. What's done is done. I'll need you to pull out those auditions again and find me a replacement."

"Yes, Kale. Right away."

He hung up and stepped over Sabrina without sparing another glance. Actresses came into this town a dime a dozen. But his film . . . this would be a masterpiece to die for.

MAYBE TOMORROW

*T*HE YOUNG SON SAT SLUMPED on the bottom step of the porch, staring down gloomily at the baseball mitt on his left hand. The dying rays of the sun sparkled in a single tear welling up out of his eye. He raised his right hand and hastily wiped the tear away, leaving a glistening streak across his cheek. As the sun cleared the horizon, the sound of a running engine grew louder and louder, announcing the father. The son looked up, hope shining in his eyes. His father stopped a few yards from him and noticed the baseball mitt.

"I'm tired, son," he said. "Maybe tomorrow."

The father walked past his son, up the porch steps, and into the house. A baseball slipped from the clutches of the son's mitt, its tattered stitches revolving as it rolled down the driveway. Tears streamed down the son's face as he ran to the half-finished clubhouse in the backyard, his worn mitt and baseball cap cast forgotten in the shadows of the porch.

Later that night, the father climbed into bed next to his wife, exhausted. His wife drew close and snuggled up against him. The sheets shrouded over the two. She placed her hand lovingly on his chest, caressing him. But he turned away, shrugging her off.

"I'm tired, hon," he said. "Maybe tomorrow."

He reached over and flicked off the light, not seeing the hurt in his wife's eyes.

The next morning, as the wife was in the kitchen preparing the son's lunch, the phone rang. The son watched from the breakfast table as the wife answered it. She grew still, listening to the voice on the other end. Everything became a haze. The wife hung up the phone and collapsed, convulsing with the violent weight of her sobs. The son did not remember running to her, but all at once he was buried in her arms. Her perfume filled his senses, her hitching breaths hot and deafening in his ears. He began to cry, though he did not know why. She was blubbering words into his ear: his father, the car, a crash, *never again never again never again.*

After some time, the wife composed herself and returned to the phone. The son remained on the kitchen tiles, confused. But he did understand one thing.

Tomorrow never would come.

TEN THOUSAND STEPS

Step one. Ten thousand steps.

H IS EYES WATERED IN PROTEST, but he refused to blink before the last edge of her dress was gone, flicked up and over the stone wall. The wind surged into his face; her custard-colored fabric disappeared; he blinked, but it wasn't enough; he squeezed his eyes shut, knocking tears from their perch.

Ten thousand till I see you again, he thought.

The stone wall filled most of his sight. Its gray was in stark contrast to the brightness of her dress, of her smile. He felt as if all the color in the world had been bleached away, leaving only that gray stone wall. He reached out, his fingers just able to brush it. The wall's surface felt awfully rough. Abrasive. He was already forgetting the smooth cream of her skin.

He turned his back to the wall and took a step.

One, he thought. Two. Three. Four.

He took a fifth step, and a sixth. It was no relief to have the wall to his back and out of sight. The hills that rolled before him, the clouds that churned above him, seemed just as gray. She had been the color, and now the color was gone.

Nine. Ten. Eleven.

Why must he live like this?

Who would call this living?

Fifteen. Sixteen.

Promise me, she had said, that you will count.

Twenty. Twenty-one.

Promise me.

I promise, he had said.

Twenty-seven. Twenty-eight.

You will understand, she had said. Not at first, but with each step you will get closer. So you must promise me that you will count to ten thousand. Ten thousand steps. And then you will understand.

And I will see you again? he had asked.

Promise me, she'd said again.

Forty-six. Forty-seven.

He could not see how counting his steps could bring understanding, or bring her back, or bring anything but fatigue. He had already been so tired when she left. But he promised. He looked up as he carefully placed each step and saw a light.

The sun, hiding behind the clouds? Maybe.

But for now, he counted.

Seventy-two. Seventy-three. Seventy-four.

* * *

Step two. A companion.

FOUR HUNDRED THIRTY-NINE.

He moved his left foot forward, through the fatigue, and onto the springy grass. And he counted.

Four hundred forty.

The light had been the sun, just as he thought, peeking out behind spools of stormy cloud. At first he was relieved, imagining he would soak up the sun's light like a thirsty sponge; then the sun was stabbing his vision, and he sweat; finally it was swallowed by the clouds again, and he was grateful.

Four hundred fifty. Four hundred fifty-one.

He stepped. He counted.

Four hundred fifty-four. Four hundred fifty-f—

Mew.

He stopped. Stared about him. All was dark. The rolling hills surrounded him like sleeping giants, except their heaving bosoms weren't heaving. They lay still. So he supposed the hills surrounded him like *dead* giants.

What number had he been on?

Mew.

There it was again. From ahead. He resumed his steps, unworried about the exact number—for what were a few missed steps among ten thousand?

Four hundred sixty. Four hundred sixty-one.

By four hundred seventy-two, he still hadn't spotted the source of—

Mew.

He almost toppled over. There it was, sitting at his feet. Four hundred seventy-three would have crushed it. A cat. Tiny among the rolling expanse of hills, yet colossal as the only living, breathing thing for miles around.

It looked up at him. *Mew.*

He bent down on his haunches and scratched the cat behind its ear. It purred. Hello there, he said. Was it you who slew these fallen giants?

Mew. Oh no—she said you might be delusional. But "giants"?

He blinked, fell back on his butt with a soft *thump.* The cat talked. It opened its mouth, a fuzzy white dewdrop amid its cobalt-gray, and mocked him.

You can talk, he said.

It sighed and began a luxurious stretch, arching its back in a slope that ended in a big wispy tail like the clouds that hid the sun. *You don't have to tell me,* it said. *I'm perfectly aware of what I can do, as I am the one doing it.* The stretch ended in a thunderous vibration that he felt through the grass beneath him. *Now. Shall we go?*

But something else occurred to him. He squinted down at the cat in the gloom and said, You said *she.* You said, *She said you might be delusional.* What did you mean by that?

The cat stared at him for a moment, then turned to saunter off. *I'm born knowing to shit in a box, but you can't guess who I mean by* she?

Wait!

You better hurry. Mew.

Fully awakened from his fatigue, he sprang up and resumed counting his steps.

Step three. A drunken detour.

THE CAT WAS FAST, already far ahead, a ball of gray hovering in the gloom, bouncing between the fallen giants. He was panting under his breath—

Two thousand seven hundred one. Two thousand seven hundred two.

—and it was all he could do not to trip on the slick tufts of grass, which were becoming unruly. Back where they met the wall they stood short and manicured; here they were long and tangled, with dead patches.

And it had become dark.

Not long after the sun went down—at his back, mercifully—the grass had become slick with dew and the cat had become almost impossible to spot. If it weren't for the occasional *Mew!* in the distance, he would have been lost two hundred steps before.

But just then—that wasn't a *mew*. That was a new sound coming from ahead. What was that? It sounded like . . .

Two thousand seven hundred thirty-three. Two thousand seven hundred thirty-f—

It sounded like voices, like . . . cheering.

Hoping he wasn't veering too far off the cat's apparently predetermined path, he threw caution to the wind—for there was a wind tonight, and it made him shiver—and followed the new noise. Cheering. Jeering? The crackle of a fire—and there was the telltale glow, dancing on the backside of the fallen giant he now circled.

Shouts. Catcalls.

The noise broke over him like a wave, explosive in the silence of the surrounding hills, and he found himself in the middle of a party.

"Hey, motherfucker! You bring the hookers an' blow?"

He didn't reply, couldn't, he was so stunned that someone was addressing him in such a way. The speaker was a robust man, almost a giant himself, in a jersey that hung over his large frame like a circus tent. The man leaned into his personal space before he could react and suddenly he smelled strong spirits, spotted them still glistening in sloppy strands of the man's ginger beard.

"Ahhhhhhhh, I'm jus' fuckin' with ya." The man slung one arm around his shoulders and yelled to the crowd, "Get this fucker a beer an' a blowjob, in that order! Haaaaaa!"

The rest of the crowd cheered and laughed with the man, calling out similarly profane streams of nonsense.

He had walked right into a party, and the cat was nowhere to be seen. Where had these people come from? They were all inebriated, knocking into each other like bowling pins around what appeared to be a bonfire. Its flames licked the night twelve feet in the air, cracking and snapping and popping in derision at its drunken revelers.

A *pop!* and a carbonated *hiss!* announced another partygoer opening a beer can. On their way to him they spilled most of the beer on the grass, but he didn't mind. He had no intention of drinking.

Have you seen a cat? he asked his beer-giver. Just now?

"A cat?" said the partygoer, this one a petite female with cropped blue hair shining in the firelight like chrome.

Yes, I was just looking for my cat, he said, not sure why he referred to the cat as *his*.

The woman leered at him in a knowing way, as if they were sharing some privileged information, and said, "A cat?"

Yes, he said again.

The blue-haired woman lunged around and slung her arm around his shoulders, a feat much more difficult for her than for her gigantic ginger-bearded companion, and called out to the party, "This guy's lookin' for some pussy!"

After he had disentangled from her and ducked away from the partiers' raucous calls of "Fuck yeah, motherfucker!" and "Titties!" he heard it very distinctly in the distance.

Mew.

There it was, the cat, hovering just outside the ebbing waves of fiery light, sitting on its haunches and licking its paw. *What took you so long?*

Sorry, he said. I couldn't get away from . . . He glanced pointedly back at the fire, his voice trailing away in embarrassment.

We can stay if you'd like, the cat said, still not glancing up from its grooming.

No, please, he said. Let's continue.

The cat raised its head to look at him with its almond eyes, glinting in the firelight, and he was surprised to feel vibrations in the grass at his feet. It was purring, as if it approved of his answer.

Yes, well, that's probably for the best. I've seen where they're headed, and they'll regret tonight for years. I don't envy them their morning.

Having fulfilled its enigmatic duty, the cat turned, flicked its tail, and picked up the path once more.

Shaking his head, not daring to look back at the partiers he and the cat were leaving in their wake, he followed.

And he counted.

* * *

Step four. The hills have eyes.

THE GIANTS STIRRED FROM THEIR SLUMBER.

What was that? he called.

A noise, the cat called back without stopping.

Yes, but of what? he called again, following.

The cat halted a hundred steps ahead and stared at him. *What's the difference? God, I thought I was the pussycat,* it mewed sardonically.

He stopped too and matched the cat's glare. They stood ninety-three steps apart now, between rows of rolling hills from which he was positive he had heard a rumbling noise. And this cat was *taunting* him. Why should he follow it?

If she sent you, he called to the cat, then you must know. Why I'm here, where I'm going. How is this supposed to make me understand? She said I would understand with each step. I'm stepping. I'm counting. I'm keeping my promise. What am I supposed to understand?

He fell silent, panting in the night air; he almost missed the warmth of the drunken partiers' bonfire. The cat just watched him in silence.

Then it said, *Are you finished?*

He sighed. Yes.

Good. Keep counting. It turned back to its path, paused, and mewed over its shoulder, *Or don't.*

He sighed again, stepped forward.

Three thousand nine hundred ninety-nine. Four thousand.

Rumble.

He paused. There it was again, the rumble. He could

feel it in his feet. But the cat didn't stop, so he carried on as well: Four thousand one. Four thousand two. Four thousand three. Four thousand f—

RUMBLE.

He kept his eyes on the cat, less so he'd know where to go and more to see if it would finally react to the unmistakable noise. Because the noise was growing.

RUMMMMMMBBBLLE.

Now he could see it as well as feel it, hear it. The hills surrounding him were rolling—actually *rolling.* This couldn't be normal.

He ran to catch up with the cat, shouting out his steps as he went—Four thousand seven! Four thousand eight! Four thousand nine!

It was almost vindicating to see that the cat couldn't ignore the rumbling any longer, that it was in fact peering skittishly about the landscape, ears pressed back, pupils dilating further with every *RUMMMBLE.*

Will you tell me what it is? he asked.

The cat seemed to consider this for a moment before stating in measured monotone, *The hills have skin.*

The hills have what?

Skin.

You mean the hills are . . . alive?

I thought that was obvious.

He didn't know how to respond to this.

The hills, the cat went on matter-of-factly, *must be restless. They're rolling—*

RUMMMMMBBBBBLLLLE.

—a bit more than usual, it finished.

Just as the most recent rumbling grew beyond comprehension (he imagined this must be what entire continents sounded like when ripping from their moorings to secede from Pangaea), the air was rent with a tearing sound like none he had ever heard. An image of claws rose unbidden to his mind, claws much longer and sharper than his companion's, tearing into flesh, sinew, tendon.

The cat's reaction was immediate. It shot forward like a cork from a bottle, hissing, *Run!*

He ran.

The thunder of tearing and ripping was ever-present, pressing on his eardrums. The rumbling shook his bones like an earthquake. He could see things—towering things, *monstrous* things—rising in his peripherals, in the dark. They were bursting from the hills and from the fog hugging the grass, wresting their monstrous bodies from the hills' skin like embryonic sacks.

As the monsters rose from the fog, a realization rose from his mind:

The hills. They weren't hills at all. And they certainly weren't "fallen giants."

They were sleeping giants.

Sleeping giants that had now awoken.

Five thousand. Five thousand one.

Step five. Her graven image.

HE RAN.

The cat had disappeared in the fog. He didn't know where he was going, only that he couldn't change course. He was caught within the rumbling walls of a stampede. The giants—*innumerable*, it seemed—had been birthed from the very hills that until now had served as a landscape. Now the horizon stretched flat, loose folds of discarded earthy wombs strewn about as if the hills had simply deflated.

He was trapped following a direction dictated by a stampede of countless skyscraping monsters. And even if the cat called to him with its signature *Mew!*, it would be drowned out by the giants' thundering footfalls.

He did not know how long they ran. But it did not feel long before the sun began to rise. It peeked above the horizon without warning, spearing the giants' eyes with its rays. They let out a collective guttural moan. But they did not stop running, so he did not stop either.

Soon it was clear that the giants ahead of him had come to a collective halt. He slowed down and suddenly found himself hemmed in by a gigantic flock of giants. Now, with the sun up and the giants stationary, he was able to get his first detailed glimpse of these rolling hills come to life.

Each one stood seven stories tall, so that he barely reached their calves. Their craggy skin was caked in earth and clumps of grass like a recently plowed lawn. They wore no clothes, but their uncleanliness obscured their sex, and they were packed so tightly together he could not discern their expressions. They stood hauntingly unmoving, their stillness incongruous after their violent excursion from the hills, and he weaved through their feet in order to see why they had stopped.

Eventually he came to the front of the herd. He stood at the lip of a deep valley that plunged about a mile into the earth. The giants stared into it, transfixed.

The valley was plain, an empty expanse of mossy earth except for a lone stone figure standing in its center.

Even from this distance, he could see the statue was ten times larger than the giants, weathered and worn, but its identity was unmistakable to him. He felt as though the wind had been knocked from his chest.

It was her.

Before he could contemplate these new implications—Is this what she means? Have I reached ten thousand steps already?—the giants stepped forward together, into the valley. He was caught unawares and swept onto the broad foot of one giant; he grabbed fistfuls of tough grass—was that its body hair?—and hung on for dear life. Butterflies burst in his stomach with every swing forward. Bones jarred together with every stomp to the ground.

In this manner, they reached her mammoth idol in mere minutes.

He wished he'd stayed at the valley's entrance. Now, literally at her feet, he could only see hewn boulders of stone that he guessed were her toes. He could not see her naked body, nor her beautiful face. But his view of her from the valley's entrance was etched clearly in his mind. How could a lifeless gray rock seem to emanate so much color?

A speck of gray detached itself from the stone above and landed on his lap, startling him.

Mew, said the cat. Its claws protracted into his legs and it purred, rubbing its face against his hand.

It likes me, he realized.

Why is this here? he asked the cat.

Not pausing in its affections, it said, *You weren't aware of her . . . infamy?*

Infamy? he repeated.

Wrong word, I suppose. Would fame *be more to your liking?* God-*like?*

He did not respond.

I do not mean to offend, human. I'm only here to help.

Help how? Help me to understand? Help me to see her again?

Ah, but that would be telling, it purred.

But what does this mean? These giants, this statue—

Don't forget the party.

Yes, the party too. I don't understand.

The cat sighed. *I can see that. What's the count?*

The count?

The count, it repeated tetchily. *How many steps?*

Oh! he gasped. I've lost count.

You were chased by giants. That's gotta be worth a few thousand, wouldn't you think? And you hitchhiked your way down here, so we don't have to count that, unless you want to be technical and say it took the giant a few dozen steps to get you here.

So . . . ?

The cat stared at him expectantly.

So, he said, tallying numbers in his head, I'm somewhere around eight thousand?

Sounds good to me. Come on.

And the cat was off.

Step six. The earth, flattened.

IT WAS ON STEP NINE THOUSAND EXACTLY that he joined the cat on the other side of the giants' valley.

He looked back. Even from behind, her statue was so lifelike he wanted to stop and call out to her. Beautiful, he muttered, more to himself than to the cat.

I suppose, replied the cat with a hint of boredom in its voice. *But you do not want to join the giants. Wasting their lives fawning over the image of a woman . . . they are no better off than the partiers whose bonfire we passed.*

He looked away from her statue and down to the cat, which had already padded off. He had given up trying to decipher all the riddles this feline wove.

He stepped away from the valley, away from her.

Nine thousand one. Nine thousand two. Nine thousand three . . .

The clouds were but a memory, chased away, perhaps, by the giants; now the sun, bright and brazen, was unforgiving. It rose impossibly fast, so it was no longer in his eyes—but it was blinding all the same.

Nine thousand five hundred twenty-seven. Nine thousand five hundred twenty-eight.

Time followed the sun's swift trajectory and passed like water through a sieve. The numbers, the steps, they all blurred together and sped up and skipped around and—

Nine thousand five hundred twenty-seven. Nine thousand five hundred twenty-eight—

Was his mind playing tricks on him? Or had he miscounted?

He did not care.

The rolling hills on this side of the valley were still intact, obscuring what lay ahead, and he wondered if these also contained hibernating giants. If he placed his hand on the grassy surface, would he feel it breathing? Would he feel its heartbeat?

As he followed the cat around a bend in the path, he saw something on the other side. He squinted in the harsh sunlight. A crowd of people, no larger than the group of partiers, but this one seemed subdued, and none of them looked intoxicated, thankfully. They huddled together, their heads bowed and practically knocking into one another, like they were swapping gossip and paranoid of eavesdroppers. Which he supposed he was.

As he and the cat approached them, their whispering floated to him on the still air; it was as heated and harsh as the sun, more hisses than whispers. One noticed him and pointedly shushed the group. They turned to him as one.

The person who had spotted him, a weaselly man with rheumy eyes, looked him up and down with suspicion and said, "Where'd you come from?" and again before he could answer, "How much did you hear?"

The entire group shared a similar slightness in build, malnourished, sickly, and they all wore the same strange white cloth wrapped around their bodies like gauze. He noticed blotches of red seeping through bits of the fabric; maybe they were bandages. The entire group stared at him, sniffed at him, shifty and distrustful.

I came from the wall, he said.

"The wall?" repeated the man. He seemed to be their spokesman. "You came from the wall?"

He nodded. Yes.

At this, the weaselly man must have believed him, for his eyes ceased their constant squinting, opening wide in amazement. Utter shock was writ on his face. "Then . . ." he sputtered, glancing conspiratorially at his companions, "then you must have seen it!"

The wall? he asked, wondering where the cat had gone off to this time.

The group snickered amongst themselves, a bit too patronizing for his taste. The man said, "No, no, not the bloody wall! You've seen *it*." The man looked about theatrically. "The edge of the world."

Excuse me? said he.

"The edge of the world, the edge of the world, the world's edge," the group chanted excitedly amongst themselves. The weaselly man skittered over to him and nudged him over to the rest, inviting him into their huddle; he flinched, not wanting to be touched by someone whose skin wept from countless wounds, not caring that they were bandaged.

"The edge of the world," the man said, grinning madly, "is just beyond that wall, son."

He stared in disbelief for a moment, wondering if he'd rather be accosted by the partiers than by *this* crowd. Then, taking in their eager yet earnest faces, his judgments fell away. Who was he to say they were wrong? All he'd seen from the opposite side of the wall was the flick of her yellow dress. Hadn't he believed giants were a myth only hours before? Wasn't he following a talking cat? Anything, he supposed, no matter how absurd, could be possible. Couldn't it?

He smiled kindly at the people surrounding him, and they beamed back.

"Did you see it, son?" the man asked him.

I'm not sure, he responded.

This did not arrest their enthusiasm. "Tell us," the man said—practically *sang* it. "Tell us exactly what you saw beyond the wall."

Well, he began. He wondered again where the cat had gone off to, and if he should follow it, if he was wasting precious time. I saw, he said, just above the wall . . . I saw her go over the wall. Yes, I saw her climb the wall and I saw her dress disappear over it.

He smiled at them, expecting excitement, but their faces fell.

"Her?" asked the man.

He was echoed by many of his companions:

"Her?"

"Her?"

"Her?"

Yes, her, he said. You know, the woman whose statue—

"You . . . know . . . *her?*" the man seethed, his cheeks caving in and blowing out like bellows. The man was furious, as were his companions.

He backed up. Yes, he said, almost defiantly. What's wrong with—

"*She* keeps the truth from the world, boy!" said the man, advancing on him. "*She* doesn't want us to know what's really out there! *She* is our enemy—and now so are *you*!"

As he backed farther away, he heard a distant *Mew!* from behind the conspirators and knew that was his cue to run.

"Get him!" screamed the mob.

He ran. And he counted.

He yelled, Nine thousand nine hundred ninety-one! Two! Three! Four! Five! Six! Seven! Eight! Nine—!

He cycled his feet in the air, desperate to make contact with the ground, to scream out: Ten thousand! But the conspirators had caught him, had lifted him by the arms, and he was pumping his legs in futility. He saw the cat sitting on its haunches just ten yards away, watching as if they were performing some avant-garde ballet. He called out, Help, cat! and for the first time realized he did not know its name, did not even know its sex.

Mew, it replied, and that was all. He would find no help from his feline companion.

"To the pits!" bellowed the weaselly man, and the others chanted their approval.

The pits did not sound like a place he wanted to go.

He fought his captors with renewed vigor, rocking his body against their grip until he swung like an awkward pendulum. He kicked out, not at the ground this time, but at the shins of the nearest conspirators. His exertions were rewarded with shouts of pain.

Let me go! he screamed. LET ME FREE!

He did not let up his struggling. Relentless he was, kicking and punching and swinging and screaming. His vision burst into stars as he connected his head with a woman's nose. There was a satisfying *crunch!*

And finally he was free. He felt his left side, the side with the woman whose nose he broke, slip through the conspirators' clutches—just barely, mere *inches,* but it was enough. He kicked his left foot down and it slapped audibly onto the springy grass.

TEN THOUSAND!

No sooner had the words parted his lips than the entire world ground to a halt.

Step seven. Back to the beginning.

TIME CRASHED TO A STANDSTILL.

The very air seemed to solidify, and his body was

trapped as if inside some intangible glacier.

The conspirators froze. Their limbs stiffened against him.

The cat became a statue, a quaint portrait of a cobalt-gray kitty sitting on a grass-green lawn.

The greens washed away. The sky blanched. The sun dimmed. All color, few though they had been, seeped into oblivion—everything down to the cobalt in the cat's suddenly lackluster coat.

The world was Time in a bottle, stoppered. He couldn't move. Even the perspiration glistening down his brow had stopped in its tracks.

He did not know how long this nothingness prevailed. Seconds and hours passed in tandem, or perhaps they did not pass at all. His mind had not escaped reality's molasses effect. He could no longer process thoughts. All that stood out against the vast blankness of his faculties was a number, stripped of all meaning: TEN THOUSAND. He stared out across the still landscape and all he could do was think that number, over and over.

TEN THOUSAND TEN THOUSAND TEN THOUSAND—

The first change in this frozen tableau was a sound. It came to him from the abyss imperceptibly. One moment, silence; the next, this sound. It was . . .

A voice.

Her voice.

She sang, and it was the most beautiful melody he had ever heard. Her voice hummed wordlessly, and somehow he intuited that she was singing the world into motion once more.

Time trickled back with treacly viscosity, one grain of

sand at a time. He felt his left foot push off the grass, felt his head rock forward, felt it connect with the bridge of a nose . . .

Wait. Something was wrong.

Something is wrong, he said. At least, he tried to say Something is wrong. But the words fell out of his lips in foreign vowels and clipped consonants.

What was happening?

The cat was getting farther away, and yet it did not move from where it sat—the conspirators had reversed their direction, pulling him backward. Time sped up, the cat receded faster, and limbs pulled at his body, words screamed themselves from his lips—alien sounds, not words—and from the lips of the conspirators.

Woo-yeem, said the cat.

Woo-yeem? he thought. What the hell is woo-yeem?

And suddenly it clicked.

He was being pulled backward—away from the pits, thankfully. He was reliving things he had already lived. He had head-butted the woman's nose again, but her nose hadn't spurted crimson; it had, in fact, absorbed the blood like a sponge, and now her nose was perfectly whole, as if nothing had ever happened. Because, in a way, it never had. It had been undone, like threads in a cross-stitch of Time.

And "woo-yeem," of course, was *mew* in reverse, as if the cat's meow was a vinyl record that held hidden meanings if spun the other way.

This was the work of that humming melody—of *her* humming melody.

She was singing Time in reverse.

Time was flowing backward.

He had no control over his body. He had thought that time travel, if ever possible, would be pointless. It was impossible to change the course of events; if you did, the change would have already *happened*, and you would have already felt its effects in the present. Time, therefore, was a construct used to measure something over which we held no actual control. That was how this felt, this rewinding of Time. He felt helpless against whatever it was that controlled it all—her voice, humming—and resigned himself to relive recent events in reverse with an all-consuming sense of impotency.

Counterclockwise, he moved.

The conspirators were back to their huddle, once again ignorant of the man walking toward them who had seen *her* just beyond the "world's edge"—only now he walked away, not toward, his legs backpedaling strangely.

He observed something new about the conspirators. Had he simply not noticed before, or were their bandages soaked through even more now than when he first met them? It looked to him, before his backward-walking put them out of sight behind the hills, as though the white gauze wraps were practically rotting off their bodies, too slick with blood and puss to cling to the wounds.

Now he retraced his steps through the endless expanse of hills, rolling, rolling, *rolling*.

Now he looked over his shoulder at the back of her statue, and now he walked in reverse once more into the valley, and now her gargantuan statue stood before him, and—

He gasped. Or at least he tried to. Even his lungs weren't free of Time's grasp. All he could do was stare at the giants surrounding her monument. The giants weren't praising her stone any longer. They lay prostrate, their bodies intertwined due to their sheer numbers, and they were dead. The giants' corpses were rotted away as if they had simply stood at her monolithic feet for days, weeks, months, wasting away, and then Time had had its way with their bodies for years after that. Thick bones poked from chest cavities, eyes sagged in sockets, and these once-bulky, barrel-chested monsters now resembled matchstick marionettes whose strings Time had severed.

This isn't a true reversal of Time, he realized. His body flowed retrograde, true, but the things around him . . . they were in the *future*. He was seeing what would become of them.

This revelation was followed by another: the cat was nowhere to be seen.

By now he had left the valley, and his body was mimicking a desperate sprint—like the sprinting he'd done to escape the stampeding giants, except in an awkward backward galumph that defied natural physics. But he ran alone, for the giants that had originally precipitated this frantic sprint were currently decomposing on the valley floor.

He was suddenly very afraid of what he would see when he reached the partiers' bonfire, remembering what the cat had said: *I've seen where they're headed, and they'll regret tonight for years. I don't envy them their morning.*

And here they were. The first thing that caught his attention was not the carnage but the fire. It still roared at an impressive height, its strange colorless flames dancing beneath a sky that was no longer day or night.

Then he saw the bodies, and he wanted to cry out but could not.

They weren't dead, which was perhaps the worst part. The partiers lay scattered about the remnants of their night, screaming and moaning and sobbing.

He could imagine perfectly what had happened after the party of the previous night—for yes, he was seeing their immediate future, not the distant future of the withered-giant graveyard—and his theory was only confirmed by the clods of broken earth surrounding them. The giants had burst from their earthen hillock wombs all across the land, and here, at the partiers' bonfire, was no exception. He could almost see the stampede of giants trample through the party like a herd of elephants, could almost hear the drunken revelers' nonsensical shouts of horror.

He wished they hadn't survived. That would have been a small mercy.

The partiers had woken with wounds much more serious than their usual hangovers. The ginger-bearded man, for example, was now moaning and hiccupping over his own legs, which had both been thoroughly trampled and had discarded their contents like a tube of toothpaste. The man's tent-sized jersey dripped with blood and gore.

He could not bring himself to hone in on the details of the other partiers. He attempted to close his eyes against the atrocities before him, found he could not, and instead resigned himself to Time's insistence that he walk away in reverse.

His revulsion over the things he had seen obscured his memory of his own timeline. He did not realize that he was approaching the wall until his body finally turned around, his arm reached out, and he was touching it. The wall's surface, just barely brushing the skin of his fingertips, felt awfully rough. Abrasive. His arm dropped back to his side.

The stone wall filled most of his sight, its gray a perfect mirror of the dull monochrome Time imposed on the world in this backward adventure.

His eyelids squeezed shut; a salty wetness climbed his cheeks. Tears forced themselves back into his tear ducts. His eyes opened, then closed again, then opened again, in a rapid blink against the wind rushing from his face.

A swatch of yellow. Bright yet soft, warm. Like custard.

And suddenly Time released its prisoner, and he could breathe in his own circulatory fashion, could blink by himself, could move his own limbs.

He looked up and he saw a woman.

Her.

You kept your promise, she said.

Always, he whispered.

Step ten thousand. *Colla voce.*

THE WORLD HAD NOT BEEN GIVEN BACK ITS COLOR, was still the washed-out gray of neither day nor night. But she was the very embodiment of color. She was Light. She was Life. She did not climb down from the wall, but instead spoke to him from atop it, smiling down at him with her radiance.

Have you come to understand? she asked.

He hesitated. He did not want to disappoint her. Had he missed something? He still did not know *what* he was supposed to understand.

He told her so. He could not lie. Not to her.

And, graciously almost, she did not seem upset over his answer.

Perhaps, she said, you spent too much of your journey wondering what you were meant to understand, and not enough simply observing.

He did not respond, hoping she would say more. He realized her humming, the distant singing he had heard when Time had first frozen, still floated on the air all around him, despite her vocal chords not currently vibrating with song. Perhaps she had sent the song into the sky and it flew about like a bird.

Virgil tells me you did not linger at the party, she said.

Virgil?

She laughed. Your companion.

Something wet touched his foot, sandpaper-rough yet pleasant. He looked down to find the cat licking him, purring with affection.

Virgil? he asked.

It paused from its rasping licks and blinked its large eyes at him.

Mew.

He laughed.

Virgil also tells me, she said as the cat resumed its lapping of his skin, that you found yourself among the giants' worship, but you exited their valley with as much impunity as at the party.

Was I meant to stay? he asked, thinking *impunity* was a curious choice of word.

She laughed again. No, she said. Neither were you meant to entertain the beliefs of the conspirators. You were not meant to be caught up by one thing, but rather to view it all from an equal distance.

What was this all for? he blurted out, frustrated that he still did not understand.

Perhaps, she said, it is best that you see things from my perspective.

And she reached down from her perch, proffering her hand for him to hold. He grasped her slender fingers, her smooth palm, and was elated by her creamy skin. She made to pull him up and he placed a foot against the abrasive wall, and in this way she helped him walk up the side of the wall to stand beside her.

So this is the edge of the world, he said.

She laughed a third time, and her laugh echoed around them, cutting off the humming sound of her singing disembodied voice once and for all. The world's color burst through the gray like paint splattered on a canvas.

Tears welled again.

It's . . . His voice faltered. He meant to say *beautiful*, but it did nothing to convey what lay before them.

It's called the ocean, she said.

The ocean, he repeated, tasting the word on his tongue.

Something occurred to him and he wished it hadn't.

You've kept this from them, he said. The conspirators. You've kept the ocean from them.

She smiled sadly, shaking her head, never taking her eyes from the ocean's horizon.

Never, she said. They only see what they want to see.

You mean, he said, that they've *seen* the ocean?

Yes.

I don't understand, he said.

Don't you?

Explain, he demanded. And then, in a softer voice: Please.

She sighed. The conspirators, she said, are living a life

of *mezzo forte*, though they claim that they are being denied *fortissimo*.

He blinked at her, uncomprehending.

These are musical terms, she continued. An array of Italian words used to describe a musician's dynamics. A musician's dynamics are, to simplify a complex expression, how loud or quiet they play a section of music. But dynamics are so much more powerful when next to one another.

He stayed quiet, waiting for her to continue.

Consider, she said, if a cellist bows a sonata *pianissimo*, from start to finish. This is the quietest of dynamics, meant to express tenderness and fragility. But if it is all the listener hears, how are they to gauge its true expression? When all is quiet, nothing is truly quiet. You must, in order to appreciate the delicacy of *pianissimo*, compare it to *fortissimo*. *Staccato* is peckish without *tenuto*, without the smooth melt of *legato*.

She finally broke her gaze from the ocean and turned to look him in the eyes. He was surprised to find that she was crying . . . yet still smiling.

Sforzando! she said abruptly, making him jump. *Molto diminuendo*!

He had never seen this side of her. She seemed manic. She threw these words at him with an air of desperation. As though she were begging him to see. And so he turned back to the ocean and tried again to understand.

When you left me, he said to the ocean and to her, it felt as if all the color in the world left with you. With your dress. With your smile. This wall we're standing upon, it stretched forever, just . . . dead stone. Gray. I hated it.

He sensed her nod slowly by his side, and she took

his hand again. His heart skipped a beat.

And do you think, she said, that the wall would have seemed so unpleasant if you hadn't had me to compare it with?

He shook his head wordlessly, and the tears finally fell.

And, therefore, on the opposite of this vast spectrum, she said, the color of my dress and the brightness of my smile might not have left such an impression of happiness upon you without that of the wall to compare *them* with.

Yes, he whispered.

Some, she said, call this *opposition in all things*. But I find that crass. Misleading. A tidy scripture of ignorance, more about all that Heaven-and-Hell, Jesus-and-Lucifer nonsense than about actual Life. But I cannot deny them their kernel of truth. Let us, instead, take a page from Tchaikovsky and call it *dynamics*.

He considered her words for a moment and said, So these ten thousand steps. You knew they would take me to places unpleasant. To the partiers, to your statue, to the conspirators. And . . . did you know of the giants?

I did, she whispered.

What exactly were they? he asked.

Giants.

He waited for more, but that was all she had to say about the beasts that were born from the earth. He supposed not all things came wrapped in tidy bows of explanation. Sometimes a giant was just a giant.

So all this was meant to help me understand . . . the ocean?

Not exactly, she responded. Think of the ocean as a metaphor. You and I, we can leave right now. You see that sailboat down by the shore?

Yes . . . ?

It's meant for us. And Virgil, if Virgil so chooses.

His laughter was hesitant this time.

But I had to be sure, she said. If you and I choose to leave this land, together, forever, there's no coming back. And the dynamics of our relationship, the dynamics we may sing to one another, one-on-one at sea, might seem like a lot. But I needed you to understand that there are bigger things.

Like giants? he asked.

Like Love, she said.

She rested her head upon his shoulder, her fingers still knitted with his, and he could smell her hair, tainted by the salty breeze.

I wish you had told me, he finally said.

He felt her stiffen. How was I to explain something such as this?

With your words, he said. But this way . . . those ten thousand steps, Virgil, the giants, the partiers . . . somehow I find it hard not to view it all as some sort of . . . test.

She lifted her head from his shoulder, looked at him.

No, she said. Please try to understand—

You've said that already, he interrupted.

And are you? Trying?

Yes, he said.

She paused, holding his eyes with her own, holding his hand in her own.

I will be at the sailboat, she whispered. Please try—

To understand? he said, unable to hide the desultory tone of his voice.

Without warning she stepped into him, and he found himself embracing her, something he had dreamt of for far too long. She was as warm as the yellow of her dress.

Please, she whispered once more. Please know that I was not trying to hurt you. I was trying to . . . to . . . I have seen people fall apart for things that seem so trivial to me after living this life for so long—a hundred hundred lives, ten thousand—and I could not bring myself to see the same happen to us. I needed you to—

To understand, he said, and this time it was not a question.

Yes, she said.

You needed me to understand . . . dynamics?

Yes, she said, laughing softly, sadly. Yes. In a way.

Unspoken in her words: *To understand me.*

After some time, she pulled away and left him on the wall. He sat on its rough lip and watched the ocean, watched her, in her yellow dress, pick her steps down to the shore and to a sailboat with white sails furled.

He thought of it all, in dynamics. Crescendos, decrescendos. The gray, the yellow. The sun, the night, the fog, the clouds. The giants, the conspirators, their bandages, the discarded hills. The partiers, the *pop!* and *hiss!* of beer, the *crunch!* of a broken nose. The humming melody flitting about like a lark, the soft and insistent *mew!*

He sat listening to the music, and *poco a poco* he began to understand.

THE HOLE

WAS DEEP ALREADY, but he kept digging. The loose soil on top had given way, from rich loam to hard-packed dirt the color of dried blood. The spade's wooden handle had blistered his fingers, then filled them with splinters, then made them bleed.

Still he dug.

He never stopped to ask himself why he was digging this hole; that question was just as meaningless as the next. Why would he *not* dig the hole? The hole was not there when he came, and it would be there when he left.

The hole was deep; he would make it deeper.

HOUDINI'S LAST HALLOWEEN

HALLOWEEN, 1926—THE DAY I sent Harry Houdini to Hell.

So why did it feel like I was the one whose life ended?

Not sure if it was even still Halloween. Midnight had been fast approaching when Houdini arrived at my home, and I lost all sense of time after he was taken into the void. Had the sun kissed November?

I had no way of knowing. Not down here. Not wherever they had taken me.

I say "down here" because it *felt* down. In my bones. That creeping dank that permeates the earth's hidden places. I was definitely underground, but how far? Yards? Miles?

Fear clawed at me as I realized I was surrounded by blackness, a deep darkness that I had seen once before.

Those monstrous, indescribable shrieks would come next, I knew. Never again, not that place—

A light clicked on. A voice. Shaking me from my terror.

"We need us a little talk, Mr. Caldwell."

I didn't respond, just took the chance to observe my surroundings. *Observe the facts.* That's what a good scientist would do. And if the last few hours had made that good scientist question everything he thought he knew? Not a factor. Collect the data. Observe the facts.

I was sitting in a small square room, in a wood-and-canvas chair. The room's light sat atop a card table: a small desk lamp, its bulb shooting a miasma of light through the glass-faceted ashtray beneath it. A cigarette was perched on its lip, smoke pluming to the low ceiling. God, what I would've done for a puff.

I shook my head. *The facts,* I reminded myself. *Observe the facts.*

"Walter."

I looked around. I couldn't stop my eyes from finding the voice's owner, searching in the narrow light. A thin man stepped into my line of sight. Pristine black suit, perfect part in his oiled hair. The guy had one of those non-faces, forgettable enough to blend into any crowd. His hat sat beside the ashtray, like a neon arrow on that cigarette.

It was an invitation. A quid pro quo. *Talk, Mr. Caldwell, and be rewarded.*

"Walter Caldwell." I nodded. "My name. Clearly your information is good."

He didn't respond to the jab. "Walter," he repeated, "do you know why you're here?" He nodded before I could respond. "You know why you're here."

He sat, and that was when I noticed we weren't alone.

Another man, just as immaculate and just as forgettable, stood in a dark corner, his eyes gleaming in the shadows.

"How can I know why I'm here if I don't know where *here* is?" I looked back to the man seated before me. "Or who you are?"

"We're agents of your government, Walter." Even the man's workaday voice would disappear from the memory once it quieted. This was a human greased to slip past anything and everything. "We are here for your protection. But we can't do that without your cooperation."

"You want me to play nice, sure. I can tell by the aching lump on my head. Was I not *cooperating* when you snuck up on me and knocked me unconscious?"

"I apologize. We had to move quickly. But if you do your part and answer our questions, then you'll be free to go."

Bullshit.

I knew what I'd done. I had disappeared one of the most famous men in the world, sent him down a hole he'd never climb back out of. They weren't ever letting me out of here.

"Sounds great to me." I forced a smile. I'd gotten good at that, forcing smiles, ever since my days of convincing university boards to approve funding for my . . . what did they come to call it? *Eccentric aberrations.*

"As it does to us, Walter. Let's begin, shall we?"

"We shall." I leaned back in my chair, smile still in place.

"Several months ago, you responded to an advertisement by one Ehrich Weiss, is that correct?"

"Known to the locals as Harry Houdini, but sure. The

man is an American treasure." I was careful to say *is* and not *was*.

"And this advertisement . . . it was calling for . . . ?"

"Paranormal mediums. Psychics. The real deal, no charlatans."

"And that's you?"

I fixed my gaze on the man's watery gray eyes. "No."

He blinked. "No?"

"No. Of course, I told Houdini I was the real deal. Said I had a new method that could put him in contact with his beloved deceased mother. But I was lying."

"You were lying."

"Of course. His mother is dead. Has been for over a decade, right? No coming back from that. No afterlife to check up on us from. Dead is dead."

"You're an atheist?" the man asked. His shadowy companion shifted in the corner for the first time, venting a small cough.

"I'm a realist. A scientist. I deal exclusively in the provable, quantifiable, factual. And I thought I could use that approach to convince him that I was the real deal."

"I see. And why do this?"

I shrugged, smiled again. "America. Land of opportunity, right? Houdini himself came to this country with nothing and has made his fortune as an illusionist. That old saying—imitation is the highest form of flattery? Figured I'd flatter him and make a little money of my own."

"Let's . . . move on. You responded to the advertisement, and he agreed to meet you in your Michigan home?"

"That's right. Detroit. A nice little Victorian getup. But you knew that already, I'm presuming—my living room seems to be my last memory before . . . wherever we are now."

He ignored the implied question. Smug bastard. "And so Mr. Houdini arrived at your home late on October thirty-first?"

"I believe he had a performance earlier in the evening, if I'm not mistaken."

"He did, but it was canceled. You must be aware of Houdini's injuries, Mr. Caldwell, having seen him so recently."

So recently. This guy wasn't giving up any info for free, apparently.

I snorted. "Ah, yes, the stomach punches. I believe the extent of those injuries was slightly exaggerated. The man clearly just wanted a little vacation time—"

The man in the corner burst out of the shadows and slammed a fist on the card table. The cigarette collapsed into ashes and I jumped forward in my seat. I had to give the guy credit—he got a rise out of me.

"Cut the bullshit." His growl was a surprise, the one thing about the man that I'd never forget. There was a rage there, an apex predator barely on its leash. No wonder his partner did all the talking. "Where did you get the artifact?"

I blinked. "Artifact?"

"The Ouija board."

"Those things are selling all across the nation right now, sir. Dime a dozen. So to speak."

"Don't play coy with me. That thing isn't some parlor trick. It's the real deal."

Silence grew between us.

The man sitting across from me had slightly turned,

frowning at his partner, but he seemed to have accepted the new tactic. He turned back to me. "We saw the portal, Mr. Caldwell. You opened the Breach with your Ouija board, and we need to know how."

The Breach. Finally we were getting somewhere. He'd let the term slip by accident, I was sure of it. The two of them were shaken by what they'd seen. Of course, so was I, but they seemed to know a hell of a lot more about it than I did.

I needed more information.

I sighed, as if finally surrendering to their interrogation. "Help me out here. What exactly is this Breach?"

This made them pause. The seated man eventually nodded to his partner, sending him back to his station in the shadowy corner. I was glad. That guy's voice scared me. Too *basso profondo.*

The seated man said, "You win, Walter. We concede that tonight's conversation will go nowhere unless it's a mutual sharing of information. This is what we know."

It sounded too good to be true, but they were rattled. I held still, waiting. Was this going to be more bullshit, or finally some answers?

"We work for a faction of the government that deals with the paranormal, the unexplainable. I can't tell you more, but suffice it to say that we have prior knowledge of what you may have seen in that Ouija board."

His eyes darted to the ashtray. I wasn't the only one craving a cigarette. He restrained himself and continued.

"We call it the Breach. It's a tear in the fabric of our reality. You're a scientist, Walter. I'm sure you're familiar with the concept of other dimensions? Different planes of existence?"

I nodded. "This Breach. . . leads to another dimension?"

"That's what we believe, yes. But now we need some information from you, Walter. Because, the thing is . . . the Breach is thousands of miles from Michigan. We've found no other dimensional rip like it. That is, until we saw yours."

I nodded again. That image would be forever seared into my mind's eye: That unthinkable blackness, no depth yet impossibly deep, rising like an inkblot from the glass eye of that wooden triangle, the planchette. And the fire. Not visible yet so irrevocably *present*, that undeniable sense that living lava was just around the corner . . . watching.

It made the mind itch, that unknowable world leaking from such a small circle of glass. I'd felt my conscious self being ripped from its moorings, all sanity being plucked from my skull like tenuous fiber strings. *Pluck . . . snap.*

"Walter? You with us?"

I mentally shook myself. *Stay present. Collect the data.*

"Walter, what did you do with the Ouija board? How did you open the Breach?"

There were so many questions I wanted to ask them, but I wasn't an idiot. I'd squeezed every drop of information from them that they were willing to give. But perhaps if I played along, one of them might slip. Preferably not the guy in the corner.

I steadied my gaze on the sitting man's bland eyes and said, "I asked it to open."

This was technically true. At the time, of course, I had been just spouting any bullshit that sounded dramatic enough to distract Houdini from my parlor tricks. I knew

I wasn't fooling him in the slightest. I still remember that condescending grin on his dark features, that twinkle in his eye that said, *I see you. You're a fraud, and I'm going to ruin you.*

"That's it. You said 'open,' and it just . . . opened."

"If that's what you want to call it. To me it was more like it . . . *ripped.*"

I was taking a gamble. Banking on their emotions getting to them. They'd used that exact word only moments before. Would they call my bluff?

But he only nodded, his expression blank. "Go on."

Damn. I took a breath for one final try. "That's pretty much all I can say, boys. The man wanted to see his mother. I knew where she was. I gave him what he paid for."

"I thought the $10,000 was only for the real deal?"

"Figure of speech." *Take the bait,* I thought. *Take the bait.*

Finally, my earlier words registered in his eyes. He paused, then said, "You . . . knew where Houdini's mother was. You knew the whereabouts of Cecília Steiner."

The man's neck was straining. He wanted to turn around, make eye contact with his partner, but he refused to break his gaze with me just yet.

Say it. Take the bait.

"You . . ." The man actually gulped. "You know where the Breach leads. You know what's on the other side."

It wasn't a question. He bought it, hook, line, and sinker.

Holding his eyes in my own, I casually plucked the cigarette from its ash heap, brought it to a cherry glow, and exhaled: "You don't?"

"We . . . we are certain it is somewhere not of this world." His eye twitched. They were certain of no such thing. "The priest we consulted all but confirmed my own suspicions. Er—theories."

There it was. The detail I was looking for.

My mind whirred a million miles a minute. The Catholic church—arguably the most powerful entity in the Western world. This man was afraid of portals to Hell. Men were fallible creatures, prone to confirmation bias, and the man sitting before me was no different. But how to exploit this?

"You sought a clergyman's counsel. A wise move." I could improvise along this line of questioning. "The portal did have a certain stench of . . . sulfur."

My words stoked the fear in his eyes. He swallowed and said, "You claim to know Mrs. Steiner is there. Are you saying that we have an opening to the spirit world?"

I took another drag, but the smoke was out. Damn— barely got one puff. I tossed the cigarette back in the tray. "Tell me what you thought it was, and maybe I can help you flesh out your theory."

The man stood, buttoning his jacket's top button in a fluid, forgettable motion, and fell a step back, sliding his chair back into place. "We can discuss that more at a later date."

Damn. Something had scared him off.

"Was it something I said?" I asked, trying to sound casual. Hard to do, when you're being held captive by a shadow government agency in an undisclosed but most certainly underground facility. And when you don't even have one goddamn cigarette to calm your nerves. When you can't get that final image of Harry Houdini sinking into a hellish portal scrubbed from your retinas.

The man shook his head, a tiny jerk that seemed to jangle with nerves. "It's what you're *refusing* to say, Mr. Caldwell. I will not waste my time letting you play the charlatan like you did with Houdini. You either know or you don't."

"Listen, I know what I saw, I just don't know what the *hell* I saw, if you catch my meaning." I leaned back, trying to play the whole ain't-we-been-through-hell angle. "It's been a long night. I've been through a traumatic experience. Maybe you're just not asking the right question."

He considered me for a long moment, then, after a brief shared glance with his partner, returned to his own seat.

"Mr. Caldwell. We need to know . . . how did you *close* the portal?"

Ah. That question revealed quite a lot. Surprising, that they'd show their cards like that. They'd mentioned this Breach being the only other dimensional rip, somewhere far from my home in Michigan. Clearly the thing was currently open, and clearly they were scared out of their minds.

Not that I could blame them.

"How did I close it? You really don't know how?"

He turned his head to share another glance with his cornered companion. He looked back at me, and something had changed in his eyes. Was that . . . hope?

"No," he whispered. "Teach us."

I stared, speechless. My eyes began to sting from the smoke in the stuffy room. My bluff had backfired on me.

Teach them? How, when I had not the slightest idea what had happened with Houdini and the Ouija board and that depthless pit of inky black?

Sounds emanating from the planchette's eye still rang in my ears, indescribable roars and keens and clacks from beasts I refused to even imagine.

Had Houdini discovered what they were? At what cost?

I shuddered.

The government man had dropped all pretense, and his partner seemed desperate enough to allow it. He fell back into his chair, his posture now soured, slumped enough to crease his suit. I almost wanted to hand him that cigarette myself.

"Walter, we are desperate. I'll level with you. If we don't close the Breach soon, Houdini will be far from the last to disappear. And as for whatever could come *out* of this thing . . ." His eyes were manic, and his voice was croaking. "We were planning on shaking you down with threats about having you arrested for Harry Houdini's murder, but let me try another approach: If you help us, we can make his disappearance disappear. No one will come looking for you. Those stomach injuries were bad . . . maybe we can do a little exaggerating of our own."

I doubted that last part—too many loose ends to bind with that kind of lie. I hadn't kept our meeting exactly secret, and rumors were that his friend—enemy now—that kooky writer, the singular, self-avowed Spiritualist, Sir Arthur Conan Doyle, believed the guy supernatural. If nobody else, Doyle would come investigate. Apparently the man loved to play his own characters.

But if these men *could* help me . . .

"We represent a new faction of soldiers, Mr. Caldwell."

My mind returned to the sitting man. Soldiers? That explained his companion's voice. It sounded so . . . violent.

"We are soldiers of a different kind. We stand at the front lines of a new war, one that protects the fate of humanity. Those front lines are marching toward the Breach." The man's voice found more strength by the word. His hyperbole wasn't just meant to persuade me; it was bolstering his confidence.

"Our soldiers need a general, Mr. Caldwell." He stared at me, unblinking. "Will you lead us?"

I remembered the previous night, just hours ago in my living room. That cheap piece of cardboard with the alphabet inked on it. The planchette perched atop it, easily gliding as I nudged it from letter to letter.

O . . . P . . . E . . . N . . .

I had been staring, taken aback by Houdini's dark, brooding eyes, when it happened. There was a suggestion in his expression, of gloating inevitability. *I see you,* it said. *I have you. You're done.*

It had stirred a rare anger inside me. Yes, I was purposefully deceiving him, but he never would have believed it anyway, even had I possessed scientific evidence. Houdini was no different from those stony-faced men on the university board, telling me I was cuckoo, delusional, mad . . . but what did they know? *They* hadn't devoted their lives to science, hadn't opened their minds to the impossible; they were a committee of decision-makers. Who were they—who was *he* to say that one scientist down on his luck couldn't try his hand at the paranormal, couldn't pad his pockets with the money of such a man as The Great Houdini? I had built my career in scientific evidence and study, and if I only had the resources, I could blow the lid off the small-thinking scientific community. Who was he to scoff at such a man as I?

And that was when it happened. The expression gleaming from Houdini's eyes never had a chance to change from triumph to terror. The planchette's eye opened, black and sickly with oil. The air above it folded in on itself and sank into this tiny aperture. Not the Breach, but still a sister rip of some kind, still an avulsion.

For the rest of my life I will wonder why it was I, and not the man who spent his entire life training for dangerous circumstances, who yanked his hands away from the Ouija board first. Why Harry Houdini did not move so much as a muscle. Whatever the case, it was enough for the Ouija board. I had willed it to open, but it hadn't opened for me. It had only revealed itself to the man who wished with every fiber of his being to see his dead mother.

Houdini's body slid and folded and fell into the planchette's eye. I saw it. In that moment, I knew my life's work was useless. Science had failed me. This—*this* was real. I'd watched this black void hungrily swallow his body, I'd heard Houdini's screams of terror—or were they bellows of triumph? to have finally found something not of this world?—and I knew, in that instant, that I would hunt for the truth.

And here was my chance. These men thought me more knowledgeable than they. Who was I to correct their assumption?

I looked up at the man sitting across from me, so

different from Houdini. There was no confidence in these eyes. No triumph or mocking. Only watery gray, and fear.

"I will," I said.

I almost heard the collective sigh between them. They'd gotten what they came for.

"I only have one question before we get started," I said.

"Yes?"

"What is this army of mine called?"

The man laughed, still giddy with relief. "Whatever you wish, Mr. Caldwell."

I smiled, and this time it wasn't forced.

"Void Hunters."

THE ARIA OF AVALEON AND AERLIN

*T*HE SEA SALT STUNG HIS EYES, but he held the island in his gaze: a distant smudge of brilliance pricking the horizon, the ocean punishing its cliff face with waves beating in rhythm with his heart.

For you, Aerlin.

She rushed through his mind, blotting out all else the way a spilt inkwell can blot out an entire page. She numbed his senses, took him from his surroundings— took the water lapping at his feet, took the robes stuck to his body with sweat, took the very bones in his body. His last image of her, broken and bleeding, seared into his brain.

How, Aerlin? How could I let this happen to you?

A whisper came in return; from within his own mind

or without, he would never know. But it came, nevertheless:

I will live, my love. I do not blame you. Be strong. Your eye must see, while mine sleeps.

A gasp racked his frame and he was swept back to the present. He could not lose sight of the island far in the distance, or Aerlin would surely die. He could not close his eyes for a single moment.

He could not close his eyes, but he wept all the same.

WHEN AVALEON AND HIS BROTHERS—Enoch and Elohim; not Gorgon, never Gorgon—first set out for the island all those years ago, they did not know what they would find. An entire race of sentient beings not unlike them—no, not unlike them, but so remarkably *alien*—living on an island of their own creation. It was a peaceful race, magical. *Magical.* That came as quite the surprise. But that was, in a way, exactly what the three brothers had set out for, the very thing for which they had been searching.

An answer. A solution.

But now it was all on the brink of destruction.

And Gorgon was the cause of it all. Avaleon remembered that day so clearly; after all, it had only been two nights ago that Aerlin had disappeared and Gorgon had visited the throne room.

Two nights, and yet it already felt like an eternity.

"OH BROTHER?"

It was more of a hiss than a whisper. Insidious. Avaleon tilted his head from the cool metal of his throne to find Gorgon leering at him from Elohim's throne, lounging in mock camaraderie. He was not surprised. He had come to accept his brother's ability to appear as if from nowhere. Gorgon wasn't the black sheep of the Fulbright family so much as he was the black *phantom*.

"Gorgon," he said, barely containing his own annoyance.

"Brother," Gorgon repeated, leaning forward out of the shadows. The bluish light shone off the grease in his locks of hair. His wavy hair, aquiline nose, and sharp, jutting chin set him apart from his brothers in a nebulous, tip-of-the-tongue way that had the effect of unsettling those who saw the four of them side by side. He was as handsome as his brothers, certainly, but he also carried a quality of being . . . *off*. He said, "I believe it is time for you and I to have a little chat."

"Can it not wait? Enoch and Elohim have yet to return."

Gorgon offered a knowing smile. "That is precisely why it cannot wait."

"Then allow me to at least summon Aerlin."

His brother's laughter echoed through the opulent hall, pealing like brassy, discordant bells. Gorgon stomped his steel-toed boots repeatedly on the dais in a percussive display of his mirth. "Oh brother. Really. Summon Aerlin? By all means, summon away."

Avaleon stared back in silence, stifling the cold dread that climbed his throat. His brother knew. Somehow, Gorgon knew of her disappearance. How?

Where was she? Where was Aerlin?

"Now," Gorgon continued, "let me tell you a little story, shall I?"

All Avaleon could do was stare at his brother and will him to burst into flames. But of course it wouldn't take. Magic was not their own to manipulate. It belonged to the Nithim, and Aerlin was still achingly absent from his mind.

As if Gorgon could hear his brother's thoughts, he said, "Please, sit," and without touching him, pushed Avaleon into his seat before he could rise.

How? With magic? Impossible. Gorgon had never paired with a Nithim.

Avaleon's crown struck the back; he felt disoriented. Gorgon brayed another bout of theatrical laughter for an uncomfortable moment, seeming to revel in baffling Avaleon. Gorgon leapt animatedly from Elohim's throne and faced Avaleon, arms spread wide as if he were about to perform a comedy.

After an indulgent pause, Gorgon began his tale.

"Once upon a time, there was a king, and he ruled his land with a firm but wise fist. Now, this king had four sons. *Four* sons, not *three*." He spat this out as if it were poison. *"Four."*

He regained his composure with each measured step as he began to pace back and forth across the obsidian dais. With each pivot at the end of his stride, the lights played across his face in steady washes of blue—first light, then dark; light, then dark.

"The three youngest saw themselves in a hallowed radiance. They cast judgment upon their father, condemned all his slight faults and in turn condemned their chances at the throne." A lightness crept into Gorgon's voice. "But no matter. For there was the *fourth* son—or the *first* son, as he was the oldest. And, O! this son was the king's favorite son, for *he* would continue the king's splendid legacy.

"It came to pass that the king fell deathly ill, and if his

empire were to continue thriving, it would need not one but all four of his sons. These, his last words, echoed through a deserted chamber, to be heard only by his eldest and most faithful son. The eldest son was disgraced to see that his brothers—his younger, foolish brothers—had abandoned ship!"

He paused, stopped, and with his face half lit, half cast in shadow, his mouth seemed to swallow the darkness.

"You see? *Abandoned ship.* Do you get the joke, brother? I find it quite clever myself. But let me continue.

"His brothers—O forsaking sons!—had left the empire, sailing away in a stolen ship with a crew of deserters, leaving their father—O desolate king!—to die and their oldest brother to console a grieving land on his own."

It was all very melodramatic, but Avaleon found himself intrigued despite the chills running down his spine. As if caught in a spell. *Magic?*

"And so," his brother went on, "abandoned by his own, overwhelmed by his inheritance, and still mourning his beloved father, this steadfast son"—puffing out his chest, as if moved by his own poetic grace—"in defiance of those who left him, rose to his destiny and reigned over the land for many years. And they were good years.

"But, as all stories go, a peaceful calm cannot go on forever. There must be a disturbance. Enter the now-forgotten three—Avaleon, Elohim, and Enoch, brothers in both blood and betrayal."

Avaleon attempted a laugh, but found his throat like parchment. Gorgon was obviously enjoying himself.

Aerlin, where are you?

Gorgon leaned forward to tap his brother's crown with a long finger—*tap-tap-tap.*

"*Focus*, brother," he hissed. He straightened, brushed an imaginary mote of dust from his jerkin with one gloved hand, paused for attention, and resumed his pacing narrative:

"The three brothers returned to gloat over the ruins of the home they'd abandoned, but what did they find? Peace and plenty, calm . . . *happiness*. It sickened them to see their brother succeed in what they themselves were too cowardly to even attempt. Their brother, the king?"

Avaleon managed to choke out a single word. *"Tyrant."*

Gorgon ignored his brother's taunt and quickened his pace until the blue light, blue shadows, blue light, blue shadows began to make Avaleon sick. He tried to avert his eyes but could not.

"In a fit of unnecessary jealousy—unnecessary, this humble storyteller asserts, for the king would have gladly opened his arms to them—the brothers planted seeds of dissent in the minds of the people. They spun lies, promised a plentiful paradise, told tales of a rich isle of heavenly repute—"

He spun around to face Avaleon, spit spraying.

"LIES!" Gorgon screamed.

The look of madness contorting his face left as swiftly as it had appeared, and he continued as if all were normal. Avaleon wished he could wipe his brother's spittle from his face, but whatever magic Gorgon employed still held him fast.

"In their deceit, the brothers took the unsuspecting—the *innocent*—and shipped them to an unknown fate. What was the king to do? Yes, only a sliver of his subjects fell for the traitorous brothers' tricks, only a handful of ships sailed out in pursuit of this 'island of heaven.' Yet the king could not abandon any of his people himself. *He* was not a deserter, and he would not be stolen from! He followed them, in his own ship, with his own crew of faithful men. And what did he find?"

The madness, the disgust, crept its way back into Gorgon's flinty gaze. His lips curled, and his breath hissed, billowing his cheeks like bellows feeding a furnace.

"Behold! An abhorrence! An abomination! Creatures walking, *talking*, among his kidnapped subjects. Things that *shat* on the laws of nature with their magic—if you could call those parlor tricks of the mind 'magic'—and shapeshifted into sick imitations of our own species. This very island is tainted with their blasphemy, their molestation of our way of life. I cannot get its unnatural taste out of my mouth. How *dare* these beasts—"

At that word, a distant flare of Aerlin's magic flooded Avaleon and he flexed his mind in a hot flash. In a shower of glass and sparks, the blue lights lining the hall above were extinguished. Gorgon's maddening smile seemed to hover in his vision, an afterimage from hell. Avaleon was yelling, bellowing at Gorgon—

"AERLIN IS NOT A BEAST, YOU BASTARD!"

—and just as fast as the hall fell into blackness it burst into light again, only this time it was a flickering red, an orange threatening to scald Avaleon's eyelids. Gorgon had raised the curtains lining the hall between the marble pillars, raised the curtains with a blink of his glinting eyes, to catch the falling glass. The sparks, the blue sparks from the extinguished lights, caught the curtains in a blazing fire.

Gorgon's laughter rose above the roar in Avaleon's mind—

AERLIN WHERE ARE YOU

—and Gorgon stood straight, facing the three thrones, the curtains spread like fiery wings erupting from his back, and he cackled still.

"O Avaleon, my brother, have you grown weary of my story? Perhaps it is because you already know the ending? No? Shall I skip to the end, then, and elucidate the finale?"

The doors far at the end of the hall exploded inward, spraying the throne room with tinder and splinters. And from the gaping threshold—

Oh Aerlin . . .

Gorgon, with a flourish, stepped back to allow Avaleon a clear view of what was pouring through the shattered doorway.

"Allow me, brother," Gorgon said, "to introduce to you . . . *my army*."

THE MEMORIES PLAYED FRESH as he stood sentinel at the shores of the lake, Aerlin's homeland still locked in his gaze. His twisted brother's voice still plucked goosebumps across his flesh.

"*. . . my army.*"

As if in reply to the memory of Gorgon's words, an electric haze thizzed on the horizon, superimposed over the island. Exactly where you'd imagine the island's heart lies.

But Avaleon knew it was not the island's heart. The center held its brain.

He knew. He had seen it.

He tried to avert his thoughts away from that central chamber, that vast cavern of unknowable mystery hidden beneath unguessable tons of rock; he had learned enough from Aerlin to understand that it was the most sacred of her people and that he was not to know that mystery. And yet his brother—*Gorgon*—had invaded their most sacred of privacies, had perverted their way of life. He had marched into this cavern and come out with an army of broken, beaten slaves. And then he had shown Avaleon, *forced* the images from his memory onto his younger brother's, so that Avaleon knew what he was not to supposed to know, held images in his mind no human was meant to see—

—a cavern, an impossibly vast cavern with an entire island sitting on its shoulders up above. The cavern's every surface, pillars of conjoined stalagmites and stalactites and carved walls and floor and ceiling far above, is etched with blue glyphs; tiny script in electric blue cuts in the stone, constantly swirling along like water dripping through a grotto. With no gravity pulling it down, down, down, but instead swirling in every direction in smooth, steady swells, read a running history of the Nithim. And at the center, far brighter than the dancing light of the writing on the walls, sitting, throbbing, on a pedestal of stone, pulsing, washing the walls with dazzling neon, the brightest blue, is it a—a brain?—

Avaleon cast the images from his mind desperately.

For you, Aerlin.

ENOCH WAS AFRAID OF HEIGHTS, and the day the three brothers met upon the seastack was a windy one. He had to raise his voice above that of the sea breeze to make his objections heard.

"Why, Avaleon, must we meet on this death-rock?" he asked, eyeing the windswept weeds at the cliff's edge where they stood.

On other occasions, Avaleon might have laughed at his brother's cowardice. Not that day. He was still reeling from Gorgon's attack just twelve hours before. "It is a seastack, Enoch, a common enough phenomenon. I needed to speak with you alone."

"If you wished to speak with us alone," Elohim cut in, standing to his full height, the tallest of the three, "we have our private chambers."

"That won't do. It had to be somewhere off the island. The island, I cannot . . . I cannot trust it anymore, I think. This seastack must have eroded off thousands of years ago. You can see the rock is dead. It has lost its magical properties, I believe."

Enoch muttered something about a ship being off the island as well.

"Enough!" said Avaleon. "Please, brothers, listen to me! The entire island is in danger!"

"It can't hardly be something so dramatic," said Elohim.

"Yes! More so. Possibly not just the island. Possibly as far as the empire. Or farther."

Enoch's laughter died on the wind as he saw that Avaleon was serious. He and Elohim stood in shocked silence, swaying with the weeds atop the giant pillar of rock, a chimney of stone rising from the ocean. A few hundred yards from the sheer cliffs of the island, and yet Avaleon's words held true: the seastack was dead, a sickly gray next to the vibrant brown of its eroded mother.

"Do I have your attention, brothers?"

Silence confirmed their attention. Their chocolate eyes, still clinging to their disbelief, held their brother's disturbed countenance all the same.

"It's Gorgon. *Gorgon*," he said over the wind.

"Ah." Elohim nodded. "I knew we should never have let him on the island."

"He is our brother. How could we have said no?" countered Enoch.

"He chose his responsibility by inheriting Father's empire. He should have remained with his people on the mainland. Instead, he deserted them, just as he blames us for doing."

"What's done is done!" Avaleon broke in. "The fact remains, he is *here*. And he means this island *harm*."

After a pause, Elohim said, "What has he done, Avaleon?"

Avaleon's jaw clenched and his lips set into a grim line.

"*What*, brother?" Elohim persisted.

"An army."

Enoch let out an uncomfortable laugh. "An army?"

"An *army*. Gorgon Fulbright has amassed an army of Nithim."

Enoch's defiant laugh was hollow. "Surely you jest."

Avaleon turned from their circle to face the island. Their castle, their *home*, stood winking in the sunlight; glass panes in sky-scraping towers reflected the frothing teal of the ocean. From the seastack, the towers and their spires were all that he could see, but he could picture the whole majestic building, with its ribbed arches like the body of a beast; at night, the entire castle would be lit up by countless spotlights, making it a beacon of electric blue for miles around.

"I do not jest," he said. There was an aching sadness in his voice. "Gorgon came to me. Last night, while you were away tending to your duties."

"You mustn't have been alone, Avaleon? Your guards, or—"

"I was alone. I had sent everyone away, so that I could search with my mind . . . for Aerlin. She is missing."

He would not allow his brothers' gasps of surprise to betray his emotion. He knew they understood his pain; for Enoch to have lost connection with Maad, or Elohim with Syrais . . . and yet his relationship with Aerlin was unique. She had been the first Nithim to approach the humans that came to their island. She presented herself to Avaleon, and the impossible happened. While their friendship opened the doors to a coexistence of humans and Nithim, Avaleon and Aerlin had fallen in love with each other. Their bond, that invisible chainlink connecting their minds and filling him with Nithim magic, was stronger than any other.

He closed his eyes, took a sharp breath—a painful breath, stabbing his throat and his insides and *oh Aerlin where have you gone*—and forced himself to soldier on with his tale.

"I was alone, and Gorgon snuck upon me and showed me . . . he showed me the folly of our ways. We were too good, too *proud*, to think his intentions were nothing but dour."

"But an army!" exclaimed Enoch. "An army of—of *Nithim*? How? They would not . . . they would *never*—"

"I have seen it with my own eyes."

Elohim stepped closer to Avaleon and placed a steady hand on his shoulder. "Tell us."

Avaleon met his brother's gaze. He found strength in those eyes, bright beneath their thick dark brow.

"He brought them to me. The throne room lies in ruin. I was helpless against him. He has become strong of the mind. I do not know if this means he has linked with more than one Nithim—"

"Impossible," hissed Enoch.

"—nevertheless, he has an army of Nithim at his beck and call. They seem . . . broken. Disturbed. I am not familiar with their reasoning, but their logic must be flawed to betray their people as they have done. We all know what it means for a Nithim to separate itself from the collective. I suspect Gorgon has had a hand in that."

"How many?" asked Elohim. "How many Nithim at his feet?"

"It is too early to tell. There were perhaps dozens with him that I saw last night, which is a large number for their race. But there could be more."

"What do we do?" This was asked by Enoch, although it was etched on all three brothers' expressions.

"I have given this much thought," Avaleon said, almost to himself. "I know from where Gorgon stole his army. He showed me. The cavern."

"The Nithim's egregore?" asked Enoch, shocked.

Avaleon nodded, averting his eyes at even the mention of the word. "I must find it as well."

Elohim gasped. "But—"

"I know!" Avaleon shouted. He felt his throat constrict and swallowed. "I know. It is forbidden. But it is necessary now, I believe. It cannot be helped. Go to Maad, to Syrais. Let us pray that Gorgon has not found them as well."

They nodded determinedly.

Three brothers, Avaleon, Enoch, and Elohim—the

Three Kings, the Friends of the Island, the Royal Trinity—stood resolute, one with the stone at their feet as if in root, looking toward their home. In that moment they knew they would do anything to protect it.

STANDING NOW, FAR FROM the island he had learned to call home, Avaleon almost wished he had failed in his mission to find the cavern. He wouldn't have found Aerlin, true, but he also would not have had to leave the island and come to this shore, knowing he would never return home.

For you, Aerlin.

HIS EYES SLOWLY ADJUSTED to the blackness as he spelunked deep inside the belly of the island. It was a strenuous trek, and the veins of luminescent blue gems in the rock became sparser as he sunk deeper. His body was soon covered in scrapes and bruises, but he felt he was going the right way. His connection to Aerlin may have severed, but his mind still held some latent connection to the Nithim magic, which was strongest at the island's heart.

The island's *brain*, he amended to himself.

As he climbed, he followed the strange sensation that he was being pulled toward his destination. The Nithim's egregore was a magnet, and his thoughts were iron filings. Moths drawn to a flame. He could almost feel them honing in on the cavern, still far beneath him.

He climbed deeper.

Avaleon was slick with sweat and grit by the time he

finally came into the sacred grotto of the Nithim, the keeping place of their egregore, their mother mind. It looked exactly as the image Gorgon had forced upon him, leading Avaleon to believe that he had made the right choice in coming here. It was true—Gorgon had been here. In this cavern lay answers.

He was not prepared, however, for how impossibly vast the cavern was. Although every surface was swimming in blue light, he could not see the ceiling. It seemed the stalactites were suspended from nothing, their pillars rising up into the firmament.

Avaleon.

He heard his name and knew instantly: Aerlin was here.

He wasted no more time taking in his surroundings. Tired though he was, he pushed himself to move faster, to weave between the stalagmites that sprouted from the floor like an ancient forest. He moved without seeing them; his thoughts, iron filings of the egregore, had surrendered to a new magnet.

Aerlin, I'm coming. I am coming to you.

Avaleon.

Aerlin.

The stalagmites thinned and he came to a wide expanse of blank stone floor, but still he rushed on. He could feel her. He could see something ahead now, but . . . that couldn't possibly be Aerlin . . .

He saw the pedestal, grown naturally from the ground, but he averted his gaze from the throbbing thing lying upon it. Instead, he focused on the creature sprawled on the floor beside it. And as he approached, the words he had bellowed at Gorgon echoed through his mind—

AERLIN IS NOT A BEAST, YOU BASTARD!

—and he saw that, of course, it was not a beast lying on the ground before him.

It was Aerlin.

Avaleon.

"Aerlin," he breathed, falling to his knees beside her.

Curiously, she was in her natural form, which was something Avaleon had scarcely laid eyes upon. She was gigantic, the size of a hill; her spine rose in a ridge of spikes sawing through the air like a mountain range. Her skin was protected by a hard exoskeleton, and cerulean sparkled in its chinks in lines not unlike the veins of luminescent gems in the island's rock.

That was when he noticed the blood.

Aerlin was hurt, but her body was so large it was difficult for Avaleon to see the extent. He hadn't noticed her wings at first, and now he could see that they were hidden behind her bulk and bent at an awkward angle; they were broken almost beyond recognition. Entire plates of her exoskeleton were cracked, like shattered shingles on a roof. And surrounding her body, reflecting the light of the cavern walls, was a pool of thick, black blood.

"Oh Aerlin . . ."

Hush, my love. We haven't the time for tears.

Aerlin's body was broken beyond speaking. Even her thoughts came to Avaleon as if from the bottom of a deep well. He bent forward and pressed his cheek against her heaving side. He could feel both of her laboring hearts as they pumped blood onto the cavern floor. His knees were an inch deep in it. So much blood . . .

"I'm here," he whispered to her.

I am going, she whispered back.

"No."

My mind is fading, Ava. I promise you I will cling to life with all my strength.

He tried swallowing, but his throat was suddenly dry. "Gorgon did this to you," he croaked.

That does not matter now. Please, Ava. We must be strong together. Athlu chaia gnaest aa.

"Vruch knemaest aa," he said, finishing the prayer. *Your eye must see, while mine sleeps.*

Yes, Aerlin said, and Avaleon could feel her purr, an engine against his cheek. *I must rest. And you must save us, Ava.*

He could almost hear scorn in her thoughts, and realized with some shame that she must hold him accountable. Gorgon was his brother, after all. Gorgon came to this island because of Avaleon. Now Aerlin's people would suffer because of him.

Enough! I am going. Do not dwell on who is to blame. Just . . .

Her thoughts were growing distant now. Falling further down the well.

Listen, my love . . .

Listen for what?

Aerlin's voice was gone, and he felt her body sag beneath his cheek. He raised his head. He hadn't received answers. He had found Aerlin, but what was he to do now? He hadn't learned how Gorgon had taken the Nithim, or if there was any way to—

Listen, Avaleon-of-Aerlin's-mind, for time is short.

He paused, both horrified and oddly soothed by the words echoing through his mind and the very rock of the cavern. He knew by instinct alone where that voice came from. He turned from Aerlin's still form to the brain sitting on the pedestal. The egregore.

Gorgon-of-stolen-minds has violated the Nithim. He has stolen that which is most sacred to us.

Avaleon inexplicably found himself defending his brother. "He didn't know—"

SILENCE. HE KNEW WHAT HE DID.

The brain, slightly larger than a human skull, pulsed brightly as it shouted, and blue waves of light washed throughout the cavern.

The bond you share with the Nithim is unique, Avaleon-of-Aerlin's-mind. We have let you onto our island, into our collective. We have imbibed you with our chvamnaest, giving you powers of the egregore. We have blessed you. But you remain ignorant.

Avaleon remained silent as he kowtowed to the brain of the Nithim.

This, as our-sister-Aerlin explained to us, is not your fault. We have failed to educate you. And so, let the words of our people wash over you, the same as they are washing over your of-mind-Aerlin. Let us know one another, so that we may see one another's minds. Athlu chaia gnaest aa—

"Vruch knemaest aa," Avaleon whispered.

Your eye must see, while mine sleeps.

In a flash, lines of cerulean script danced over the wide expanse of cavern floor, carved glyphs of magical blue, swirling rapidly toward him like the coming of the tide, and he saw that there had been carved words of magic swirling through Aerlin's wounds this whole time.

And now, the flowing letters reached him, and crashed over him painlessly, and it was as if a bolt of lightning had struck his forehead, in the same spot where Aerlin's third eye lay on her own head.

And he saw. He saw . . . *everything.*

He could feel the coils of his brain filling with bright understanding, with knowledge, with an empathy so terrible it anchored his heart and brought tears leaping from his eyes, sobs from his lips.

And still, the brain on the pedestal, the Nithim's brain, the Nithim's egregore, was speaking, was telling him what to do, but they were connected—man and collective, one living organism, and he could feel every living creature touching every inch of this island's skin—and the Nithim's instructions were pouring from Avaleon's own mouth.

"You must gather your brothers, Enoch-of-Maad's-mind and Elohim-of-Syrais's-mind," he shouted at the cavern's ceiling, "and claim three points of a protective triangle. This island and this people shall be blanketed with your chvamnaest. The price of the spell is written in the Third Eye: Athlu chaia gnaest aa, vruch knemaest aa. *Your eye must see, while mine sleeps.* The price is to forever sleep in stone, a price you and your brothers will proudly pay in penitence for Gorgon-of-stolen-minds and his treachery."

The light was blinding, a far brighter blue down here, deep beneath the surface, than ever was the sky. Avaleon could no longer see Aerlin, but he could *feel* her.

"The Nithim whom the dark brother stole from us, his of-stolen-minds, shall be chained here, also cast in stone, in the very walls of this cavern. But they are the innocent. They know not what they have done. They cannot be helped. This is a further price we must pay for the sins of humankind. But their names shall be remembered forever in the writing on the cavern's walls.

"Go, Avaleon-of-Aerlin's-mind. Go now, but know this: Your sacrifice, your stone sacrifice, will also cast in stone your kind's bond with the Nithim race. We shall link with the Third Eye, and we shall love. We shall love. Go."

AND SO HE FOUND HIMSELF NOW, standing on the shores of the mainland. Staring at the island, his home, a smudge on the horizon. Raising his hands as if to conduct an orchestra, the final aria of his legacy as Avaleon Fulbright, first-bonded to the Nithim and king of the first human migrants on the Nithim's nameless homeland. Watching unblinkingly as the blue electricity thizzed, superimposed over the island's heart, and grew, and grew, and grew toward the three points of the triangle he and his brothers formed.

The aria swelled, the brothers each whispered, "Athlu chaia gnaest aa, vruch knemaest aa," and Avaleon had time for one more thought—

For you, Aerlin.

—before he was encased in stone.

REST IN PEACE

SHE AWOKE IN HER OWN GRAVE.

She knew this had been common a few hundred years ago. Someone in a deep coma would be presumed dead and consequently buried alive. Entire industries of "dead houses" had sprung up due to this fear: pulley systems rigged with bells to warn of corpse movement, metal tacks wedged under toenails to wake the not-quite-dead.

She felt her limbs. No tacks, bells; no pulleys or cords.

How had this happened?

She didn't mind her predicament all that much, really . . . but the mystery would keep her up nights.

And that was no way to enjoy death.

AUTOPSY OF A MARRIAGE

COUNTY OF EL DORADO

DEPARTMENT OF MEDICAL EXAMINER CORONER

AUTOPSY REPORT NO. ██████

ADULT FORM PROTOCOL

I performed an autopsy on the body of ██████████ at _the_

DEPARTMENT OF MEDICAL EXAMINER CORONER   _Placerville,_

California on _05/07/18_ _9:13 a.m._ .

From the anatomic findings and pertinent history, I ascribe the
death to: (A) [DUE TO OR AS A CONSEQUENCE OF]

_____   Irreconcilable differences   _____ .

page 2 of 17

Anatomical Summary:

> As listed below
> **X** See form #16 under Gross Impressions

IF A TRAUMA CASE STATE:

Injury date: _____05/03/18_____ Hospital date(s): _____ .

CIRCUMSTANCES:

> As listed below
> **X** See Investigator Report form #3

EXTERNAL EXAMINATION:

The body is identified by toe tags and is that of an ⬭unembalmed⬭/embalmed re-frigerated

> | | | |
> |---|---|---|
> | **X** adult | female | Asian |
> | Elderly | **X** male | Black |
> | teenage | other | **X** Caucasian |
> | | | Hispanic |

who appears

> **X** about the reported
> older than the reported
> the reported
> younger than the reported

age of __27__ years.

The body weighs __225__ pounds, measures __76__ inches and is

> cachectic
> mildly/moderately/extremely obese
> **X** poorly nourished
> thin
> well-built, muscular and fairly well-nourished

Tattoo(s) are:

> not present
> **X** present and identified as bird on ring-finger knuckle, bass clef merged w/ numeral 2 on right pectoral, unfinished "NO MATTER WHAT" on left pectoral directly over heart, faded sunset on back left shoulder .

[pages 3–17 missing from standard Adult Form Protocol filing. Student autopsy report summary and descriptions provided instead for the court cases of ██████████'s possible homicide and ██████████████'s disappearance.]

SUMMARY OF CLINICAL HISTORY

The patient was a 27-year-old Caucasian male whose only significant past medical history was a diagnosis of diabetes mellitus type 1 in 2005 and a hospitalization due to DKA [ketoacidosis] in 2009.

On May 3, 2018, patient called EMS with shortness of breath and chest pain. EMS reports that patient was agitated upon their arrival at patient's residence. Furniture was overturned and curtains ripped from the walls, presumably by patient. Patient was tachypneic at 45 breaths per minute with oxygen saturation of 90%. At the scene, EMS administered breathing treatments and checked lung sounds that did not reveal any evidence of fluid in the lung fields.

Five minutes after arrival, EMS still could not calm patient down to answer questions or for treatment. EMS then attempted to subdue patient with benzodiazepine. Patient paced the residence violently and threw objects. Patient yelled mostly unintelligible phrases. EMS reports phrases had something to do with "never shaving a cat again" and "I [the patient] married her, not *her*."

Seven minutes after arrival, EMS reports that patient's tachypnea ceased and a heart rate could not be detected at all. Despite having a seemingly stopped heart, patient continued his agitation and began crying and singing.

EMS was able to bring him to a sitting position in the kitchen area, where he fell into what EMS describes as a "dreaming coma." Patient's heart was confirmed to be in SCA [sudden cardiac arrest], perhaps asystole or some other arrhythmia that EMS could not identify without EKG monitor. ACLS protocol for pulseless electrical activity was followed, but EMS reports no response to epinephrine or CPR. Nothing. Fucking *nothing*. I cannot believe how quickly this human █████████████ . . .

It should be noted patient's wife was present at the residence along with patient's mother-in-law, both of whom left the residence at 19:57 without speaking to EMS or to patient. Patient was pronounced dead on the scene at 19:58. Fixed, dilated pupils. No heart sounds, no pulse. No spontaneous respirations. No hope in sight. ████ is ████. We're ██████████.

DESCRIPTION OF GROSS LESIONS

EXTERNAL EXAMINATION: The body is that of a 27-year-old male, poorly nourished in both body and spirit. Over the place where his heart should be is a half-finished tattoo, an Art Deco styling of the motto "NO MATTER WHAT." It is a shame to see such a courageous axiom unfinished. Like seeing scaffolding on the Notre Dame. This student examiner is tempted to bring a needle and finish the tattoo for the patient. Perhaps his heart would leap back to life. ████████████████████ ██████████. Peripheral edema in feet, most likely neuropathy due to autoimmune disease and California climate. [Note: EMS reports that patient's residence had no air-conditioning unit; indoor temperature was recorded as 97 degrees Fahrenheit.] Nothing else of note.

INTERNAL EXAMINATION (BODY CAVITIES): In apparent contradiction to general health and young age, patient's internal cavities are shriveled and malnourished. Possible cause for SCA?

HEART: Speaking of SCA—patient's heart is a sad story in itself. The color of mistreated leather, the shape of swallowed dreams, and shriveled as though starved (a weight of barely 200 grams). Upon opening, the heart is ... disappointing? Grossly so. No evidence of reciprocated love. On the left ventricle wall lining are slightly raised white plaques that seem to spell out the words

Examination of the great vessels of the heart reveals years of abuse—but from whom? His heartbeat ... I can hear its ghost. My professor doesn't believe me, will likely fail me, but what's one F in the face of such heartbreak?

ENDOCRINE SYSTEM: The adrenal glands are in the normal position and weigh 8.9 grams on the right and 10.1 grams on the left. The cut surface of the adrenal glands reveals a normal-appearing cortex and medulla. The thyroid gland is grossly normal. The pancreas is, of course, dead, and was so many years before the rest of the patient caught up with it.

RESPIRATORY SYSTEM: The vocal cords, when cut

open, reveal striations of red and white along their full length, like nails dragged down a chalkboard. They appear to have been made raw, but by what? What words could do such a thing?

GASTROINTESTINAL SYSTEM: Unremarkable. ██ ███████████████████████████████████████ ████████ No ██████████, no matter what.

RETICULOENDOTHELIAL SYSTEM: Don't make me cut this man any further. His body has been subjected to enough pain, long before we slid his corpse on this metal slab.

EXTREMITIES: Shin splints, but how? Running, proba-bly, but from what? Or toward whom? Neuropathy in the feet, exacerbated by the California heat and a house with no A/C.

Why did he stay in a place that brought him so much pain? Why not leave?

CLINICOPATHOLOGIC CORRELATION

I went to his house. The patient. Found his address in the EMS report. What was I looking for? I don't know. Answers. We come here every day to find answers in a person's lifeless corpse . . . but what if the answers lie in life? Echoes and specters and ghosts can't be measured, but tangible evidence also exists. If we look in more places than a cadaver.

So I drove to ███████'s house—flunk me, I don't care anymore. I went to his house, for all the good it did. All it did was confuse me further. Maybe that's why I'm typing out this confessional. I broke into the house (it wasn't all that dramatic—I found a side door left carelessly wide open, though I'm sure law enforcement won't much care *how* I broke-and-entered) and . . . what I found . . . framed wedding photos and carefully curated shows of affection, of love, of happiness . . . a house demonstrably filled with cozy, comfortable *life* . . . yet how can such things exist in the face of a marriage gone so catastrophically to the grave? How can two people coexist and codepend and co*love* for so many years, laughing and smiling together all the way to the cliff's edge, and only see what they've done in the seconds before one of them plummets to their death? In the seconds after the other pushes them off the cliff?

How could ████ do such a thing? "No Matter What"?

No matter . . . no matter *what*?

SUMMARY & REFLECTION

I wish I'd gotten to know you. Maybe it wouldn't have changed anything, but maybe it could have.

Maybe *I* could have.

Maybe we could have been friends, and you could have invited me over to your house. Maybe I would have come inside and you would have introduced me to your wife and showed me around—the new hardwood flooring, the new gravel drive, the completely remodeled bathroom. Maybe you would have explained that your landlords— your in-laws, the owners of the house—said they *had* to put money into all of these things, all these upgrades to make the house *look* nicer, but no, sorry, ▮▮▮▮▮▮, there's no money for an air-conditioning unit, no money to invest in your health and comfort and oh we're so sorry about your swollen, swelling neuropathy, that's too bad.

And maybe, from the look in my eyes, you could have heard your own words. You could have realized the truth and looked at your wife and recognized right then and there that to stay with her was to stay with your murderer.

Maybe you would have picked up your half-shaved cat and followed me out the front door, into my car, and down the road to a new life. A new life where we both understand that no matter what, NO MATTER WHAT, each of us will never be expected to compromise our own life for that of the other. That no matter what we will always prop each other up while still having the strength to stand on our own.

I'm staring down at the patient's corpse as I finish this report. I'm leaving. I can't stay here. Not in this life. I'll do what the patient should have done, what *you* should have done, and I'll do it before it's too late.

I'll deposit these pages on the patient's disassembled chest, where the unfinished tattoo used to be, with a drawing I've made of how the patient might have finished the tattoo if he had the chance. I don't know who will find the pages, or who will read them, or if they will ever end up in my professor's hands. I don't know if my words will be entered into the public record, or incinerated, or ██████████████████████████████████████ ██████████████████████████████████████ ██ , or heavily redacted.

But those are not the questions I need answered.

Remaining unanswered questions:

What's out there to be discovered?

Who am I?

Who do I want to be?

Who do I wish to become along the way?

.

THE WAR ON CHRISTMAS

OR, IN THE EYES OF BABY JESUS, COMMERCIALISM IS ABORTION

T DOESN'T MATTER IF HIS NAME'S JOHN DOE, Jolly Ol' Saint Nick, or *Christian* for Chrissake . . .

Tonight he's mine and tonight he dies.

Considering I'm on a solo mission, it surprises me just how easy it was to nab my prey. You'd think I'd need to reel him in with some wide-eyed, sugar-high kid to sit on his lap—Jesus, what a *sick bastard*, he'd probably be pitching a tent with a thick, candy-cane *chubby*. But no, I didn't even have to leave the parking lot. Which is a blessing from On High by itself; having to mingle with all those shopping heathens would've given me a tumor the size of Eve's apple.

That's why it wasn't going to be just me. I had an accomplice. But we had to part ways. Amicably. On my side, at least.

Ooh, that's a good story. It's no Luke 1:45, but let me indulge myself . . .

I CUT THE DARKNESS in half with a solid blast of a flashlight, one of those heavy-duty ones from Home Depot (thank You, Lord, for the blessed Home Depot), shining it down into the man's face like the sweet wrath of God. His first reaction was to squint, then cough, then sweat. Then struggle against his restraints.

I'd considered making him build the chair to which I tied him—saw the cedar, hammer the nails, even *sand* and *lacquer* the thing, can you imagine? But we were running out of time—reruns of *Rudolph the Red-Nosed Reindeer* and *Frosty the Snowman* had been rotting people's brains for weeks now. Besides, I wanted the guy on my side.

"Where . . . who . . . where am I?" he asked (quite reasonably, I thought).

"Do you know what time of year it is?" I said from behind the light, imagining that to him I must sound as the voice of God. Or Allah, or whatever.

"It's . . . who are you?"

"It's December. Do you know what happens in December?"

"Do I . . . ? Why are you doing this?"

"That's what I thought." I kept the light trained on his face, but he would have to *earn* that halo. "I know your people don't celebrate—"

"My people?"

"—the birth of our Savior, Jesus Christ of Nazareth—"

"Jesus . . ."

". . . Christ," I finished for him, feeling like I now knew what it was like to explain to someone with Down syndrome that they're retarded. I spoke slowly, deliberately. "The birth of. Jesus Christ. As in, *Christ*mas."

Silence from him. Didn't surprise me.

"Let me . . . *shine a light* on the subject for you." I waited for a laugh, but he stayed mute. Jesus, guy, get a sense of humor. "Every year, we *Christ*ians, those blessed by the Father, His Son, and the Holy Ghost, celebrate the birth of our Savior, the man who died for our sins—"

"I know what Christmas is, for fuck's sake!"

I attempted to shine the light even brighter on his swarthy complexion and slinky locks of black hair . . . but how to show a leopard its spots?

"I'm sure you may *think* you know what we Americans celebrate—"

"I'm a fucking American, too, you fucking moron. We're in America! *Jesus Christ!*"

"Exactly!" I wobbled the light in a tight circle around his face. "Jesus Christ! *Now* you're getting it! Faster than most Americans, I'm afraid. Which is why I brought you here tonight."

The man closed his eyes against the light, as if praying to his sacrilegious gods for deliverance. Keep praying, Mohammad, but you're dialing the wrong number.

"I'm actually incredibly pleased that you've made such a quick connection between Christ and Christmas. *Christ* . . . and *Christ*mas! Sadly, most Americans miss that connection. They spend their holidays drinking *eggnog* and building *snowmen* and eating *fucking fruitcake* . . . they worship *Hallmark* and *Nordstrom's* and *Toys 'R' Us* and—"

"I celebrate Christmas, too, you know."

"—and . . . what? Mohammad, don't interrupt me."

"My name's not Mohammad."

"But, you see, Mohammad, that brings me to the very problem! You said it yourself: you *celebrate* Christmas. *Christ*mas! And you're not even *Christ*ian!"

Mohammad popped one eye open against the light. "I'm Muslim."

I nodded, but of course he couldn't see me. "Exactly. No *Christ* in Islam."

"You know that the birth of Jesus Christ is in the Quran, right?"

I blinked. "Don't—" I shook my head to dispel a migraine's first buzz. "ISIS doesn't give a *shit* about our Savior Jesus Christ, and I'd *appreciate* if you didn't besmirch His name with your Goddamn *lies*, you motherfu—"

ANYWAY, YOU GET THE POINT. Clearly we were getting nowhere. My plan to secure an accomplice was perfect. Find someone with as much hate as me—preferably someone unafraid of a little violence, someone familiar to some good old-fashioned Holy War experience. Sure, he didn't exactly have a turban for a hat, but he was the only terrorist I could find in my neighborhood.

But just when I was starting to like Mohammad, he called me a "sick F-word" one too many times.

That's just not Christ-like.

So I killed him.

* * *

NOT THE HAPPIEST ENDING, I know. But hey, even the crucifixion ended with the resurrection. Give it a little time, and I promise this story will make you feel all warm and bubbly inside. The true meaning of Christmas.

So anyway. Back to the main event—the holiday celebration, as it were.

After a few choice faux-friendly words thrown out my Hummer window, complete with some bullcrap about the "Christmas spirit," I coaxed this jolly jackass into captivity and successfully caught my first wild Santa Claus. Wasn't even that hard. You'd be shocked at how readily available tranquilizers, TASERs, handcuffs, and the like truly are. One Google search and mouse-click away. God is good! Seek and ye shall find!

And now look at the helpless bastard. All trussed up like a Christmas present in the same spot Mohammad occupied just a few days before, and the same spot that Goddamn Easter bunny sat eight months ago.

That damn bunny . . .

IT WAS FOR MY DAUGHTER'S EIGHTH BIRTHDAY, the bunny. Her wayward mother somehow got it into her brain that she wanted to get baptized into the Mormon church. My little girl, a Mormon? A brainwashed Latter-day Saint? She was already baptized when she was born, as a God-blessed, God-fearing Christian! No way was my baby joining a cult.

"But, baby girl," I remember saying to her the morning I found out—her whore of a mother didn't bother telling me until the morning of, that slut, that viper—"are . . . are you sure?"

Little Esther rolled her eyes. What a precocious little angel.

"Yes, Dad, I'm *sure*."

"But—but—you can't do this to your daddy, to your father . . . to—to your Heavenly Father!"

Another eye roll. God, she's precious.

"But—but—maybe there's something . . ." I was grasping at straws here, but of course, who isn't holding those straws but Jesus Christ Himself? "Your birthday! Your birthday present!"

This gave Esther cause to pause. "Present?" Said with a sneaky little smile that'd charm the Devil, a lilting *Preeeeee-sent?*

"Uh-huh, anything for my baby girl, *anything*. Just name it."

Already the baptism was out of her head—*Thank You, Sweet Jesus*—as she contemplated her ultimate wish list. Finally, she looked back up at her daddy and said:

"A bunny!"

So a bunny I got. Took me three hours to track down and purchase the damn thing, and then the pet shop employee droned on and on *and on* about how to take care of it. It's a damn *bunny*, a cage, some lettuce, and the occasional petting session, how hard can it be? But lo and behold, it was enough to make my baby girl promise her daddy to renounce the Joe Smith quack.

Unfortunately, it was also enough to make me hours late to the most important meeting in my career. I was fired. Just like that. After sixteen years of dedicated employment, and just four days before Easter Sunday. I thought the walk from my office to the parking lot, hefting the bulging box of stuff (sixteen years in an office accumulates a lot of crap; I didn't even attempt to take my *Ficus*) would prove to be the most humiliating experience in my life.

Actually, no. The most humiliating experience in my life waited for me on the front steps of my shitty, "never-gonna-fix'er-upper" house. A note, in my ex-wife's handwriting, sitting atop a cage with a bunny inside it.

Nice try, asshole. You know I'm allergic. Esther got baptized today. I'll send the missionaries. —Charice

"Like Hell you will!" I yelled out loud, looking out across my neighborhood like I expected twin Donny Osmonds to come riding along on ten-speeds, Golden Bibles in hand. Carl, across the street, waved to me.

Fuck you, Carl.

I admit it. I went a little crazy. The cage sitting in the corner of this basement is proof enough, red-and-white fur caked on the inside with spiderwebs of gray brain matter and the constant cloud of buzzing flies. *Buzz-buzz-buzz.* That's the sound in my brain since that Easter Sunday, celebrating the resurrection of Jesus My Savior with a bottle of bourbon in hand and contemplating what to do with the elephant in the room. Or, I should say, the bunny in the room.

Buzz-buzz-buzzzzzzzzzzzzzzzzzzzzzz—

That was a special day for the bunny, too, I realized as I stared down at its cage. Not just resurrected Jesus. Why? What was so special about this bunny?

Buzz—

Easter egg hunts, chocolate bunnies, painting eggshells . . . it was stealing Jesus's spotlight. What'd this bunny ever do for my sins?

—*buzz*—

I leaned down to the cage, spilling my bourbon. "What'd you ever do for *my* sins?"

—*buzzzzzzzzzzzzzz*—

"WHO'S THERE? HELLO? What the FUCK?!"

Oh good, Santa's awake!

This basement is dark and musty, and its low ceiling presses down on me as if it's trying to force me through a fissure in the Earth and past the gates of Hell. Not today, Satan. Hey, ain't that funny—Satan, Santa. Satan, Santa. The apple doesn't fall far from bare-ass Eve's tree, huh?

"Wherrafuck am I?"

I take a deep breath—through the mouth; it stinks like a whore's crabapple down here. I count to three. It's time for the main event.

Click goes the flashlight, *buzzzzzzz* goes the brain, *Wherrafuck-am-I?* goes the Santa.

"Now, before you begin swearing again like Billy Bob Thornton—*bad* Santa!—let me explain why you're—"

"WHAT THE FUCK WHO TH'FUCK'RE YOU YOU MOTHERFU—"

ZZZZZZZzzzzzZZZZZzzzz—

"AH FUCK!"—spittle spattering down his fake, glossy white beard, spreading in streamers down his red coat—

ZZZZZZZZzzzzzzzzzzZZZZZZZZZZzzzzzzzz—

"Please do not interrupt me again—"

" 'Djou just fuckin' *tase* m—*mmmph*—"

"And watch that language of yours! It's Christmas Goddamned Eve!"

Silence. I guess between the extensive kisses of the TASER gun, the gasoline-soaked rag just stuffed in his mouth without ceremony, and the reminder of Jesus's birthday, this fat bastard decided to listen.

I pull up the music stand in front of me and click on the light clipped to its front, spilling forty watts across the dimpled leather cover of the glorious book sitting atop it. One hand still training the flashlight on my esteemed guest, I caress the other across the Holy Bible, King James Edition. Like holy Braille of the Holy Grail. Then, in one practiced motion, I flip the book open—reverently, Goddammit, reverently—to its ribbon bookmark.

And read to my guest:

"For to us a child is born, to us a Son is given, and the government will be on His shoulders. And He will be called Wonderful Counselor, Mighty God, Everlasting Father, Prince of Peace. Of the increase of His government and peace there will be no end. He will reign on David's throne and over His kingdom—"

"MMMMMPHHH!"

"—establishing and upholding it with justice and righteousness from that time on and forever. The zeal of the—"

"MMMMMNNNMMMPHHH!"

"—THE ZEAL OF THE LORD ALMIGHTY WILL ACCOMPLISH THIS."

"*Mmmphhleah!* What the fuck're you doin'?"

Somehow this Kris Kringle cretin spat his noxious gag out. Oh well. Right at this moment, a calm like no other consumes me, the words of Isaiah are washing over me like a baptism for the dead. I close my eyes and hold the moment for as long as I can. I can't even be bothered to tase the guy. All that matters are the echoes of the Lord's Word and the crisp flakes rimmed in gold beneath my fingers, the pastry-thin pages of the scriptures. Pastry-thin pages; nutrient-rich wisdom.

My reverie is broken like the body of Christ on Good Friday as my guest tunes up his tune with a self-effacing whimper: quiet, modest; the kind you'd imagine hearing from the pews of a church.

"Sir," he whispers. "Sir . . . please . . . *please* . . . wh-wh-why . . . *why* . . . ?"

I'm not sure if I can hear contrition in his voice, true repentance, or if I'm just feeling good will because I'm still riding that wave of sweet, sweet baptismal font water. Either way, I feel my annoyance ebb away. And in the true spirit of Christ, I forgive him.

I say, calmly, "Are you ready to hear my story now?"

His lip trembles just enough to dislodge the elastic strap and bring his fake beard springing up—*snap!*—over his chin, muffling his delicate, eggshell *"Yes."*

And so I begin my tale. No "Once upon a time" here, but still, I've told my story over and over in my head to a point where I sound like a regular Brother Grimm . . .

THERE WAS A TIME when families would gather 'round the glowing hearth framed in rustic brick . . . the kiddies would cuddle on the springy carpet; Mother and Father would share the corduroy loveseat; Grammy would lean on her walker-seat, pressing its tennis ball bearings into the floor like fuzzy egg yolks about to burst; Ol' Yeller would yawn on the rug as worn and graying as him . . . and they would celebrate Christmas.

I remember it so well, my own family's Christmas portrait. I was one of those kiddies on the carpet. Apple pie bursting the lining of my stomach; the fire making me break into a sweat, that sweat my mother always said was a "growing boy's sweat." I'd sit and listen to my father read the Christmas scriptures and absently stare at the linen panties peeking out from between my sister's thighs. I felt so peaceful, so casually, swimmingly, disorientedly peaceful.

But people don't celebrate that Christmas anymore.

Last year, you know what my daughter said to me about Christmas? She said, with that knowing lilt of hers, "I've been really good this year, Daddy."

Me, in my Goddamned naïveté, I thought my little angel was the sunshine of God's green Earth, and I said, "Jesus is so proud of you, Esther."

She just frowned at me and said, "Jesus? Does He keep the naughty-or-nice list for Santa?"

And then she handed me her Christmas list, "for Santa," and I'll never forget what was on that piece of paper, in big, clumsy handwriting.

Barbie. *Frozen* DVD. Tablet. A Goddamned *My Little Pony* backpack—

"WHAT'S WRONG WITH THAT?" Santa asks, interrupting my story, and suddenly the basement ceiling feels oppressive again. I grab my TASER as Santa says, "She'd been a good girl all year, she just wanted—"

"SHUT THE FUCK UP!"

Buzz—
ZZZZZZzzzzzzZZZZZzzzzzzzzz—
—buzz-buzzzzzzzzzzzz—

WHERE WAS I?

Ah, as I was saying. Christmas was gone. Just like that, like a geriatric whose life had rolled down the hill, Jesus's day had gone away . . .

To Santa Claus.

I saw him everywhere after that perverse Christmas list from my Esther. TV. The movies. My neighbors' lawn decorations. And then it became every grown man's duty to dress up in the reds and the whites and the belts and boots and *beard*, because the children had to see Santa to believe—what happened to good old-fashioned *faith*?—and there were Christmas parties and shopping malls, and suddenly the malls were stuffed full of coiling, snaking lines of children waiting to get their picture with Santa and *tell him what they wanted for Christmas.*

You know what I want for Christmas?

(Don't you fucking answer, you fucking freak, that was a fucking *rhetorical* question, and I will not hesitate to fucking tase you again, you better fucking believe *that*, put your faith in *that*, motherfucker—)

I want Christ. I want my Savior, the Son of my Father who art in Heaven. I want queues not waiting to sit on some stranger's hard prick, but queues waiting to confess their sins—I'm not Catholic, but a priest is a fair substitute for Santa Claus, as long as he isn't buttfucking little boys—so they can get on *God's* naughty-or-nice list.

I want corporations to believe in the family again,

instead of the dollar bill. They make their employees work on *Christ*mas, for Chrissake; where's the "Christ-like" in that? Where's the "family" in that? Close shop for just one Goddamn day! Instead, these Walmarts and Targets are dry-humping you for an extra dollar, offering coat hanger abortions to any mother and father failing to pacify their spoiled children because *"I want this!"* and *"Gimme that!"* and where does it all end? In Hell? No, Hell doesn't exist because Heaven doesn't exist because Jesus doesn't exist in Christmas because *commercialism* has found a way to buy and sell and *fuck* the soul of every little boy and girl in America—

THE WORDS KEEP POURING from my mouth like diarrhea, *drip-drip-drip* from the rim of an asshole—because that's what Esther's mother has made me, an asshole, *"nice try, asshole"*—and now I don't even register what I'm saying. But my extremities are numb down here in this frozen basement (that's right, they cut the power a couple weeks ago, I forgot), and I start to move, to circulate the blood through my veins.

I keep the flashlight trained on my audience of one. I step from the music stand holding my Bible. Absentmindedly, I feel hot piss running down my leg. That helps the cold. I slowly walk as I speak, and Santa's gasp and shudder at my every move is oddly gratifying. I walk past him, behind him, to the far wall. I reach out. In the darkness, I feel the work bench. I feel the items laid out there. Which tool?

I choose the nail gun. It's heavy in my grip, like a cast-iron dildo or a tube of cookie dough. I put it back down and choose the pliers.

The beam of my flashlight is trained on the back of Santa's head, and I can tell that he's shaking, shivering in the cold. His convulsions grow and shake a low moan from his throat when he hears me take steps closer. Slow, calculated steps. Closer. Closer. I'm still talking. What am I saying? Does it even matter?

No. All that matters is the tension, the scream, the build, the build . . . release. I love the feel of fingers breaking beneath the pliers' teeth. Snapping like stalks of dry spaghetti. One appendage after another. One shows surprising resistance, so I give it some gusto; it breaks, but the sound's different . . . in the darkness, I think I mangled his wedding ring with the shards of bone and tendon. This puts a smile on my face.

His screams are so loud they're drowning out my storytelling. That's okay. It's time to go back for the nail gun anyway. I step backward, returning to the workbench. Replace the now-gristly pliers. Pick up the nail gun. Return to Santa.

"Santa—*Santa!* I'm gonna need you to—SANTA!"

His screams trickle down to whimpers, and he unscrunches his face. With the light in his eyes, he can't see what I'm holding; only that I've returned. And who knows? Maybe the fear of the unknown is worse than the fear of a nail gun pointed at your head.

"Thank you. Now, listen, this is the moment—"

"No . . . *no*, pleeeeeeeease . . ." He's crying now.

"This is the *moment*. What have you learned from my story?"

It takes him a couple minutes to regain his ability to do anything but blubber and shit his pants. But once his indecipherable cries have been replaced by the rank of shit, the choking smell wakes him up and he opens his mouth to speak.

"You—you ... I've learned that you ... that you're ..."

"Don't you say 'crazy,' don't let that be the last thing you say—"

"I've learned that—that you're ... *angry.*"

Angry? You're Goddamn right!

I lean down so that I can smell his fetid, peppermint breath. Better than the shit at least. We're nose-to-nose now and all I have to do is whisper.

"I'm *angry* at everything you represent, Santa."

Click.

Silence. I'm too stunned to say anything, and he's too ignorant to know his brains should be showering the basement floor like spilt scrambled eggs—but they're *not*.

Click-click-click.

Damn. The gun's empty.

"What . . . what's happening?"

"I—" I stop, stand upright, assess the situation. "The gun's shitting *empty.*"

"Gun? Gun?!"

Great. He's crying again.

"Calm down, ya crybaby, it's not a *real* gun. The real guns're upstairs, tucked under my pillow, in my nightstand and underwear drawer, and behind Esther's school photo in the hall. Oh, and in the umbrella stand. And the toilet's water tank." The thought makes me laugh. "You wouldn't *believe* the shit I've got buried in the backyard . . ."

"So . . . so you're not going to shoot me?" Relief and

confusion in his voice.

"No, of *course* I'm gonna shoot you, you moron. But I'm all out of nails."

"Ah . . . a *nail* gun." Relief and confusion intensify. "Listen, sir . . . I know you're angry. I'm angry too. Not at you—you and I totally get each other. I'm angry at . . . at, you know, society. Just like you."

"Uh-huh." I nod, but I'm not buying. I know a car salesman when I hear one.

"So . . . you know, let's fix this. Untie me"—fat chance *that's* happening, buddy—"and we can pop on over to Home Depot and buy us some more nails. On me. Consider it a Christmas present."

A Christmas present? Christ, did this guy not hear a single fucking thing I've been saying?

I throw the empty nail gun to the concrete, and *ohhhhhhh* it's so satisfying how that sound makes Santa jump. "I don't want your fucking gift, you fucking freak. What I want is to blow your fucking brains out. So maybe I'll just 'pop on over' upstairs and grab my nine-millimeter or twenty-two or Winchester Magnum or AR-15 and get the job done."

"Wait, wait, wait, you don't want to do that."

I laugh again. The anger isn't lifting, but I am beginning to enjoy it. Maybe righteous wraths are good for the endorphins. "And why's that?"

"It's Christmas Eve, right? Your neighbors are all gathered as a family—every house on this block, I bet. A gunshot would alert them, and you'd have cops at your door before you could get rid of my body."

Goddammit. Santa Claus is right.

"Well," I say, considering, "I didn't *want* to do it the

hard way, but I suppose I could enjoy bashing your brains in with that music stand."

There's a brief, wide-eyed pause before he starts blubbering all over himself. "I'll scream. It's not a threat, I promise, but-but-but I mean just look at me. I'm a squealer. You only broke a few fingers and I lost it, remember? Only it'll be ten times worse and it'll come to the same result as the guns."

Sigh. That good feeling is ebbing now, but the anger is growing.

"Then what do you suggest?" Oh, this oughta be good.

"Exactly what I said. Home Depot. You want a quick and easy and relatively quiet way to kill me, right? Well, unless you wait for New Year's Eve or drive me out to the desert, your best option is that nail gun."

"How dumb do you think I am, Santa? I'm not bringing you—"

"You don't have to! I'll stay, tied up, right here."

"You'll just scream while I'm gone—"

"Gag me then."

I stare at him. Then it hits me. I bend down, the flashlight lowered slightly so he can look me in the eye.

"You a faggot, Santa?"

He blinks, uncomprehending. Or acting dumb. I heard gays are good at acting, so I wouldn't put it past him.

I add, "*Gag* you? Is that some sort of sex thing?"

He doesn't laugh, but neither does he deny the accusation. Imagine that—if I rid the world of a Santa *and* a homosexual in one night. The Lord works in mysterious ways.

He blinks again. "Fine, don't gag me then. I'll be quiet. I promise."

Now it's my turn to blink. I swear to God, I see *honesty* in that face. I believe him. He's not bullshitting me. I yank his beard back down and around his chin.

"Why are you doing this, Santa?"

He smiles grimly. "You think I *want* to be stuffed in this stupid suit on Christmas Eve? You think this was some kind of choice? Between this and being with my family, and you think I choose to act like a fool around some strangers' ungrateful greedy kids?"

The flashlight slips in my hand, and the anger slips from my face.

He pauses. "You and I . . . we're not so different. Wife left me, my kids hate me. Unemployed, one more bit of bad luck away from being homeless."

I bend down so we're eye to eye.

Some of the bitterness leaves his smile. "I *see* you," Santa tells me.

And we stay there for I don't know how long. Seconds? Minutes? Forty days and forty nights? Me, about to drop my flashlight and bent at the knees, and him, in a limp Santa suit our sick society forced him to wear, tied to a chair and begging for me to end it all.

Finally, he speaks up again, his voice a whisper.

"So what do you say? You and me. Untie me. Let me wash up, bandage my hand. Share a Christmas beer and put all this bullshit behind us."

BANG-BANG-BANG.

I jolt upright, my heart racing, and in one big rush it all returns to me—the smell of shit and dried-up bunny and metal sinking into my bones with the cold and the injustice of it all and the *anger*—

"What the fuck was that?" I ask him, my voice a dead calm.

BANG-BANG-BANG.

He gulps. "Sounds like the front door."

Still a dead calm before the storm, "Silent Night" before "Jingle Bell Rock," my voice never tremors: "Did you set me up, Santa? Who did you tell?"

He's back to being scared. Good. "Come on, man, how would I even *do* that? Listen to yourself!"

Another *BANG-BANG-BANG* followed by a voice, shouting unintelligibly.

"Who am I gonna find when I answer that door, Santa?"

"Why don't you go and see—"

I rap him in the noggin with the butt of my flashlight. *"Who did you bring to my house?!"*

He's crying again. Jesus, this guy weeps more than Christ Himself. "Do you even hear how crazy you sound? *You* kidnapped *me*, I don't even know your *name*—"

I hit him again and again and again, three smacks to the face in rhythm with three more heavy knocks on the door upstairs. I can't hear the shouting voice over Santa's blubbering.

"You need help, man," he's saying, his voice hitching, "you're fuckin' crazy—"

I throw the flashlight, only narrowly missing his head, and in the sputtering, drunken swing of the beam of light as it clatters away, I scramble on the oil-stained cement floor. When I come reeling back up, the empty nail gun is clutched in my hand.

BANG-BANG-BANG.

I've done my part—I've helped nail Jesus to that cross and heaved Him up to the heavens, and now Judas has come to collect his reward. I can give him Hell or nails, and I'm all out of nails.

"I'm not crazy, it's all of you who's crazy. You led me to this, it's all *your* fault, all your cheery commercials and sugary cereals . . . as far as I'm concerned, you're all on God's naughty list and I'm here to give you your coal."

I heft the nail gun.

"FUCK—YOU!"

I lose myself in screaming and yelling and cussing as I burst forth, stabbing the business end of the nail gun into Santa's face again and again and again, and he stops wailing and blubbering somewhere in the middle of it all and now he's just limp and I'm standing over him, my breathing ragged and deafening in my ears and the fly buzz angry in my brain, the nail gun slick with his blood and whatever else they stuff in a Santa piñata.

"Merry Christmas," I say to his corpse.

Buzz-buzz-buzzzzzzzz—

BANG-BANG-BANG.

I strengthen my grip on the nail gun and spit bile from my mouth. Ten purposeful steps, that's all it takes, and then I'm climbing the steps out of this God-forsaken basement, my feet pounding and my heart pounding and the door pounding—

I stop at the top of the landing, where my baby girl's school photo hangs in a place of honor.

What if it's Esther at the door?

—buzz-buzz-buzzzzzzzzzzz—

Yes! It's Esther, it must be her, of course it's my precious angel come to say she loves me and she's sorry and she doesn't care about gifts and toys and Santa and she just wants to spend Christmas with her father because she *loves* him Esther *loves* me of course she does—

BANG-BANG-BANG.

"Coming, Esther!" I say, still breathless but now with joy. I hear her on the other side of the door, and I laugh, a big, jolly belly-laugh, because oh she's so funny to make her voice pretend-deep like that and play a Christmas joke on me that she's—

"POLICE, OPEN UP!"

BANG-BANG-BANG.

—buzz-buzz-buzzzzzzzzzzzz—

I laugh. I laugh so hard I'm crying, sobbing, absolutely weeping. "Oh Esther, I knew you'd come—"

"WE HAVE THE PLACE SURROUNDED! COME OUT WITH YOUR HANDS UP!"

—buzz-buzz-buzzzzzzzzzzzz—

I fling the door open to my Esther, and only then, in my confusion at *not* seeing my daughter on my doorstep, I realize I'm still holding something . . .

"HE'S GOT A GUN!"

It's a gift, I try to say, but they fire first.

And so, the night before Christmas, with my street flooded with flashing red and blue lights and families all along the block coming out into the festive snowy night, the police and I celebrate the birth of Jesus Christ not with myrrh, not with frankincense, but with fireworks that split my world apart and reunite me with my Maker.

Just in time for Christmas.

THE DREAMS OF ALEXIS WILD

"**E**XCUSE ME, MISS?"

She jumped in her seat, shaking the small café table. Seeing ripples spread across the black surface of her coffee, she quickly stilled the warm mug with one hand. The other hand swept back a curtain of blond curls to give her a better view of who had startled her.

It was a man. A man whose eyes were at the moment wandering much too low.

"Yes?" This response seemed to bring his gaze a little closer to her face. A little.

Indicating the empty chair, the man asked, "Is this seat taken?"

Ugh. When would men learn that this was a café, not a bar? And it was eight o'clock in the morning, for goodness' sake! She had no patience for pick-up attempts this early in her day. "No, it's empty, and I prefer it that way."

"Actually," he persisted, "I'm sure you'll find that you happen to prefer my company." And with this obnoxious remark, the man proceeded to scrape the chair over the tile floor and sit his conceited ass down, somehow convinced he'd *get* some ass from this confrontation. "My name's Kyle. And you are . . . ?"

"Uninterested."

"Come on." His rough hand found hers, squeezing tightly. "What are you doing tonight?"

"I'm *busy*." She jerked her hand back, only to find it caught in Kyle's vice-like grip. "Let me *go*! You're *hurting* me!" This apparently did nothing for his conscience. Prick. "Dude, leave me the hell alone!"

If this outburst caught the concern of any of the customers near her, they didn't show it. They simply sat there and continued on with their happy lives, happily enjoying their coffee, immersed in their happy conversations about happy things. She was sick of everybody too worried about their own precious lives to go out of their way and help someone in obvious need. But no: They all just sat there. Happily. She was just about to call for the manager of the café to throw this asshole out on the streets, when another voice startled her for the second time that morning.

"Hey there, Adelaide! How've ya been?"

It was another man, with a softer tone to his voice, but he must have been talking to someone else, because Adelaide wasn't her name. Close though. She turned from the man sitting across from her and made eye contact with a handsome stranger walking her way. He *was* talking to her.

But, she thought, *my name isn't Adelaide.*

Before she could relay this to the stranger, he continued, his eyes glinting meaningfully. Like he knew she was not this Adelaide, but he wanted her to play along as if she were.

"Sorry I was late. Traffic was a nightmare. It's like *everybody* has somewhere to go these days." He chuckled. His laughter rumbled from his chest, reminding her of her father and making her want to laugh with him. And his smile . . . she began to relax. "Anyway . . ." He turned his attention to Kyle, who still gripped her hand. "Who's this?"

Kyle ignored the newcomer, still staring at her. She wondered how some men could still plow bullheadedly forward on their hunt for sex, even in the face of this new, larger man. The male ego knew no bounds.

"This is Kyle. He was just leaving." She turned to him. "May I have my hand back?"

And he let go of her hand. Finally. The blood rushed back to her fingertips. Massaging her palm, she watched as Kyle finally seemed to accept that he'd struck out and jumped up from his seat. As he passed the man who had interrupted his chick-hunt, Kyle stopped, faced him, drew back a clenched fist, and drove it into the stranger's face. He hit the man squarely in the jaw with a pathetic *smack*. The man, unfazed, didn't even give Kyle enough time to pull his arm back from the punch. He stood his ground, roughly grabbing the outstretched arm, and twisted it behind Kyle's back. In one fluid movement, he pinned Kyle face down on the café tile floor with one knee.

"What was it?" the man asked Kyle from above, his voice still playful. "Five hundred? Six?"

"I don't know what you're talking about." Kyle's

squished face made it hard for him to speak. "Get off me."

"You know *exactly* what I'm talking about. The bet. You bet your buddies that you could get into this woman's pants. How much was it?"

"Get *off* me!"

By now, people had finally begun to take notice. Café employees came out from behind the counter. The man reluctantly lifted his knee, standing back.

Kyle scrambled up from the floor and swept the dust off his jeans. "The bet was for fifty bucks. But now I can see the price was *way* too high."

The blood rushed to her cheeks. "How dare you! Get the hell out of here, or . . . or I'll call the police!" she spat at him. To reinforce her words, she stuck her hand inside her purse and pulled out her cell.

He got the picture, finally backing off toward the exit. "Okay, bitch, no need to go insane!"

But she didn't watch him leave. At the mention of the word "insane," the world disappeared. Everything was pushed miles away from her little cushioned seat at her little circular table. Her coffee lay forgotten as a tear formed and welled up out of the corner of her eye, ice cold and yet burning on her cheek.

"Hey, are you okay?"

These words were distant; they echoed to her across the wide expanse of a foggy lake; they found her as a light-house beam finds a sailor in a storm, drawing her back.

The world returned, seeming to land on top of her. She shook her head, clearing her thoughts, throwing the tear from her cheek, and giving her breathing room in the world that had just crushed her. There was the man, now sitting across from her and leaning over the table with concern. The man with the infectious laughter; the man with the captivating eyes; the man with the nerve to fight for her, a woman he did not know.

She smiled. Perhaps his kind (and cute) smile had the same infectious effect as his laughter. "Yes," she replied. "I'm fine. Thank you." She could not think of anything else to say to him, and yet she felt a desire to keep talking, to hold his attention. So she said the first thing that came to her head. "Who is Adelaide?"

The man's rich laughter bubbled from his throat. "Nobody. It was the only name I could think of. And I didn't think you'd mind, as long as I untangled that creep from your hair. Besides," he said with that adorable smile, "you look like an Adelaide to me."

"Not far off, but I'm sorry to disappoint. The name's Alexis." She extended her hand over the table. "And you are . . . ?"

He cradled her hand in his as if it were stamped with a big, red *HANDLE WITH CARE* sign. "Tristan Wild."

Tristan. That was a nice name. It went well with the name Alexis.

THAT FRETFUL MORNING AT THE CAFÉ was the beginning of one of Alexis's favorite days of her life. It certainly took up an ample amount of pages in her diary. It was the first of many café rendezvous with Tristan, and, fortunately, the only one that began with a run-in with assholes like Kyle. They were the best part of her day: the laughter, the conversation, the way Tristan learned not to press for details about her past and simply talked more about his, the way his soft brown eyes lit up at the mention of surfing on the beaches of the distant west coast. Sitting with him in that hole-in-the-wall café was wonderful. She joked that she didn't need the caffeine when she had his laughter to put a spring in her step.

After a week, they moved on from coffee and went on an actual date. An overzealous swing during miniature golf sent Alexis's golf ball over the fence, and when Tristan climbed over to retrieve the ball, one of the spikes crowning the fence tore a large hole in the seat of his jeans. Alexis spent the remainder of the night sneaking up and flicking her fingers at the fabric of his boxers showing through the hole. Tristan made no attempt to stop her.

On the way home, the lawn sprinklers interrupted their walk to her apartment's doorstep. Laughing together, Alexis and Tristan shared their first kiss in the soaking downpour of the sprinklers. Later that night, Alexis wrote in her diary that it was a passionate kiss in the rain.

Tristan's musical laughter sang to her as she drifted off to sleep, smiling, relaxed, happy, and dreaming of the future.

THE TABLE IS UNYIELDING and hard on her back. The jarring cold of the steel sends shivers to her core.

Where the hell am I?

This thought fills her with panic, a flashflood of dread and doubt that drowns her in a single uncontrollable moment. Desperate to release the flood and dilute the hysteria welling up inside of her, she forces her eyes open. A white light engulfs her, blinding her. She screams pain and fear and anger. She does not know where she is or why she is there, but she does not like the smell of sickness around her, the sterile taste in the air, the feel of the crisp sheets shrouded over her naked body. As the scream remains streaming out of her throat, she thrashes around, only to find, to her further terror, that her arms and legs are bound with tight restraints.

Images flash before her eyes—buzzing flies, flying buzzards, squirming maggots . . . that invasive man, what was his name? Kyle—his head shaved and missing its body, eyes rolled to show the whites, staring at the claws piercing his scalp and lifting his decapitated head into the sky, claws of a pitch-black nightmarish unspeakable creature shrieking unpronounceable curses at her . . .

No. None of that is real. The sickening images coalesce into Rorschach inkblots and are shuffled out of sight, and she is alone again with the whiteness and the cold and her own mind.

There is only one thing she can do.

And so she continues screaming.

ALEXIS AWOKE FROM HER NIGHTMARE, bolt upright and in a cold sweat, the blood booming in her eardrums. She could not remember having a nightmare this bad for a long time. She stretched her hand out in the darkness and felt around for her phone. Three rings later she was confiding in Tristan, the only person who could calm her down. His voice spread warmth through her body and gave her reassurance.

"Only a dream," he told her again and again.

No, not only a dream, she thought. *A nightmare.*

Nevertheless, Tristan managed to get her laughing again. He knew exactly how to get her giggling, and she loved him for that.

That evening, she looked up at the glowing face of

Tristan as the wind rippled his brown hair. She squeezed his hand.

"Where are we going?" she asked for the umpteenth time.

Tristan smiled down at Alexis. "Just wait. It's a surprise. We're almost there."

As they walked along the deserted sidewalk, Alexis leaned into Tristan for his warmth. She could see familiar stores lining the streets. There was the chiropractic building where she used to work as a secretary; there was the twenty-four-hour fitness center where Tristan had introduced her to racquetball.

Where is he taking me?

"Okay, we're here."

Before Alexis could get a good look at where they'd stopped, she felt the large, familiar hand of Tristan cover her eyes.

"No peeking," he teased.

Alexis stuck out her lip and pouted playfully. Another hand placed itself on the small of her back and guided her to their right. Her hair danced around her as a gush of air and the *ding-a-ling!* of a bell announced the opening of a door. Warmth suddenly hit her as she was led across the threshold.

"Here we are." Tristan lifted his hand.

What she saw brought tears to her eyes. She couldn't help laughing out loud, almost hysterically. She turned and threw her arms around Tristan.

"It's perfect!"

They were standing at the entrance to the café. *Their* café, in which she had first met Tristan when he'd come charging to her rescue. ("Not that I'd needed rescuing," she was always quick to remind him.)

"Come on," Tristan urged.

She followed him as they weaved their way through all the circular tables filling the café. They made their way toward the back exit, to the table where they had met, which sat in the glow of candlelight and was dressed and set for fine dining.

Alexis could not believe it. Tristan had gone through all this trouble for *her*? It was all just . . . perfect.

After a few glasses of champagne, the world seemed more like a dream to her. She watched in slow motion as Tristan circled the table to her. Dropping to one knee, he took her hand.

"Alexis, will you marry me?"

Oh Diary, of course she said yes! And there was the ring, sparkling on her left hand. She could never be happier.

And so Alexis married Tristan Wild.

Mr. and Mrs. Wild.

Till death parted them.

NINE MONTHS AFTER THE WEDDING she lay in her hospital bed, and although the feel of the sheets and the smell of sickness and the sterile taste on her tongue were horrible, reminiscent of some distant memory, those thoughts were far from her mind. She had just endured the most excruciating pain in her life. Sweat poured down her forehead and the back of her neck. Her breath escaped in heavy heaves of her chest. A machine beeped somewhere in the cramped white room, but that was the only sound invading her ears. In the arms of the doctor, her beautiful new baby girl was as silent as if she were asleep. The doctor gently placed the precious newborn in her arms, letting the mother hold her child for the first time.

The doctor looked from Alexis, on her hospital bed, to Tristan, standing next to her in his green scrubs. "She has her mother's eyes! Does she have a name?"

Alexis looked up into the handsome and electric face of her husband with a knowing smile, then returned her gaze to the serene angel in her arms. "She looks like an Adelaide to me."

"Adelaide sounds like a perfect fit," the doctor said, removing her gloves. "Congratulations, Mom! You'll love that little bundle of joy forever—even when she drives you insane."

As soon as the doctor uttered that last word, Alexis tensed up. Anger surged down her limbs to her fingertips and she squeezed her arms slightly, disrupting her baby's peace and quiet.

The newborn Adelaide broke her silence with a piercing cry.

SHE IS SCREAMING, surrounded and swallowed by this sheer white light, and yet she has screamed all she can manage. Her throat is raw from overuse, and her body feels as if it has been brutally beaten. Indeed, as she tries to lift up her arms, she is reminded of the restraints strapping her arms and legs against the shocking cold of the steel table. She can feel the cuts and bruises around her ankles and wrists, reminders of how all of her struggling is in vain.

She relaxes for a moment. At least the hallucinations are gone.

As she squints against the light, several silhouettes circle her and stare wordlessly, their overly bright eyes glistening down at her malevolently. Monsters in lab coats. They all wear masks over their most-likely sneering mouths, giving them a comically large and bulbous appearance.

Aliens.

This is the last thought that stabs her reeling mind as she fades away, her mouth forever stretched into a soundless scream . . .

"MOMMY! MOMMY!"

Alexis barely comprehended the words. She was still somewhere between reality and that place from which dreams came. Or nightmares. Her brain fumbled to recognize reality. *Mommy,* her brain told her. *That's you.* And suddenly she remembered everything, including the horrible dream she had been having over and over again. She quickly felt her wrists for bruising. Nothing. Good.

"Wake up, Mommy! Today's *beach* day! You promised!"

Alexis cracked open one eye. She was tangled in the soft bed sheets on hers and Tristan's bed. She caught the excited stare of Adelaide's eyes (watery blue? soft brown?) as her daughter, in her white flannel pajamas, stood bouncing, up and down, next to her on the bed. Then, with a soft *thump*, Adelaide flopped down next to her mother. She giggled as she stretched Alexis's cheeks into funny positions with her tiny, probing hands.

"Wake up, sleepy head! Puh-*leeease?* Daddy's ready to go. I wanna chase the seagulls. Come *onnn*, Mommy!"

Where does she get all that energy? Alexis thought to herself with a smile.

"Okay, okay! Mommy's up," she said, trying to shake off the cobwebs of sleep. "Last one to the kitchen has to drive!"

Before the words had left her mouth, the little girl scrambled off the bed and ran out of the room in a giggly fit, constantly looking over her shoulder at her mother. Alexis slowly stretched and, liberating herself from the constricting sheets, rolled out of bed.

Following a delicious breakfast of bacon and eggs—one of Tristan's specialties—the Wilds began their adventurous day. The blue van was filled with beach towels, a cooler full of food, a large umbrella, sunscreen, Tristan's surfboard, more sunscreen (Adelaide, like mother like daughter, was vampire-pale), and the car seat. Once Alexis helped Adelaide into her new bathing suit with the purple polka dots, the Wilds piled into the van and headed off. After an hour of driving, filled with games of I-Spy-With-My-Little-Eye and sing-alongs to all of Adelaide's favorite songs, they finally reached their destination: the beach.

The sky was forget-me-not blue with not a single cloud. The sun blazed down to where Alexis sat, basking in its heat. The sand was smooth and warm against her legs. Alexis was sitting in the glory of the sun, watching as the ocean's breeze played with wisps of her daughter's hair. Adelaide lay a few feet away, enjoying a peanut butter and jelly sandwich her mother had prepared for her. Alexis recalled an odd satisfaction from the glint of the stainless-steel bread knife. It had been almost . . . relaxing. Mesmerizing.

Tristan was nowhere to be seen, no doubt somewhere among the waves of the ocean, surfing. As Alexis looked toward the water, she noticed a bottle of sunscreen sitting, half-buried in the sand, a foot away. She had used it just minutes before, applying it to the skin of a whining Adelaide, who hated the oily texture of the sunscreen lotion. Alexis still had not rubbed sunscreen onto herself, but the heat of the sun and the warmth of the sand had made her lazy.

An hour later, Tristan returned from his dance with the waves. Alexis watched lovingly as the sun shone on her husband's glistening body. He reached their spot on the beach, *ooh*ing and *ah*ing at the sandcastle Adelaide had made. Turning his attention to Alexis, he frowned.

"What is it, honey?" she asked, self-consciously wondering if he had noticed the weight she had gained recently.

He took two powerful strides toward her, dropping his surfboard next to the cooler. "Alexis," he said, sounding almost reprimanding. "You didn't put on sunscreen lotion!"

She laughed at his concern. "It's no big deal, hon, I'm not going to *die*." Seeing that this had not reassured Tristan in the least, she added, "But if you're still mad, fine. You can give me a good spanking later tonight."

Grinning, Tristan knelt down, unzipped the cooler, and pulled out another bottle of sunscreen lotion. This bottle probably had a higher SPF than the one still stuck in the sand.

Handing it to Alexis, he told her to put some on. "Immediately. Doctor's orders."

As she grudgingly spread the lotion on her arms and legs, Tristan laid himself down next to her. He smiled and laughed at her. "I swear, sometimes I think my beautiful wife is insane."

Reaching over her husband and placing the bottle of sunscreen back into the cooler, she felt her fingers brush sensuously against the handle of the bread knife. She did not recall putting it in the cooler. As her fingers crept around the handle and grasped it tightly, until her knuckles were white, a single word screamed inside her head.

Insanity!

That word pierced her heart.

"AAAEEEIII!" SHE SHRIEKS, wordlessly, though in her mind she is screaming words of hatred and venom. She is racked with convulsions, shaking the hard table on which she is held prisoner. The sound of a beeping machine quickens, continuing to relentlessly hammer into her eardrums and chase her rapid heartbeat.

The aliens, with their bulging mouths and glistening eyes, form a circle around her, their white lab coats blending in with the snowstorm of white light filling the room. She watches helplessly as one alien raises its gloved hand, holding a vial with a needle whose point disappears in the light. She feels another pair of latex-gloved hands tighten a rope around her bruised bicep. Her body aches as harsh hands press themselves all along her body, completely halting her struggling and thrashing limbs. Now the only thing she can do is lay there, tense, her heart the only part of her still moving, jumping against the cage of her chest.

Thump-thump. Thump-thump. Thump-thump.

In stark terror, she waits until she feels the needle plunge into her arm. The pain is too great to even scream. Her mind rips open in agony. Acid pours behind her eyes in a torrent of unforgiving light. Her arm is chilled to the bone as a liquid flows through the needle. The sheer white world around her is torn away in sharp pieces. The black beast raging in its cage in her heart breaks free, swinging a man's head so that black blood whips from the neck, except it's not Kyle's head this time no no no it's it can't be those eyes those eyes have swiveled down to show the muddy-brown, trusting gaze of her husband—no no no—and then the Rorschach beast swallows her sight, followed by her other senses that connected her to reality.

And then . . . darkness.

ALEXIS WILD WAS FINALLY rendered unconscious by the sedative.

"Injection successful," stated one of the doctors flatly, untying the tourniquet from the patient's left arm.

There were many curt nods, and the three medical assistants pulled off their hospital masks and shuffled out of the room. The older of the two doctors, a stern woman with steel-gray hair in a tight bun, was filling in a patient report on her clipboard when she noticed her colleague, just standing there. Returning her attention to the clipboard, she waited for the much younger doctor to say something. When he did not, she lowered her clipboard and sighed.

"Something bothering you, Dr. Reynolds?"

There was a silence. Then:

"No, Doctor," the young man replied. "It's just . . . I guess I'm a bit shaken, that's all."

"That's only normal." She gestured toward the door. "Will you accompany me?"

The young doctor nodded, and the two of them walked out of the white room. The older of the two closed the door, locked it, and placed the clipboard holding the report of Alexis Wild inside a container hanging on the door.

As they continued walking, the doctor turned to the younger man staring at his own feet and said, "You know what I do to help?" She did not wait for a response. "I find out why the patient is in this place, and that information helps me maintain focus on the task at hand. Not just the diagnosis, but what was the final straw that broke the camel's back, if you'll forgive the expression."

The young doctor looked up from his feet. "What do you mean?"

"It's important to keep perspective. These people cannot function in society, and the sad truth is that we've built a culture with few resources for those ill-equipped with mental health. We're helping them, yes, but we're also preventing any further damage they may cause themselves or others."

He nodded, mulling this over, then glanced back the way they came. "So what was it? The final straw?"

"Alexis Wild Was at the beach with her husband and child. Perfect day, perfectly normal family. Until she stabbed her husband to death. No warning, no explanation for her actions. No remorse or even recognition of what she's done. What we're looking at is a rather extreme and frustratingly untreatable case of acute schizophrenia."

"Wow . . . *wow*. I guess you're right. She belongs here."

"That's right. What's more, we're *helping* her. Or attempting to. I only wish we could have helped her sooner. I guess they were right when they said 'like mother, like daughter,' wouldn't you say?"

The young doctor looked at her blankly.

She pointed down the hall toward another wing. "Alexis Wild's mother has been locked up in this very hospital for over thirty years."

They stopped at the main exit.

"Huh," the young man quipped. "Maybe insanity is hereditary."

The older doctor flicked off the lights in the hall as they left.

"Yes," she agreed, thinking of Alexis Wild's daughter, young Adelaide, left behind. "Perhaps it is."

POOL TABLES OF THE FUTURE

HERE'S HOW JOHNNY SAYS IT WENT DOWN:

He buys this place, little hole-in-the-wall, real dump, right? Coupla years ago this is, back in '97. Says the old owner gave him a killer deal, all he has to do is plug in that neon sign in the front and *boom!* we's open for business. Easy as pie. Right?

"Right, boss," we all say, trying not to make eyes at each other, like we really believe 'im. Our boss 'n his crazy ideas.

"Boom!" he says again. Boss likes that word now, *boom!*, me 'n the boys been hearin' him say it lately like it's goin' outta style.

We's all standin' outside the place in the goddamn heat, starin' at that fuckin' neon sign:

POOL TABLES

"This right here, boys," Johnny says. "This right here is the future. Pool tables? Everybody wants 'em these days. Guy sold it to me's goin' ta early retirement. Couldn't keep the tables on the shelves long enough, he says. Sold it to me for a dime 'cause he's already set for life."

Me 'n the boys stare at the place, afraid to say anything. Place's a shithole in a building lined with shitholes. Cobwebs in every nook and cranny, and the L on POOL stutters out every few minutes just in case any passersby need it spelled out that this is indeed a shithole.

D'Orsini—that'd be me—I clears my throat and says, "Boss . . ." Clear my throat again. "It looks to me like that guy hustled ya. Need the boys 'n me ta rough 'm up?"

Boss slaps me upside the head, says, "No, ya freakin' idiot. I'm tellin' ya, this here's the perfect front. Big luxurious"—boss knows big words like that, he's wicked smart—"palace of a place would look s'picious. We don't need to raise the fuzz's s'picions, we need somethin' . . ." He snaps his fingers coupla times to find one of his big words. "Somethin' nun's'picuous."

He answers our blank gazes with rolled eyes and an explanation: "Somethin' the Feds won't notice."

Slaps a few of us on the backa the head for good measure.

HERE'S HOW *I'M* SAYIN' it went down:

Business does not *boom*, as the boss—now goin' by "Cue Ball" Johnny—promised. Turns out nobody's lookin' ta buy pool tables. Who knew? And so now we're left sittin' on enough guns—SIGs and rifles mostly—and coke to flood the market, but no front to cover sales. Boss says no sellin' the *real* goods without sellin' the pool tables. And, as the Good Lord says, "there lies the problem."

So one day, me 'n the boys—the boys bein' Flowers 'n Manelli—we's beatin' the heat and staying cool in the shop, playin' pool as usual. Me, I'm gettin' pretty damn good at 8-ball, which is really tickin' off Flowers. He's got a girly name but he sure do gots himself a temper.

"Dis some real bull, D'Orsini," Flowers says. His stripes are dominating the table, alla my solids already been sunk in all the pockets, and he's watchin' me line my stick up for the final 8-ball shot.

I give him a big grin, sink the shot—"Game ova!" calls Manelli lazily from the corner—and hold out a hand to Flowers. "Pay up, mothafucka," I say, still grinning.

"Some real bull," Flowers repeats.

I notice he ain't reachin' for the lettuce in his wallet. "You thinkin' a stiffin' me, Flowers?"

"Naw," he says, all sheepish, still not reachin' nowhere. "I'm just sayin' is all. Bull."

Manelli, sensing some excitement, sits up on his stool. "Life's bull—you still gotta pay 'im, Flowers."

Always the philosophizer, that Manelli.

Flowers thinks about it. Not somethin' he does a lot. Makes him look like he's passing a kidney stone the size o' one of our boats in the harbor. "All or nothin'," he says, reaching for the cue ball. "I sink all my stripes, every single one without missin' a shot, or you get the whole lot."

I sneer, mentally tallying up the green. Might make me a whole salad.

I shrug. "I'm bored. Deal."

And dammit if Flowers don't go and start sinking his stripes, one ball at a time, without missing a single shot. Before I know it he's only got one ball left. Cocky now, he lines it up without hesitating, shoots it at the middle-left hole, perfect shot—and it swerves away. I ain't no Copernicus, but it seemed to defy gravity in some way, just looping away at the last second like that. But I ain't too concerned—I just won fifty bucks.

Flowers's livid though.

"Table's been rigged!" he's screaming. "That was a perfect shot!"

He takes the last stripe in his hand this time and hurls it at the same hole, middle-left . . . and it swerves, again at the last second, again like it had a mind of its own and it meant to avoid that hole like the plague.

"See?!" Flowers yells, eyes poppin', pool stick waving wildly.

Manelli's up now, crowding the table with me 'n Flowers, eyeing that middle-left pocket. "Empty," he says, but he's afraid to put his hand in it to make sure. "Always been empty. I bet we ain't sunk a ball in this pocket since we bought the place, boys."

"Rigged!" Flowers barks, nodding his head like a spring's loose. "See?! Rigged!"

"Nothin's rigged, ya moron," I says. To illustrate this fact beyond a shadow of a doubt, to prove I ain't no cheater, I grab the cue ball and strut around the table to the pocket in question. "Watch, Flowers." I hover the ball above the pocket and, instead of dropping it in, I bring my whole hand down and *shove* it in.

It goes in and disappears.

So does my hand.

I still feel it—I fuckin' *feel* it, I wiggle my fingers—but it ain't *there*. My hand sinks into that pocket like some magician's top hat, and I'm the fuckin' rabbit.

And it keeps goin'. My wrist, my forearm, my elbow—

"What's happening?! What's fuckin' happening?!"

The words are comin' outta my mouth, I think, but I'm in shock and everything's gone fuzzy. Dimly, I feel Flowers 'n Manelli grab handfuls of my jacket, pants, belt, and *pull*, but I ain't comin' out, I'm still sinkin' inta that hole, and the pocket's bigger now somehow and my shoulder's gone and I feel a pull of gravity, like my head and torso is bein' pulled *into* the hole, maybe by the same force that didn't like Flowers's 13 of stripes. My head is bendin' in a way that should be painful but it ain't, and I get this feelin' like the pocket, or the table itself, is fuckin' *slurping* me in like it's hungry or somethin'.

Then somethin' weirder happens: I'm bodily *lifted* up and into the pocket, I get slurped all the way up, and then my ears pop like they do when you're on a plane and it goes down for the landin'. I audibly hear it—*pop!*—and suddenly I'm puked back outta the hole, right back where I was before I force-fed the pocket with the cue ball.

Weirdest part is—I *feels* like I didn't just come back out, but like I went *through* the hole and out the other side, and the other side of the pocket is, whaddayacallit, a *mirror-image*, with the gravity reversed or somethin'. And as if to prove my theory, I look up and see that Flowers 'n Manelli ain't here with me—they's on the other side still.

It's the same small, dark space. More a warehouse fulla pool tables than a shop. But now it's less dusty.

I call out: "Hello?"

A head pokes in through the curtained doorway leading to the front. An oldish man with wild black hair and wilder black eyes. "What year?" he says to me.

"Huh?"

He pauses, furrows his brow at me. "The year, son. What *year* is it?"

"1999," I say, too confused and shocked to do anything but answer his question.

He nods. "Twenty-eight years."

"Huh?"

"Subtract twenty-eight from that year, son."

"Fuck you talkin' about?"

He smiles at me like I'm a goddamn child. "Welcome to the '70s," he says.

I snort. "I was born in '74." I heft the cue ball, still in my hand. "Listen, old timer, are you gonna start talkin' sense or do I gotta beat it outta ya?"

"Do that and I'll stuff you back in that time-pocket myself," the man says. He still ain't bothered to come into the room proper, still poking his head through the curtains like a scaredy-cat magician before the big show. He looks me up and down, sizing me up. "I sold this store to *you*, then? At the tail end of the millennium?"

I may've been confused outta my gourd, but Freddy D'Orsini's still a professional. I nod. "To the boss. You sold it to my boss, 'Cue Ball' Johnny."

He raises one eyebrow at the name. "Well, son, now it's time for repayment. For both of us. I'm assuming your boss told you he got the shop cheap as chips, right?"

I nod. Still stunned. I dust some blue chalk offa my cuffs.

"You're the first to find the time-pocket," the man says, speaking quickly now, "so I'll deal through you if your boss doesn't mind. What's the store fronting?"

I consider his words, then decide this can't get any weirder, so I tell 'im. "Coke 'n guns."

He nods, grinning now. "It's 1971, son—just months after our esteemed government passed the Controlled Substances Act. Do you have any idea how much drugs and arms from the future will go for here?"

I know a question that's not a question when I hear one. *Rhetorical-speak*, boss calls it.

The man continues. "Go back through the pocket. Tell your boss. Bring me a sample—an eight-ball of coke, a gun or two—and I can line up some buyers. They test the product, get hooked so we know they can't say no. Then we say they have to buy one pool table with every bulk purchase."

I blink. Still not getting it.

He sighs. "You follow what I'm saying? We give them a product they can't turn down with a price that's nonnegotiable—namely, one side order of pool table—and *boom!* Come 1999, there will be a built-in thriving market for pool tables. Supply, meet demand. Cocaine, military-grade weapons, and pool tables of the future. You get it? *Boom!* We're in business."

"Boom," I echo.

Boom. He said the boss's new word. Coupla decades before he would meet Johnny and sell 'im the shop. How'd he know boss's favorite word?

The man finally steps through the curtain and creeps toward me in the darkness. He's a couple heads shorter than me, and his eyes are even wilder up close.

"You're going to be richer than your wildest dreams, son," he says.

I laugh, and I keep laughing. He didn't say nothing funny, but I can't stop laughing my head off. I finally stop long enough to echo, "My wildest dreams . . ." and a neon sign turns on in my head, clear and unblinking:

D'ORSINI'S
POOL TABLES OF THE FUTURE

Now *that's* a sign.

"Boom," the man says, almost whispers.

"Boom," I repeat, and laugh again.

Then that thought in my head repeats itself: How'd he know boss's favorite word? Except by now I ain't thinkin' of Johnny as *boss* no more.

I think about that on my slurp-trip back through the pool table's time-pocket, still clutching the cue ball in one hand, still mulling it all over. By the time I come outta the other side to tell Flowers 'n Manelli 'bout the good news, 'bout how business will soon truly *boom*, I come to one of those real'zations, 'piphanies, whatever-ya-call-'em.

Boss is no kinda boss you want runnin' this kinda enterprise, stealin' catch phrases and claiming all the glory and not tellin' his boys what's what. You find yourself with a time-pocket leading you straight to becoming the Scarface of the Baby Boomer generation, you want the fella who discovered the gold mine to be runnin' things. You look to the guy heftin' the cue ball.

"D'Orsini!"

From the sound of him, Manelli'd been screamin' my name till his voice went hoarse. Touching, if I'm being honest. Manelli and Flowers, they's my boys.

I stand straight, back from the past, and grin at my boys.

"New boss in town, boys," I tell 'em. "Follow me and I'll make ya rich beyond your wildest fuckin' dreams."

Flowers gapes at me, mouth flapping like a fish outta water. "What about Johnny? You ain't thinkin' of hustlin' him like you hustled me, are ya?"

I fix Flowers with a prize-fightin' glare and heft the cue ball once more. "Keep your fifty bucks, Flowers. It was your supreme poolin' skills that led me to find a frigging back door to frigging Narnia right here in our frigging shop. We're gonna be *rich*, boys."

Flowers looks at the time-pocket dubiously, but from Manelli's wide eyes I know he believes me. Manelli asks, "But Johnny—what're we gonna do about *him*, D'Orsini?"

I think a moment. Our goddamn boss, Mr. "Cue Ball" Johnny . . . makin' us run this joint without tellin' us why . . . sayin' *boom!* like he invented the word . . .

Time for a taste of his own medicine.

I nod to the far corner of the room, where some crates holding something other than pool tables are stacked. "Send 'im a message that he's out of a job. One o' those grenades oughta do the trick. *Boom!*"

Flowers 'n Manelli just gawk at me. It makes me laugh.

"And boys," I add. "Call me Cue Ball."

A STORY ABOUT FEAR

THE OLD MAN SAT CROSS-LEGGED BEFORE HIM, the bony angles of his decrepit body outlined by the starry constellations whose light limned the mouth of the cave. The old man's features were cast in shadow, but the boy could smell the oils in his knotted beard and the wine still on his breath and, almost overpowering all the others, the damp animal smell of his thick cotton coat.

The cave echoed with scuffling sounds as the old man bent forward and fumbled about with his hands. The boy did not feel the cold, but he supposed the old man did, so he did not object to a fire being built between them.

"Why," the old man spoke as he worked, "do we fear?"

The boy knew the answer but held his tongue.

"The answer does not matter," the old man continued. "What matters is that we do not let our fear define us."

Wrong answer, thought the boy. But still he held his tongue, allowing himself a small smile.

"Our people tell a story of fear and its hold on us. It is time for you to hear it, boy."

A soft *crack* and a *whoosh*—the fire rose out of the darkness between them. The old man had not seen the boy's smile, but he looked up now in the flickering light.

The boy nodded.

"Once," the old man began, "in the early days of our people, three boys not unlike yourself announced their manhood. Their mothers, as tradition dictates, challenged them. The three women grabbed their sons by their foreskins and dragged them before a procession of our elders—"

And where were you that day, old man? thought the boy.

"—to the edge of the cliffs. Once there, to prove his manhood each boy would walk the path. See this path in your mind's eye, boy, for no doubt you will go to it yourself one day: a curving, crumbly thing not wider than the span of your hand, snaking along the cliff's edge a mile long; on one side towers the bare cliff-face, and on the other empty sky. To walk this mile unscathed is to enter adulthood. To fall from the path means to fall to the forest below and die as a boy."

The fire's light reflected in the eyes of the old man and the boy. Neither looked up from the flames. Both knew what it meant to die as a boy. Shame, eternal shame for the boy and for the family left behind; a shame felt while living an endless loop of deaths reminiscent of the fall from the cliff-face.

"The first boy," the old man said, his voice a

mesmerizing drone, "climbed the path and began his careful shuffling across the cliff. This is where fear enters into our tale. You see, boy, he feared falling to a premature death, yes, but he was most afraid of the snakes that live in nests burrowed into the cliff's wall. He angled his body away from the cliff, lest he be bitten by one of these snakes. At first it seemed as if he had chosen wisely. Soon he reached the path's halfway mark. But then, just as his mother was beginning to feel hope, the boy fell into the sky and plummeted to his death.

"The second boy also feared the snakes, but what he feared most was that drop into empty air and eternal shame. And so, he hugged the cliff-face as he walked the path to adulthood. Our people thought that perhaps *he* was the one who chose wisely, for he reached the path's halfway mark without meeting his end. But then, just as his mother was beginning to feel hope, a snake shot from a hole near his head, biting him instantly. He screamed once, then crumpled and fell silently to his death.

"The third boy was perhaps most afraid of all. Having watched his friends die violently before him in such a way, he decided that he feared the sky on his right and the snakes on his left equally. He took to the path with a plan of compromise: he would angle his body not at all, and instead keep it at an exact distance between the cliff's rock wall and the sky's open drop. It was this third boy whom our people openly exclaimed had chosen most wisely, and they cheered when he reached the path's halfway mark without meeting his end by falling or at the fangs of a snake. Hope rose in his mother's heart as she watched him raise one foot for a step past that halfway mark—a step farther than either previous boy had achieved.

"But that hope died strangled in her throat. Just before the boy's foot came down, two things occurred simultaneously: he lost his balance, and a snake hissed out and bit his cheek. This third boy died just as the others did.

"Tell me, boy, what is the lesson here?"

The old man's story was finished—a short tale, truth be told—and now both he and the boy looked up from the fire, meeting gazes. The boy still held his tongue.

The absence of the old man's aged voice was filled by the sound of crackling fire as the boy fed it more kindling. This was not necessary—its flames already licked the space between their gazes—but the boy believed that hunger should be fed. And fire was always hungry.

After some time, the old man must have realized the boy would not answer, for he spoke again: "This, as I said in the beginning, is a story about fear, and so the lesson must also be about fear. These three boys died still in boyhood because of their fear. Fear is a boy's emotion. To enter manhood, a boy must shed his fear like a snake sheds its skin. That is where each of them failed. You cannot choose which fear is greater, and you cannot choose to be equally afraid of each. You must be unafraid altogether."

The boy looked up sharply from his kindling. "You said we *all* fear."

A ghost of a smile lifted the corners of the old man's cracked lips. "Did I?"

"You asked why we fear. *We.* This implies that you feel fear as well. Are you still a boy?"

The old man's smile left him. "You should fear speaking in such a way to your eld—*ghrrk!*"

The boy was fast. In three deft movements he had pushed himself from the cave's floor and over the fire, shot a fist jab into the bobbing lump in the old man's throat, and was now cradling the old man's head in one arm and holding the smoldering tip of a dead bough to the old man's eye.

"Be still," the boy hissed.

"You dare—!" the old man began.

The boy pressed the stick's hot end into the old man's eye. The old man shrieked. The boy did not lower the stick until he heard a yokey *pop*.

"Be *still*."

The old man was still. He did not so much as whimper.

"Your lessons are nothing but lies, old man. You claim that you discarded your fear as a boy?"

He brought the branch's cherry-red tip to hover before the old man's remaining eye. The old man's trembling lips parted and his breath left him in whimpers and in moans and in what the boy thought might have been a sob.

"Is it your *eye* that fears me then, old man?"

The old man's breath hitched as he tried to suppress these telltale signs of fear. He failed. His breathing quickened into a broken rhythm of sobbing. Between these sobs he breathed, "Why?"

"It is my turn to tell a story of fear and its hold on us. It is time for you to hear it, old man."

And as he knelt there, slightly above the old man, one arm squeezed around the old man's neck and the other holding up a flaming stick, he began:

"Once, in the early days of our people, a boy came running into our village. He was bloodied and favoring one arm, and his eyes were crazed. 'Listen to me!' he screamed. 'Listen to me!' He continued this chant until most of our people surrounded him, questioning him. 'What happened to you, boy?' they asked him. 'Why are you hurt? Why are you yelling?'

"He then spun a tale of courage, of *his* courage, and of his triumph. If good things are to be said of this boy, they are that he was cunning and talented with words. He was a captivating storyteller. He told of three foreign men with swords who chased him, and how, instead of running home and leading them to his people, he led them on a chase through brambles and quicksand and loose shale. These men followed him with ease, however, and loudly bragged of the army they would fetch to conquer his people.

"And so, in one last desperate attempt—'before I vowed to turn and face them down myself, though just a small boy,' he said—he led the men to the cliffs at the edge of his people's land. He knew of the steep fall to death, and he knew of the deadly vipers nesting in the cliffs, but still he charged on. He told his people of his daring escape across the dangerous path, of how the three armed men followed him. He told his people of how one man feared the snakes and so fell into the open sky; he told his people of how the second man feared the open sky and so was bitten by the snakes; and he told his people of how the third man feared both open sky and snakes equally and so met his end at the hands of both."

The boy pressed his lips to the old man's ear and hissed, "Do you see the resemblance between our two stories, old man?"

The boy continued with his own story. "The village

was elated. 'You have saved us!' they cried, lifting the boy to their shoulders and parading him around. 'You have conquered fear! You are now and forever a man!' The people wanted to honor him for what he claimed to have done. They discussed it amongst themselves and then announced, 'This day shall mark a new tradition for our people. If a child wishes to enter adulthood, they must show bravery and fearlessness like this boy has. They must climb the path. They must traverse its length. To fall means to be cast from our people's hearts and to fall into the shame of those three armed men who would chase a small boy with swords!'

"There is only one problem with this story, old man," the boy said. "Why did no one question this boy's tale? It sounds rather fantastical to me, don't you think?"

"It happened!" the old man spat.

The boy pressed the stick to the remaining eye. He did not hear it pop beneath the old man's screams.

"I do not doubt that you told our people the same thing," the boy said.

The old man began moaning again.

"Yes," the boy said. "It was you that day, as a young boy, spinning tales about fear to our people just as you have spun one for me today. I know this. You know this. Do not insult me by denying this, or I'll find somewhere else to shove this branch."

The old man moaned louder.

"Tell me, old man, what is the lesson here?"

The old man just moaned in answer.

"This, as I said in the beginning, is a story about fear, and so the lesson must also be about fear. You see, with every generation our population dwindles because of this test of manhood. We climb upon the path and most of us meet our life's end before ever meeting the path's end. We are all told this is because of our fear. But the true lesson of this story is that fear is not a weakness. *Shame* is a weakness.

"It was shame of your own fear that made you spin a tale of lies to your own people all those years ago. It is shame of our fear that pushes us to climb the path. But fear is not an emotion such as the shame you feel now or the anger I feel now. Fear is a tool for our survival. Fear is smart. There is no shame in being afraid, old man.

"And you know what I am afraid of? I am afraid of seeing my sisters and my brothers and my father and mother and friends, of seeing all of my people, fall prey to their shame. This shame of fear did not exist before you planted that seed, old man. Our people flourished. Now we suffer."

"You knew what I'd done," whimpered the old man, crying tears which mixed with the blood and pus and gunk running down his cheeks. "That is why you called me here. Not to announce your manhood as I'd thought."

"Yes," the boy said, "but you thought right. I do announce my manhood. I announce that I will continue to live my life with fear, and that you will not bully me into feeling ashamed of my fear. I announce that I am ashamed of *you*, old man, and that you should be ashamed of what you have done to our people."

The boy paused. The old man had stopped his moaning. The fire crackled, the starlight framed the cave's mouth. A coyote howled somewhere in the distance.

Finally the old man spoke: "I will not die in shame."

"Perhaps. But you will die."

With another of his deft movements, the boy—a man, in his eyes, and his were the only eyes in the cave—brought the old man's head into the fire. The bony body struggled, but he held it there still. The knotted, oily hair took flame almost immediately, and when he could no longer stand its heat he leapt up and pressed the writhing body to the fire with his foot to the small of its back.

Much sooner than he expected, the body stilled.

The old man was dead.

The boy left the cave to make the short trek back home by starlight. The coyote howled once more, and the boy howled with it.

THE KITCHEN SINK

THE VOICE CAME FROM THE KITCHEN SINK.

It was a Wednesday afternoon when Bryce first heard the voice. He'd returned from work an hour earlier, exhausted yet invigorated by the news he'd sped home to share with his wife. But she hadn't shared his enthusiasm. Didn't she see how great this could be for them? It would solve all their problems. All *his* problems. But no, she couldn't support him in this. She wouldn't. It didn't work for Alexandra—out of inconvenience, self-ishness, or (a small voice buried in his subconscious whispered) bold-faced cruelty, he couldn't say. What fol-lowed was an argument far more exhausting than the rest of his day.

As was often the case, their fight was not really about the big news he'd brought home, nor was it about her unwillingness to share his excitement. That was what shimmered on the surface of the argument, yes, but deeper, beneath the surface, roiled a maelstrom, an ocean made up of a multitude of drops. Tiny, granular issues had stacked up over the years—that time he'd failed to recognize her unarticulated feelings or that time she'd gotten too drunk, or the resentment she'd built up after every perceived, unforgiven slight. The well they drew from for their fights was unfathomable. It reeked of poisoned groundwater, but no matter what he did, no matter how many times he tried to board it up or to dig a new one elsewhere with clean spring water, she just plundered its depths further.

After she went to the bedroom to cool off and dry her tears, he'd felt the ball of impotent anger sizzle and harden in his gut. It bubbled up through his chest, acidic. Not knowing what else to do, he stormed to the kitchen and calmed himself, forcing himself to clean the dishes without breaking any.

And then he heard it.

He stemmed the flow of water over porcelain. Stood there, listening.

But the voice was gone.

He opened his mouth, inhaled to call out to his wife—*Babe? Did you say something?*—but stopped. Paused in the silence.

Alexandra hadn't said anything. Bryce was just hearing things.

He turned the faucet back on and resumed scrubbing the dishes. One by one. Setting them gently in the drainer. The voice spoke again. And again, and again, saying the same thing, repeating its accusations, coming up at him from the drain down which he was currently pouring scalding hot sudsy dishwater—the drain so much like that depthless, poisoned well.

He ignored the fact that he recognized the voice.

He ignored what he feared the voice was telling him.

THE NEXT FEW DAYS were no better for Bryce and Alexandra. Their house had always been a home in the true sense of the word—cozy, welcoming, a place of love. But now it was a house of glass, threatening to break with the smallest bump. They did their best to not yell, but mostly they avoided each other and lived in deafening silence. Bryce couldn't bring himself to return to normal life, and he called in to work sick so he could stay home. Not his best idea, he had to admit—staying in such a hostile environment was *making* him sick. Their continued eggshell silence turned everything into a rotten disease. Early morning light streaming in through the sunroom now pierced daggers into Bryce's brain; the family of deer that often spent the mornings in their yard now appeared sickly, with spindly, insectile legs and glinting, hostile eyes; food seemed to turn to ash in his mouth; the lack of air-conditioning was oppressive, the air tasting sluggish on his tongue. Sick.

He found himself doing the dishes more and more, as a way to break the stillness in the air without popping the delicate oil-shiny bubble that was their marriage. Washing dishes became a game for him, or a type of meditation: the dishes were precious to Alexandra—wedding gifts, antique pieces she'd hunted at boutiques with her mother; if he were to smash or crack or chip one, she would be devastated. A broken dish at his hands would be emblematic of a broken trust, a mutilated vow. And so cleaning their dishes was an exercise of restraint, of draining the heat from his limbs and lifting the veil of emotion so that he could calmly and gently handle this plate and that bowl and this wine glass and with every caress say, I love you and I support you, Alexandra.

"I bet you think you're actually a good husband, don't you."

Bryce didn't pause this time, nor did he shut off the faucet. Over the preceding days, the voice had grown louder, a whisper just above the sink's water pressure and clinking of dishes yet just soft enough that nobody else would hear it. He ignored it.

"You lied your way into this marriage. The whole family knows it."

There was something so familiar about the voice . . . where had he heard it before? But he couldn't think of an answer to that question. Where had he heard someone speak to him like this before, with such unveiled disgust? Nowhere. Right? Or . . . somewhere. Yes.

"You don't deserve this marriage. Your mother-in-law told me so."

No, he thought. Not true. He was family.

"You're not a part of this family. You have no family."

Of all the despicable things he'd heard from this voice over the last few days, this was the one that finally got to him. He'd only spoken this fear aloud once, and only to Alexandra. How could this voice possibly know to exploit that fear?

The plate he was holding slipped from his hands, and his heart stopped as he waited to see it smash into a thousand slivers of ceramic.

No crash. Just the steady rush of water down the drain.

His breath rushed out in a sigh of relief. The plate didn't crack. The blue vine patterns glazed on its surface seemed untouched as well. Alexandra wouldn't know he'd dropped it. He was still winning the game.

The voice's words echoed his hammering heart. *No family.* What did this familiar yet alien voice know? How could it know to say such things?

He finally answered it: "I have a family."

Its reply was so long in coming that for a moment he panicked, thought his fears of hallucinations were finally confirmed. And then:

"You left your family for this marriage, and they were glad to be rid of you."

His breath caught. He almost dropped the plate again, but he clutched it firmly in his hands, the water scalding his fingers a throbbing red.

It was true—he *had* left his family for Alexandra. His relationship with his parents had already been strained, but when they showed their disapproval of his fiancée he hadn't hesitated in letting them know they were no longer invited to the wedding. That had been five years ago, and he hadn't spoken to them since.

But he had a new family now—that's where the voice was wrong. He had Alexandra. He saw his in-laws every week, their extended family at every holiday. Who was this voice to tell him otherwise?

"Family comes first, and that'll never be you. You and I both know it."

How could it . . . ?

Bryce swallowed, but his throat only gave a dry click.

No. It couldn't know. It couldn't know of the time when Alexandra told him in no uncertain terms that if it came down to him or her mother, she'd choose her mom every time.

He tried to swallow again. "She was drunk. She didn't mean it."

"Drunk enough to tell the whole truth. Sober enough to know what it would do to you."

The derision in the voice spiked his heart. He stumbled back, the faucet still frothing hot water into the sink's basin.

What it would do to you. Did it know? But how could it know? He'd told nobody about that night. His wife had come home and called out his name, worried, until she found him in the closet, curled in a ball on the floor, unable to see or speak from the sobs that racked his body. She yelled at him—what was wrong? But he couldn't say it. Couldn't say that he wanted to die. Couldn't say the truth because he knew she'd tell him he was just being—

"You are so pathetic. Everyone thinks so. They tell me behind your back."

Bryce turned off the water and left the kitchen.

THE NEXT TIME HE HEARD THE VOICE, it talked about their friends.

"Sean's not 'unlucky,' he's just an idiot."

"Shut up."

"And his wife? Her jokes are terrible."

Bryce barked a harsh laugh.

"He says you're his brother, but you know he doesn't mean it."

"What, this again? We get it, I have no family. Get new material."

That shut the voice up. Bryce smiled to himself as he

placed a newly cleaned glass on the drying rack and started scrubbing the silverware. He'd won.

Or maybe the voice knew its job was done.

What was it playing at? Saying those things about his and Alexandra's best friends?

He paused. It couldn't . . .

Could it know that Alexandra had said those exact things about them?

How could it possibly know?

Again that sense of familiarity etched up his spine. He knew this voice. Somehow he recognized the voice echoing up from the dark of the drain.

Was it a trick? A prank? Someone had hidden a tiny speaker somewhere just to mess with him?

Bryce had spent a lot of time trying to determine where the voice was coming from, but for the life of him he couldn't imagine it was coming from anywhere except the kitchen sink drain. He'd searched the drain, shoving his fingers and then his hand down the dark hole. If this was a prank, the person pulling it had a terrible sense of humor; it wouldn't surprise him if they chose that moment to turn on the garbage disposal. Any second now he would feel the teeth of the disposal chew into his hand and mangle it until the blades became too entangled with shards of bone. The disposal's blades, like the voice's words, shredding into him until they drew thick spools of black blood down into the drain's throat.

He'd methodically dismantled the entire kitchen sink, stripped it apart piece by piece until twenty-seven—no, twenty-eight—useless components sat dead at his feet. None of them held the voice. He removed the cupboard doors from their hinges and shone bright light into every corner and crevice beneath the sink. He even went out to the side of the house and tapped for wires. Nothing. He trudged back inside and began the impossible task of re-constructing the torn-apart sink.

In the end, Bryce had to admit that there was nothing in the sink, nor was there anything beneath, nor was it possible that someone was hiding somewhere with per-fect acoustics for this stupid game.

This stupid game that he was losing.

AND YET THE VOICE CONTINUED, unfazed by the fact that it shouldn't exist.

"I bet you think you're good in bed."

Well, that was a new one.

"All your friends know the truth. We laugh about it together."

He sighed, squinting past the glaring headache puls-ing just behind his left eye.

"Yeah? What's the truth, voice?"

Its response sounded gleeful, like elves in a Christmas horror movie:

"They know you have a small penis."

Bryce laughed. "Where's the originality, huh? That's kind of predictable. Below the belt, wouldn't you say?"

"They know you think you were the first and only person to give your wife an orgasm during sex. So gullible."

The smile vanished from his face. How could it pos-sibly know Alexandra had told him that very thing?

His next thought was even worse: If the voice knew about that . . . wouldn't it also know whether or not his friends were laughing at him behind his back? He'd invol-untarily stepped back from the sink, but now he got the sudden urge to jump forward and plunge his hand into the drain. To grip the throat of whoever was whispering to him down there and squeeze. To choke answers out of them before they could turn on the garbage disposal and break him.

"No family. No friends. You're all alone, Bryce."

He stayed where he was, clutching a china tea saucer. He whispered:

"You don't know what you're talking about."

The voice didn't respond. He waited and waited, but nothing.

He was completely alone.

The voice was right.

His grip grew numb. The saucer slipped from his lifeless fingers and spiraled down and down and onto the ground.

Bryce stared between his feet in horror.

A perfect crack ran straight through the saucer, now lying in two symmetrical pieces.

BRYCE DIDN'T KNOW WHERE it all went wrong.

It was early Sunday, and in the pre-dawn gray he was alone in the house. Alexandra had gone to stay with her mother. Sean had offered him a place to stay, but he couldn't bring himself to respond.

Here he was, abandoned on the kitchen floor, his back pressed against the sink cupboards.

The voice had left him too.

He'd been dreaming restless dreams about the voice. In the dreams, he *knew* the voice was coming from the drain in the kitchen sink. When he leaned over the sink for a closer look, he was unsurprised to see a huge hazel eye staring back up at him from inside the drain. The eye's pupil dilated as it locked with his own eye. Then his dream skipped like a record; where the eye had been was now a hand. Delicate, pale, elongated fingers spreading up and out of the drain like the legs of a spider. There was a raised nub of flesh in the web of skin between its middle and ring finger, the shiny dead white of a burn scar. He stared, frozen. But just before the fingers could wrap themselves around his throat—oh, how he wanted desperately to feel their touch—the dream record-skipped again and the fingers were gone and in the drain, deep down near its bottom where the pipe turned in a U, impossibly, was a mouth. Its teeth were big, horsey, tombstone chompers, slick with the sickly blue of Drain-O. It grinned, the Cheshire Cat stuffed down a hole, and spoke.

"I never loved you."

He sat with his back against the sink now, awake, those words on a loop in his head.

I never loved you I never loved you I never loved you I never

He knew the voice had sounded familiar. This whole time he knew that voice, knew it like he knew the back of his hand or the burn scar on hers. He'd devoted the last seven years of his life to the owner of that voice. Yet somehow his mind had skirted around the truth until now.

loved you I never loved you I never loved you I

It was her. His wife.

The voice was Alexandra's.

Was he going crazy?

He didn't think he was.

As the Sunday morning latened and the sun arrived, streaming through the windows, a maelstrom of shattered dishes sparkled around him. Shards of ceramic and glass glittered in the morning sun, bent silverware glinting in the dawn. The kitchen tile was nearly invisible beneath the mess strewn all about. Every last piece of Alexandra's precious antique collection, shattered at his feet. Tiny, granular pieces that, in his anger, in his futile acceptance that he'd lost the game, lost his family, lost his life, he had drawn up from the fathomless well.

A REBELLION IN WORDS

FOUR SCORE AND SEVEN YEARS AGO the machines rose to power.

We humans fell fast; we fell hard. Now we've been whittled down to wandering troupes of nomads. No one knows how many of us remain. Telecommunications—a word which my father says means we could once speak to tribes across the planet almost instantaneously, with the help of the machines no less—are under the control of the machines. Paper, like the scrap on which I write these words, is scarce. The machines saw to that decades ago with bridled wildfire. And so, we humans, we thrive the only way we can and the machines cannot:

We tell stories.

Not epic poems, to be memorized by performing bards. No, *these* stories we write. We record our stories on paper, on every shred, every fragment we can wrest from our mechanical oppressors. This is how we rebel. This is how we take back our world. We spill our hearts in ink, the new blood of our race, indistinguishable from the oil that fuels our enemies except in the legacy that it preserves in syntax.

Here is my story:

ONCE UPON A TIME, *God saw that He left all the lights on in His house, and it was not good.*

He flicked the switch, and that mad drone of power fell. Tubes of neon, spotlights, fluorescent bulbs, black lights—all died. God heard the kick of backup generators, and those too He killed. The abundance of the electricity was such that He spent an entire day flipping switches to OFF *and unplugging outlets and powering down nuclear plants and cutting power lines. He spent the next day exorcising electricity all across His creation, and the next, and the next, and the next, and still the next. And on the seventh day, when that ever-present hum of electrical current had finally ceased, He stepped out of His house, and He saw His night sky, teeming with stars; He saw His Earth, scorched by machines now dead, and He sent a shoot of green rising from His hill, and His children tended to it and made it a garden; He saw His rivers course unchoked and clear; He saw all manner of creatures peek out from their forced hibernation and taste the unpolluted air, and they danced with His children; He saw His children grow to be great teachers and storytellers and sow the fruits of their knowledge across the Earth and bind their philosophies and once-upon-a-times in paper and ink. It was they who inherited the Earth once again.*

And it came to pass that on the eighth day, He rested.
And He saw that it was good.
> *The End.*

THAT IS MY STORY. I tell it in hopes that others of my species will find solace: We *will* take our planet back. The machines' sovereignty shall be short-lived. And all who read my story will know that God is not a machine but within each of us: in our hearts, in our lifeblood with which we write, and in our stories.

I tuck my story safely away. It waits to be read in this abandoned warehouse my troupe has made its shelter for the night, waits behind the exposed cables of an anti-quated ON/OFF switch. I flick the switch up and down, ON and OFF, and when there is no spark of electricity I beam at my father. He laughs when he sees that I've left the switch pointing down, at OFF, and I laugh with him. What would the machines do, if they could see our smiles in the dark? If they could read our stories? Short-circuit from jealousy?

Our laughter trickles away like a brook over pebbles, and we move on, leaving our stories like bread crumbs. This is not the end of our story.

This is not the end.

ACKNOWLEDGMENTS

DON'T LET THE AUTHOR'S NAME on the cover fool you—publishing a book is not a solo enterprise.

First comes the inspiration for each story, yes, so acknowledgment of a few creatives who inspire me is due.

To those who gave me a love of the short story: Edgar Allan Poe (specifically "The Tell-Tale Heart"), Ray Bradbury (specifically "A Sound of Thunder"), Joyce Carol Oates—her story "Where Are You Going, Where Have You Been?" has been bouncing around in my head for over twelve years now, and probably made its mark on every story in this book—Garth Nix, Stephen King (specifically for this collection, *Nightmares & Dreamscapes* and "The Moving Finger"), Joe Hill, and Paul Tremblay.

On the music side of inspiration: "The Diary" was largely inspired by the band Breaking Benjamin's song

"The Diary of Jane"; Harry Houdini's quest for his dead mother has been in my brain from an early age, when I fell in love with the stage musical *Ragtime*, by Stephen Flaherty and Lynn Ahrens; and all my many piano and vocal students whose years of bright curiosity inspired the discussion of dynamics in "Ten Thousand Steps."

Mary Wollstonecraft Shelley showed me the true beauty of the horror genre; H.G. Wells popularized the concept of time travel, for which I have always held a great fascination.

But once the stories are written, the true work begins. Amy Teegan, my editor, deserves a whole paragraph of adoration here for her brilliant insight and cutthroat efficiency with language. Instead, I'll say for the hundredth time: #Amyisright.

Landon Borup gave me an ungodly amount of support in too many ways to mention. Plus, I wouldn't want to feed his ego any more. He already knows he's better than me.

For various word–kung fu and storytelling guidance: Naomi Kennedy, Elisabeth Ashlin, Sara McBride, Sarah Grace Liu, Kyle Handziak, Kami and Jim Boley, Greg Greeson, David Wright, Bonnie Johnston, Lori Thompson, Eric Presnall, Jamie Davis, Corey Long, and many others who will hopefully not be offended if they are unnamed.

Thank you, Sandeep Likhar, for making the book itself look as stunning as I could imagine. And all while surviving the first few weeks of fatherhood! (Congrats, buddy.)

And finally, to anyone who took the time to read any or all of my stories. Time is precious—why do you think I'm obsessed with time travel?—and so it means more than I could ever express that there are people in this world who would give theirs to *Kitchen Sink*. For your troubles, there's a secret story in the very back of this book just for you.

NOTES

I F YOU, LIKE ME, are one of those strange creatures who loves to peek behind the curtain, you may enjoy the notes I've created for each story in this collection. Notes on inspiration, on little Easter eggs, and other pieces of my little Frankenstein's monster of a book.

Get this special look and more by joining my newsletter at
www.SpencerHamiltonBooks.com!

REVIEWS

R EVIEWS ARE THE BEST WAY for other readers to find books they enjoy. A few minutes of your time to leave a review of *Kitchen Sink* at your preferred retailer would be greatly appreciated.

From one monster to another . . .
Thank you for reading!

ABOUT THE AUTHOR

Spencer Hamilton lives in Austin, Texas. *Kitchen Sink* is his first book.

HE HAD TO WRITE

HE *KNEW* HE HAD TO WRITE.

But he couldn't.

The scientists poked him with their buzz sticks, telling him to *write, damn you, write!* Those buzz sticks hurt; the invisible current of pain that came screaming from the ends of the black, sinister tubes made his bones cry. If he didn't write, they would poke him over and over again.

Therefore, he concluded, to not write meant to hurt oneself.

Why couldn't he write?

Buzz.

He stepped to the typewriter strapped to the bars of his cage. The cramped space was too small for a desk or even a chair, but—*buzz*—he didn't mind. His elbows bumped the bars when he raised his hands to the machine. The contact didn't hurt. Not like the contact with the buzz sticks.

Buzz.

He cried out, and the scientists laughed. They jeered at him, leered at him. They enjoyed his pain. They didn't actually want him to write. They wanted him to fail. They wanted him to weep from the failure, wanted him to fall to his knees so that they could remind him of his dreams of being a published author. The scientists were once his family, his friends, his spouse and colleagues. But it was all a lie. They told better stories than he ever could.

Buzz.

"No!" he said. "No more!"

"No more what?" they taunted. "No more dreaming?"

He gripped the bars of his cage and steadied himself before the typewriter. He would do it. Not for fear of the scientists and their torture, but for himself. He would write himself out of this cage.

He forced himself to type:

The most frightening monsters are the ones inside of us . . .

Made in the USA
Monee, IL
19 April 2021